C000127022

A Serving of Deceit

**A Cubley's Coze Novel
Book Two**

By

R. Morgan Armstrong

First Printing

Copyright © 2023

All rights reserved. No part of this book may be reproduced or transmitted in any form or by any means, electronically or mechanically, including photocopying, recording, or by any information storage and retrieval system, without the written permission of the Publisher.

Author - R. Morgan Armstrong

Publisher
Wayne Dementi
Dementi Milestone Publishing, Inc.
Manakin-Sabot, VA 23103
www.dementimilestonepublishing.com

Cataloging-in-publication data for this book is available from The Library of Congress.

ISBN: 979-8-9872295-1-4

Front cover design: Rebecca Myrtle-Razul

Back cover design: Jayne Hushen

Graphic design by Dianne Dementi

Printed in U.S.A.

A Serving of Deceit is a work of fiction. References to real people, events, establishments, organizations or locales are intended only to provide a sense of authenticity and are used fictitiously. All other characters, incidents and dialogue are drawn from the author's imagination and are not to be construed as real.

A SERVING OF DECEIT'S MAIN CHARACTERS

The Gunn Family ~

William Boyer Gunn	Billy Gunn, BB Gunn, or BB - age 12
John Douglas Gunn	Billy's father
Laura Jane (Harris) Gunn	Billy's mother
Scotty Gunn	Billy's little brother - age 2 1/2
Grandma Harris	Matilda Harris is Billy's maternal grandmother

The Clark Family ~

Kent Farnsworth Clark	Superman - Billy's best friend - age 12
Sally Ann Clark	Kent's mother - a widow of Korean War

The Cubley Family ~

Charles Matthew Cubley	Matt Cubley, widower, former prosecutor, and new owner
Janet Cubley	Matt's wife, deceased, killed by a drunk driver
Jack Cubley	Matts son, deceased, killed by a drunk driver
Grandpa Cubley	Matt's grandfather and builder of Cubley's Coze Hotel
Uncle TJ	Thomas Jefferson Cubley, hotel owner, now deceased
Matthew Lee Cubley	Matt's father

Cubley's Coze Hotel and Resort Staff ~

Matt Cubley	Hotel owner by way of inheritance from his Uncle TJ
Chuck Tolliver	Hotel manager
Cliff Duffy	Night clerk
Boo Skelton	Dining room waitress & peacemaker of the kitchen

Maddie Johnson	Chief cook, fluent in French & English
Connell Washington	Cook with an alcohol problem
Toby "The Cleaner" Stanley	Dishwasher with mental issues
Richard Baker	Grounds supervisor
Rose Baker	Richard's wife, Maddie's daughter, & housekeeping supervisor

McCulloch Family

Big John McCulloch	John Louis McCulloch, big boss & main county employer Little John's father, Lou's grandfather
Mary McCulloch	Big John's wife and Lou's grandmother
Little John McCulloch	Police sergeant, Lou's father
Willa McCulloch	Little John's wife & Lou's mother
Lou McCulloch	Little John's son and a main bully to BB and Kent

The Bullies

Lou McCulloch	Ringleader of the three
Dickie Lockhart	Brother to Carl, 1 year older, but held back in school
Carl Lockhart	Dickie's younger brother, meanest of the three

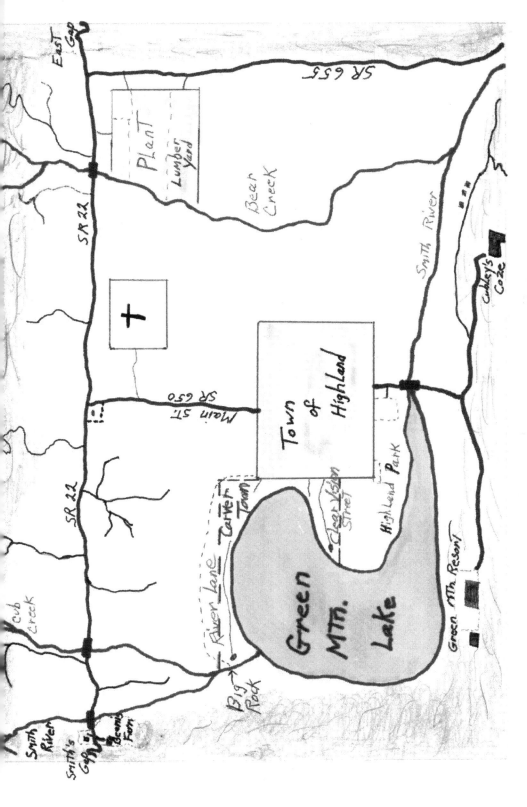

CUBLEY'S COZE MAP LEGEND
For The
TOWN OF HIGHLAND

Building #	Building Description
1	Frank Peters & Son Grocery
2	Highland Hardware
3	Top Hat Theater
4	Highland Furniture
5	Frank Dalton, Attorney at Law
6	Highland Five & Dime
7	Mountain Drugs
8	The First National Bank of Highland Ben Southwall's Law Office – Second Floor
9	Highland Volunteer Fire Department
10	Highland Methodist Church
11	Green Mountain Baptist Church
12	McCulloch Chevrolet Dealership
13	Black Panther Grill
14	The First Baptist Church of Highland

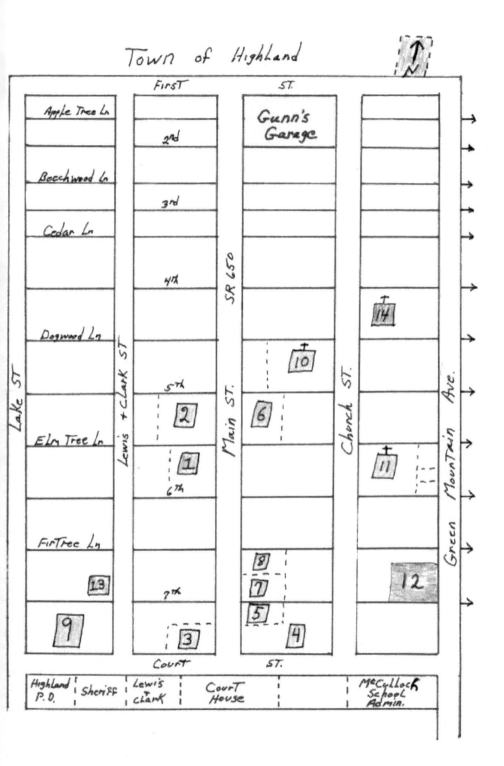

Town of Highland

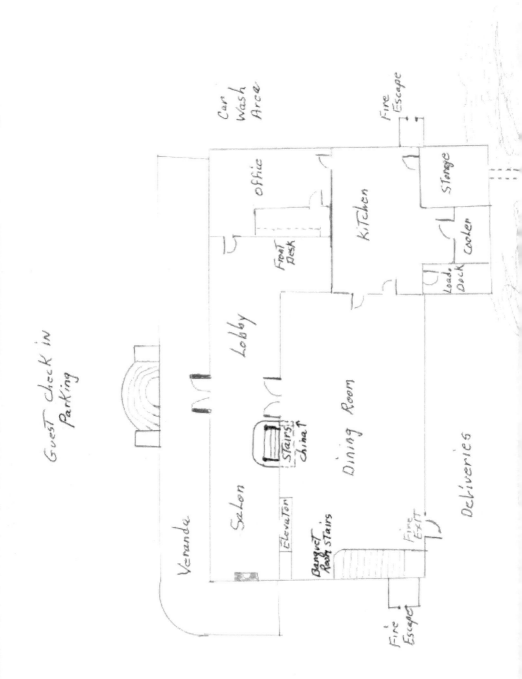

DEDICATION

This novel is dedicated to my son,

Robert Charles Armstrong.

ACKNOWLEDGMENTS

Thanks to the following family friends at Wintergreen Resort for critically reading the first drafts of this novel: Sue Carlson, Sallie Singletary, and Terri Brooks. A special thanks to the first editor who helped tremendously with the storyline and grammar, Lynn Hilleary, of Nelson County, Virginia.

I am grateful to the artist, Rebecca Myrtle Razul of Staunton, Virginia, for the design of the book's cover and the little emblem of the tow truck, Blacky, which repeatedly appears to show a shift in time or location.

I am indebted to my final copy editor Gail Blankman of Wintergreen Resort, for getting this novel ready for publication. I found her suggestions and criticism invaluable. However, since the author did the final edit, any errors are mine and mine alone.

Author's Notes:

This novel's plot and the characters portrayed are purely fictional and are not based on any person, living or deceased. However, many of the scenes come from similar experiences of the author as a prosecutor, trial attorney, and Virginia General District Court Judge. And the dialogue by police officers is language heard by the author while a 1972 intern police officer for the City of Virginia Beach while on summer break from law school or serving as a supervisor to the Virginia State Police, Henry County Sheriff, and local town police officer's special High Intensity Target Unit. Also, the author researched the weather, music, movies, songs, and prices for 1955.

When the title of a chapter contains the word Billy, the point of view of that chapter is twelve-year-old Billy. When his name is absent, the point of view is that of the omniscient narrator.

Author's Disclaimer:

In this novel, conversations between characters of different races often reflect what is unacceptable language today. However, such language is historically correct, and the prejudicial attitudes of certain characters have been used when required by the plot. The intended purpose of this novel is to demonstrate why such language, prejudicial attitudes, and deceit in all forms should be avoided and condemned.

CUBLEY'S COZE MYSTERIES

A SERVING OF REVENGE
A SERVING OF DECEIT

The car coasted toward the drop-off with an unconcerned occupant behind the wheel. Unconcerned because he had bullet holes in the back of his head. The first shot had deprived the gentleman of life, and the next two were for insurance. Now, propped upright in the driver's seat, the deceased was only along for the ride. The car did a nosedive into the creek, the rider's head smashing headfirst into the windshield, rendering the face almost unrecognizable. Landing first to the feast were flies, but an arm hanging out of the open driver's window would soon attract larger scavengers.

CHAPTER 1

BILLY'S DANGEROUS MIRROR
Monday, July 11, 1955

Being fourteen and all grown up, I've spent a lot of time trying to decide which is worse, lying or getting friends in trouble by telling the truth. The way things went down two years ago, I'm not sure I know the answer. But I'll tell you what happened, then you can choose.

My best friend, Kent Clark, and I were twelve years old the terrible summer of fifty-five. I remember it as if it were yesterday. After a sniper murdered several supervisors at McCulloch Wood Products, killed our chief of police, wounded the plant owner, Big John McCulloch, and burned down the plant, he kidnapped Kent and me. He also kidnapped Richard Baker, the hotel groundskeeper and maintenance man for the Cubley's Coze Hotel and Resort. The three of us were working at the hotel when we accidentally crossed paths with the killer.

My buddy and I were worried. Not about that sniper because our boss had rescued the three of us from the sniper. Those adventures were old news. No, we were concerned about three older boys who were after us. And they were mean!

This problem with the bullies had begun in June, and things were getting worse. That Monday in July, Kent and I were upstairs

1

in my room discussing which of the three bullies was the most dangerous when Mom interrupted.

"Billy, if you and Kent leave the house, be sure to tell me." She had just brought some clean towels upstairs for my bathroom and stopped at my bedroom door to remind us. Again.

"Yes, ma'am," I answered, hoping Scotty, my little brother, who was almost three that summer, stayed downstairs with my grandma because I needed to discuss serious business with Superman. My best buddy's real name is Kent Farnsworth Clark, but calling him Farnsworth is a sure way to get punched. We all called him Kent or by his nickname Superman. Also, I'm called Billy Gunn instead of my full name of William Boyer Gunn, but my friends prefer BB Gun or just BB.

Kent and I had been kidnapped for a short time, and that's why our moms had a new rule. Each time we left our homes, we had to tell an adult where we were going and what time we'd return— prisons kept looser rules. Our moms thought they were keeping us safe, but that's not how things turned out.

I needed to ask Kent something without my mom hearing me, so I began to whisper.

"Superman, do you think a mirror can have supernatural powers?"

"BB, you keep worrying about that stupid wish you made a month ago on that dumb old mirror. Things like that only happen in the movies, not in real life. Speaking of movies, I can hardly wait until this Saturday. Mom said I could go."

Kent had gotten off the subject, which he often did, but I was concerned about my mirror and needed to get Kent back on track. "Come on, Superman, stick with me on this. I'm serious. I know stuff happens in the movies, but I'm talking about real life. Do you remember in June how bored I was?"

"Yeah."

"How I followed the advice of those high school guys and made a wish on my bathroom mirror for an adventure."

"You told me you did. I thought you were a big spoofer, but things did go crazy."

"Yeah, a big wreck happened, people began getting shot, we got into one scrape after another, tangled with bullies, became witnesses in court, and got kidnapped—all of that happened the first half of the summer."

"I know all that. I was with you, remember? What's got you up a tree anyway?"

"I'm worried the mirror's not going to leave us alone."

"Okay. So, what's happened lately?" Kent asked, flashing his crooked smile, the one he got from the sledding accident. When the stitches came out, it left a small scar, and the corner of his mouth stayed stuck in one position. So now, when he smiles, it's only on one side.

"Well, nothing," I answered, but so much had happened after my wish, I was still worried. "If it isn't the mirror, then what's going on?"

"BB, I agree it's strange, so, to be safe, don't make any more wishes. If you're responsible, gosh, every kid in town was grounded during the murders because of you."

"Holy smoke, I didn't think of that. Please, don't tell anyone!"

"Okay, if you promise, no more wishes!"

"I promise! I ain't never going to make any more wishes on mirrors!"

"William Boyer Gunn, stop using ain't," Mom corrected me, passing by my door with a second load of clean towels.

"Yes, ma'am. I'm trying, but sometimes, it just slips out."

"Mrs. Gunn, BB's trying. I know 'cause I correct him whenever I hear him slip up," announced Kent and flashed me his crooked grin.

I began aiming eyeball daggers in his direction and mouthed, "I'll get you for that."

"Billy, pick up those dirty clothes you wore yesterday and put them in the laundry hamper, please," Mom ordered as she went back downstairs.

"Yes, ma'am."

I picked up the dirty clothes, balled them up, and stuck them on the top shelf of my closet. They weren't ready for the laundry. I considered them shelf-dirty, having worn them only one day, and not laundry-hamper-dirty—no need to rush things. Besides, most of the mud would brush off.

Kent came close to look at the wound on my head. My injury was the result of getting whacked by one of the bullies.

"BB, how's your noggin?"

"About healed up, the same as your eye. Okay, perhaps my mirror didn't cause those bullies to attack us those times. Lou McCulloch has it in for me and knows he can get by with it. Carl and Dickie Lockhart are plain mean and don't need no mirror to come after us."

Mom had snuck back upstairs with a load of sheets, and she let me have it.

"Billy, first it's ain't. Now I hear you using double negatives. You would try the patience of a saint. Please, don't make me correct you again!"

"Yes, ma'am. I mean, no, ma'am." I hoped Mom understood. Things had been relatively quiet in the house today. I wanted them to remain that way. Grandma was no longer fussing that we would all be murdered in our beds by the killer, and she had stopped demanding we move to West Virginia to live with her sister.

I lowered my voice so Mom couldn't hear me and asked Kent, "Superman, do you think Lou and the Lockhart brothers will leave us alone? I busted Lou's nose pretty good at the Green Mountain Resort."

"Well, they better. Being witnesses because of something we saw involving the Beamis incident, we should still be under that witness protection thing. Maybe that will keep those bullies away from us."

"I don't know about that with the local chief of police being dead. The rest of the cops might not protect us since the trial's now over," I said with a shrug.

"Well, I don't plan on taking night strolls by their houses. Not even Superman's going to look for that much trouble," Kent remarked.

"Trouble has moved here to stay. That's what people stopping by Dad's garage are saying."

"More trouble, we don't need."

"Kent, since the plant burned down, most of the men are out of work. If Big John McCulloch doesn't rebuild it, the Town of

Highland might dry up and blow away. I even heard Dad tell Mom that our garage and towing business might have to close."

"Gunn's Garage? No way."

"Dad depends on the workers at the plant. The rich big wigs use McCulloch's Chevrolet, and they all work for Big John on salary. It's the regular workers who aren't getting paychecks."

"More bad news is in the air. I overheard a teller at Mom's bank say that folks are drawing out all their savings. Also, one old farmer told my mom that he wanted his money before there was a run on the bank."

"You think that might happen?"

Kent shrugged his shoulders as he tossed the comic he wasn't reading on my bed. He began shooting imaginary birds in the air with his finger, making gun noises of "pow... pow."

I threw my comic on top of his and started looking for my tennis shoes. I knew they were here somewhere unless Scotty had tossed them in the toilet again—the little turd.

"Superman, I don't think Mr. Cubley was happy when he had to kill the sniper during our rescue. He warned him to give up, but that only gave the guy time to shoot. Heck, Mr. Cubley could have been killed instead of getting winged."

I pulled my tennis shoes from the trash can beside my desk. My little brother was playing tricks again.

Kent stopped shooting and answered, "Yeah, I've noticed the same thing. I'm glad the bullet just grazed our boss's arm."

Kent got up, walked over to the window, and looked outside. A car had just pulled into the garage parking area. My dad's garage and our house are on the same lot, which is good and bad. The garage gets a lot of business but often at odd times.

"Mr. Cubley said he wished things had turned out differently. I'm sure he was talking about having to shoot the sniper," I added, joining Kent at the window.

"Isn't that our old teacher?" Kent asked, turning to look at me.

"It is, that's Miss Jones. Let's go see what she wants."

We ran down the stairs two at a time until Grandma shushed us for making too much noise. She had Scotty on her lap, and he was about to doze off. We instantly stopped running and started tiptoeing across the living room and kitchen. Then, we ran outside, but I stopped and grabbed the screen door just in time to keep it from banging. Mom was watching me from the laundry room.

Both Kent and I had had Miss Jones as our sixth-grade teacher, and she was swell! I liked her the best of all my former teachers. The letter, telling us which of the seventh-grade teachers we would get this fall, was due any day now. Kent and I were hoping we would be together again, and maybe our old teacher could tell us something.

"Hi, Miss Jones," we both said.

"Well, if it isn't BB Gun and Superman!" Miss. Jones responded with a big smile.

This was the first time she had ever used our nicknames. In school, it was always Billy and Kent unless I got in trouble. Then, like my parents, she'd call me William. I didn't care much for William at home or in school, but my teacher seldom had to use it.

"I came by to see how you boys were doing. Since you're running through the house, I guess you're fine—right?"

"Yes, ma'am. We're fine as frog hair. Not shot anywhere," I said and was proud I hadn't used a double negative. Mom must have been proud, too, because she stepped out on the back stoop to pat me on my shoulder.

"Virginia, how nice to see you," Mom greeted her with a smile.

"Hi, Laura Jane. My goodness, it seems like the whole town is talking about these two brave boys. I'm so relieved that they're okay." Miss Jones was starting to make Kent and me blush.

My dad walked out of the garage with a rag, wiping his hands as he walked, and spoke, "Miss Jones, would it be possible to start school tomorrow or the next day? Certain parents need a break."

"John Gunn, don't you go putting notions into the school board's heads. I cherish my summer vacation. It keeps me out of the nuthouse."

I knew that Miss Jones was joking because she had this big grin on her face.

Mom interrupted with, "Virginia, I don't know how you do it. Keeping two boys entertained and knowing where they are all the time is almost too much for John and me."

I think Mom was serious.

"Laura Jane, I know you and many other parents are feeling the same. I hope better days are ahead. It's like there's a black cloud over this town. All of a sudden, too. People are all saying how it's very strange."

Miss Jones had gotten all serious, and I started to panic. Did she know about my wish?

"Virginia, come inside and let me fix you some iced tea. I won't take no for an answer." Mom smiled and opened the screen door for Miss Jones.

"Laura Jane, I will, but before I do, I have some bad news for Billy and Kent."

I noticed she looked serious, but there was a hint of a smile at the corners of her mouth—something I had picked up on last year in school.

"Has my boy been causing you trouble?" Dad frowned and gave me a stern look.

"No, John. I'm being moved to the seventh grade this year, and both Billy and Kent are in my class."

"Yippee!" I got out first.

"Yes! Yes! Whoo, whoo, whoo, whoo!" Kent yelled as he broke into a war dance, bouncing first on one foot and then another in time with his whoo, whoos.

Dad shook his head and went back into the garage. As I yelled into the air, I glanced at the big sign over the door, "Gunn's Garage and Towing Service." My joy suddenly crashed. Would this all still be here in a year?

Mom and Miss Jones retreated into the kitchen, as Kent and I sat on our picnic table to talk in private. This fall, we would be together and have Miss Jones as our teacher. This was great! Superman and I would have a ball, except for tests. Miss Jones did give hard tests and could pile on the homework, but not on weekends. Working hard during the week and playing hard on the weekends was her motto.

"BB, things couldn't be better. Miss Jones for the seventh grade and the best is yet to come—a triple feature," proclaimed Superman, all excited.

"What did you say?" My mind was half thinking about Dad's business.

"This weekend, the Top Hat Theater is showing the *Bowery Boys Meet the Monsters, Them,* and *The Snow Creature.*"

I knew I had to correct Kent; he was all wrong. "That can't be—they were on last weekend. This weekend's a double cowboy feature."

"That's what I thought, too. I thought that I would die since we missed our three monster movies because of the plant burning," Kent told me, all serious.

"Kent! Die, really?" I said with a fake frown on my face.

"Sad, I mean that I would be sad. It was awful how the town lost its electricity during the fire, which shut down the theater—no electricity meant no monster movies. Now that they got the electricity back on, the monster movies are held over. Isn't that great?" Kent hopped up and began doing his little war dance again.

"Sounds too good to be true, but I wonder how many kids will get to go. A lot of the parents are talking about no paychecks for some time with the plant closed," I answered him on a somber note.

We talked some more about the Town of Highland falling on hard times because of the fire and how our friends would suffer. "But Kent, you and I are lucky. Mr. Cubley says we still have our jobs washing cars for his hotel guests. Being working men, we'll have cash for the movies. Let's ask Laura and Judy—our treat." I knew that Kent would love to have a date with Judy, but he was too shy to ask.

"Well, as long as it's not a date or anything. I guess it would be alright. You ask them," requested Kent.

"Okay, if we see the girls, I'll do the asking. Come on, let's get our bikes and cruise. We need to double-check the movie theater and ride up to the hotel to see if there are any cars to wash tomorrow. I also want to be sure that Mr. Cubley's arm is okay. He did get shot by our kidnapper, you know," I said with a smile.

"Yeah, remember? I was there. But it was just a graze," Kent added with a finger pointing to his left arm. "Besides, Mr. Cubley was a Marine. Those guys are as tough as Superman," Kent concluded.

"Let me tell Mom we're off. I sure hope Mr. Cubley's at the hotel. I wonder who else is in Miss Jones's class?"

I waved to Dad, who was bringing out an oil pan to wash around back. So far today, he had not asked me to help out in the garage. I guess being kidnapped by a notorious killer was still working for me. I wondered how long it would take for Dad to get back to handing out chores.

It took us five more minutes to tell Mom we were leaving. I didn't want to interrupt her while she was talking to our teacher. Even at twelve, I knew better than to interrupt an adult in front of company, especially when the company's your seventh-grade teacher.

While I stood waiting just inside the kitchen door for a break in their conversation, I was thinking about no more wishes on my bathroom mirror.

Kent might not believe it, but I did, and I wasn't going to take any more chances—too dangerous. I just hoped my mirror was done with us. In the first part of June, I only asked for one adventure, only one, but it had given us enough adventures for years and years.

Little did I know my bathroom mirror wasn't finished. It was just getting started.

CHAPTER 2

BILLY'S DAY OFF
Monday, July 11, 1955

F inally, I was able to speak to Mom, and then, we were ready to cruise.

Kent and I got our bikes from behind the garage, and I said, "Superman, let's ride out to the plant to see if the fire's out."

"You know our moms won't let us ride our bikes on State Route 22—too much traffic."

Kent minded his mom when it came to stuff that he knew would upset her if she found out. She often found out because Kent couldn't keep secrets from her.

I had a solution. "Okay, we can ride on Main to the Highland Cemetery and see the plant from the top of cemetery hill."

"Yeah, that's okay, if traffic's not too bad on Main," cautioned Kent, always the worrywart.

Having that decided and seeing traffic was light, we rode north on Main toward the Liberty Bell Gas Station. Nearing the service station, we got up speed, made a wide right into the driveway to the cemetery, and started pumping hard up the steep hill. We didn't get far before we had to push our bikes.

It's a great view from the top, with the site covered in grass and only a couple of trees in the way. We each picked a tombstone, leaned our bike against it, and figured the occupant wouldn't complain.

The McCulloch Wood Product's main plant, rough end department, maintenance building, and the lumber yard were nothing but piles of smoking rubble. That angry worker had left only the water tower, boiler room, and the office building standing, but all those structures had burn marks from the fire. The log yard was okay because logs don't catch fire as quickly as lumber, and the firemen saved them. Today, all the fire trucks were gone, leaving a couple of workers with hoses connected directly to hydrants to wet down the rubble.

If you squinted your eyes, it was possible to see some flower bouquets in front of the plant where Police Chief Obie Smith had been shot and died. For the present, the Town of Highland didn't have a chief of police. That's when I noticed a freshly dug grave nearby. We walked over and looked in. No casket, just a hole. It had to be for Chief Smith because several nearby tombstones were Smith family markers.

The cemetery had several other new gravesites, but these were covered with dirt. Two of the three people shot at the plant were buried here, as was a deputy sheriff. I had been within thirty feet of the deputy when it happened. Mr. Skelton, Dad's mechanic, and I were on a tow. Blacky, Dad's big black tow truck, blocked my view, but I heard the shot and later saw the body covered with a sheet.

I remember how creepy it felt on our visit to that cemetery. I talked to the man who killed all these people, our kidnapper, for over an hour the day he captured us. First, he was alive, and then, he was dead. I also noticed there was no gravesite for him. We heard later that his family buried him in another town. No one in Highland has had anything good to say about the sniper. However, there are two sides to every story. I've often thought about how badly he and his family were treated before he began killing people.

My dad has this saying: "When revenge is out of its cage, it'll rampage like a wild animal and not know when to stop."

We didn't stay long looking at the plant—nothing much going on.

"Okay, let's race to the bottom of the hill," I called out but didn't wait. I got a cheater's head start. After almost wrecking in some loose gravel, I watched Kent cautiously make his way down the slope. He finally rode up and asked, "Where to now?"

"Let's go see Mr. Cubley."

"To Cubley's Coze Hotel and away!" he shouted and took off. This time he got the cheater's start.

We raced down Main Street and sailed past my house without stopping. When we got to Beechwood Lane, where Kent lived, we hung a left to cross over to Green Mountain Avenue. Then, we turned right onto Green Mountain Avenue and sped to the bridge built on top of the Smith River Dam. Green Mountain Lake was to our right, a deep blue color that day with ripples on the water, but not a soul was using the town park.

I looked over my shoulder for police cars. Not for us, we weren't going that fast. I checked to see if the Highland Police were pulling over delivery trucks bound for Mr. Cubley's hotel. Big John McCulloch was trying to ruin Mr. Cubley's hotel so that Mr. McCulloch's hotel would not have the competition. The special police on the McCulloch company payroll had orders to harass the delivery trucks bound for Mr. Cubley's hotel. The recent shootings and fire had diverted the cops to more critical matters, but now that things were getting back to normal, I figured they would resume their dirty tricks. But today, I didn't see any trucks pulled over, which was good news.

I passed Kent, slid into the entrance drive for Cubley's Coze Hotel, almost wrecked, had to hop off my bike, and began pushing it. Kent passed me but had to hop off his red Columbia just up the hill. He waited for me to catch up, and we chatted as we pushed our bikes—our race forgotten.

"Wonder who'll be the next police chief?" Kent asked.

"Well, if Sergeant McCulloch doesn't take over running the plant, I'll bet you that Big John gives him the job as police chief."

"You really think Big John would turn the plant over to Little John?"

I thought for no more than five seconds. "You're right. Sergeant McCulloch isn't sneaky or smart enough." I was getting out of breath and stopped talking until we made the top of the hill.

Once there, we rode the last quarter mile at a normal speed and talked about the monster movies coming to the Top Hat. Then, we stashed our bikes around back in the woods behind the hotel kitchen and went inside.

Maddie Johnson, the hotel's chief cook, was the first to see us. She broke into a big grin and yelled a warning to Boo Skelton, the maître d'.

"Boo, look who showed up on their day off. Some people are just too dumb to enjoy a vacation day dropped right in their laps."

"You boys look all hot and worn out," exclaimed Boo when she saw our flushed and sweaty faces. Then she added, "Are you boys hungry?"

Maddie turned, waving a spoon, "The first one of you rascals who even looks at that batch of chess pies cooling on the counter will get a poke in the ribs." Then she looked down at our feet. "Y'all clear out of my clean kitchen with those dirty shoes."

Maddie Johnson had traded in her grin for a broad smile. I looked behind us and knew she was joking. The floor behind us was spotless.

"Now, Mrs. Johnson, you are unfair. How could we stay away when the wonderful smell of your little cupcake-sized chess pies is flowing down off this mountain and filling the valley with its fragrance? Kent and I could smell them clear over to my dad's garage." I was throwing in some big words we had learned from Polecat, the hotel's newspaper delivery guy, who spoke like the King of England.

"Don't you think you can charm a chess pie off me, boy! Boo, you keep an eye on these two, and be sure you count those pies when they leave."

Boo was the temporary maître d'. The regular one had quit to take care of her sick brother. When fall arrived, Mr. Cubley would have to find someone permanent after Boo returned for her final year at the university. "Boo" was the funny nickname for Beverly Olivia Skelton. When she was in the first grade, and Halloween was near, all her friends began calling her "Boo the Skeleton," much to the dismay of her parents. The nickname, however, stuck but was shortened to just "Boo."

Then, Boo called out, grinning, "Maddie, I just noticed two of these chess pies are leaking filling where their side crusts have cracked. It wouldn't be right to serve them to guests. My goodness, we can't let our guests get their fingers sticky, so I'll just toss them in the trash." Boo was starting to reach for two of the cupcake-sized tarts while looking to see our reaction.

"No!" Kent and I both yelled. We heard Mr. Cubley get up from the desk chair in his office and open his connecting door into the kitchen.

"Well, well. I figured with all this racket that it had to be you two or a couple of highway robbers. I thought I told you boys to take today off?"

Kent broke out with his crooked smile and responded with, "Mr. Cubley, we are off. We just came by to be sure you were okay, not to wash guests' cars. Gunshot wounds are serious."

"Kent, this is hardly a gunshot wound. It's a mere scratch. Two stitches are not worth you coming up here to check on me."

Mr. Cubley walked over and looked closely at the tray of chess pies.

"Boo, did I hear you say you had two chess pies you needed to toss out? I'll take them," Mr. Cubley said while trying to hide his smile.

"Mr. Cubley!" I complained, and that's all I was going to say on the subject. My frown said the rest.

"Here, boys, take them and get yourself a couple of Dr. Peppers out of the cooler." Mr. Cubley waved as he walked back into his office, laughing.

Boo handed us the little treats on napkins. The filling was like pecan pie filling but without the pecans and were they deliciously sweet. I used to think that I could eat six of them with no trouble, but one day, I found out that four could make a person sick.

Boo motioned her head toward the cooler as she returned to the dining room. Kent and I grabbed our drinks and took our bounty out onto the loading dock. Before we had finished, Mr. Cubley walked out to the loading dock.

"Well, you two have your fun today because tomorrow you do have cars to wash. Come on in at the usual time."

"We'll be here bright and early. Are things back to normal?" I asked, finishing up my chess pie and licking my fingers to get the wonderful goo off. I wasn't about to use the napkin.

"This is so good," Kent added, also licking his fingers.

"Billy, with the plant shut down, the town is holding its breath. No one knows if Big John's going to rebuild or not. With so many jobs hanging in the balance, I would say nothing will be back to normal for some time," Mr. Cubley had a sad tone in his voice.

"Any news on how Mr. McCulloch's doing?" Kent asked.

"Polecat heard at the police department that the doctors are hopeful. It's going to be another day or two before they can say for sure. You two watch yourselves. Polecat also heard Lou McCulloch boasting about how his dad's going to clean up the town's juvenile delinquent problem. Lou bragged that he might help his dad with that problem. I would guess that he's talking about you and Kent."

I spoke up, "We'll be careful. Kent and I will stick together like glue. Right, Superman?"

"Yeah, I'll protect you," Kent promised.

Mr. Cubley, like all adults, warned us twice. "Just be careful, 'cause with his dad being at the hospital with Big John, Lou's loose and roaming the town."

Kent decided to bring up the other two who were after us. "What about Carl and Dickie Lockhart? Dickie might be the older brother, but Carl's three times worse."

"I think Mr. Lockhart had a 'heart to heart' with Dickie and Carl, but you stay clear of them, too. They're both older and bigger and not known to mind their father."

Mr. Tolliver, the assistant hotel manager, came out to tell Mr. Cubley that he had a phone call. The two of them went back into the hotel, so Kent and I followed and peeked into the kitchen. We had to make sure there were no more damaged chess pies! Maddie caught us looking. She acted like she was going for her big butcher knife, so Kent and I took off and grabbed our bikes to ride to the Top Hat Theater.

The theater was closed during the day, but the marquee promised three monster movies for this Saturday. Satisfied, we walked our bikes over to Lewis and Clark Street when we saw Polecat selling papers on the corner.

"Hey, Mr. Smith, how are you doing?" I asked, knowing never to call Mr. George Washington Smith by his nickname, "Polecat." That would be rude since he was our friend. But Polecat was what everyone called him behind his back. He hated that nickname and was not shy about letting people know how much. I tried to stop upwind of Polecat—the reason for his nickname—and not be obvious about it. I misjudged the wind's direction and caught a strong smell of body odor. I tried not to let on. Kent was luckier; he stopped in an upwind spot.

Polecat greeted us with, "Well, if it isn't the heroes of Highland. I hope you have becalmed yourselves after your recent brush with death at the hands of Highland's assassin. Why are you boys roaming the streets when you should be engaged in remunerative endeavors at the hotel?" This flowery language was so typical of Polecat, a newspaper delivery boy who was very intelligent and could recite conversations, word-for-word, years later.

Kent smiled at Polecat and explained, "Mr. Cubley gave us the day off. I think he wanted some peace and quiet, so here we are."

Of course, I had to add, "Yeah, off today, but back to work tomorrow. No rest for us working men."

"Any news?" Kent asked.

"Mr. Clark, have you ever encountered me when I was not overburdened with a conglomeration of headlines and press releases?"

"No, sir. I never have." Kent gave me a wink, but I already knew he was playing with Polecat.

"The *Highland Gazette* is replete with follow-up articles on the sniper's rampage and the glorious exploits of Matthew Cubley, rescuer extraordinaire. There are quotes from every important person in town. Today's paper contains one in-depth article from a state psychiatrist on the psyche of Highland's despicable sniper. However, there's not a word about his maltreatment at the hands of the plant officials and the local constabulary. Among us three, I think the basis for the misfortunate conclusion to this entire matter may be blamed on the policies and procedures at the plant that drove him to kill all those people." Polecat smiled, and his yellow teeth proclaimed he was quite satisfied with his opinion on the matter.

"I concur," I responded with a word Polecat had taught Kent and me.

"I join my colleague in a similar pronouncement," Kent added. I was amazed by how he used the words correctly. I think Polecat was also impressed.

"Indeed," he said to Kent.

"Any news about the McCulloch Plant?" I asked.

"Much too early to even speculate, Master Gunn. My periodical is silent on the matter. I suspect a delay of one or more weeks before those in authority resolve the matter. The McCullochs may need new sources of funding," Polecat concluded and placed a bundle of papers in his bike's basket in preparation for departing.

"See you later, Mr. Smith," said Kent.

"See you in the morning at Cubley's Coze," I threw in as he left.

"Where to now, BB?" Kent wanted to know.

"We could backtrack to Mountain Drug and check for new comics. I'm behind in my reading," I stated, getting my right foot on my bike pedal.

"Let's ride. Up, up, and away," called out Kent, pretending to be Superman as he got the jump on me.

I made a fast U-turn with my rear tire sliding a little while Kent circled more slowly. We rode back down Court Street to Main Street, where we stashed our bikes at the Highland Furniture Store next to some garbage cans directly behind Mr. Dalton's law office. We walked to the Mountain Drug Store up the street.

Laura Akers and Judy Peterson were at a table with milkshakes. Both wore sundresses and sandals. Laura's dress was light blue, and her blond hair looked so soft against it. Judy had on a forest green dress, and her blond hair contrasted with the darker color. Kent and I walked up and greeted them. They both smiled and asked us to join them. Kent's face turned pink, but not mine.

Kent ordered a Coke float; I ordered a chocolate shake and a hot dog. After our snack at the hotel and now ice cream at the drugstore, that's all I could eat. Kent added a hot dog to his order. We offered to buy hotdogs for Laura and Judy, but they said they weren't hungry. They thanked us for the offer with smiles. I blushed when Laura looked me in the eyes; I looked away at the comic book rack.

Judy spoke to Kent, "I read all about you getting kidnapped by the sniper. Weren't you scared?"

"Well, s…some," he stuttered.

I could not believe Kent just admitted to being scared. That one came out of left field.

Laura looked right at me with a question. "Weren't you scared, Billy?"

Now I was stuck. If I said no, Kent would be mad. If I said yes, the girls would think I was yellow.

"Some, I guess, but not much." I figured I had better stick with some of what Kent had said.

Judy took her long spoon and chopped up a chunk of ice cream in her shake. "Oh, I would have been terrified. He shot all those people and then to be kidnapped by that killer. I would have died of fright," Judy said, sitting straighter in her chair with a look of concern and waited for me to answer.

I blurted out, "Actually, he never hurt us at all. I was more afraid for Mr. Baker."

I was fast getting into trouble with this conversation. I took a big swallow of milkshake—a big mistake. I almost choked, and milkshake started dribbling out of my nose. I grabbed a napkin to hide it.

Laura tried to suppress a giggle. "Oh, you boys always act so brave, even when you shouldn't." She pretended not to see the mess I was making, but she did slide her paper napkin to me.

I wasn't having much luck hiding the milkshake spill. I noticed Judy was also trying not to giggle.

"So..." snort. "Did they get in any new comics?" I responded, trying to change the subject.

Judy answered with a frown and a shake of her pretty blond curls. "I think they're the same ones from last week. I know the Daisy Duck one isn't new. The cowboy comics, I don't read because the cowgirls never do anything except get tied up."

Before I could reply, the door opened. There was Lou McCulloch with Dickie Lockhart and Carl Lockhart following him. They were coming inside and talking loudly. I tried to duck behind my milkshake glass, but Lou spotted Kent and me right off.

He turned, grabbed Dickie by the arm, and pushed him backward and out of the door. Carl was behind them and got pushed back, as well. I heard him yell, "Cut it out," but Lou blurted out, "Stupidman and BB big butt are in there, big as life. Here's our chance!"

The three bullies stood in front of the drugstore, talking. I could guess what the conversation was about.

Laura made her next statement more to Judy than to Kent or me. "Those bullies are so mean. Why don't they leave you two alone?"

Judy joined in and turned to look to see if they were gone. "Yeah, those three are just terrible. I hope they leave and stay gone."

"I'm not scared of those three—not one bit," Kent said, but he looked to see if they were leaving. They weren't leaving. We were cornered.

I frowned and voiced my wishful thinking. "Well, maybe they'll get tired and leave. I would hate to have to bust Lou in the nose again."

Kent backed me up with, "You did pop him good last month. His looks might improve because they sure couldn't get worse."

I remembered the comics and decided that was how we could wait out the bullies. "Hey, I see a couple of Roy Rogers comics that I think I'll read again."

Before I could get up, Laura put her hand on my arm, "Boys, we must meet Judy's mom at the dress shop. Come with us, please!"

Kent looked at me but didn't respond, so I did.

"No, we'll be fine. Once we finish our drinks and comics, we'll head on home." I was trying to sound brave. I was certainly not going to let a girl help me out of a scrape. I sounded more daring than I felt, but at least Lou didn't have a ball bat with him this time. When he attacked me in the park on the Fourth of July, it took days for me to get rid of my headache.

"Yeah, we can take care of ourselves. Thanks," Kent bragged to Judy, but his voice cracked.

The girls got up and left arm in arm. The bullies backed up and let them pass. Kent and I sat looking at each other.

"Now, what?" he asked.

"Let's wait 'em out," I said, looking at the clock. "We can read a couple of comics. It's okay because we both have some drink left in our glasses. Just don't drink fast," I counseled Kent.

We killed thirty minutes until we finally finished our drinks, one small sip at a time. Once we finished them, the rule was that we had to put our comics back on the shelf or buy them. The place was starting to get crowded with lunch customers. It was time to go before we were asked to leave. I just hoped Lou, Dickie, and Carl had gotten tired of waiting for us.

I opened the door, looked, and stepped out onto the street. Kent was right behind me. No bullies in sight. Thank goodness. We walked over to where we had stashed our bikes, but they weren't there.

"You dunces looking for these?"

Lou was holding Kent's bike. Carl was holding mine. Dickie was the one doing the talking, "Why don't you come on over here and take them from us?"

CHAPTER 3

BILLY, BIKES, AND BULLIES
Monday, July 11, 1955

L ou McCulloch was holding Kent's red Columbia bike. He mounted it, rode it in a circle, and tooted the horn for good measure. Carl Lockhart had my green Schwinn Hornet by the handlebars, bouncing it up and down on the front tire. He was bouncing it harder and harder.

Dickie, Carl's brother, was enjoying the show and looking smug when he yelled, "Take back your bike from Lou, Superman, I mean, Stupidman!" Dickie was taunting Kent, hoping he would fight Lou, who was older and bigger.

"Give me back my bike," Kent yelled as he tried to block Lou from riding his bike in a circle. Lou just swerved around him, stood up on the pedals to pick up speed, and zoomed out of reach. The bully swung wide on his next circle, keeping farther away from Kent.

I was both scared and mad but shouted like I was just angry.

"Not funny, Carl. Stop it before you bend a spoke." I walked up to Carl, balled up my right fist, and looked up into his eyes. He was a head taller than me. He stopped bouncing my bike and glared at me to see if I would back down.

"You gonna fight me, BB big butt?"

Carl threw my bike to the side so hard that it bounced—not good for the paint. I wasn't aware Dickie had snuck up and quietly gotten down on all fours behind me. When I glanced at my fallen bike, Carl lunged. He hit me in the chest with both hands.

I went backward, falling over Dickie, who was still on all fours behind my legs. My feet left the ground, and I fell faster and faster. I remember thinking, *why is it taking me so long to hit the ground?*

Then, wham!

My head hit and bounced, just like my bike had, but I saw stars exploding. The last thing I remembered was another blow.

Somebody kicked me in the head. I saw the shoe coming out of the corner of my left eye just before everything went dark.

"Billy, Billy, can you hear me? Billy, can you hear me? Sally Ann, he's still not conscious. I'm not sure he's breathing!"

Miss Martin, Mr. Dalton's legal secretary, was leaning over me. At least, it looked like her. Only one of my eyes was working.

"Whuh ham I? Miss Marthun, ish that..." Things were all fuzzy. I couldn't see anything out of my left eye. My headache was back, worse than when Lou had clobbered me with that ball bat a week ago. I closed my eyes because it even hurt to think.

"Billy, do you know where you are?" asked the second lady, who sounded like Kent's Mom.

"No. A shoe flew...?"

"Sally Ann, I hope Billy's mom and dad get here soon! He's not talking right!"

Was Miss Martin talking to Kent's mom, but that was nuts? Mrs. Clark should be at the bank. Was it Saturday? Why was the bank closed? Where was I?

Suddenly, I remembered and opened my right eye.

I started to sit up, but the bullies were holding me down by the shoulders. I started swinging. They let go.

"Billy, it's me. Calm down! It's Carol, Carol Martin!"

I looked, and it was Miss Martin. She was leaning back away from me, and both her knees were on the gravel. I thought, *gee, that's gotta hurt.*

I whispered, "Miss Martin, where's Kent—our bikes?" I was whispering, but I think it was too soft for her to hear me. I panicked and spoke, "Kent?"

It felt like a cherry bomb exploded in my brain. I was not going to repeat that mistake. I quit talking, stayed still, and closed my eyes tight.

Miss Martin leaned down and spoke softly. "Billy, you boys are behind the office. Kent says some older boys jumped you and stole your bikes. Do you remember?"

It was coming back to me. "Yeah, they did," I said softly, despite the horrible pain.

Miss Martin began to explain things without me asking. "Kent's over there with his mom. I called her when I found you two. Just lie still. Your parents are on the way." Miss Martin began rubbing my chest in little circles, which felt good but did nothing to help my headache.

"BB, you okay?" Kent asked me from ten feet away.

I didn't want to speak, so I gave him a thumbs down.

"They took our bikes! I tried to stop them, but Carl and Dickie held me while Lou beat on me. When I finally got my breath back, they were gone. They took our bikes!"

His mom said, "Hush, don't worry about the bikes. We need to be sure that you two boys are okay,"

I turned my head and saw out of my one good eye Mrs. Clark wipe a smear of blood off Kent's face.

Kent would have none of it. "Mom, that was my Christmas bike. I know how you saved, skipped lunches even, to get it. I'm going to kill them. I'll find me a gun and kill them."

"Kent, stop talking like that. You're not going to kill anyone. We'll get your bike back or buy you another one. Stop worrying about your bike and lie still!"

Mrs. Clark was trying to calm Kent, but I felt the same way. I knew there was no way she could afford to buy another bike for Kent.

A man suddenly spoke to me. "Billy, here's an ice pack for your head."

I recognized the voice. It was Mr. Dalton, the attorney, and he handed his secretary, Miss Martin, a paper bag with some ice in it. Then, he gently removed a towel that somebody had wrapped around my head. It was full of blood and ruined. Next, he applied a thick compress to my wound and wrapped a gauze bandage around my head several times to hold the compress in place. Miss Martin then placed the ice bag over my eye and began stroking my arm.

I whispered, "Mr. Dalton, they took our bikes. They'll smash 'em or sell them." I tried to get up, but when I tried to move, I got dizzy and threw up. Used milkshakes and hot dogs don't taste good.

Mr. Dalton held my head while I finished making a mess. "Billy, please don't move. Your dad's on the way. Let's let Sheriff Lawrence get your bikes back. Son, I think you have a concussion, so don't move."

Mr. Dalton made sense. I knew if I tried to stand, I would throw up again. One mess in front of Miss Martin was bad enough.

I looked out of my right eye. Kent's mom was still trying to clean his face. Miss Martin was holding a new towel to my head with ice in the bag over my left eye. She kept telling me to lie still and close my eyes. That sounded like good advice, so I did.

I heard a car pull up and then another. I peeped out of my one good eye. Mom and Dad were hurrying over.

"Billy, are you hurt?" Mom asked in a high-pitched voice.

I decided not to let her know how I really felt. "No, just a little headache. They took our bikes!"

Kent spoke up. "Mr. Gunn, Mrs. Gunn, it was Lou McCulloch, Carl Lockhart, and his brother Dickie. Those older boys knocked Billy out, beat on me, and took our bikes."

Kent left off, "Let's kill them."

I wanted to add that they deserved to be shot, stabbed, and scalped, but my head hurt too much to speak.

"Billy, who did this to you?" Dad asked me like he didn't believe Kent.

A whisper was all I could manage. "Lou—Carl—Dickie."

Mom took over from Miss Martin, who was now standing beside Mr. Dalton, and I saw that she had blood on her. Real blood looks so different from movie blood!

Miss Martin began to give Mom a report. "Laura Jane, I found the boys when I brought out the trash. Kent was awake, but he had been badly beaten. Billy was out cold and remained that way for five or ten minutes. When he did wake up, he was all confused, talking about flying shoes."

Mr. Dalton spoke up, "Sheriff, those three are out of control. You need to charge them. This is way beyond kids having a schoolyard scuffle. Besides, these two youngsters are under the protection of the court, aren't they?" Mr. Dalton was talking to Sheriff Lawrence, and I didn't even know the sheriff was here. That must have been who drove up in the other car, I heard.

When the sheriff spoke, it was not good. "Frank, we have a problem. The case was dismissed this morning, and the witness protection order for Billy and Kent as alibi witnesses went out with the case," reported the sheriff.

"Well, this is still a crime, and the second time Lou has attacked Billy. Lou should have been charged when he hit Billy with the baseball bat at the Fourth of July celebration."

"Frank, you know I can't get a warrant for anyone high up in the McCulloch organization without permission from Mr. Albert Winston Brown. I'll talk to him, but this is out of my hands." Sheriff Lawrence was talking to Mr. Dalton about getting permission from the county prosecutor to charge the bullies, but it was my dad who answered him.

"Sheriff, I warned Little John what would happen if one more thing happened to either one of these boys. I don't give a toot on a tin horn about Big John, Little John, or the county prosecutor. You better do your job and forget about the bigwigs."

"Now, John. I understand how you feel. I'd feel the same if it were my boy, but I can't go arresting Big John's grandson without the county prosecutor's okay. You know how things work in this county,"

"Sheriff, if you won't fix this, I will!"

"John, don't you go doing something you'll regret. I'll go see Mr. Brown first chance and explain things. He's the Commonwealth's Attorney and sworn to follow the law. I think, this being the second attack, he'll issue a warrant, but I can't go off half-cocked and get Big John riled."

Sheriff Lawrence was trying to help, but I knew my dad. When he made up his mind, that was it. Only Mom could talk to him then, and even she didn't always win when he got stubborn.

That's when Mom butted into the conversation. "John, help me get Billy to Waynesboro Memorial for stitches. You can fuss with the law later!"

Mom was ready to leave with or without Dad. My dad was mad, but Mom was boiling and not to be crossed.

At least they weren't mad at me. Dad was going after Lou's dad, and the fact that he was Big John's son and a police sergeant for the town would make no difference.

"Sheriff, I'll be back and do what I need to do. Laura Jane, let's go. Sally Ann, do you need to take Kent? You're welcome to ride with us. We have room."

Kent's Mom usually didn't like to ride with other people, but this time she surprised me. "John, that would help. Kent's nose is still bleeding, and I don't think his eye looks right."

I felt better when I heard Kent and I were going to the hospital together. My head was hurting worse, and I still couldn't see out of my left eye. I hoped Mom was wrong about me needing stitches.

Dad knelt beside me. "Frank, I'll be by in a day or two and replace those ruined towels."

My dad surprised me. He was doing the same thing as the Beamis brothers had done when they replaced the sport coat Mr. Cubley ruined when he covered their dad's body at the wreck last month.

After my wish on that darn mirror, that wreck started everything happening this summer, and I guess my mirror wasn't done with me yet. I never intended all this from a single wish for one adventure on my bathroom mirror because I was bored. Those high school boys, who told me to make a wish on a mirror, sure gave me a bum steer!

"Sheriff, I'll expect those bikes back by dark," Dad stated as he picked me up. He just picked me up like I weighed nothing."

"I'll do my best," replied Sheriff Lawrence, and he walked with Dad over to our car. The sheriff opened the car door and held it for us. Dad leaned in and put me down in the middle of the front seat.

Mom slid in beside me. When Kent and his mom got in the back, Dad drove us to the garage, where Mom put some old sheets on the seats since both Kent and I were still bleeding. Dad drove, and the ladies talked a little, but Dad didn't say anything until we got to the hospital. He parked right in the front where it said, "No Parking" on a big sign. He ran inside and got some nurses.

I was hoping they would let Kent and me stay together, but they took Kent into a separate room and put me in a room all by myself. The nurse, who came in to examine me, was way old. Heck, she was almost as old as my grandma. She took her thumb, opened my right eye, and shined this big flashlight into it. She did the same to my left eye. That's when I threw up all over the floor.

I was glad Mom and Dad were outside in the hall, or I might have gotten whacked for the mess I made. The nurse left for a couple of minutes and told me to lie still. She got this colored fellow, dressed all in white, to come back with her, and he brought a mop and a bucket. I thought it was for me to clean up my mess, but he cleaned it up like it was no big thing. The nurse didn't even fuss at me.

My doctor was Doctor Benfield. He asked me all sorts of dumb questions like I was stupid. He wanted to know where I lived, what day of the week it was, and the date. I keep up with dates. In fact, his questions were first-grade easy. He finally asked me what had happened. I told him about Lou, Carl, and Dickie beating me up, two words at a time and whispering. When I told him I was getting tired of getting beat up, his expression changed.

"Son, what do you mean? Has this happened before?"

Well, then I whispered how Lou hit a homer off the side of my head in the park on the Fourth of July. I told him if the bullies would switch sides whacking me in the head, it would help some. The left side of my head had taken about all I could stand.

He then asked my mom and dad to come into the room. They talked about me like I wasn't even there.

"Mr. and Mrs. Gunn, your boy says this is the second time he's been hit on the left side of his head. Is this true?"

"Of course, it's true," Mom said. I could tell she was irritated.

"Have the authorities been notified?"

This doctor must not read the newspapers. Mom was going to get in his hash if he kept this up.

"Doctor, we not only notified the authorities, but Kent and Billy are supposed to be under the protection of the court. They were witnesses in a criminal case, and their testimony contradicted the evidence of some local cops. Then, the son of one of the local policemen and two of his buddies beat up the boys. We think it was to stop Billy and Kent from testifying in court and messing up the policeman's case. On top of that, they got kidnapped by a sniper, who burned down our main industry!" Mom was answering. Dad was just looking madder and madder.

"Are these the two boys who were in the papers? The ones who were kidnapped over in Green Mountain County?" the doctor asked. Now he was finally starting to catch on.

"Yes! It's been in all the papers!"

"It sure has. I've been reading about your Billy and his little buddy. I should have paid closer attention to their names. Sorry!"

"All we want is to be left alone and go home in peace!" Mom was starting to get louder.

"I understand, but Billy has a concussion. We'll need to keep him until tomorrow. Also, I need to stitch up the wound on the left side of his head. That wound has some parts that are fresh and some old. To heal and not leave a bad scar, he needs a few stitches."

I didn't need stitches. I've never had any before and didn't want any now. I sure didn't want to have a sleepover in this hospital. No, sir, no way.

"Doctor, in that case, I'm going to stay here with him." Mom was making her wishes known. I thought I would try.

"Doctor Benfield, can Kent and I room together?"

The doctor explained Kent's injuries were not serious, although they were going to be painful and look bad for a few days. He would be discharged and could go home shortly.

Dr. Benfield looked at Mom. "Mrs. Gunn, it might be better if you left Billy with us, went home, got a little rest, and picked him up tomorrow. He should be fine; this is more of a precaution." The doctor was trying to help and make this easy on Mom, but I knew what was about to happen. I was right.

"Doctor Benfield, I'll not leave Billy here or anywhere else. If I can't stay with him, I'm taking him home."

Mom said about what I thought that she would. She's so predictable; it's scary.

Dad decided to finish the conversation. I didn't expect that. "Doc, I'll just gather his things. You tell me what we owe."

"No, no. Billy needs stitches, and he should stay here overnight. Mrs. Gunn, if you're that concerned, of course, you may stay. I'll admit him to the children's ward, and we have an empty double room there. The second bed will be very short, but you're welcome to use it, or we can move in a chair that reclines."

Mom's face softened. "Either is fine."

"I'll notify the nursing staff to bring in the chair." Doctor Benfield was a smart fellow.

Mom started slow and picked up speed on her orders to Dad. "John, when Kent and Mrs. Clark are ready, take them home. Tell Grandma that Scotty may sleep with her tonight, or he'll cry since Billy's not there. Have her put clean pajamas on him."

Dad asked, "Okay. Anything else?" I knew there was a lot more coming.

"Tell her that supper's in the fridge. Just warm up what we had last night. There should be plenty. Remind her there's ice cream for dessert. Pick us up in the morning, early—first thing. You have your man, Mr. Skelton, handle the garage." Mom was giving Dad orders like Joe Friday did to his partner on *Dragnet*, and that was that.

The doctor came back with a nurse. He told Mom I had to go with him for just a little while. He leaned over, explained stuff to me, but not all he said was the truth. He promised me that the stitches wouldn't hurt—not one bit. He claimed he had special medicine to numb the pain.

Doctors are tricky; they hold back the bad stuff. He was right; the stitches didn't hurt at all. The three shots he gave me so that the stitches wouldn't hurt were what he kept secret. I thought someone had kicked over a hornet's nest, and they were stinging the fire out of me when he put in the "it won't hurt" medicine.

When he was finished sewing up my face, they put me back on a gurney (a bed with wheels). Two young nurses wheeled me down the hall, up an elevator, and into a room on the second floor. Mom was waiting.

"Mom, where's Kent?" I was worried about him.

"Your father took him home. He wanted to say goodbye, but Dad needed to get back to the garage."

"Can he come to see me tomorrow?" I asked.

"Yes. His mom's taking off work, and he can visit you after you get home. The doctor says he'll discharge you when he does his rounds in the morning."

Mom was at the sink in the room, trying to get some of the bloodstains off her blouse. I'm not sure how much blood can run out of a person, but I think I was about on empty.

"Well, how is our little hero doing?" A pretty nurse asked me. She had a smile that reminded me of Boo.

"Okay, but I ain't no hero," I said without thinking.

"Billy Boyer, just because you got a bump on the head doesn't mean you can start using ain't. I don't want to hear it again." Mom wasn't going to let a little thing like almost bleeding to death slow down her grammar lessons.

"Sorry, Mom. Miss, I'm not a hero." I answered correctly but was totally embarrassed. This nurse was swell and not old. She was maybe nineteen or twenty, making her older but not too old.

"Aren't you the famous Billy Gunn that I've been reading about in all the papers? Here you are on my ward. It sounds to me like you're pretty special."

"It was Mr. Cubley who rescued Kent and me from the killer. He's the hero. He even got grazed on the arm." I had said about all I wanted to say. My head was still telling me to shut up.

"Billy, that makes you brave in my book. If you need anything, I'm on the evening shift. They have you on a light diet, but I bet I could find some cherry or grape Jell-o. How does that sound?"

"That sounds good. I like grape best. Can I have a Dr. Pepper to go with it?" I asked, thinking she just might be a good person to know.

"Billy, you may have some hot tea or tap water," Mom piped up, ruining my order for a cold Dr. Pepper.

"One grape Jell-o and a nice cup of tea. Mrs. Gunn, would a little honey to make it taste good be okay?" the nurse asked Mom.

"I think a little honey might be just what the doctor ordered if a certain little boy would stop talking and rest."

Mom gave me a half frown.

"I'll bring two cups. Also, I'll bring you a gown, and if you give me your blouse, I'll see if the laundry might be able to get those stains out. I'll have it back by ten tonight. Our laundry does a good job on bloodstains."

"Oh, that would be wonderful. I forgot to pick up an extra blouse at the house. We were in such a rush to get the boys over here."

After the tea, I tried to go to sleep, but it wasn't my fault that I couldn't. Nurses kept coming into the room all night long.

I found out in a hospital that nurses don't want anyone to rest. If they have to be up working, then no one should be sleeping. They not only woke me every hour for no reason; they took my temperature and put this thing on my arm called a blood pressure cuff every few minutes. The cuff thing had a balloon that they wrapped around my arm and pumped up. Near dawn, another old nurse came in after Mom was sound asleep. I thought this nurse was going to squeeze my arm right off with that cuff thing. She pumped way more than the other nurses, but the numbers stayed the same. I don't think that old nurse knew how to read the numbers. If you pumped up a tire, the numbers went higher on the tire gauge. As I said, I don't think that old nurse knew how to work that cuff thing because her numbers never changed, no matter how hard she tried to pump it up. I was sure glad when she gave up and left.

The doctor sent me home the next morning with a bunch of instructions that he gave to Mom. When Dad picked me up, I asked about my bike. I knew the answer by the look on his face before he even said a word. The bikes were still missing.

Riding back to the garage in the car, I worried the whole way. I closed my eyes and thought about all the good times we had had riding our bikes. I guess Mom and Dad thought I was sleeping. Mom asked Dad what they ought to do about the bullies. His answer scared me.

"Laura Jane, don't ask me again. I should have handled it the army way when Lou hit Billy with the bat in the park. I thought the court would protect him, but that was a mistake."

Dad was into one of his quiet moods. They generally were dangerous for me, but this time he wasn't mad at me. I was afraid he was angry at Mom and might hit her.

"John, the boys and I need you. Don't you go getting locked up in prison!"

"Laura Jane, I can be just as deceitful as the law in this town. Don't say another word to anyone about this! I can't afford you messing up what has to be done."

I peeped without opening my eye much and saw how Dad gave Mom a look I had never seen before.

Mom remained quiet the rest of the way home. I tried to figure out what Dad meant, but I fell fast asleep. I slept until we got home since there were no nurses to keep waking me up.

CHAPTER 4

BILLY HAS VISITORS
Tuesday, July 12, 1955

S cotty woke me from my nap. I was so tired from my night in the hospital that the first thing I did when I got home was to go to sleep. I almost bopped the little ankle-biter for waking me. He was right beside my bed when he leaned over and kissed me on the cheek.

"Billy, if those boys hurt you, you come tell me. I'll shoot 'em with my cap pistol. Okay?"

"I'll do that, Scotty."

"I missed you when you didn't come home."

"I missed you too. I had to stay at the hospital."

"I don't like that hop-stable," Scotty said with a frown.

It was rare that we talked like this. Usually, we were fighting. Scotty leaned close and whispered. "Don't tell Momma. Grandma let me stay up late and watch TV. She let me have two scoops of ice cream after she put me in my pajamas."

I knew why he didn't want Mom to hear him. I was surprised that the two scoops didn't keep him up all night.

"It sounds like you and Grandma had fun. Where was Dad?"

I was curious about Dad not putting a stop to ice cream at bedtime.

"Da Da worked in the garage. I think he was mad at somebody. He wouldn't talk to me—not none. I stayed with Grandma all night 'cause you were in the hop-stable."

"I would rather have been home with you, little guy."

"I'm not little. I'm big."

"Billy, here's your breakfast, some cream of wheat and dry toast," Mom announced as she came into the room carrying a tray with a dab of cream of wheat in a bowl, a cup of something hot, and one slice of toast with nothing on it on a plate all by itself.

"Where's the butter and jelly?"

I was starting to get a sick feeling about breakfast. Breakfast in bed was so rare that I thought this might be the third time in my whole life. But with a breakfast like this, thank goodness it was unusual.

"No butter or jelly until tomorrow, and you're to stay in bed and rest today—doctor's orders."

"Aw, Mom. I need to get with Kent and find my bike. It's important." I had a second gloomy feeling that I was more than grounded. I was on room confinement. Drats!

"No running around for you today, but I'll go down to Mountain Drug later and pick you up a comic book. You can tell me what you like a little later."

Mom was trying to be nice, but I wanted my freedom. Then she finished with a surprise for me.

"Oh, Mr. G. W. Smith brought you a get-well card. I need to clean it, and then I'll bring it up. Scotty, you come downstairs with me. Billy has to rest."

I almost didn't understand who Mom was talking about. Kent and I were not used to hearing Polecat being called Mr. G. W. Smith. Smith maybe, but not Mr. G. W. Smith.

My curiosity got me to thinking. There was no telling where he got the card. Gosh, he must be worried about me if he went to the trouble of getting me a card. I never heard of Polecat giving anybody a get-well card, ever. In fact, the only time he handed out cards was at Christmas, and those were for the people he wanted to hit up for a bit of Christmas money. I decided to make a point to thank him the next time I saw him.

Then, I heard a car drive up. Dad called out to Sheriff Lawrence, followed by the noise of several people coming into the kitchen. I slipped out of bed, opened the closet door, and hopped back into bed. Now, I could hear them through the heating vent that connected to the first-floor vents. It was my secret way of hearing stuff going on downstairs without my parents or Grandma knowing that I was listening.

"Uh, John, Mrs. Gunn, you know my chief deputy, E…Ed Barnes. We wanted to come by to, you know, talk."

Sheriff Lawrence sounded nervous, and I didn't hear them getting bikes out of their patrol car. I knew my bike was still lost because when you put a bike down, it makes a bike sound.

"John, I spoke to all three boys. They claim they never saw Kent or Billy yesterday, and they don't know anything about their bikes. I stuck my neck out on this one for you. I talked to Lou McCulloch without his father being present. Sergeant McCulloch's going to be madder than hell at me for going behind his back. I doubt he'll buy that I had no choice because he was at the hospital with Big John. I'm surprised you didn't run into him." Sheriff Lawrence was doing his best to make himself look good.

This was junk. Laura and Judy could tell the sheriff that Lou and the Lockhart brothers were lying. Lou started into Mountain Drug, saw Kent and me, and pushed the Lockharts back outside. That's when they found our bikes, and the rest was obvious.

I heard Mom and didn't need the vent, "Sheriff, those boys are lying. This is the third time this summer that Lou has attacked Billy. It's the second time all three bullies attacked Kent and Billy. You were in court when the judge told us that Kent and Billy were under the protection of the court. I want those monsters and their parents arrested."

Mom was mad and didn't care who knew it.

The sheriff lowered his voice to speak, "Ma'am, the judge's order expired yesterday. I have to talk to Prosecutor Brown before I can get an arrest warrant for those three boys."

"When are you going to do that?" my dad asked.

"John, I don't know," said the sheriff.

"Dammit, Dick. I've known you for a long time. Don't tell me you don't know," Dad began loud and then ended quietly. When he got quiet, that meant someone was about to get whacked.

The sheriff's answer surprised me. "Mr. Brown's missing. No one's seen the Commonwealth's Attorney since he left court yesterday. His car's gone, and he didn't go home last night. We have a BOLO out for him."

I knew a BOLO was "be on the lookout" in police talk. Polecat taught Kent and me a bunch of police talk during the time of the sniper.

35

"How about the bikes?" Dad asked. "Have you searched their houses?"

"John, we can't go around searching the homes of the most influ... some of the most im...John, we can't go busting in on citizens without probable cause. I got to go by the book." Sheriff Lawrence was floundering.

"You better do something!" Dad was so quiet; I could barely hear him.

Chief Deputy Barnes spoke up with, "John, we have every deputy looking for the bikes. We'll find them. It'll just take a little time." Barnes was trying to help the sheriff but not doing very well as far as I was concerned.

"Dick, Ed, you boys go on. I got work to do." I heard Dad but just barely. Someone opened the screen door, and I listened to the shuffling of feet, and some idiot let the screen door slam. I assumed the sheriff and Mr. Barnes were not wasting much time leaving.

People in town often talk about how strong my dad is. I know. I got the scars on my back from his belt to prove it. I think my dad even scared those cops since they left in such a hurry.

Next thing, I heard Mom coming upstairs to pick up my breakfast tray. I didn't have time to close the closet door.

"Mom, was that the sheriff?" I asked, trying to sound groggy like I'd been resting.

"Yes, Billy. The sheriff and the chief deputy."

"Did they bring my bike back?" I asked, leading up to something that I needed to tell Mom.

"No, son. Not yet." Mom answered with what I already knew.

"Mom, Judy Peterson and Laura Akers saw Lou, Dickie, and Carl come into Mountain Drug yesterday. The bullies saw Kent and me, and then they went right back outside. That's when they hunted up our bikes. Lou was lying when he said he never saw me yesterday."

"William Gunn, how do you know what Lou told the sheriff?" Mom wanted to know with a frown crossing her face.

I had made a stupid mistake. Mom was about to discover my secret, and there the closet door was wide open.

I thought fast and blurted out, "Uh, I came downstairs to get some water. I heard the sheriff tell Dad about it. I came right back upstairs when I saw we had company. I'm feeling much better. Honest."

I felt terrible about lying to my mom but needed to keep my vent a secret. Knowing what was going on kept me out of a lot of scrapes.

"I'll tell your father, but you stay in bed, young man. Don't you be sneaking downstairs to snoop!"

"No, ma'am. I'll stay right here. Would you tell Dad that I don't want him thinking I don't tell the truth?" Gosh, I was getting in deep, what with lying about the vent and now acting all truthful. I better quit before God turned me into a pillar of salt or something worse.

"You stay in bed, or I won't bring you a new comic book!"

"Yes, ma'am, stuck like glue, won't move an inch."

I told her which comics were my favorites. After she went downstairs, I was desperate to get out of bed and hunt for my bike. I was afraid Kent might be out there hunting on his own. I needed to be with him for protection.

Just as Mom got to the kitchen, another car pulled into the lot. In a few moments, I heard Mr. Cubley ask how I was feeling. Mom told him to go right up and to talk some sense into me about staying in bed. I quickly closed my closet door and hopped back into bed, just in time. This was turning into one busy morning for a kid who was supposed to be resting.

"Billy, I guess one day off wasn't enough. You had to figure out a way to get two days off." Mr. Cubley was smiling, so I knew he was joking with me.

We talked about Lou, Carl, and Dickie, and them stealing our bikes. He said he had his chief informant on the case.

"Mr. Cubley, guess what? Polecat brought me a get-well card."

"Well, the old boy must like you." He went on to say that Maddie had sent over a spice cake for the family. Then he ruined it, typical for an adult. He said I would have to wait until tomorrow to eat it because I was on the doctor's special diet, and spice cake wasn't part of it.

I complained about trying to get well on a starvation diet. I asked if he would smuggle me a saw blade for an escape.

He laughed. "Sorry, the warden's a friend of mine. You'll just have to wait for your official release date."

"I guess," I groaned more than said.

"Kent's mom called me before I came here. She almost had to give him a spanking for trying to sneak off, so, I need you to promise to behave, stay in bed, and get well. I'll stop off at his house when I leave here and make him promise the same."

"Mr. Cubley, I never heard of Kent ever doing something like that. He minds his mom almost all the time," I said, all serious like.

"Yes, she told me how hard it was for her to save enough money for his bike. Those three bullies have gone too far this time. I tried to talk to your dad, but he won't talk about it. I don't blame him for being angry, but I hope he lets the police handle it."

"Mr. Cubley, Kent wants to shoot them, and so do I. My dad won't shoot anybody, but he might not wait on the cops."

"Billy, the police and the grown-ups will have to handle this. If the bikes are returned, I bet you won't feel so bad."

I could tell that Mr. Cubley was trying to get my spirits up, but I knew better. I was afraid if we let the police handle it, our bikes were goners.

"Mr. Cubley, the sheriff told Mom and Dad that Lou, Carl, and Dickie swear they didn't do it. They're saying they weren't at the drugstore. That's a lie! Two girls in my class saw them, but nobody believes us. It's hopeless!"

"Sometimes, it does appear that people don't believe the facts. Instead, they believe lies from those who have wealth and political power. Don't give up yet, son. I'll talk to the troopers. They might be able to help."

"I'm starting to feel like no one cares."

"Billy, sometimes the people who should help, don't. It's up to the good people to put things right. You just get well. Let the adults figure out how to make things right. Okay?"

"I guess so." I said it, but I didn't believe it.

Mr. Cubley walked downstairs and out the back door. I could hear him and Dad talking by the garage, but I couldn't hear what they were saying. Mr. Cubley left, and I went back to being bored.

Later that morning, Mom brought me a Roy Rogers and a Scrooge comic. She was nice to get me two. They cost a dime each, so I knew she felt bad about me getting hurt.

Lunch was a piece of toast and some soup. Supper was not much better, but she did let me have a small, and I mean a tiny, piece of spice cake. Two bites, and it was gone. I licked the frosting off the plate.

I read my new comics for the tenth time and was about to fall asleep when I heard Dad on the phone. Since it was too late for him to be calling a customer, I opened my closet door and listened.

"Bruce, how have you been? Yeah, I should have, but things have been busy around here. I guess you heard about the sniper. I thought things would calm down, but I got trouble. Bad trouble."

Dad told him briefly about what the bullies had done to Kent and me over the summer and explained that Lou's father was the town's police sergeant. He went into all the details about what happened behind the furniture store and our injuries. Dad and Bruce spent a lot of time talking about each of the town police officers, the missing Commonwealth's Attorney, and where Sergeant McCulloch lived. I almost fell asleep, but then he said something I didn't quite understand.

"Bruce, do you think the boys will help? I hate to ask, but I just don't know what else to do. If I do it, my wife and family will suffer more than me.... Yeah, you and I think alike—a midnight formation, the army way. This kid, Lou, he's the ringleader. No, I don't want to kill him or even put him in the hospital.... That's right. You understand exactly what to do to him.... What? Do you mean Lou's old man? Hell, I don't much care if you did, but doing that to him might complicate things. It's going to be hard enough snatching the kid. Let's keep it simple.... Don't worry. I'll fix up an alibi, just tell me when.... I'm in their debt, big time. You tell that crazy master sergeant not to get too wound up.... Oh, also, they took the boy's bikes. I'll send you pictures and descriptions, so keep an eye out for them…. They sure do, in the worst way. Yeah, talk to you later."

I was going over in my mind what Dad had just said. I knew he was going to do something to Lou, but I had no idea what exactly. I knew what an alibi was. Dad was going to have to cook one up. He would need a good one when the police showed up to question us. This would give me a chance to learn how to invent an alibi that would fool cops.

Dad was friends with some sergeants in the Army. These guys were together during something called the Battle of the Smudge or Budge or something like that. Dad hardly spoke about it, but sometimes at night, he would wake us all up yelling. Mom told me that it was because he had bad dreams about the war. When Dad hurt me that time, she explained it was because of the war, and it wasn't his fault. I learned to avoid Dad whenever he stayed out all night and came home in a quiet mood.

He was going to get these sergeants to do something and maybe even get our bikes back. I didn't care if they did hurt Lou. He deserved it!

CHAPTER 5

BILLY IS BOTH BETTER & WORSE
Wednesday, July 13, 1955

Wow, my head sure was hurting, but I wasn't about to tell Mom. The rest of me felt like I had been run over by "Blacky", Dad's big black tow truck. Today, the calendar date was the thirteenth—never a lucky day for me. Plus, it was raining.

Last night, my mom announced that she wouldn't let me work today because of my busted head. But now that it was raining, there would be no cars to wash. I was afraid that I was still on room confinement. I needed to get the word out to someone for help. I was being starved to death on bread and water in my bedroom prison.

Scotty was back to being a brat. Grandma was fussing about how this town was going to the dogs. I had to agree, but I didn't think the dogs would take it.

Breakfast smelled good, so I brushed my teeth, washed my face, brushed my hair on the right side and a little on top, but then gave up. My hair was cut short for the stitches on the left side. Guess I would have to live with looking like I had gone sideways into a buzz saw.

Mom, for years, refused to give me a Mohawk haircut. However, the hospital just did, but only on one side. When I asked her about cutting the other side to match, well, another battle lost. Kids have no rights at all, and to make my day a total failure, I remembered that my bike had been stolen.

Okay, because I was dizzy, I slowly took the steps downstairs one at a time and pretended nothing was wrong. I tried to act normal so Mom would forget about starving me to death.

"Hey, Mom. What's for breakfast? Something smells good."

"Good morning, Billy. How's your head?" Mom asked as she flipped some French toast in the iron skillet.

"Doesn't hurt at all. Any news on my bike?" I kept my fingers crossed for two reasons: my little lie about my head wouldn't be noticed, and my bike would show up.

Dad was the one who gave me my answer. "No, son, your bike may be a lost cause. I'll check with the sheriff, but don't get your hopes up."

Grandma added, "I don't know when the both of you will learn that this whole town is a lost cause. First, snipers, then they burn the plant down, everyone's out of work, and it's not safe for children to walk the streets. Muggers, killers, and thieves roam free! I guess you'll sell out and move after we're all dead and buried." Grandma Harris was looking for a fight. Mom or Dad might give her one this morning.

Mom went first. "Mother, we all feel bad enough without you adding to it. We're doing the best we can. Please, drop it."

"Drop it! Drop it! You speak to me like I was a dog, just like a dog. I wouldn't treat a dog the way you treat me. Stingers and bouquets are all I hear around this house. As much as I do for you, and you treat me worse than dirt."

Grandma was bouncing Scotty on her knee while going on a rant. She was bouncing him so hard that his head was bobbing forward and backward. I was worried that a major fight between Mom and Grandma was brewing. We hadn't had one in a week and a half, so a squabble was due.

I figured Dad would chime in, but he didn't. He just sat there. He wasn't in one of his "quiet moods" from staying out late because he had been home last night. So, perhaps, no big family fights this morning. I could live with a little one.

"Billy, here's your French toast. Get some orange juice out of the fridge. You can eat what you want today. Just don't overexert yourself."

Mom gave me two pieces of French toast and took a close look at the side of my head. I pretended it didn't hurt when she poked around the edge of the bandage with her finger.

"Can I have a piece of spice cake to go with breakfast?" I asked, thinking I might be able to trade on my injury for a nice hunk of cake. I found out that I had pushed Mom too far.

"No, you may not. Eat your breakfast and be content. Children in China would love to have your French toast. Clean your plate and stop that whining and turning up your nose over this lovely breakfast."

I said nothing, quickly got my orange juice, and sat back down.

Grandma started to say something, but the phone rang. Mom picked it up on the first ring.

"Hello, Gunn's Garage. Oh, hello, Sally Ann, is everything okay? Sure, he can come over. Now? No problem. What did he want? That is odd...Oh. Sure, bring him on over." Mom hung up the phone with a glance at me.

"Was that Kent's mom?" I asked, but I knew it had to be.

"It was. The bank president asked her to come in early for a meeting, but he wouldn't tell her why. She's going to drop Kent off here, so he won't sneak off to look for his bike. Billy, I expect you to set the example. No sneaking off!" Mom gave me her mom stare. "Billy?"

"Yes, ma'am. No sneaking off. I gotta set an example and behave." I was so glad to know today would not be a total waste. The warden was letting me have a visitor. The best news, I was off bread and water rations.

I noticed Dad reading Monday's paper. The front page was just the old news about what started all my adventures. The collision between the McCulloch log truck and Mr. Beamis was the wreck Dad worked, and he let me go with him. Poor Mr. Beamis was dead, and the paper was still saying it was his fault, which wasn't true at all. My boss, Mr. Cubley, saw the wreck happen and was told by the driver that the faulty brakes on the log truck caused the accident.

Dad turned to the sports page, which was the end of me reading the news. I munched on my breakfast and decided I didn't want any more news or adventures. I just wanted my bike back. I kept thinking about getting a gun and forcing Lou, Carl, and Dickie to return it. Kent felt the same. The problem was that I had no way of getting my hands on a gun. Dad's guns were rifles and shotguns. I wouldn't get far, toting a rifle down Main Street—not after a sniper killed all those people.

"Hey, BB, how's the noggin?" Kent let the screen door slam with a bang. I was lost in thought and jumped. I hadn't even heard his mom drive into the lot. Then, a new worry started bothering me. Could a concussion make a person go deaf?

"BB, you asleep at the switch?"

"Hey, Superman, you look awful," I answered Kent, and he did look awful. His face was all kind of lumpy with dark bruises. He looked worse than me.

"Thanks, beautiful. You look like Chief Red Cloud scalped you, but only on one side," Kent said with his crooked grin.

Mom interrupted our conversation. "Kent, would you like some French toast? I have extra."

"Yes, ma'am. It smells good." Kent was not one to turn down food. I bet he had a big breakfast at home, but a second one was okay by him. I never understood how he stayed thin when he ate so much.

"Billy, get Kent some orange juice," Mom told me with a wave of her spatula.

"Kent, it's in the fridge," I told him.

"Billy, I told you to get it. That's no way to treat company," Mom scolded.

"Heck, Superman's not company. He's family," I said as I got him his orange juice. The whole time, I saw Kent trying not to laugh. When he healed up, I would get even.

Kent and I finished breakfast and went up to my bedroom. I gave him my two new comics to read. I was going to kill Scotty. The skunk had ripped the cover off my brand-new Roy Rogers comic. It was impossible to have anything with a little brother in the house.

I told Kent about the phone call Dad made last night. His response was, "I don't care what they do as long as they find my bike!"

We talked about where those three might have hidden our bikes. Kent reminded me that Lou snatched his tennis shoes last winter. He looked all over, but no luck. Like his shoes, he didn't think he would ever see his bike again. Kent looked like Sad Sack in the comic book.

The phone rang a couple of times. We could hear Mom talking to her friends about how I was healing up and thanking them for calling.

"Kent, it would be better if people would send over get well stuff like candy, comics, or baseball card bubblegum," I said and smiled.

"Yeah, hey, you got any cards to trade?"

Kent and I looked through my baseball card collection. He had brought over some of his extra cards, so we did serious trading, which took us until lunch.

He and I got spice cake for dessert. We even helped Dad and Mr. Skelton in the garage. That's how bored we were. The afternoon dragged along as slowly as waiting for the three o'clock bell in school.

When Kent's mom picked him up, she came into the kitchen in a bit of a huff. Kent and I were sent upstairs, which caused us to sit in my closet to listen.

"Laura Jane, I've never been so mad in all my life. The nerve of that man. Telling me my son better stop telling lies about Lou McCulloch. He even intimated Kent and Billy were troublemakers, getting into fights all over town, trying to pass the blame off on their betters. I almost smacked his face!"

Mrs. Clark was talking so loudly that we didn't need the vent. We could hear her plain as day.

"I don't see how you held your temper," Mom replied.

"I had to. I wanted to tell him off and quit. Quit, right on the spot. But I couldn't. I can't afford to lose my job at the bank—even with what they pay."

Mrs. Clark had gotten quiet, and then we heard her blow her nose. Afterward, she said something too low for us to hear, so we moved closer to the vent.

"…he better be done with false accusations?" But we missed the first part.

"What did you tell him?" Mom asked.

"I told him Sheriff Lawrence was looking into the stolen bikes. I was going to leave it up to the sheriff. I did tell him my boy was a good boy. He was no troublemaker."

"Well, good for you. What did he say to that?"

Mom was making something in the kitchen by the sounds of it. I thought she must be making tea or coffee.

"He said this was a friendly warning. But, if I wanted to keep my job, I better get my boy under control. He then told me I was dismissed. Dismissed…like a schoolgirl. That man needs to be dismissed with a beating like they gave my little boy."

"Little boy," I whispered to Kent. I had to put a hand over my mouth to keep from laughing.

He acted like he was going to punch me but didn't. Instead, he just gave me a dirty look.

Superman and I decided we would try to get another piece of cake from the kitchen. When moms are upset, sometimes they let kids have stuff they usually wouldn't. Just because it didn't work at breakfast didn't mean it wouldn't work now.

Well, it didn't work this time either. Both Mom and Mrs. Clark said, "No, you boys are not going to ruin your suppers," right off at the same time. Kent's mom told him to get in the car.

A few minutes later, after the Clarks left, I walked over to the garage just as Mr. Cubley pulled into the lot in his Chevrolet Bel Air. If I couldn't get a jeep like Nellybelle, a car like Mr. Cubley's would be my second choice.

"Hey, Billy, how are you feeling?" Mr. Cubley asked me as soon as he saw me.

"I'm fine, Mr. Cubley. How are things at the hotel?"

"Picking up. Not full but picking up. When the weather breaks, if you're feeling up to it, we can use you, boys. Just let me know."

"I hope to be back tomorrow or the next day at the latest," I said as I followed Mr. Cubley into the garage. I was hoping to pick up more news.

"John, how goes it?" Mr. Cubley asked my dad.

"Matt, I guess okay. It can't get much worse. I hope it doesn't get much worse." My dad was not happy. It showed in his voice and face.

Dan Skelton, our new mechanic, walked out from the parts cage. He greeted Mr. Cubley.

"Dan, good to see you," Mr. Cubley said in return. Mr. Skelton walked over and extended his hand to Mr. Cubley.

"Matthew, always a pleasure. That daughter of mine still doing a good job in the dining room?" Mr. Skelton was in a much better mood than my dad.

"Boo is doing a fine job," Mr. Cubley answered.

I noticed he called Boo, Boo. Mr. Skelton didn't like his daughter's nickname; he preferred Beverly Olivia Skelton, but her dad was starting to accept her nickname. I even recently heard him use it once or twice.

"John, the reason I came by was to pass along a little information. This tidbit, I picked up from an informant of mine."

I knew Mr. Cubley was talking about Polecat, who knew all kinds of things. He delivered papers for the *Highland Gazette*, which meant he was all over town every day. The man was so odd that people thought him a little crazy. Paying him no mind, they said stuff in front of him, like he wasn't even there, but he could remember everything he heard, and the man was brilliant. Jeepers, creepers, he made a great informant. Mr. Cubley let him eat breakfast at the hotel for free every morning in exchange for information.

"What information might that be?" Dad said back to him. I noticed Dad traded his moody look for a curious one.

"Lou McCulloch was seen riding a red bike on Monday afternoon, late. Carl and Dickie Lockhart were following and riding double on a green bike. Now, this informant says those bikes were exact matches to Kent and Billy's bikes."

Mr. Cubley smiled, so I knew the chances of Kent and me getting our bikes back just went up. Way up.

"Okay, so why are you telling me this?" Dad asked, throwing a rag on the workbench, giving Mr. Cubley his full attention.

"Well, I want you to pass what I'm telling you along to the sheriff. I can't because my informant must remain in the shadows. That's how he works."

Mr. Cubley looked at me and held his hand up like he was taking an oath. I knew what that meant. He sometimes made Kent and me take oaths to keep quiet about hotel secrets we sometimes heard by accident or on purpose. Being employees of his hotel, Superman and I always kept those secrets, well…secret.

"How will that help me get them back? The sheriff said he wouldn't search their houses," Dad said with a frown starting to form on his face.

Mr. Cubley grinned, "This informant saw the three riding on Lewis and Clark Street toward Highland Hardware. Ten minutes later, he saw them walking on Elm Tree Lane toward Lake Street. They were laughing about something and had no bikes with them."

I knew what he was saying. It was easy to figure out where they had stashed our bikes. Richard Lockhart, who was Carl and Dickie's dad, ran Highland Hardware for Big John McCulloch. If they rode our bikes north on Lewis and Clark to the hardware store, mystery solved.

The hardware store kept a bunch of new bikes and bikes to be repaired in the basement. If the bullies hid them there, no one would pay any attention to two more used bikes. They could put repair tags on them with bogus names and future repair dates. No one would bother them for weeks and weeks. Bikes are easy to sell if crooks wait until the cops stop looking for them.

"Matt, I'll certainly pass this along. No one will know the source. You can be sure of it," Dad answered, but I could see what my dad was thinking. Mr. Cubley noticed too.

"John, just promise me that you'll let the police handle it. Right?" Mr. Cubley was concerned that my dad might get them back on his own.

"I will guarantee you that I'll not do a thing but pass this information along. Satisfied?" Dad asked Mr. Cubley.

"I am. Billy, do you swear?"

"Mr. Cubley, I know what a secret is. I will. I do. I mean, I won't," I said, holding up my right hand just a little to let him know his secret was safe with me. He taught me all about taking the oath to tell the truth when I was to be a witness in court.

I figured on another late-night phone call, and I was right on the bull's eye. I tried my best to stay awake, reading a comic under the covers with a flashlight.

It was late, but I heard Dad on the phone and listened. Mom was asleep, and Dad was in the kitchen talking softly, so softly that I could barely make out what he was saying.

"Bruce, something else for the guys. The bikes are in the basement of the Highland Hardware. You'll find it on Main between Fifth and Elm Tree Lane. Can't miss it."

Dad gave this Bruce guy a complete description of the bikes. He described the inside of the hardware and told him he would mail him a diagram of the hardware and a street map of the town. This Bruce guy must have asked about a security guard. Dad told him the big boss owned the hardware, and the town police were in his pocket because they were on the plant's payroll. These special cops checked his businesses regularly. Big John didn't need to pay for a watchman. Also, the Highland Police Department was short of men. The night shift only had one cop manning the PD office and one on patrol. A diversion at the plant would take care of the town car for thirty minutes or longer. Plenty of time to get in and....

Dad's voice grew dim, and darn, suddenly, it was the middle of the night, and I was in my closet where I had gone to sleep next to the vent. I missed the end of the call. I got up, fell into bed, and was asleep right away.

CHAPTER 6

BILLY AT THE CHIEF'S BURIAL
Thursday, July 14, 1955

I awoke and opened my eyes one at a time. Scotty was standing beside my bed, holding my new Scrooge comic book. The cover and some inside pages were on the floor behind him.

"Scotty, leave my stuff alone. Give me that!"

I grabbed his arm and squeezed until he let go. He started to cry, so I gave his arm a push. He turned and ran down the stairs, yelling like I had pulled his arm clean off. Grandma asked him what was wrong, and he told a tall tale about how I was beating on him, but I was mad and didn't care what he said. I got up, picked up the cover and pages off the floor, and tried to Scotch tape it all back together. It wouldn't hold. Two new comic books and Scotty had ruined both within as many days.

Perhaps a circus or traveling fair might come to town. I would give it my stash of fourteen dollars to take the brat. Then, he could clean up after the elephants or sell bottles of elixir to pay for his keep on the road.

Going into the bathroom, I wrote "BB" in the water of the toilet and flushed. I looked in the mirror, the one that was causing all the trouble. I only saw myself, nothing spooky, so I sighed, washed my face, and brushed my hair on one side and the top. Finally, I gave up on the hair and got dressed.

Another awful day to mark off the calendar. Today was the funeral for Chief Obie Smith, who had been killed the day of the plant fire. Mom told me yesterday that our family was to be in the church by one o'clock, but the funeral wasn't until two. She expected a crowd to fill not only the church sanctuary but the Sunday school auditorium on the first floor. Grandma was keeping Scotty at home, thank goodness. Mom said I had to go to the funeral, even after I had begged to stay home and help look after the evil monkey.

The First National Bank of Highland was closing at one o'clock for the funeral, so Kent and his mom would also be at the church. She and Kent were members of the Methodist Church, but Mrs. Clark had been ordered to attend Chief Smith's funeral at the Green Mountain Baptist Church, or her pay would be docked for the entire day.

When we got to the church, although we were an hour early, only a few seats were left. So, when Kent and his mom arrived, they had to sit downstairs.

Fifteen minutes before the funeral started, a whole crowd of police marched into the sanctuary. They all sat in the reserved section. I saw Trooper Giles, and he smiled at me. The other troopers had very stern expressions. Not one of them was smiling; in fact, they didn't even look around. The Smith family came in last and took up the first two rows.

I fell asleep during the service, which earned me a punch from Dad and a dirty look from Mom. Staying up late listening to Dad's calls to his army buddies made me sleepy. Plus, the preacher was going on and on about some poor man getting robbed on a dusty road. I thought the preacher said the guy's name was Sammy Terian. This Bible story sounded like Kent and me getting beaten and robbed. But that's when the preacher proclaimed Chief Smith had good qualities, the same as this Sammy Terian, which was not true. The Chief never helped Kent nor me with those bullies. That's when I dozed off and got punched.

Going to the cemetery was fun. There were police cars in a long line in front of us, and all of them had their red lights going. Also, every intersection had cops blocking the road as if we were the governor or somebody important.

It was raining, and the cemetery was muddy. I stepped in two small puddles on purpose, but Mom didn't fuss at me for getting mud on my shoes because everyone was walking in mud.

Back at home, Dad pulled the car up close to the kitchen. Mom made us all take our shoes off at the door. Scotty was sound asleep on Grandma's lap, but when the screen door slammed, it woke him up, and I got blamed. My fingers were wet; it slipped, and how was that my fault?

It was a quiet afternoon only fit for reading or building my new model airplane without help from Scotty. I had just glued on a wing when a car pulled up.

Dad left with a stranger in that car and was gone for more than an hour. I knew when he returned because I heard the kitchen door slam. Dad let the door bang, but no one fussed at him.

I was gluing on the landing gear when my parents started talking in the kitchen. Grandma was in the living room with Scotty, watching a soap on TV. I had to listen at the vent.

"John, what are you planning? You need to let the police handle this!" Mom was saying. That's what got me interested.

"What do you mean? You're the one who said for me to do something. I'm doing something. It's gotta be done, and I'm not going to call it off." Dad was speaking softly, and I could just barely hear him with my ear next to the vent.

"Tell me what you are doing."

"No, Laura Jane. I'm taking care of business. Now leave me to it." I could hear Dad's footsteps as he walked into the bedroom.

Dad got a call after supper that wasn't a tow job. It was Sheriff Lawrence.

After the call, Mom asked, "What news did the sheriff have?"

"I don't know if he's lying or just stalling. He says he can't do anything until they find the Commonwealth's Attorney. Brown remains missing. No one's seen him, his car can't be found, and his family is frantic. The police have run all the roads looking for him, clear down to Roanoke and past Charlottesville. No sign of him or his vehicle."

"How strange." Mom sounded concerned. "I hope they find him."

"I don't care if they find him or not. I'd rather handle this myself. The law's not going to go against Big John, Little John, or Lou. The McCullochs run this town. The sheriff only cares about getting re-elected, and he knows if he crosses Big John, most of his campaign funds go out the window." Dad was angry and frustrated. I could hear it in his voice.

"I know, but I don't have to like it. I just don't want you getting arrested. You're who I care about. This family needs you," Mom said in a softer voice.

"I'll not only be careful, but there won't be any way they'll be able to tie me to it," Dad added a little louder.

"I'm praying that you're right."

"Laura Jane, is there any more of that spice cake?"

When I heard that, I scooted down the stairs trying to think up an excuse for going to the kitchen.

Both Grandma and Scotty were napping with their soap still playing on the TV. Dad was sitting down with a piece of cake when I got to the kitchen.

"What are you doing down here?" Mom asked me with a very suspicious look.

"I got thirsty. May I have a glass of water? Wow...Dad... cake. May I have a piece of cake?" I asked, all innocent-like.

"That boy has radar or something. He shows up whenever cake or candy is even mentioned," Dad said with a chuckle.

I got my cake and kept my vent a secret. Hiding the truth was getting easier the more I did it. I got the last piece of cake and Scotty missed out. Little kids often sleep through the good stuff. Too bad. He got what he deserved for ruining my new comics.

Matt was sitting down with a cup of tea and a piece of spice cake at the employee's table in the kitchen of Cubley's Coze. He was thinking about the old hotel and all the good times he had spent here with his uncle, Thomas Jefferson Cubley. However, no one called him by his proper name, only his nickname, "Uncle TJ." Being his uncle's only nephew, Matt had recently inherited the place. However, after working through several hotel calamities, he was starting to think of Cubley's Coze as his own business.

Two waitresses were talking about the recent funerals. Matt had skipped the funeral for Chief Smith. Funerals were still too painful because of the recent death of his wife, Janet, and their son, Jack. They were buried together in Roanoke in a shady part of the cemetery. The city where they had been so happy until a drunk driver took it all away. His salvation had been Cubley's Coze, which was keeping him occupied.

The original name of the resort hotel was Cubley's Cozy Inn and Tavern, as named by Matt's grandfather—Uncle TJ's father.

When, as a small child, Uncle TJ couldn't say all the names but could only get out, "Cubley's Coze," the name stuck. Grandpa Cubley liked the sound of it, changed all the signs, and that's how the hotel got its unusual name.

Matt's mind was picking up random thoughts like a child grabbing puzzle pieces. A big black tow truck, little Billy Gunn helping his father work the Beamis wreck on the day he arrived in town, all the unusual people of Highland he'd recently met, and dramatic events were crossing his mind like a holiday parade.

After that wreck, a sniper had come to town. One murder after another confused the local police until the state police joined the investigation and asked Matt for help. Having been a drill instructor at the Marine Corps Sniper School during World War II, one of the state troopers, a former student, came to him for advice. Thus, Matt had landed right in the middle of the police investigation.

The final tragedy was when the sniper burned the plant, killed the local chief of police, shot Big John, and took Billy, Kent, and the hotel groundskeeper, Richard Baker, hostage. Matt had freed the boys and Richard, but he had to kill the sniper in the process. The killing had been justified, but it troubled him.

Presently, his days were spent trying to keep the hotel profitable. The town boss, Big John McCulloch, was causing Matt all sorts of trouble. Matt's Grandfather had owned Green Mountain when the McCulloch patriarch moved into the county. The McCulloch family had built a newer and larger resort on the west side of the mountain on land leased from the Cubley family. Cubley's Coze was on the eastern side of that same mountain. The lease favored the Cubley family, causing Big John to do all he could to buy Matt out or run him out of business and off the land.

The two brightest lights in his dark world were Billy and Kent. Hiring the boys to wash cars at the hotel had brightened his days. Although, when it came to Kent, he felt conflicted. Kent reminded him of his dead son, Jack.

He had become fond of the boys in a short period of time. But the three bullies had turned on Billy and Kent because they worked for Matt and were scheduled to testify as alibi witnesses. The boys had seen something that would show Little John and the local cops were charging the wrong people for the shootings. So, Lou McCulloch had targeted Billy and Kent to stop them from ruining his dad's case.

The town police were in Big John's pocket, and the county sheriff was caught in the middle and worried about the election. The state police were doing what they could, but Big John had a direct line to the governor, a former corporate attorney for McCulloch Wood Products, who had ordered the troopers to lay off. Circumstances over the stolen bikes had made their recovery complicated.

"Matthew, you look troubled," Chuck Tolliver, Matt's loyal hotel manager, commented.

Matt focused on Chuck and whispered, "I told John Gunn about the bicycle lead Polecat had given us. I was afraid if I told the sheriff, he would figure out my informant was Polecat."

Matt took another sip of tea and asked Chuck to follow him. Leaving his empty cake plate, he rose, and with Chuck following, they moved into the lobby beside the front desk where they could speak in private. No guests were in the lobby.

Chuck began with, "You think John might try to go after Lou or Lou's dad on his own?"

"I don't think so. He promised to pass the information along to the sheriff or maybe the state boys," Matt explained.

Chuck nodded in agreement and added, "Well, the officers of the Highland Police Department are out of it. They aren't going to arrest the son of their sergeant, and Sergeant McCulloch isn't about to arrest his own boy."

Matt took a final sip of tea and continued, "I'm hoping that the sheriff will do the right thing." Matt stated and put down his empty teacup.

"So, what now?" Chuck asked.

"I guess we wait and pray that John will give the sheriff a chance to work this out. Maybe Albert Winston Brown will turn up and do his job, or things will all go to hell, the plant will not be rebuilt, the town will die, and we will all move to Florida and go fishing." Matt's joke wasn't funny, but it wasn't meant to be. He departed from the front desk, took the stairs to the second floor, and sought refuge in his private apartment.

Chuck took their cups and saucers back to the kitchen. He handed them to the dishwasher, Toby, "The Cleaner," who was still working away on the dishes from the evening's seating. He never left until every last dish, pot, and pan was spotless and put away in its proper cupboard. Thus, his nickname.

Chuck no sooner resumed his position behind the front desk when a gentleman came into the lobby with an old Army duffle bag that was as old as the hills—World War II vintage or older.

"May I help you?" Chuck asked the potential guest.

"I hope so. I'd like a room for the night. Do you have a vacancy?" The man was a bit scruffy looking, but with open rooms, Chuck was reluctant to turn away a paying guest.

"I think we have a room. The kitchen's closing. Do you need supper?" Chuck asked, trying to take the measure of the man.

"No, I ate in Lexington, but thank you. My business meeting ran later than I expected, and I thought I'd better stop for the night. I hope you have a vacancy. I'd like to avoid driving into Charlottesville as sleepy as I am."

"I noticed your duffle. Are you military?" Chuck was fishing. The man's face suddenly flashed suspicion, but then it was gone in an instant, and he smiled.

"I was a first sergeant in WW II, Europe. I still like to use the old duffle. I know it looks pretty beat up, but it has sentimental value. I hope that doesn't cause a problem with me staying here. I'm happy to pay cash-in-advance. I was told you ran a nice place by a friend of mine." The man was trying to be friendly, which changed Chuck's mind about him.

"No, glad to have former military stay with us. My boss was a Marine, so you're very welcome here. Who was the friend? I might know him," Chuck asked, and this time he was just being Chuck.

"No, I'm sure you aren't acquainted. He heard about this place from a friend of a friend. As I said, I'm just passing through." The man's tone had changed slightly to more guarded.

"Well, I can put you in room 312, nice view, and should be quiet. I'll need your name and address for the register." Chuck pulled out the register, but as was Chuck's procedure, he insisted on writing the guest's information first. He only let the guest sign in the final column. Chuck liked things neat, orderly, and readable.

"Bruce Waters. My address is 1431 South Street, Denver, Colorado. Where do you want me to sign?" Mr. Waters asked.

"Right here." Chuck showed him, pointing to the line to the right of the address. Chuck noticed the man took his time with his last name, being careful to fashion each letter.

Mr. Waters took the key and quickly climbed the stairs, two at a time. He didn't use the elevator. Chuck walked into Matt's office and looked out the window to study the cars in the guests' parking lot. The newest arrival's vehicle was near the light pole, a 1950 Buick with Tennessee plates. Chuck wrote down the number. He would make certain that Mr. Waters paid his bill before checking out. He even scolded himself for not taking the man up on his offer to pay in advance.

Chuck's worry was needless. Bruce would pay his hotel bill with cash, and his room would be left in perfect order. A night fog creeping up the mountain from the river would leave more of a trail.

CHAPTER 7

A MISSING PERSON
Friday, July 15, 1955

Matt was troubled. On his way to bed last night, he'd given Cliff Duffy, the night clerk, the latest list of con men and deadbeats for delivery to the Green Mountain Resort. Big John had been trying to run him out of business by stealing portions of his guest registry and luring his guests away, but Matt was returning the favor by dishing out something worse. Having been a prosecutor in Roanoke, Matt was able to get public records on minor criminals. Several of the prosecutors, his previous colleagues, were happy to supply him with the information he was sending to his competitor.

He tried to rationalize his trickery by telling himself he was keeping Duffy's wife from being fired. Big John was forcing Cliff to steal guests' information to lure them away from Cubley's Coze. Cliff's wife, the family's major income producer, worked as the account for several businesses owned by Big John.

Rather than fire Cliff, Matt turned him into a double agent. Supplying the other resort with the names of crooks, Big John was being duped into inviting criminals to book reservations. However, this trickery bothered Matt, especially at bedtime, his usual time for prayer.

He had to admit that his spy-trick was working, perhaps too well. These criminal guests at the Green Mountain Resort were skipping out on room rents plus stealing towels, bedclothes, and lamps from the rooms. The Highland Police were running frequent calls to the rival resort, and one need not mention how these "special guests" were causing general mayhem for the staff.

Just before dawn, Matt's guilty feelings over another recent event had spawned a terrible nightmare. He dreamed that he was checking in a hotel guest when the guest suddenly screamed. Matt looked down to find both his hands covered in blood.

His dream caused him to send Richard Baker back up to the hunting lodge to bleach the remaining bloodstains from the front porch. These stains came from the man Matt had killed during his rescuing of Richard, Kent, and Billy. The shooting was unavoidable, but it continued to bother him.

Coming down to the lobby after his miserable night's sleep, Chuck reported his worry over last night's late arrival. He gave Matt the details, which caused Matt to peek at the guest in the dining room. But to Matt, all seemed normal. He was, however, relieved when the man left ahead of the checkout time and paid his bill in cash. Chuck was excellent at spotting guests who needed watching, but Matt guessed Chuck had missed it on this particular person.

Trooper Mike Quinn next arrived for breakfast and a chat. Since Matt had been a central figure in the recent sniper investigation, all the local troopers, except for the sergeant, were now very friendly.

"Morning, Matt. Will you join me for breakfast?" the trooper asked Matt.

"Don't mind if I do. I hear this place serves a decent breakfast," Matt joked, trying to pull himself out of the blues.

"Yeah, that's what I hear from the other troopers. I thought I would check it out for myself. It's always good to double-check things." The trooper said with a smile.

"I noticed how thorough you are. This makes, what, your tenth test breakfast since I inherited the place last month?"

"Matthew, you exaggerate. I think it's only number nine," the trooper replied, enjoying the banter.

Boo came over, gave each man a cup of black coffee, and took their orders.

After she left, Matt asked, "Mike, what's on your mind?"

A frown crossed the trooper's face. "We seem to be back in the thick of it. I guess you heard Mr. Albert Winston Brown is missing. He seems to have dropped off the face of the earth—not a clue. He's now been declared a missing person, officially."

"Yeah, I hear his wife is under the care of Doctor Hill. I wonder if she knows something or in the dark?" Rumors from his staff and local guests in the dining room were divided on what the lady might know.

"Matt, if she knows something, she isn't sharing. The sheriff's been talking to her because I don't think she trusts us troopers. Her husband always kept us at a distance. Normally, Chief Smith could help, but with him dead and Sergeant McCulloch at the hospital with his dad, the Highland Police Department is almost useless."

Matt noticed his breakfast was about to arrive and quickly said, "I have a feeling Mr. Brown, being a prosecutor, has more than one or two enemies. You may be in for a long investigation with plenty of suspects."

Boo delivered their breakfasts and swiftly left. She was waiting on Matt's table instead of the regular waitress and was careful to give the two men their privacy. Boo was astute at reading guests and especially her boss when privacy was desired.

The trooper leaned over his plate and spoke softly, "We're in a bind. The governor's on Sergeant Oliver's case, big time. Not directly, of course, but the current load of manure is coming down through the upper ranks and landing on Oliver's desk. Sarge is taking Richmond's 'BS' and not passing it on—good man that he is."

One thing about the local troop, they were loyal and thought a lot of their sergeant. Hearing this, Matt felt even more guilty about disobeying the sergeant's orders not to go on the mountain to rescue the boys and Richard, but, despite suffering from guilt, he would do it again in a second.

Matt was curious and asked, "Why is Richmond dumping on Sergeant Oliver?"

The trooper stopped eating and answered, "I believe the governor thinks that we should have solved the sniper case sooner and before Big John's plant was torched."

"Yes, and while Sergeant Oliver and you boys were at it, maybe you could have stopped the Communist threat and solved the hunger in China," Matt replied.

The trooper smiled, then added, "We're also hearing Richmond is blaming Bobby Giles for wrecking his state-issued car when he caught that bootlegger. So that puts Trooper Giles toward the bottom of the gold star roster and high on the brass's shit-list."

"What? He made an important arrest and made you guys look good at the time!"

Bobby Giles had become Matt's instant friend when he had loaned him an untraceable pistol that Matt had used in his rescue mission at the hunting lodge. This was something both men had kept secret.

Trooper Quinn sighed and went on to say, "You're right. We did the best we could, but Richmond needs someone to blame for a blue and gray patrol car ending up on the junk pile. Second-guessing is their trademark. But you need to know that this whole division gives you the credit for stopping that killer before he could hurt those boys and Richard. That, my friend, has not changed."

"Yeah, but I feel bad about having to kill him," lamented Matt.

"You shouldn't. The guy's no longer a threat, and things are better, except for our missing Commonwealth's Attorney," Mike Quinn added as he finished eating and pushed back his plate.

Matt started to take a final forkful of his own but paused. "You think maybe Brown took off for some personal reason? A woman, maybe?"

The trooper whispered, "No girlfriend as far as we can tell. The public says that Brown's always been loyal to his wife. I never heard a single rumor about him not being faithful. Speaking of loyalty, that man's done everything Big John ever told him to do, and he's never strayed from the company line. His two vices are greed and sucking up to Big John tick tight. But hey, most folks in Green Mountain County wouldn't cross the big boss—present company excluded. I hear he has very little influence over you, which puts you last on his Christmas card list."

Matt laughed. "Yeah, well, I have a real knack for making the McCullochs mad at me." Matt finished and pushed back his plate.

He decided to change the subject. "Mike, did you hear about Lou, Carl, and Dickie beating up Kent and Billy?"

"Yes, I did. How are the boys?" Trooper Quinn asked.

"Billy got a concussion, and those bullies beat up Kent badly. It's a good thing that Little John's over at the hospital with his dad. John Gunn could become a major problem for Little John and Sheriff Lawrence," Matt said with concern.

"I was talking with Bobby Giles about John this morning. I think Billy's dad will eventually go after Little John. It will be the type of fight where two go in, and only one comes out," Trooper Quinn concluded.

"I hope I fixed it, so that doesn't happen. John's a good person, but we all know he has a temper. I told him that I overheard where the boy's bikes might be hidden but made him promise to let the sheriff handle it," Matt paused while Boo and the regular waitress for their table cleared it.

Matt began again after they left with the dishes. "Sheriff Lawrence told John that he had to get an okay from the Commonwealth's Attorney before he could make arrests. Now that Albert Winston Brown's missing, I hope John and Sergeant McCulloch don't meet until the sheriff can at least recover those bikes. Any chance you state boys can do something?"

"Not a chance. Orders have come down from upstairs. We are to concentrate on the main highways and back off working the Town of Highland unless the local police ask for our help. That puts us out of the picture," Trooper Quinn said with a frown.

"I guess having the governor in your pocket lets you get what you want when you want it." Matt was deeply troubled by this news.

"It sure seems that our governor will do about anything Big John wants," said the trooper as he rose from the table. He continued with a smile, "I better shove off before dispatch calls me a missing person. I've been ten-seven too long, but thanks for hearing me out. I needed to unload."

"Mike, I'm always willing to listen, and good luck finding our missing prosecutor."

"Say, if you hear anything, give Giles or me a call. That's one case we still have the authority to pursue. I know how you seem to know stuff before we do."

"I'll do that," promised Matt.

"Before I leave, Matt, tell me, what is your secret?"

"No secret. Hotel owners just hear things. Murder breeds talk. You'd have to be deaf not to pick up tidbits of local gossip," said Matt, who was not about to reveal the value of a polecat by the nickname of Polecat.

The two men parted, and the trooper's conversation made Matt ponder. So far, all the killings this summer were hot entrees of revenge served up as blue-plate specials, and the town was choking on the consequences. It would take time for the Town of Highland to return to normal even if Brown turned up alive and well.

If it weren't too late, Matt would try to corner Polecat for today's news. He glanced at his watch as he walked into the kitchen, thanked Maddie for another fine meal, and grabbed a second cup of coffee. He was in luck. Polecat was still on the loading dock, his private dining room, finishing his breakfast.

"Mr. Smith, how are you this fine Friday morning?" Matt called out as he grabbed a chair and moved it upwind of his prized informant. He tried not to be obvious about its placement.

"Mr. Cubley, a glorious morning to enjoy the beauty of the mountains. The abominable stench of the conflagration has dissipated, and one may now inhale clean and gentle breezes. Join me in partaking of God's gift of an unpolluted atmosphere."

"Mr. Smith, as always, you have captured the moment. I, too, am relieved the smoke from the plant fire has left us. I was happy to see the wind out of the southwest this morning. How are things in town?" Matt instantly began fishing for information and hoped this conversation stream would provide something.

"The constabulary continues to be confounded over the disappearance of the county prosecutor. Mr. Albert Winston Brown has broken with his customary habit of being predictable. His disappearance is without explanation, according to police discussions, official and unofficial."

"Of which police agencies are you privy?" Matt asked, trying to focus on particulars.

"My good sir, I apologize. I obfuscate. My excursions into the Green Mountain Sheriff's office on my morning paper deliveries reveal sparse information of merit, and they are the main investigative body at present."

"That's not good. How about the local officers or the state boys?"

"The Highland Police Department officers are in such disarray over the recent shooting of Mr. John Louis McCulloch, Sr., the killing of Chief Obie Smith, and the absence of Sergeant John Louis McCulloch, Jr. from their ranks that they are impotent.

I am, at present, devoid of adequate contact with the state police. They no longer occupy the elementary school for a command post. Consequently, I have lost the ability to eavesdrop on their deliberations. Excuse me; I must replenish my morning infusion of caffeine."

Polecat got up and went into the kitchen for a second cup of coffee. Matt's chief cook, Maddie Johnson, and Polecat exchanged pleasantries. Polecat was instructed to take his refill from the most recently brewed urn of coffee. Maddie Johnson was one of the reasons that Matt enjoyed informative discussions with Polecat. She fed him well and looked after him despite his appearance, flamboyant speech, and lack of hygiene. He returned with a steaming cup of coffee.

Matt decided his informant was holding something back and began to push harder. "Okay, so the police have no leads on the disappearance of Mr. Albert Winston Brown. What do you pick up from the gossip mill?" Matt asked, using Mr. Brown's full name since Brown always spoke of himself in this way.

"Matthew, I opine that there are three levels of gossip in this locality: high, middle, and low. The high gossip comes from the ladies' beauty parlor, to which I am only slightly privy. No hard information at that level, only speculation of dubious merit." Polecat took a sip of the steaming coffee and seemed to enter into a meditative state for a few moments, making Matt wait.

"The middle-level gossip comes from the fire station and other businesses around town. I also derived gossip from my newsroom at the *Highland Gazette*. All the middle-level news I must categorize as not fit to print, as papermen say. A cacophony of innuendo, but when all of it is distilled, the residue contains nothing worthwhile." Polecat took another pause from their discourse. Matt knew this was done to build tension. Polecat usually saved the best for last to tease his audience.

Polecat sat a little straighter and smiled. "The lowest-level gossip comes from the pool hall and those places of ill repute that only certain people of low moral fiber are wont to visit. I include certain of our county leaders, who have vices and tastes toward the illegal and immoral. Now, this is where I discovered noteworthy information about a person known to you and one for whom you were present at his arrest. I do believe the odor of the moonshine lost in the capture of this individual still lingers on the flora at that locus." Polecat stopped and looked to Matt for a reaction. He got it.

"What? You don't mean Doc Hathaway, do you? He's in jail and has been there since I watched Trooper Giles and him wreck. The breaking of all those jugs of moonshine made one awful stink. Besides, he was just a driver, not the real bootlegger. How is he involved in Brown's disappearance?" Matt was stunned.

Polecat winked and then, smiled. "A prisoner is not free to roam, but while that be true, his thoughts may freely fly to the borders of the kingdom. Upon their return, his brain may well bear the facts you seek. Capture his thoughts, young sir, capture his thoughts! His body is dross, but the value of the prisoner's thoughts are beyond what can be measured by the banker's scale!"

CHAPTER 8

BILLY'S FAMILY IN TURMOIL
Saturday, July 16, 1955

T he family was around the breakfast table, but I could tell right away something was wrong. Mom didn't speak, nor did Dad. Dad not speaking was normal. Scotty and Grandma playing the airplane landing in the hangar game with a spoonful of glop; that was normal. Scotty holding the spoon with his mouth while Grandma tugged on it to get it loose—well, that was normal. But Mom usually greeted me when she handed me my breakfast and asked me my plans for the day. Today, she said not a word. Plus, she had a frown with that little crinkle on the top of her nose—and that crinkle meant trouble.

That's when Grandma broke the silence. "Laura Jane, I don't understand how you and John can sit idly by while the town bullies brutalize your son. I guess you're going to wait until they kill him before you act."

Grandma was looking for a fight. It was going to be a major, major one, and I was the cause. I remember thinking, *should I say something or keep quiet?* Mom never gave me a chance to speak.

"Mother, now don't you start. All you want to do is cause trouble. Sheriff Lawrence is looking into the matter. Just as soon as the Commonwealth's Attorney returns, he'll arrest those boys." Mom said it in a firm voice, but she looked worried.

"If you wait for that jackass to do something, Billy will be grown or in his grave. You better mark my words before it's too late. I don't understand why that husband of yours doesn't make those bullies leave little Billy alone. There he sits, like a lump on a log."

Grandma had stopped feeding Scotty his glop about halfway through this last rant. She waited for the explosion because we all knew the fuse was lit. We weren't wrong.

Dad took his right arm and swept his plate and coffee cup right off the table. His dishes and food hit the kitchen wall with a crash. The cup bounced intact onto the floor, but the plate shattered.

Dad jumped up so suddenly that his legs propelled his chair backward with a clatter. He drew back his fist, and I thought Dad was going to hit Grandma. Instead, he stopped, looked at her, then his fist. In an instant, Dad turned, went through the open kitchen door, and slammed the screen door so hard it cracked the wooden part on the handle side. I couldn't believe it! He broke the screen door!

Mom looked at Grandma, said nothing, rushed from the kitchen into Mom and Dad's bedroom, and slammed the door. She didn't crack the bedroom door, but it made a loud bang—so loud, I jumped.

Scotty was cranking out the start of a scream. His face was red and scrunched up. When it erupted, if the neighbors across the road couldn't hear him, they weren't home.

"Well, I never!" Grandma said in a huff, got up, picked up Scotty, took him upstairs to her room. She slammed her door. Mom's slam beat her slam by twice, but for Grandma, it was a respectable slam.

I looked around. I was suddenly alone. My fork was suspended in midair with a piece of egg on it. That's the moment the egg decided it was time to dive for the plate. It landed on a piece of toast. I gently put the fork down and looked out the busted screen door. There was daylight shining through the crack. I couldn't see Dad, but I heard him in the garage beating on something with a hammer. I hoped it wasn't a customer's car.

This was all my fault. I should have known that Carl and Dickie would do something sneaky. If I had been paying better attention to what Dickie was doing, I wouldn't have fallen over him. Getting on all fours behind someone was such a common trick that any idiot should see it coming. Only a dunce would trip and fall backward. Well, I was a first-class dummy. Perhaps, if I had jumped high enough when I got pushed, I wouldn't have gotten knocked over. Even when I was down on the ground, I could have grabbed that foot before I got kicked in the head. Maybe Kent and I should have hidden our bikes better.

I had caused Dad to break the screen door, and I decided that I'd better buy a new door to make amends. I could hear Mom crying, and that made me feel terrible.

I took a sip of milk and decided I wasn't hungry. Carrying the dishes to the sink, I scraped the leftovers from each plate into the trash. I figured this breakfast was done. I picked up Dad's coffee cup off the floor and put it in the sink. I picked up the broken plate, being careful not to cut myself. The mess on the wall was more challenging. I wiped the wall with soap first, then water. The egg came off, mostly.

I washed and put away all the dishes. I looked at the door, but the split would not go back together, even pushing on it.

Scotty finally stopped screaming, and I could hear Grandma singing to him. I figured she was lightly bouncing him up and down as she walked back and forth across her bedroom—back and forth, back, and forth—footsteps on squeaking boards.

Now what?

I went over to my parent's bedroom door. I softly knocked. I guess Mom didn't hear me. I knocked again a little louder. I heard her get up off the bed; it made a squeak. She turned the knob and opened the door just a little.

"Mom, I know it's all my fault. I'll pay for the door. Please don't cry."

There must have been something in that dishwashing soap because my eyes were starting to water.

"Billy, this isn't your fault. Do you think this is your fault? Oh, my dear little boy. Why do you think that?"

"Mom, I shouldn't have let Dickie and Carl fool me and trip me. I could have grabbed that foot. If I had been quicker, stopped it, before he kicked me, hidden my bike better, I'm just not ...."

The rest got muffled because Mom grabbed me and hugged me so tight my mouth sort of got smashed against her. I couldn't talk or hardly breathe.

"Billy, you're not to blame. Please, don't think that. Those boys are just mean. I should have been there." Mom was crying. Now I was crying for real.

We sort of just stayed like that for about half a minute. Finally, Mom pushed me back a little and looked at me as I wiped some of the tears away. I was not only at fault, but now I was ashamed of being a crybaby.

"Billy, you're my big boy, but some things are up to your father and me, not you. This problem is for grown-ups, so don't blame yourself. I love you. Always remember that you and Scotty are always in my heart. Now stop crying."

I got a kiss on the forehead. Mom pulled away, and she went into her bathroom. I could hear water running in the sink. I went back out into the kitchen to check on the screen door again. It was still cracked.

Mom came into the kitchen, and I heard her stop at the door.

"Billy, did you clean up the kitchen?" she asked.

"Yes, ma'am. I tried real hard, but the egg left yellow on the wall. I pushed on it, but that crack in the screen door won't close up. If we go to the hardware, I bet they can order us a new one. I'll pay for it. I got money from my job."

"Billy, your dad can fix it. He broke it!"

"Mom, please don't be mad at Dad. It was my fault, not his!"

"Billy, this was not your fault. Stop saying that! Grandma shouldn't have said that about your father. You know how Grandma says things she doesn't mean. She blows up and gets over it. Now, you go call Kent. You and he should plan something to forget all about this."

Kent and I wanted to see the movies at the Top Hat, and Mom says to have some fun, so I better.

"Mom, may I ask you something? It's really important."

I was thinking, *If I'm going to get to see those three monster movies today, this is the perfect time to work it out with Mom.*

"What?" Mom asked, and I knew she had no idea what I was about to ask.

"Mom, you know how when the plant burned down, it knocked out the electricity to the whole town?"

"Yes, I remember." Mom said, but she started to sound suspicious.

"Do you remember how Superman and I were all set to go to the Top Hat Movie Theater to see those three really great monster movies the day the plant burned down? The ones we had been waiting to see all summer? You know, the *Bowery Boys Meet the Monsters, Them,* and *The Snow Creature*? If we don't get to see

them this afternoon, Kent and me will never, ever get to see them."
I was pleading and laying it on pretty thick.

"Billy, you are something else. It's Kent and I will never see
them again, not Kent and me," Mom said, shaking her head.

"Kent and I. Got it. They may not ever come back here again.
We'll die if we don't get to. All the kids are going. We'll be the only
ones in the whole town who won't have seen them. Please, Mom."

"What am I going to do with you? Call Kent and let me
talk to his mother. Your Dad and I will take you boys and pick you
up. One of us will talk to Mr. Stone to make sure nothing happens.
When the movie is over, you wait inside until you see us pull up."

Mom was putting down some tough rules. Superman and I
would miss getting our pea shooters and suckers at the dime store,
but if things worked out, we would get to see the greatest monster
movies ever made.

I called Kent. We were lucky; his mom agreed to let him go,
so long as Dad got Mr. Stone to watch out for us. Now, Mom had to
work things out with Dad.

She went out to the garage, where they talked for ten minutes.
When she came back into the house, she said Dad would drive us,
and that was that.

I called Kent back. Mom let us talk for ten minutes. I still felt
guilty about the big fight this morning, but Mom and I had patched
things up between us. I think she and Dad were okay. Grandma,
well, Grandma would be mad for at least another day. That was the
way things worked at the Gunn house. I guess everyone has to suffer
through fights between grandmas and moms and dads.

About an hour later, Trooper Quinn drove into the garage lot
with Trooper Giles riding shotgun. Both troopers got out and went
inside to find Dad. I figured I better check on things as well. Walking
into the parts cage, like I was looking for something, I could hear
what Dad and the troopers were saying.

"John, I think the sergeant is going to assign his car to me.
I'm off Tuesday and Wednesday, and if you aren't too busy, I'll drop
her off." I knew that Trooper Giles was leaving his patrol car for
Dad to soup up.

Trooper Giles was going to get Sergeant Oliver's old 1950 Ford instead of the new 1955 model he had been promised. The brass were punishing Trooper Giles because he had totaled his old car, which wasn't fair. The trooper had been doing his job.

Trooper Giles was known as the best driver with the fastest car in the division. The reason he had the fastest car was because he paid my dad, the best mechanic in Virginia, to soup it up.

Dad responded, "Sounds good to me. I guess the sergeant is getting the car that should have been yours. Will they still let my little improvements slide? I don't want them to get reported." Dad asked Trooper Giles.

The trooper leaned against a car and answered. "I'm going to make the changes, then risk what happens, but it won't come down on you, just me. By the way, how is your son doing?"

"He's healing, again! I'm damn tired of this and having to put up with shit from certain people. First, a sniper, and now, bullies." Dad had a lot of pent-up anger in his voice. The troopers both heard it, which caused Trooper Giles to put his hand on Dad's arm.

"John, you and your family are in my prayers. I mean that. No one should have to put up with what you've been through. It's hard, but at least be thankful that your boy escaped that sniper with his life." Trooper Giles was trying to make Dad feel better.

Dad looked like he was going to say something, but then stopped. He looked mad but he just stared, first at Trooper Giles and then at Trooper Quinn. Finally, he appeared to decide something and took a deep breath.

"Bobby, you're right. I am thankful. It's just that I'm worried. I've got to find a way to stop the attacks on Billy before he gets seriously hurt. You boys said if he had more trouble, you would help us."

I was surprised to hear what those troopers told my dad. Things had changed because the governor had ordered the state police to avoid handling minor crimes in Highland. They could work the state roads, but the town was off-limits. Trooper Quinn explained how Judge Carlton's witness protection court order was no longer any good. I thought Dad would get mad, but he never said a word. I wanted to yell because I felt a lot madder than Dad over the way things were turning out.

The troopers stayed a few minutes, but things were awkward. They left sooner than I thought they would have normally. Dad saw me watching him and came over to me.

"Billy, your mom says you want to go to the movies with Kent."

"Yes, sir. We really want to see those movies today. This may be our only chance." I tried to make it sound important, not to miss them.

"Well, your mom thinks it would be good for you boys to have some fun. I'm going to take you, and I think she's going as well. You must promise me that you'll stay inside the theater the whole time. You are not to leave. You hear me, son?" Dad was looking at me in the eyes.

I looked him right back in the eyes. "Yes, sir. We'll do exactly what you say."

"William, this is not your fault. Mom said you think it is. I want you to be careful, but it isn't your fault. Understand?" Dad never stopped looking me in the eyes.

"I understand," I said, but I was confused. I still thought it was my fault. I wished it hadn't happened. I really didn't understand Dad. He called me William. I can't remember the last time he called me William, and I didn't get whacked right after.

When Dad was frustrated, he got mad and broke things—like at breakfast. But when he talked to the troopers a few moments ago, he was too calm. I thought about the phone call with some guy named Bruce. Dad was up to something. What would the family do if Dad went to prison? I could wash cars, but how many car washes would it take for me to pay for all the stuff this family needed? I had to grow up faster, a lot faster!

CHAPTER 9

THE CALM BEFORE THE STORM
Saturday, July 16, 1955

M att was sitting in his office, thinking what possible connection Doc Hathaway could have to the local prosecutor's disappearance.

The Hathaway family had a long history that Matt had only recently learned. Doc had been framed on a false charge of stealing payroll checks from the plant by Big John after Doc had mentioned forming a union at the plant. As a result, the man was thrown in jail, his family evicted from their company house, and his wife and their two boys suffered greatly. When Doc got out of jail, he began to drive for a Waynesboro bootlegger, the only job he could find.

Matt had been riding with Trooper Lusk, giving him advice on sniper techniques, when Lusk and Trooper Giles tried to stop Doc as he was hauling a load of bootleg liquor. Doc swerved into Giles, causing both to crash in the woods, with both vehicles ending up as total losses. Although Giles was scheduled to have his old patrol car replaced with a new one, he was getting the sergeant's old car as punishment. The brass first praised him for Doc's capture. But now, those same officials had turned on Giles because Doc was only a minor whiskey runner, not a big fish in the criminal pond like they initially thought.

In another turn of events, Matt recently learned that Karen Hathaway, Doc's wife, had experience running a restaurant. Matt had decided to hire her, despite her husband's record because Matt had gotten to know her and her two boys when her sons came to the rescue of Billy. Lou had attacked Billy with a baseball bat on the Fourth of July, and Skip and Barry Hathaway had come to the rescue. Now that his current maître d', Boo Skelton, was leaving to go back to the university to finish her final year, Matt needed to replace her.

Some local troopers were even working to clear Doc of those original false charges. Now Polecat was telling Matt that

Doc might have information about the disappearance of the county Commonwealth's Attorney. Matt knew Doc had been in jail since the wreck which happened on the first of this month. Since the Commonwealth's Attorney had just disappeared a few days ago, there was no way Doc could have been directly responsible. But could he help the authorities?

Chuck Tolliver, his hotel manager, interrupted his thoughts with a knock on Matt's door.

"Morning, Chuck. How's the house count?" Matt asked, hoping it was up. Unfortunately, between Big John McCulloch trying to lure his guests over to his resort and guests canceling reservations because of all the recent killings, Matt was having difficulty trying to run the resort he had just inherited.

"Our house count is better. We expect a crowd for lunch today. John Gunn called to make a reservation for his family for dinner. He wasn't sure if Grandma Harris would attend, but four places are reserved for certain." Chuck was amused at John's uncertainty about the last member of the Gunn household.

"Chuck, I get the impression Grandma Harris gives John a good dose of mother-in-law-itis on a frequent basis. His sweet wife makes up for it, but he does have an interesting mother-in-law."

"Not sure I would say interesting, but she seldom goes unnoticed," Chuck smiled at his own comment.

"Maddie has been quiet, and isn't the kitchen staff working smoothly?" Matt leaned back in his chair and stared out the window.

"Yep. Since you rescued her son-in-law, Richard, Maddie has been more understanding of the kitchen staff, and Boo is a miracle worker at calming her when she gets irritated. Things are almost too good. I hope it's not the calm before the storm."

Chuck was wont to worry, but the last five days had been pleasant without a single murder, wreck, fire, or shooting. A nice change from recent history.

"Matt, there's a guest who has invited you to join her and her friend for lunch," Chuck was smiling.

Matt turned to look at Chuck. "Let me guess, Miss Carol Martin and Mrs. Linda Carlisle. I believe I will. Have Boo set me a place. Carol was the one who found Billy and Kent behind Dalton's law office. I'm curious about what she saw."

Chuck wagged his finger at Matt. "You promised me no police work for the rest of the summer. Wasn't catching a sniper and getting shot enough for you?"

Matt shrugged. "Chuck, it was a graze. Besides, I'm concerned about Billy and Kent. Someone better fix this bully mess, or Billy's dad may go too far. John isn't going to put up with much more."

"I think you're right," agreed his hotel manager.

Matt rose and walked to the connecting door from his office to the kitchen. "Chuck, I think I'll go to the post office. Do we need anything from town?" Matt asked.

"Not a thing. Oh, we do have a flower delivery that's late. You might see if the Highland Police have him stopped. I hope they're not up to their old tricks of harassing our deliveries." Chuck no more than got this out when the delivery truck driver came into the kitchen with the flower order.

Matt called out, "Chuck, your flowers are here. The gods are smiling on you."

The sun traveled across a cloudless sky until it reached its zenith. Guests began to arrive for lunch, and two of the prettiest ladies in Green Mountain County walked into the lobby. Carol Martin was a blond who many of the single men in town were trying to catch. Linda Carlisle, a Korean War widow, was her best friend. She was equally sought after. Carol was trying her best to perform some matchmaking between Matt and Linda. However, she was meeting with only limited success.

Boo Skelton seated the two ladies and then notified Matt that his presence was needed in the dining room. Matt wasted no time in joining the ladies. He walked through the kitchen and tried to check, without being obvious, what Maddie had prepared for lunch. Her Saturday specials were almost as good as her Sunday specials.

He then darted through the kitchen door, narrowly missing a busy waitress carrying a loaded tray. The dining room was filling, and the staff was wasting no time.

"Ladies, I was quite pleased to hear you wanted a third for lunch. May I join you?" Matt asked, knowing Carol would answer first, and she did.

"Matt, sit down. How's the arm?" Carol asked without a second wasted.

"Just a scratch. I've done worse, sliding headfirst into home plate," Matt said, trying to brush off her concern. "Linda, nice to see you again. Have things slowed down at the courthouse?"

"No, things at the courthouse have been hectic. The judge is even at work today, but he told me to take Saturday off. I expect my desk will be loaded when I get back on Monday." Linda's smile had captured Matt's gaze. His face blushed when he realized he was staring.

Matt diverted his gaze to Carol and asked a couple of questions about the attack on Billy and Kent. She provided him a detailed report, and even Linda joined in with some information she had picked up at the courthouse. Being the judge's secretary, she was privy to facts not available to the average person, and she often shared these with Carol if they weren't privileged. Today, Matt was being included in her inner circle.

"The three bullies are insisting they never laid eyes on Billy or Kent on Wednesday. Knowing those three, most of the town's not buying it. Sheriff Lawrence told me that two young girls, schoolmates of Billy and Kent, saw the three bullies at Mountain Drug right before the attack."

The topic moved to the latest events concerning the McCulloch family. Big John had been released just that morning from the Waynesboro Memorial Hospital. The Koehler Funeral Home ambulance, owned by one of his relatives, drove him home. Some of the neighbors whispered about all the cussing going on as the stretcher hit some bumps as it was rolled to the McCulloch mansion. Both Mary, Big John's wife, and Willa, Little John's wife, were staying at the "big house" to take care of Big John. Lou was at home with his dad, so that he wouldn't disturb his grandfather.

The Highland Police Department remained in a state of confusion because no one knew if Little John would become chief or move into the plant to help run things. Their jobs depended on whether Big John intended to rebuild the factory. If the factory wasn't rebuilt, the Highland Police Department might be reduced in size or even disbanded.

Carol leaned closer and whispered, "Lou and the Lockhart brothers are running wild."

Linda asked her, "How so?"

"They're avoiding adults by hiding out in the woods or the park until after dark. A couple of kittens were found burned to death in the park this morning. Their owners reported the atrocities, but the Highland Police claim they're too busy searching for Albert Winston Brown to fool with dead kittens."

The two ladies discussed more pleasant topics with Matt, such as the weather and what movies were popular. Matt and Linda exchanged several lingering looks. Carol was sure these two would be a perfect match. However, Linda wasn't ready for romance, and Matt felt guilty whenever he even thought of Linda in that way. He could not consider a new female in his life, other than as a friend held at arm's length.

Lunch was served, and the three ate, drank, and talked quietly. People arrived, ate, and departed all around them. When Matt noticed the time, it was after two o'clock. Boo was pleased that Matt was enjoying his lunch. She made sure the three were undisturbed by the other waitresses.

The two ladies noticed the time and made a slow departure to do some shopping in Waynesboro. Matt decided he would enjoy a little time on the veranda to continue his pleasant Saturday.

Rocking on the veranda, he could not help thinking about the local prosecutor. Having been an assistant Commonwealth's Attorney, he knew the dangers of that office. Albert Winston Brown either had taken off for some reason that he wanted to be kept secret, or he'd been murdered. But where was the body? Where was the man's car?

His other concern involved Kent and Billy. Lou McCulloch was out to get the two boys—a feud was obvious. Carl and Dickie Lockhart were mean, and with Lou's cloak of protection because of his grandfather, there was little to stop those three. Lou's dad was of little help in controlling his son. Little John's conduct was more a model of bad behavior, and Little John was supporting Big John in his vendetta against Matt, which had spilled over to include Billy and Kent. What a mess!

The dining room was half full by seven-thirty when John Gunn drove up to Cubley's Coze with Laura Jane and little Scotty in the front and Billy and Grandma Harris in the back seat. The family of five made their way across the parking lot to the steps of the veranda with John carrying Scotty. Matt greeted them, and this time Scotty smiled at him.

Matt thought, *well, well, I'm making progress with little Scotty.*

"Me like ice cream and pie," Scotty said to Matt as John set him down to walk.

Strike that progress stuff. It's not my charm but the ice cream and pie that has captured his attention.

He smiled at Laura Jane and shook hands with John and Billy.

"I hope you got that spider web off your door. It looks like a man running a hotel would not let it run down," Grandma Harris instructed, squinting upward to see if the spider web that she had spotted on her last visit had been removed. It had.

Billy's mom instantly responded with, "Mother, for goodness sakes."

Matt smiled inwardly; *Laura Jane Gunn sure had to put up with a lot from her mother. Tonight, was no exception.*

Matt noticed John gave his mother-in-law a look that would have chilled most people. Not Grandma Harris, who continued with, "Well, it's gone, so there. Stop dawdling! I'm hungry! And where are we going to sit?"

Grandma Harris was walking toward the dining room with purpose. She was not waiting for her family. Laura Jane had Scotty by the hand, almost dragging him, to keep up, and John followed three steps behind them.

Matt leaned down to Billy after giving the bandage on the side of his head a closer look.

"Looks like we both have war wounds, don't we?" Matt said in a whisper to Billy. He didn't want to stir up the father's emotions, but he wanted Billy to know he was supportive.

Billy smiled up at him. His dad had walked on ahead, so it was safe to comment. "I guess we do."

John Gunn was generally friendly, but usually, his friendliness was limited to a smile, nod, or wave. Matt noticed tonight that he stopped to talk to friends he knew as he crossed the dining room. John even went out of his way to speak to a stranger. He was working the room like a politician.

Matt made sure the Gunn family was seated to Grandma's satisfaction. He had bread and iced tea delivered to Grandma Harris before she could ask. Laura Jane mouthed "thank you" to him when she saw what he was doing.

Being the good host to all his guests, he made his rounds of the dining room, always keeping an eye on the Gunn table. John usually ate quickly, but he was taking his time tonight. He consumed his meal so slowly that the family had to wait on him to finish before placing their desert order.

It was a little after nine o'clock when the Gunn family was served dessert. In the distance, the town siren sounded, calling the volunteer firemen to answer a Saturday night fire. John checked his watch but returned to his dessert, maintaining his leisurely pace.

When everyone was finally finished, Matt invited the Gunn family to enjoy the veranda and chat, not expecting an acceptance. John readily accepted his invitation and asked the waitress if she would bring him a cup of coffee.

This was a first. The family and Matt gathered on the veranda, and John was in such a good mood that Matt decided to speak to him on what might be a sore subject. Matt maneuvered his seat next to John's. Scotty came over to Matt, climbed onto his lap, and proceeded to ask for more ice cream. Laura Jane told him the hotel had run out, but they could come back another day for the treat. Scotty said, "Okay," and proceeded to go to sleep on Matt's lap.

"John, you doing okay?" Matt asked.

"Doing fine. Boo's dad has taken the load off me at the garage. He's a good mechanic."

"I was surprised the Chevrolet Dealership let him go."

John leaned closer and spoke softly. "Dan Skelton's a good man. You know he was fired when Big John heard Boo stepped in as maître d' to help you out. Dan told me that his boss at the dealership said if she didn't quit her job here, they would be forced to let him go. I hired Dan on the spot, and the rest is history. I got a good mechanic, and you got to keep your Boo."

"Do you have enough business for two mechanics?" Matt asked.

"Business could be better, but even with the plant shut down, I'm behind. How about you? You doing okay?"

"I'm making it, but I miss Billy. In fact, I miss both the boys. They both healing up?"

"They seem to be," responded John.

"And the parents, how are things?" asked Matt.

"Billy's driving his mother crazy, wanting to come back here to work. She broke down and let him go to the movies today. Both he and Kent went to see some fool nonsense about atomic bombs and giant ant monsters."

"Sounds like something those two would like. I think the picture's called *Them*."

"I suppose—a dumb name for a dumb movie. Laura Jane made me drive them to keep them out of harm's way. I thought it was a waste of an afternoon going to see movies. He had chores waiting at the garage, but he does seem happier after we let him go. I expect when they do come on back to work, someone will have to drive them."

"If you can't, I'll get one of the hotel staff to do it," Matt offered.

"No, it's not that big of a bother, but I'll need you to be sure Kent and Billy stay put. Both their mothers don't want them wandering off," John Gunn said with a questioning look.

"I'll watch them and make sure they don't leave unless they're with an adult."

"Thanks, that should keep them safe."

"Any news from the sheriff on the bikes or the charges?" asked Matt, getting up to the subject he wanted to discuss.

John frowned, "Nope."

Matt knew from that short answer that John was not going to tell him anything. After more silence, the fire siren on top of the fire station sounded for a second time. Chuck came outside and commented about two fires on a single night.

That's when Billy's mom spoke up, "John, don't you think we better get on home? Scotty's sound asleep, and I'm sure Matt has better things to do than hold him."

"I've been ready to go home since dessert, but no one asks what I want," Grandma Harris spoke from her rocker. Matt had thought she was sleeping, but nothing got past Grandma Harris.

"What time is it?" John Gunn asked.

"It's almost ten." Matt said, looking at his watch.

"John, did you forget your watch?" Laura Jane asked her husband.

"No, I have it. I think it's running slow. Just wanted to be sure of the time." John stood and took the sleeping Scotty from Matt. The family made its way down the veranda steps and over to their car. John slowly drove past the front of the hotel. When he passed the veranda, he stuck his arm out of the car window and waved at Matt. The large grandfather clock in the lobby chimed ten o'clock.

CHAPTER 10

A MIDNIGHT FORMATION
Saturday, July 16, 1955

T he Skyline Parkway Motor Court office, right beside the Afton Mountain Howard Johnson, was busy with guests checking in. Six men in six cars stopped at an overlook on the Blue Ridge Parkway near the motor court to decide how to arrive at the motel. Over the next three hours, they checked into three guest rooms, two at a time.

Keeping to their plan, none used their actual names nor gave valid addresses. Promptly at five in the afternoon, they all met in the leader's room to be briefed.

Master Sergeant Casey O'Malley was accustomed to the group paying attention to him, but that had been during the war. He wondered if he still had their respect. "All of you pay attention. First Sergeant Williams has done an outstanding job of recon, so listen up." The talking stopped, and each man instantly focused on Williams, which showed that O'Malley was still the boss.

The battalion sergeants had been tight in Europe. These were the lucky few from A, B, and C companies who had made it back alive. However, they hadn't gotten together as a group since being discharged after World War II. They kept in touch. A few would meet for a beer or a game of golf, but not the whole group, until now.

"Thank you, Master Sergeant," responded First Sergeant Bruce Williams. He looked at each man as he got out his maps and papers. His gaze first fell on Master Sergeant Casey O'Malley, who everyone called Crazy Casey behind his back. O'Malley still looked like a master sergeant—clean-shaven with white sidewalls and a distinct military bearing. Bruce had let himself go, not bad, just long hair and often a two or three-day-old beard. But it was to his advantage to look more civilian and less military for tonight's work.

Next to Bruce Williams sat Staff Sergeant Joe Lincoln, Bruce's roommate, who would assist him with this briefing. By the door sat Sergeant Frank Smallwood, and on one of the beds sat

Sergeant Duke Stricker. On the other bed sat Staff Sergeant Jackson "Jack" Foley, who was quiet but deadly. O'Malley was pleased they had all answered the call. Seeing them all attentive, O'Malley motioned for Bruce to begin.

"First Sergeant John Gunn has requested our help. Master Sergeant O'Malley has decided the solution to John's problem is to use a midnight formation with three objectives. First, create a diversion at the McCulloch Wood Products Plant to get the local cops busy and out of town. Second, penetrate and reclaim two items from the local hardware store. Third, kidnap and scare off the little brat who's led the attacks on the first sergeant's boy. After the last attack, the brat and his two helpers put John's boy in the hospital. Also, the three bullies are one or two years older than John's boy, and it's time for outside help."

Bruce asked Joe to pull out the first two sheets of instructions and hand them to him. He began to talk and pass the documents out to the others.

"Duke, you have the Highland Hardware store. Your 1953 Dodge station wagon should fit the bill. The bikes are a green Schwinn Hornet and a red Columbia. Will they fit?" Bruce handed Joe Lincoln the papers and waited for an answer.

"Two bikes, yeah, they'll fit with no problem. It says here no night watchman, are you sure?" Joe asked.

"First Sergeant Gunn assures us, there's no watchman at the hardware. The building gets checked by the town's one patrol car. Currently, there's only one cop at the PD and one on patrol. If the master sergeant does his job, that patrol car will be tied up at the plant, trying to figure things out." Bruce wished he could watch the chaos that Crazy Casey would initiate. It should be spectacular.

Sergeant Frank Smallwood loved to needle Duke, and he interrupted with, "Duke, think you still have the knack to bust in without waking half the town?"

"Frank, I'll do my job and be out in two shakes of a lamb's tail. Do you need me to hold your hand while you snatch the boy?" teased Duke.

"You tend to your mission, and I'll handle mine."

"Stow it, you two! I need to get through this," Bruce gave them a cold stare, and the two shut up.

"Now, Duke, since you claim to have plenty of time after you get the bikes, I need you to set off a noisemaker and a small fire to ensure the cops know the hardware was broken into before ten o'clock. Timing is critical, and it has to be done no later than ten," Bruce insisted.

"Should be some trash and boxes I can set off with a delayed fuse. I'll add gunpowder packed in a small glass jar that should get the attention of all the neighbors. Will that do?" Duke asked.

"Between the master sergeant and you, the Highland Fire Department should be hopping like teenagers at a hillbilly dance," Bruce commented.

Bruce gave Duke Stricker a detailed handout describing the two bikes and a map of the hardware store layout. Several questions were asked, but no problems surfaced.

"Master Sergeant, you clear and ready?" Bruce asked Casey O'Malley.

"This is going to be fun. I have a trunk full of stuff that will drive the plant's night watchman into nervous fits. In the end, it'll look like kids having a little fun. The town cop should be tied up for at least an hour until he figures it out," answered O'Malley

Bruce turned to the last three men, "Okay, I'll be lead on the penetration of the McCulloch house. I got the layout from First Sergeant Gunn. He got invited to a party there several years back, but he thinks the info is still good. We got to go in just after dark and be out no later than ten," Bruce informed his team.

"Who's going in?" Frank asked.

"Hold on, Frank, parade rest," Bruce replied.

Frank was the opposite of Jack, talkative, where Jack was quiet. Jack had been called "Jack the Knife" by some of the troops. No one knew how many enemy sentinels he had killed with his razor-sharp knife. Deadly and quiet was Jack.

Knowing these men, Bruce cautioned them that this mission had to be "a slip-in and slip-out with minimal damage." He stressed that no one was to be hurt—much—scared, yes, hurt, no!

"Jack and I will deal with the boy. Frank, you and Joe will stand watch. If the master sergeant causes enough ruckus, I think the brat's dad will go charging off to the plant. You two will be our lookouts and backup if he returns before we exit."

"Who else might be with the boy in the house?" asked Jack, which was rare for him to ask anything.

"Word is the wife is over at the grandfather's mansion, helping take care of the old man. Our intel is the boy will be at home by himself. This should be a walk in the park."

"You sure?" asked Casey.

"I'll leave early and recon the house. If the kid's off somewhere, we'll come back another night for the boy. John's son and his best friend put a lot of stock in these bikes. Getting them back is a big deal to the first sergeant. So we recover the bikes tonight, with or without snatching the brat. Any questions?" Bruce asked.

Of course, Frank had several. Jack, none.

Bruce left first. After two hours, the others left according to the time they needed to arrive for their missions.

Master Sergeant Casey O'Malley drove to a spot near the plant. He parked on a farm road across the highway from the entrance. He didn't know it, but he parked almost in the same spot as the sniper had used the night before he set the big fire, murdered the Chief of Police, and shot Big John McCulloch.

Crazy Casey would set off enough fireworks to bring out the town fire department and the cops. He got out five hundred firecrackers, twenty M-80 large firecrackers, plus two jugs of gasoline. He put several packs of cigars, duct tape, extra fuses, and the explosives in an old army knapsack. He carried the two, one-gallon-jugs of gas in his hands.

Carrying the two one-gallon jugs of gasoline, he worked his way over to the log yard. Then, Casey wedged the glass jugs of gasoline with two-minute fuses between logs near the top row. He wound a bright yellow ribbon to the neck of each to mark its location. He needed bright markers to find the fuses quickly during his escape.

Along the ridge on the other side of the log yard, he placed many strings of twenty firecrackers with cigar timers of different lengths. Those cops would think a platoon was firing down on them!

Between the strings of firecrackers, he rigged M-80s with cigar timers, also set for different times. The cops would be busy ducking and dodging imitation pistol and shotgun fire from the ridge, leaving the town open to the ex-military men's real mission.

One cigar on a string of firecrackers, he lit and immediately put out. This string he left for the cops to find intact. It was sure to lead them to believe this was just a bunch of kids having fun.

Now came the tricky part. Before dusk, Casey slipped down next to the boiler room to set the rest of the large M-80s. Each had a one-minute fuse stuck in the end of a short stub of a cigar, which he duct-taped to two windows on the side of the boiler room. The windows would shatter, with only the glass striking the side of the boiler. He didn't want to hurt the night watchman, just scare the devil out of him.

Other M-80s with longer fuses he taped to the windows of nearby buildings, so when they exploded, glass would fly into the building and all over the desks. No workers should be working at night, but what a mess this would make.

Crazy Casey now hid in a shed and waited for it to get dark. When he checked his watch, it was almost eight-thirty. Planting the fireworks had taken longer than he had planned, but he was ready with a little time to spare.

The night watchman made his rounds on the half-hour, right on schedule. Casey waited until the man returned to the boiler room, and it was totally dark. He wanted to thank the man for keeping to his schedule. Crazy Casey was also ready to begin on time.

He checked his watch, and it was time to light off the first fuse. He sneaked down to the boiler room, unobserved.

Casey lit each cigar fuse and made sure each was embedded firmly. Each of the cigars attached to the M-80 fuses should burn down until the firecrackers went off as if someone was running away from the area, shooting out windows as they went.

Next, he lit the cigars attached to the strings of firecrackers and M-80 fuses up on the ridge. These had longer fuses, set to explode at different times over thirty minutes to an hour. Now he was jogging for the stacks of logs.

There was an explosion at the boiler room, and it sounded like someone with a shotgun had just blown out a window. Right on time, the watchman ran outside, looking to see what was going on.

Casey waited for the second M-80 to blow. When it blew out the second window, the watchman stood stunned. Then a third explosion. Thinking he was under attack, the night watchman dropped and crawled back into the boiler room to phone for help. Casey lit off the fuses to the gasoline bombs and made good his escape while the night watchman was busy calling for help.

Casey heard other M-80s going off in sequence, blowing out the windows of the office building. M-80s were going off every few minutes as Casey drove out to State Route 22, turned left, and drove east past the plant, over East Gap, and on to the motel on top of Afton Mountain. Arriving at the motel, he opened a can of beer with his old army church key to wait for the rest of the team to report in.

The frantic call from the night watchman arrived at the Highland Police Department just as Officer Roger Younger was getting a cup of coffee. He called to Zeke Barnes, who was napping instead of being on patrol, to catch the phone. Zeke picked up the phone and almost dropped it.

"What did you say? Stop yelling, talk slower...I can't understand you. What?"

Zeke started shouting, "Roger, the plant's under attack—men with shotguns. Sweet Jesus, they're trying to destroy the boiler room and the main office building."

Zeke started to run for the back door and his patrol car, leaving Officer Younger dumbfounded. Seeing the man just standing, he screamed at him to move. Younger dropped his coffee cup. It shattered on the floor.

Zeke stopped at the back door to be sure the other officer was responding. He wasn't, so he added, "Roger, damn you, call Little John! Get him to the plant, now! I need backup! Call the sheriff. Hell, call the state police. Call everybody!"

Zeke ran to the rear lot, jumped into his patrol car, hit the lights and siren, and with tires throwing gravel, tore out from behind the Highland Police Department building. He almost ran over a young couple crossing the driveway. They were leaving the park hand-in-hand and had to jump back to avoid being struck. Zeke never slowed for them but slid in a broadside slide into Court Street. He was going full out, headed east toward Main Street and the plant.

Officer Roger Younger called Sergeant McCulloch at home. When Lou answered, Officer Younger demanded to know where his dad was. Lou said, "He's at Grandpa's. Say, who is this?"

Roger had already hung up and was dialing Big John's house. When Officer Younger told Sergeant McCulloch about the emergency, the sergeant yelled to his wife that he was going to the plant, drove home, told his boy not to leave the house, and jumped into his patrol car. He sped to the plant with siren wailing.

Officer Zeke Barnes arrived first and slid to a stop in the plant parking lot. The watchman yelled and pointed that they were shooting at him from the log yard, so Zeke drove there just as more fireworks went off. He radioed Sergeant McCulloch, "I need covering fire. I'm pinned down in the log yard."

Zeke's broadcast went out over the police net, and it was too bad that the master sergeant couldn't watch the ensuing chaos. The recent business of the deadly sniper left all the police in the area on edge. When Officer Barnes, Sergeant McCulloch, and two deputies arrived at the state road that ran beside the log yard, it was quiet. But when they all got out of their cars, they began to hear what sounded like shots. Ducking for cover and looking in the direction of the sounds, they could see flashes on the ridge. Every officer opened fire.

When another deputy arrived, he got out his high-powered rifle and fired off a round. The bang startled Zeke, and he almost turned and fired on the deputy. Each was now in danger of shooting the other.

Sergeant McCulloch began to suspect that these weren't pistol shots that he was hearing. The sound was wrong. He started yelling for everyone to stop firing. As luck would have it, the current string of firecrackers stopped, having run out.

"Zeke, get your sorry carcass up there and check that ridge," ordered McCulloch.

"Little John, are you nuts? I'll get shot," Zeke responded, not wanting to join Chief Smith in the ground. He was hunkered down behind his patrol car and wanted to stay there.

"Hey, I'll go! You guys cover me," said one of the new deputies. It had been quiet for almost a minute, and he wanted to show these old guys he had the stuff.

The deputy ran hunched over and got about twenty feet ahead of the other officers when one of the longer fuses burned to the end, and an M-80 went off, followed by another string of firecrackers.

The explosion and pop, pop, popping startled the deputy so much that he flinched and fired off a pistol round by accident. His gun had just cleared his holster, and he shot himself in his left thigh. Thinking he had been shot from the ridge, he yelled, "Help me, I'm hit bad!" and he fell to the ground.

Two more explosions went off, and suddenly the middle stack of logs in the log yard was aflame. This fire was behind the police, and being backlit by the flames, they were perfect targets for shooters on the ridge. One of the deputies crawled to his car, put out a call for the fire department, and began begging the county dispatcher, "We need more help! Officer down! Officer down! My Lord, he's shot! Snipers on the ridge, and we're pinned down!"

The siren on top of the firehouse began its wail, calling the volunteer firemen. The county dispatcher began calling for troopers and deputies from other jurisdictions.

The officers at the plant opened fire and kept firing until they ran out of ammunition. All available police officers, which initially only amounted to five on-duty officers until more were called out from home, were now headed to the McCulloch Wood Products Plant. This diversion was better than any of the sergeants could have imagined.

The state police, who were following orders to work the main roads and stay out of the Town of Highland, had their single, on-duty trooper way out on State Route 29 just south of Charlottesville. It would take him half an hour to reach the plant. The Town of Highland was now vulnerable for the second part of the sergeants' plan.

When the two Highland patrol cars and the three deputies from the sheriff's office left town with sirens wailing, Duke waited until after the fire siren went off on top of the firehouse. Then he drove his station wagon right into the Highland Hardware parking lot, coasted across it, and parked by the side door. He got out of his vehicle with a hammer, a rag, and some tape.

After placing strips of tape on one of the panes of glass, Duke placed the rag on the glass, over the tape, and tapped the glass. It broke with almost no sound and stayed in place. Pushing on the broken glass with the rag, it fell all taped together and hit the floor with a muffled clink. Next, he reached inside and opened the door. He was inside.

Going straight to the basement door, he went down the stairs, and there mixed in with the other bikes, he found the two bikes he was there to collect. He had them in his car within two minutes of arriving at the hardware. It was easy to pick up the taped glass, rag, and hammer and put them in his car. All these implements were going into the first river he crossed.

Duke quickly emptied the hardware's two refuse barrels left behind the store for pickup into a mound of trash. The pile was large enough to make plenty of fire and smoke but not close enough to catch the store on fire.

Finally, he placed a quart jar packed with gunpowder in the middle of the parking lot, away from the pile of trash. He inserted a long fuse into a hole that he had drilled in the metal top of the glass jar. He wanted a lot of noise but didn't want to spread the fire.

Duke started his car to ensure he could make a quick exit from the parking lot. He lit the trash first and made sure it would burn; then, he lit the fuse to the gunpowder, hopped into his car, and exited the hardware parking lot. He was a block away when he heard the loud boom.

He drove to Gunn's Garage, and as he pulled into the lot, the volunteer fire department siren began to wail for the second time that night. It was 9:40 p.m. His noisemaker had done the trick.

He checked First Sergeant Gunn's house by knocking on the door, but no one was home. It was as he had expected.

He took both bikes and placed them inside the unlocked garage. Following his instructions, he locked the door and got in his car. He drove out of town to the Liberty Bell Gas Station and turned left to avoid the excitement at the plant. He went the long way around to the Blue Ridge Parkway and on to the motel. His part of the plan was finished.

The remaining four sergeants were in hiding around the McCulloch house. It was dark when they watched Sergeant McCulloch fly into his driveway to pick up his patrol car. They also heard him yell to his son to stay home. When the sound of McCulloch's siren died in the distance, Bruce Williams and Jack Foley pulled on black hoods with eyeholes cut in them and went to the basement door. Using two pry bars with tape over the ends, they broke in. The door didn't look damaged, just sprung a little.

They found Lou McCulloch in the den listening to a baseball game on the radio. A hood with no eye slits went over his head before he knew anyone was behind him.

They took him to his bedroom and tied him to his bed. Leaving the boy's hood on, Jack began to inform the boy how his life was about to change.

"John Louis McCulloch the Third, we're here to warn you, we don't like what you've been doing. You've been tried by the Brotherhood and found guilty." Jack was whispering, and that was much scarier than yelling. Jack's voice was spooky, mean sounding when he whispered.

"Who the hell are you people? Do you know who I am? My father..." Lou tried to finish, but a rap on the top of his head with a sap filled with lead shot got his attention. It stung but didn't cause real harm, and the mark was hidden by his hair.

Then Bruce struck him hard in the stomach with a rolled-up newspaper. The blow was loud, hurt a lot, knocked the breath out of Lou, but just left a red place that would fade.

"You speak again, boy, and I'll cut out your tongue, fry it, and make you eat it. Then, I'll cut you, so you'll be able to join the girls' choir and sing with the sopranos. Please say something else.

I love to hear little boys scream," Jack was even starting to scare Bruce. This midnight formation was to scare the kid, not cause him to have a heart attack.

A midnight formation was a tool used by sergeants in the military to discipline a particularly troublesome soldier unofficially. It was used when the standard code of military conduct process would embarrass and maybe even hurt the company commander's record, or the soldier was not responding to his prior punishments in proper military fashion.

Midnight formations were also reserved for the troublesome soldier who was endangering his squad, platoon, or an entire company. They were under the sole purview of company sergeants: used rarely, but when needed, a useful tool. No record of the procedure was left if done correctly. No officer found out about it or admitted they knew of it. It was done in such a way that no evidence was left. Most soldiers, who had been the subject of a midnight formation, never mentioned it. For the really bad cases, the body was made to look like death by enemy fire, if the body was found at all.

Lou McCulloch, this night, was a quick learner and remained silent. However, he was so scared he wet his pants.

The whispers continued from Jack, "Lou McCulloch, you attacked Billy Gunn and Kent Clark on several occasions. This is a warning. If you or your two accomplices repeat any violence on our protected brothers, we will come back. There is nowhere you can hide from the Brotherhood. No one can protect you from the Brotherhood. The Brotherhood will know because we have spies watching you." Jack was bent over, whispering in Lou McCulloch's right ear. Lou was quiet but shaking.

Suddenly, Jack screamed, "Do you understand?"

Lou McCulloch was not expecting a scream. He went rigid and almost broke the bonds.

"Do you understand?" Jack whispered.

"I do! Please don't kill me! I won't go near them. I'll give them back their bikes! I will! I promise! Please believe me!" Lou was sniffling, sobbing, and begging.

Now Jack and Bruce knew the final point would imprint the scare in Lou McCulloch's mind.

Jack was ready for the climax of tonight's show. "The Brotherhood saw you hide the bikes at the Highland Hardware Store on the day you took them. We have them. If you ever speak of this night, we will know. We will return." Jack was back down beside the boy's ear.

"I promise! I promise!" cried Lou.

"Listen to me. We are going to put you in the closet with the hood over your head. We'll untie you, but you will count to one hundred, slowly. If you come out of the closet before you reach one hundred, it will be the last thing you ever do. People disappear in this town and are never found. Even important people—official people. The Brotherhood knows."

Lou was terrified now. When they said important people disappeared and weren't found, he knew they meant that they had Mr. Albert Winston Brown.

"I will do what you say. I will." Lou was so scared that he could hardly breathe.

"After you finish counting, you will go to your grandfather's house and wait there for your father. You will tell them you got scared and wanted to be with your mother. We will be watching." Jack waited.

Lou realized he needed to answer. "I will. I promise!"

Jack took his knife and cut the boy loose but left the hood on his head. Lou did not attempt to remove it. They picked him up, tried to avoid the dripping urine from his shorts, and they dumped him into the closet. Jack took his knife and tapped three times on the closed closet door.

"Count out loud, slowly, or die. The Brotherhood knows." Jack said in his spooky low voice.

The two men slowly and quietly stepped back to the bedroom door. When they were sure that Lou was slowly counting out loud and following their instructions, they quickly went out the way they had entered. They even locked the basement door; it held loosely, but it held, and they retrieved their pry bars.

They waved to their two buddies, Frank Smallwood and Joe Lincoln, who had been lookouts. That's when the four heard a distant boom from the direction of the hardware store—right on time.

The men removed their hoods, and picking up the pace, they walked a half-block down the street, around the corner to a vacant lot, where their car was parked. They climbed in, and Bruce started the car. He drove another two blocks with his lights off. They proceeded normally across to Main Street and heard the fire siren go off for the second time that night.

Bruce checked his watch and said, "It's just after nine-thirty, so First Sergeant Gunn's alibi is watertight. We did well, and it only took us thirty minutes."

Bruce drove side streets to be on the safe side until he had to take Main out to State Route 22. Once going west on the highway, the long way back to their motel, Bruce Williams again spoke to the men. "You know, I hate scaring kids, but I guess it had to be done."

"I don't hate it one bit," Jack spoke, which got everyone's attention. "That boy's father's the law, and he should be making his kid mind—be setting the example for the other youth. Instead, the whole family's the problem. If this doesn't fix things, we might just have to make his old man disappear for real!"

"Jack, you do know the local Commonwealth's Attorney is missing?" Bruce asked.

"Yeah, I know," Jack said.

"When you told that kid, you would come back, and he would disappear like a local official, no wonder he peed his pants," Bruce said in an accusing voice.

"You're wrong, Bruce. He peed his pants when I told him I would cut out his tongue, fry it, and make him eat it. Then I told him I would cut him so he would sing with the girls' choir. That's when he wet himself," Jack said without a hint of mirth.

"Jesus Christ, Jack. I hope you didn't scare him to death," Frank Smallwood commented.

"We left him counting to one hundred. He's fine," Jack answered and let his head drop back on the back of his seat. The rest of the ride back to the Skyline Parkway Motor Court was a quiet one, except for Jack lightly snoring in the back seat. The Brotherhood had come to town and gone. The question that remained: would the Brotherhood have to return?

CHAPTER 11

BILLY FINDS A SUNDAY MIRACLE
Sunday, July 17, 1955

I was sleeping in, as were most of the family. Our dinner at the hotel had kept us up until after eleven. The only one moving around was Dad. Even Grandma, if awake, was being quiet in her room.

I heard Dad go out to the garage at dawn, but I decided to roll over in bed and snooze a while longer. I was dozing off when our phone rang. Dad picked it up on the second ring. He was quick because he didn't want it to disturb the family. But we were used to hearing the phone ring at odd hours, which was one of the problems of running a towing service. After no more than a couple of minutes, I heard him start Blacky and drive out of the lot. No two blasts on the air horn to let Mom know he was on a call this morning. It was too early for that signal.

I popped open one eye because I was sure Scotty had heard Blacky. I was afraid that the little toad would be up to no good. I was wrong. Scotty was still asleep in his bed with one arm hanging off the side of his bed and his feet on his pillow. He slept in the funniest positions. I heard Blacky backfire in the distance as Dad changed gears.

I eased out of bed, tiptoed to the bathroom, threw some water on my face, dropped my pajama pants, and shot a long stream into the toilet—too early to flush—I just left it. I walked softly down the stairs in my pajamas and got a muffin out of the breadbox. This would hold me until breakfast. Mom made special breakfasts on Sunday, which made up for having to go to church. She was strict about church, except for Dad. Dad went with us most of the time unless he had a job. Me, well, I was forced to go to church every Sunday, rain or shine. I also had to wear a white shirt and tie. Religious strangulation should be against the law, but apparently, it wasn't.

Sometimes we went out for lunch after church. However, since we had eaten at the hotel last night, lunch today would be fried Spam sandwiches on loaf bread, which was fine with me. They were good with ketchup and mayonnaise.

Then, I remembered our bikes. My mood barometer dropped into minus numbers. Our bikes had been gone one day short of a week, and I figured we would never see them again. Too much time had passed.

I heard the toilet flush upstairs. That meant the terrible almost-three-year-old was up and getting into mischief, or he would have come downstairs. I hurried back to our bedroom, and sure enough, Scotty was destroying, not reading, one of my comic books. He had it upside down. The ankle-biter was tearing out the pages, not turning them. I tossed my muffin on the dresser and went after the snot.

"Scotty, give me that! You can't even read!" I was in no mood to put up with the shenanigans of a little brother. I grabbed both his arms and squeezed. He dropped the comic book and began to cry.

"Scotty, hush. If you stop crying, you can have part of my muffin."

I retrieved the partial muffin from the top of the dresser and gave him a bite. I knew he wasn't hurt because he stopped crying to chew. This kid had a cry, don't-cry switch, and he flipped it off for a bite of muffin.

While Scotty was eating his bribe, I donned a pair of shorts and a t-shirt, slipped into my tennis shoes, and went into the bathroom to see if I could do something about my curly hair on one side and bald spot on the other. I tried, but no luck.

I stared into the bathroom mirror, the one with the supernatural powers. I knew such stuff was foolish, but events were about to convince me otherwise. Anyway, no one believed me, but something strange sure happened each time I made a wish on that mirror! I had gone so far down this magic path that I figured I would risk adding one more little request.

"Mirror, Mirror, if I ask you for a miracle, would you just do one more? Please, not a bunch. I just want one." I paused, took a deep breath, and proceeded. "I would like for you to return our bikes to either Kent's house or mine—Amen." I was hoping this wish, if carefully worded, would prevent crazy stuff. We didn't need any more trips to the hospital or property taken by the bullies. I just wanted our bikes back.

I peeked out my bedroom window. No bikes.

Scotty was getting fussy. The muffin was history, and he was bored, so I took him downstairs. I was fortunate because I met Grandma in the living room. I turned Scotty over to her, got a glass of orange juice out of the refrigerator, and walked out to the garage.

Dad had left the side door of the garage unlocked. So, I went in to see if he'd left a note for Mom or me, telling us where he'd gone.

Then, I saw them!

My bike and Kent's bike were right in the middle of the garage! I ran over and touched them to ensure they were real, spilling half my juice on the garage floor. Then, I ran to the telephone, put down my half-empty glass, and called Kent's house. Lucky for me, Kent answered. His mom wouldn't have appreciated having to get out of bed to answer the telephone on Sunday morning.

When Kent answered, I yelled, "Superman, they're here!"

"BB? Is that you? Who's here?" Kent wasn't picking up on what I was telling him, not at all.

"Superman, your bike, my bike, they're here. Right here in Dad's garage. It's a miracle. I asked the mirror to return them, and it did! No, my dad and his...never mind, they're here!" I was yelling so loudly that I knew poor Kent was in danger of going deaf. I bet his mom could hear me without being near the phone.

"BB, if this is a joke, it's not funny," Kent complained. "Is this for real?"

"Kent, this is no joke. Our bikes are here. I'm looking at them right this minute. You've got to come over and see for yourself." I was happy beyond belief!

Kent dropped the phone. I could hear him yelling for his mother. He was trying to get dressed and tell her what was happening at the same time. It was funny, listening to them and them not knowing that I was listening. Kent's mom tried to calm him down but gave up. Finally, I heard them leave the house with their phone still off the hook.

I met Kent as he and his mom drove into the garage lot. I had his bike so he could see it. He jumped out of the car and hugged his bike like it was a pet. Kent's mom had on her bathrobe and street shoes—outside and on Sunday. I wouldn't have believed it if I hadn't seen it.

The noise brought Mom to the kitchen door.

"Sally Ann, what in the world! Is that Kent's bike? Where did you find it?" Mom asked as she came outside in her bathrobe and slippers. I sure hoped the neighbors weren't watching!

"We didn't. Billy did. Billy, where did you find it?"

Mrs. Clark thought I had found the bike.

"Not me! Both our bikes just appeared in the garage this morning. I have no idea how they got there. Well, I do, sort of. No, I don't." I knew I was about to get someone into trouble, either Dad or me.

"William Boyer Gunn, you tell me the truth, young man! What did you do?" Mom had used her angry voice, which meant I better explain and do it now.

I had to fib, so Dad didn't get into trouble or go to jail. "I made a wish on my bathroom mirror, and poof, here they are."

I shouted this as I ran into the garage, grabbed my bike, and rode it into the yard. I smacked the right handlebar on the door frame coming out but missed my fingers, so I didn't care.

Grandma came outside with Scotty to see what all the commotion was about.

Mom didn't believe me. "Billy, there's no such thing as a magic mirror. Whoever took your bikes must have returned them."

"Yeah, that's what happened," I agreed, much relieved. Mom's excuse was better than mine.

Kent was shaking his head; no! "You think Lou McCulloch or the Lockhart boys would return our bikes? Do you really think that?" Kent said it before I could shush him. The boy was slow, and I wanted to smack him.

Kent's mom spoke up. "Laura Jane, he does have a point. I can't imagine those boys returning them unless they were forced into it. Maybe Little John found the bikes and made the boys bring them back," Mrs. Clark was saying with a smile on her face.

"Well, however they got here, they're here. Come inside and join us for breakfast. We have to get these boys fed and ready for church." Mom announced her church sentence, then motioned us towards the kitchen.

"Mom, our bikes are back. We need to check them out. Do we have to go to church?" I asked, with Kent joining in as well. We were both reduced to begging.

"Yes, you do. You can thank the Lord for bringing back your bikes. I expect the reason lies in that direction rather than in some foolishness about a magic mirror." Mom's mind was made up. I knew missing church was out of the question, but Dad's secret was safe for now.

We were about finished with breakfast when Dad drove into the lot, pulling a wrecked Ford. He reported that some tourist had hit a deer, swerved off the road, and smashed his car's front end. He didn't seem as surprised as the rest of us, finding the bikes in the garage. He commented, "The thieves must have brought them back."

Kent and I both rolled our eyes at each other.

I felt better about telling my fib because Dad and Mom had told a tale to cover up Dad's secret plot. Anyway, the bikes were back, and despite some scratches, they looked okay. Kent and I would have to try them out to be sure, but we were back in business!

Just as Mrs. Clark and Kent were ready to return home to dress for church, Sheriff Lawrence drove up with a deputy.

"Morning, John," Sheriff Lawrence greeted my dad, but his face was stern.

"Morning, Dick," my dad called the sheriff Dick and not by his title.

"John, Mrs. Clark, I need to know where your boys were last night." The sheriff asked, but he looked like he expected trouble. He got it from Dad.

"And why would you be needing to know that?" My dad asked before Mrs. Clark could say anything.

"We had trouble at the plant last night. Looks like kids were involved. They set off firecrackers, broke out a bunch of windows, and set fire to the log yard. One of my men is in the hospital." Sheriff Lawrence had taken off his hat and held it beside his right leg. He was banging the hat against his leg, over and over in time with each word he spoke.

Mom walked right up in front of the sheriff, put her hands on her hips, and did she look riled!

"Sheriff, you have your nerve. Billy was with us last night. He's not over his concussion that he got from those bullies. The ones who are still running wild! No thanks to you!"

"Ma'am, we're …"

Mom interrupted him in mid-sentence, "I'm sure a bunch of fireworks going off at the site of a burned-down plant is much more important than arresting the bullies who attacked my boy! Well?" Mom was mad. Not a little mad, but a whole pile of mad!

That's when Mrs. Clark joined in. "Sheriff, why don't you go arrest some real criminals and leave the few good kids in this town alone? Kent was home with me last night, recovering from his injuries, or have you stopped believing the good citizens of this town?" Mrs. Clark was building up to being as mad as my mom.

"Now, ladies, I got to do my job. Some kids did some serious mischief, and I must investigate. If you say, the boys were with you, okay. No need to get your feathers ruffled." Sheriff Lawrence thought he was finished when he spotted the two bikes leaning against the garage. "Say, aren't those the bikes y'all claimed were stolen?"

Dad decided he wasn't going to let the ladies have all the fun. "Dick, you're about to piss me off. Yeah, those are the bikes that were stolen. The thief returned them last night. I found them first thing this morning when I came out to run a tow job."

The sheriff straightened up just a little. "John, where were you between, say, seven and ten o'clock last night?" Sheriff Lawrence asked, and the deputy stepped a little closer to Dad. I saw him reach for his handcuff case on his wide belt.

"Where were you, Dick?" Dad asked him right back, and he turned to face the approaching deputy. My dad was about to whack somebody.

"Now, John! Don't you go getting smart with me! Answer the question!" Sheriff Lawrence ordered, and he was getting angry at this point.

Dad turned back to face the sheriff. "Dick, if I get smart, I'll be the only one between you and me, suffering from that condition. I was with the family in the main dining room of Cubley's Coze Hotel, having dinner. We were there all evening. Do you think I was shooting off fireworks at the plant? Okay, I confess! I was in two places at the same time!"

"You got a witness that can vouch for you?"

"Are you as stupid as you sound?" Dad was trying to get Sheriff Lawrence riled, and he was getting the job done in fine fashion.

Mom thought it was time to stop Dad from going to jail. "John, I'm sure the sheriff has his reasons. Sheriff, we were having a family dinner, and I can vouch for my husband."

"Ma'am, I'll need to know what time because the hardware got broken into last night, just before ten o'clock. First, we had a problem at the plant after dark, then trouble at the hardware. Were the boys and your husband with you all evening?" Sheriff Lawrence had turned to look at Mom and was trying to avoid looking at Dad.

Mom smiled, but there was no warmth in it. "Billy and my John had nothing to do with either of those things. We were all at Cubley's Coze until after ten o'clock in front of a hotel of witnesses."

"Mrs. Clark, where was your boy?"

"He was at home with me all evening."

"Is that right, Kent?" asked the sheriff, pushing it, and drawing a frown from everyone who wasn't a cop.

"Yes, sir! I was watching TV with Mom!" Kent announced almost in a shout.

Mrs. Clark reached for Kent's hand. "Now, unless you have something important to discuss, I'm taking Kent home to get ready for church." Kent's mom escorted him over to their car, opened the passenger door, and gave the sheriff a cold look.

"Yes, ma'am, you go on. John, Mrs. Gunn, I guess that's all I have for right now. Sorry to have bothered you." Sheriff Lawrence put his hat on and motioned for the deputy to get in the patrol car. They followed Mrs. Clark out of the lot and back towards town.

Mom turned to me and said, "Billy, please put those bikes back in the garage and lock the door. Then, come to the house. It's time to get ready." Mom gave me the "do it now" look. I put them up without making a fuss.

I paused in the garage to think. I knew for sure that Dad and his army buddies returned our bikes. Their plan worked. The fireworks and fire at the plant got all the cops out of town, but the fire at the hardware didn't make sense unless it was a warning. But a warning for whom? Why set a fire at the hardware? I had no answer for that one, so I locked up the garage and hurried into the house.

We all went to church, even Dad. We were a little late because Dad had to get cleaned up. The sermon was all about a king trying to decide who was the real mother of a baby when two women claimed it. He was smart. He told the two women he would just cut the kid in two. Each could have half a baby. I got to thinking about how that might solve my Scotty problem if I could find a second mother to claim the little monkey. It was too bad the king ended up saving the baby. Maybe if we could find a king like Big John, I bet that baby would be in pieces before you could say Jackie Robinson.

I sort of nodded off as the Bible story ended because the preacher had given us the same sermon a year ago. He sometimes repeated old sermons after he came back from his summer vacation. He threw this one in without having had a vacation.

One time, Miss Jones assigned the same homework a second night in a row. That almost gave us a free night until dumb old Sarah Foster told her what she'd done. Sarah got several punches in the arm on the playground. That may have been the reason none of the adults told the preacher that he was using an old sermon. They didn't want to get punched in the arm. Keeping quiet was sometimes the best way.

CHAPTER 12

BILLY EAVESDROPS
Monday, July 18, 1955

K ent and I arrived at the hotel loading dock as prisoners in my mom's car. Our parents were not about to let either of us ride our bikes to work. The bikes were safely stored out of sight in Dad's garage. We knew it was best to keep quiet and not fuss about it. I tried to hide my feelings and waved goodbye to Mom, but she didn't wave back; she was worried about Dad and the cops.

Kent and I announced ourselves to Mrs. Johnson and came out with full breakfast plates. We were just in time for Polecat's morning briefing to Mr. Cubley on the town news, gossip, and his predictions for the future. The speculations of Polecat about Highland's destiny were more accurate than the Farmer's Almanac on the weather.

Polecat launched right into the recent disturbance at the plant. The same one that had my mom so worried.

"Saturday night was a rendition of the Keystone Cops, Highland style," Polecat joked as he was balancing a full plate on one knee, eating, sipping hot coffee, and talking, all at the same time.

All of us were watching Polecat juggling his breakfast, expecting a crash at any moment when Mr. Cubley asked, "Have there been any arrests?"

Polecat gave him a grin and answered, "None. Not a single arrest. Apparently, some town children set off M-80s and fireworks at the plant. The M-80s were duct-taped to windows. Smaller firecrackers were strung out on an adjoining ridge to make it look and sound like people were firing guns down on the plant. One of the deputies got excited and shot himself in the leg. Then, two small gasoline bombs exploded and set a stack of logs on fire. That's when the volunteer fire department joined the police in *Much Ado About Nothing.*"

Polecat used the title of one of Shakespeare's plays to make his point. He would do that from time to time. I read that particular play last year, and it was funny once you got past the goofy way they talked. Polecat sometimes spoke that way when he got wound up on a major news story.

Polecat cleared his throat and resumed, "Next, when things began to calm down, a real bomb went off at the hardware. The firemen had to wind up the hoses on old Pumper Number 1 and go to the hardware, while the new pumper remained at the plant to extinguish the flaming logs. Pumper Number 1 lit out for town at top speed. The top speed being forty-five miles per hour. The fire chief complained to his barber that he had been worried because the truck's water tank was down to fifty gallons. Fortunately, it was a minor fire at the hardware, and fifty gallons had been plenty."

Polecat set down his empty plate and began in earnest on his mug of coffee. He blew and sipped as he talked.

"Now, the firemen discovered, after they put the fire out, that the hardware had been burglarized. Zeke Barnes left the plant to investigate the hardware break-in, while Little John and the rest of the boys remained at the plant."

"What were all the cops doing at the plant? I thought you said it was just some kids pulling a prank?" asked Mr. Cubley.

"It was, but at first, the cops thought World War III was starting, and once every constable within thirty miles arrived, confusion reigned. I have it on good authority that when Little John discovered that the gunfire was a hoax, he was apoplectic. Several of the firemen remarked how his use of certain expletives was quite inventive. The sergeant then relocated to the hardware, thinking his professional services were obligatory there." Polecat paused to make sure everyone was ready to listen to the good part.

"Mr. Lockhart, the manager of the hardware, was ordered from the warmth of his matrimonial boudoir, leaving his spouse partnerless. Alone, he drove to the cold environs of the hardware store to inventory the stock. He, Little John, and Zeke Barnes labored until dawn. Much to their chagrin, every tool and implement was in its assigned place and accounted for."

"Mr. Smith, are you saying nothing was stolen?" asked Mr. Cubley.

"Nary a nut nor bolt," responded Polecat. "And, to add insult to injury, when Little John returned to his abode, his son was missing. A frantic search revealed the boy reposed in the bosom of his mother at his grandfather's mansion. Master Lou McCulloch revealed he had been suddenly afflicted with what his dad described as an unreasonable and abiding fear of unseen forces. On the contrary, no amount of coaxing could alter his disposition or convince him to return to his father's residence. His father is mired in consternation over his boy's continued anxiety, even in daylight, over going home."

Polecat rose with the dignity of the King of England departing from his throne room. He carried his dirty dishes to the hotel kitchen door, where they were taken by a waitress. Giving an eloquent thank you to the entire kitchen staff, he left the hotel on his bike with a lingering odor in his wake.

Mr. Cubley picked up the stack of newspapers Polecat had delivered to the hotel. Then with the papers under his arm, he deposited his dishes in the kitchen on the way to his office.

Kent and I finished our breakfasts and began washing the first of several cars that were waiting. Then, just after nine-thirty, the telephone rang in Mr. Cubley's office.

"Linda, is he coming here? I can come down there. No, that's fine. I'll be waiting." Mr. Cubley ended the conversation and hung up the phone.

Kent and I could hear his side of the conversation because his office window was open. Since this is where the hose pipe was located, we were often privy to certain private discussions. Mr. Cubley knew we could hear, but he trusted us to keep what we heard secret.

An hour later, Mr. Tolliver announced Judge Harland was there to see Mr. Cubley. Kent and I were working on our second car of the morning near the open office window.

"Judge Harland, a pleasure to see you, sir. What may I do for you?" I knew Mr. Cubley was speaking to the circuit court judge. Heck, everyone knew who this guy was.

"Matthew, there are several matters we need to discuss. They best be done away from the courthouse. I also thought I might enjoy an early lunch from the Cubley kitchen. I hear you're keeping up the fine traditions of the place," said the judge.

"I have to thank Mrs. Johnson and the kitchen staff for that." Mr. Cubley called to Mr. Tolliver, who came right in, and the judge's reservation was made.

"Matthew, I need to ask you for a favor. We're in a real jam at the courthouse. I guess you know the Commonwealth's Attorney is missing. So far, the police are getting nowhere. The man has disappeared off the face of the earth, and the local court dockets are getting behind."

"Judge, I'm new here, and ..." Mr. Cubley didn't get too far.

"Matthew, just hold on. I know what you told me last month. I hate to ask a second time but calling in substitutes from other jurisdictions is a poor way to do business. If you aren't willing to step in, I understand. However, I saw your work in Roanoke. I need a good prosecutor to do the job until things are resolved. I won't keep you in the position any longer than I must, but will you take the position until we can find a more permanent solution?" Judge Harland paused. I knew this is what grown-ups called, twisting somebody's arm.

"Judge, I guess you know that Big John McCulloch and his boy are not my biggest fans?" Mr. Cubley was right about that! Worst enemies would be more like it.

"Matthew, that's one of the reasons I'd like to appoint you. I'm tired of people thinking Big John runs the court. He's run Mr. Brown for years, but he doesn't run this court, nor does he run Judge Carlton's court. Will you do it?"

"Judge, I don't know what to do!" Mr. Cubley responded with concern.

"Matthew, the county needs you. Judge Carlton joins me in this request." Judge Harland was making it hard for Mr. Cubley to refuse.

"Judge, I'll do it until we can get a better replacement or Mr. Albert Winston Brown turns up. I may need a few days to get up to speed on the cases, and I'll have to break the bad news to Mr. Tolliver. We were starting to get things straightened out at the hotel with me halfway learning the resort business," Mr. Cubley finished.

Kent and I went back to scrubbing the tires on the guest's car because the owner told us he wanted to leave by noon. We heard snatches of some dull court case details as we worked, but that was boring.

I scrubbed and thought.

Mr. Cubley being appointed as the Green Mountain County Commonwealth's Attorney, wow! That was going to make some important people go nuts. I would love to see Big John McCulloch's face when he hears about this.

After the judge went to lunch, we heard Mr. Cubley talking to Mr. Tolliver.

"Chuck, what in the world have I gotten into? What am I going to do?" Mr. Cubley was talking to Mr. Tolliver more like a friend than a boss to his employee.

"Well, I guess you're going to prosecute cases for the county and run a resort in your spare time. This ought to keep you out of the pool hall."

I knew Mr. Tolliver was kidding. There was a pool hall in Highland, but only bad types played pool there.

"Chuck, I don't know if the Highland Police Department will even work with me," Mr. Cubley said with a sigh.

"What choice do they have? If you're the Commonwealth, they have to work with you, or better said, for you. So maybe you can get them to start acting decently towards the plant workers," Mr. Tolliver said in a reassuring voice.

Kent squirted me with the hose. He said it was by accident, but that got us going at each other. We played for a minute but then got back to business. I heard Mr. Cubley say to Mr. Tolliver that he had to go down to the courthouse to fill out some papers for Mrs. Carlisle. I knew he would like that. He was fond of her, and she liked him. I had seen her kiss him on the cheek at the hotel celebration party after the sniper case was solved.

Mr. Cubley would be working on a bunch of Green Mountain County cases. Then, maybe, he would prosecute Lou, Carl, and Dickie for beating up Kent and me. I sure would like to see them get lengthy prison terms for stealing our bikes.

Kent and I were working on our fourth car when Mr. Tolliver told Mr. Cubley that Mr. John Louis McCulloch, Sr. was on the phone and wanted to see him right away. Mr. Cubley left for his meeting, and that was when the owner walked up to check on his car. He asked us to take out the spare tire and clean under it. We found hundreds of seeds scattered in the spare tire well and trunk. Superman got that cleaned out by borrowing the maid's vacuum cleaner from the third floor. I got it back before she missed it.

We were finishing up this last car when Mr. Cubley returned from seeing Big John McCulloch. Kent and I listened in as he reported what happened to Mr. Tolliver. Since the window was open, what else could we do? We had to listen.

"Chuck, I was wrong."

"Big John didn't order you to turn down your new job offer?"

"No, he doesn't know about it. Also, he's forgotten all about me rejecting his offer to buy Cubley's Coze. He told me he needed to withdraw his generous offer, claiming the funds he was going to use were needed to rebuild the plant. He laid it on pretty thick, how it was for the good of the community. I didn't know what to say. I think the drugs he's taking have addled his brain."

Kent looked like he was cranking an imaginary eggbeater with his hands.

I almost laughed out loud.

Mr. Cubley continued while we cut up.

"I decided I would just go with it. I thanked him for letting me know his decision. Actually, I was quite happy to learn that he's going to rebuild the plant. A lot of people will be pleased with the news," Mr. Cubley ended on this cheerful note.

"Matt, that is good news. I just hope he treats the workers right during the construction. I wonder who he'll hire to replace the plant supervisor that the sniper killed? He didn't say, did he?"

Mr. Tolliver asked the question that I wanted to ask.

"No, he never mentioned the details or who he might hire as the new plant supervisor. Then, of course, there's also the business of replacing Chief Smith. I think his boy will get that position."

Kent groaned, and I held my nose.

We heard Mr. Cubley get up and walk over to the window. "You boys get all of that?" He asked with a big smile on his face. He knew all along that we'd been listening.

Kent was closer to the window and responded. "Yes, sir. I guess we need to take that oath on pain of death that we won't tell nobody nothing." Kent realized what he'd just done.

I had him. He knew it. He had made such a big deal correcting me when I made the double negative mistake. Now, he had said it, and I was going to get him back. But Mr. Cubley got him before I could.

"Kent Clark, I can't believe Superman is using double negatives. What would Perry White or Jimmy Olsen say?" Mr. Cubley was ribbing Kent. I was loving it.

Kent was already red in the face and getting redder. That's when he turned the hose on me for a second time. I smacked him on the arm with my wet rag twirled into a rat's tail. We both got fussed at by Mr. Cubley for messing around when we should be working.

We went back to finishing up the last car and behaved for the rest of the day.

When we went into the hotel to collect our money, my share was one dollar. Mom would get half for my college fund, which left me fifty cents. Now, on top of that, there was a dollar in tips from the four cars, which left me with a whole dollar for the day. Not too bad for a day's work. A dollar would get me into the movies four times. Kent and I were doing all right, despite that stupid college fund.

Trooper Bobby Giles pulled into the hotel lot right after I called Mom to come to pick us up. He spoke to Kent and me, but right away, he asked Mr. Tolliver for the key to the hunting lodge gate. Mr. Cubley asked him what the matter was.

"Nothing Matt. We're checking all the roads in the county, trying to find Mr. Albert Winston Brown's car. I remembered that road up to the lodge and thought I had better check it out. Have you been up there since last Monday?" Trooper Giles asked.

I knew that last Monday was the day Mr. Brown disappeared, and the police were about out of places to look for him.

"Chuck, have Richard come around. I'm pretty sure he went up one day this week. I sent him for a second try to clean up the bloodstains off the lodge porch."

Richard Baker, the hotel maintenance man, came into the lobby from the kitchen. During their conversation, he told Trooper

Giles that he had driven to the lodge on Wednesday but didn't see any cars off the road, going or coming. He explained, "I didn't look over the banks or in the woods because I had no reason to."

And that's when Trooper Giles decided he would thoroughly check it out and got the key from Mr. Tolliver.

I looked at Kent and started to ask Trooper Giles if we could ride with him and blow the siren. That's when Mom showed up, which messed up our getting a ride in the trooper's car. I knew Dad had just souped it up. I sure would have liked to ride in it.

Dad fussed all the time about what a rotten deal Trooper Giles had gotten because he wrecked his old blue and gray. Dad showed me the new improvements he put into the sergeant's old car assigned to Trooper Giles.

I remembered his exact words. "Billy, that old heap is fast. When Trooper Giles and I tried her out—they had refused to let me go with them—it hit one-forty at top speed."

I could see how proud my dad was. The new car the sergeant was now driving with the stock motor wouldn't touch Trooper Giles's souped-up hand-me-down blue and gray.

On the way home, Mom passed Lou, Carl, and Dickie riding their bikes. When Lou saw our car, he yelled something to Carl and Dickie. They turned into our church parking lot and lit out for Main Street. They were riding away from Mom's car as fast as they could pedal.

"Superman, did you see that?" I asked Kent.

"Yeah, those three lit out toward Main like their tails were on fire," Kent said, but he said it too loud, and Mom heard it.

"Kent Clark, don't you use that sort of language. Your mom and I want you boys to speak civilly. That way, people will think better of you," Mom said it in sort of a nice way. Nicer than when she corrected me.

"I wonder what those boys are up to? They got into some kind of a hurry when they saw my car," Mom said to no one in particular.

I gave Kent "the look." He gave me "the look" right back.

The bullies stopped behind some tall boxwoods near the Green Mountain Baptist Church.

Dickie began, "Did you see them? Riding with BB's momma, all cozied up. We need to dish out a double dose that'll put them in their proper place for good."

"Yeah! That last beating we gave them wasn't near enough. We need to get them good this time! Let's leave them with fewer teeth," said Carl.

Lou replied instantly, "No way! It's too dangerous!" Abandoning the argument because the Lockhart boys didn't want to make Lou mad at them, the boys rode their bikes to the mansion of Lou's grandfather. Then, changing into swimming suits, they silently drifted on air mattresses in the grand pool behind the tennis court. The three boys ignored the wind, which was creating ripples on the water.

CHAPTER 13

A CHILLY FOG IS BANISHED
Tuesday, July 19, 1955

Matt rose early and looked at his wall calendar. A large red circle showed that today was the first day he would take over the Commonwealth's Attorney's Office for Green Mountain County. Before the death of his wife and son, he'd been an Assistant Commonwealth's Attorney in Roanoke, but now he was going to be the boss. Matt laughed at himself because there were no other attorneys to boss since the office consisted of one attorney—him.

He did have a secretary, and he knew from talk downtown that she was very loyal to Mr. Albert Winston Brown. He wasn't sure if she'd accept him or how to handle the situation if she were hostile.

Counting backward from today, the nineteenth of July, he marked the eleventh of July with a large "X." That was the day Brown had disappeared. Despite a massive police effort, there was no trace of the man or his vehicle. A dead body would be in bad shape after more than a week's exposure in this heat.

He glanced out of his apartment window for a view of the valley. There was no view. There was only fog. He could just barely make out the hotel's front lawn and entrance road. The rest was a gray blur.

He dressed in a dark suit and went to the hotel kitchen for breakfast. Matt planned on eating in the dining room until he saw Polecat on the loading dock. He decided to join him despite his court attire.

Billy and Kent would not be washing cars in this weather. Matt always felt a little down when the boys weren't around. And now that he was the acting Commonwealth's Attorney, it meant several more days a week that he wouldn't be around the hotel to see them.

"Good morning, Mr. Smith. How are you this dreary morning?" Matt asked Polecat, using, of course, his proper name.

"There blows an evil wind upon the moors, this morn. It's a good day to remain by the hearth and perhaps enjoy a cup of ale with friends." Polecat said with a yellowish grin.

"I wish I could, Mr. Smith. I fear I must attend to the criminals of the county. What matters of concern do you have for me this day?" Matt said, digging into a stack of flapjacks with extra maple syrup, trying not to spill drops on his tie.

"No news of your predecessor. His countenance has not been seen, lo, nearing a fortnight. His heirs are without hope and are in a state of mourning. The constabulary is confounded and floundering in a swirling morass of foggy confusion."

Polecat sounded like a bard of the Elizabethan period, but that was his style. Matt enjoyed the intellectual challenge of figuring out what Polecat was saying.

A resort guest had recently mentioned how sad his paperboy was an imbecile. Matt knew better.

Possessing an incredible memory coupled with superior intelligence, Polecat was Matt's chief informant and foremost freeloader. The complimentary breakfasts at the hotel granted Matt information worth ten times the cost of the meals. Moreover, the information delivered was extremely valuable on local matters. The marvelous thing about this informant, he was able to gather information from both the police and the underworld in equal measure.

"Mr. Smith, you mentioned that Doc Hathaway might be able to help find Mr. Brown. What did you mean by that?"

"Mr. Cubley, the worth of Doc Hathaway will become clear in time. But at present, his incarceration will prove to be an insurmountable obstacle for you. I suggest you focus on certain places of lucre that are frequented by those who seek riches but often exit as paupers."

Polecat was being obtuse, but when Matt asked for an explanation, Polecat declined by switching to another subject.

"Of more importance, Mr. Cubley, today is the day that Big John McCulloch is to start rebuilding the plant. If it's not too inclement, the construction equipment should arrive by noon. After that, the plan is to start clearing debris left after the fire."

"That is news," responded Matt.

"Ah, but I'm not done. There will also be an announcement of a new chief of police." Polecat paused. He was most pleased with himself. Delivering papers to the Highland Police Department and lingering outside the door to Little John's office had afforded him news so fresh that he was fourth in line to hear. Little John had been the first to know when his dad told him last night. Then, Little John informed Frank and Roger Younger in the police station this morning, where Polecat overheard the news, making him fourth in line of news nobility.

"Mr. Smith, who is it?"

"Ah! The next chief of the Highland Police Department will be John Louis McCulloch, Jr. His street name to all who love him will remain Little John. A reference to his intellect, not his size." Polecat raised his cup of coffee with his little finger out to the side in salute, then took a sip.

"Mr. Smith, you have just ruined my day! I think Judge Harland talked me into the worst set of conditions imaginable." Matt stopped eating and just sat there for a few moments, absorbing the information, and looking dejected.

"Mr. Cubley, the ship of state is listing hard to starboard. Perhaps, as its next pilot, you will be able to shift the ballast and bring the USS Justice to a more even keel. While your efforts will not be pleasant, they are imperative." Polecat looked into Matt's eyes with a combination of concern and expectation.

"Mr. Smith, I fear that she may capsize, and I will go down with her."

Matt pondered his fate until he thought of another question, but Polecat gave him an answer before he could speak.

"Mr. Cubley, the answer is "no." I'm not aware the selection of a new plant superintendent has been made," Polecat informed Matt.

"How did you know that was my next question? Can you read my mind?" Matt asked in wonder.

"Your last line of inquiry was leading to the obvious, so there was no need for me to use clairvoyance," Polecat answered with his alligator smile. His lower canines were enlarged and made his smile look quite dangerous.

"I guess you're right," Matt answered. He slowly took his dishes into the kitchen. Each step felt as if he was dragging a ball and chain.

Matt noticed Boo introducing Karen Hathaway to the kitchen staff. She was here for her scheduled job interview.

He concentrated on improving his mood. Successful to some degree, he greeted Karen Hathaway and asked her into his office. After a brief conversation, he invited Chuck and Boo to join him. Matt wanted them all to participate in her interview for the position of maître d'. The interview lasted thirty minutes. After the meeting, Matt asked Mrs. Hathaway to wait in the lobby for a few moments.

"Do you all think we can make a decision now, or should we ask Mrs. Hathaway to come back later?" Matt asked Boo and Chuck.

"I think she will fit in nicely," Chuck said almost instantly.

Boo spoke next. "Let's give her a week or two to work with me. I want to be sure I leave things in good hands," Boo requested.

Boo was young, but she was very good at her job. Matt hated to lose her, but he knew it was her mother's dying wish for her to finish at the university.

"Boo, that sounds like a good plan. Let's see if she can start tomorrow. I think I'll begin her at the wage of a waitress plus what's fair for lost tips. Working with you, she'll miss out on them. If she works out, I'll raise her pay to two-thirds of your pay. You just let me know how she does."

Boo was considerate, knew the quirks of the job, and was hardworking. The question was, could Karen Hathaway handle the hotel's temperamental cook and the demanding guests?

Matt gave Mrs. Hathaway the news. She departed smiling and promised to report for work first thing in the morning.

Matt left the hotel for the office of the Commonwealth's Attorney, which was located on the second floor of the Green Mountain County Courthouse. The secretary occupied a desk in the waiting room with the prosecutor's office next to it. That was it—two rooms—nothing like his Roanoke office suite.

The secretary, Mrs. Sarah Louise Harvey, was in her sixties. She had a stern countenance and kept her salt and pepper hair in a tight bun on the back of her head. She was rail-thin, always dressed in dark clothing, and reminded him of his third-grade teacher, who was quick to rap the knuckles of any student foolish enough to cause trouble.

Matt walked into the office and smiled.

"Mrs. Harvey, good morning. My name's Matthew Cubley, but please call me Matt."

"Mr. Cubley, I know who you are. I shall call you, Mr. Cubley," she announced without any hesitation.

Matt decided to tread cautiously. "Mrs. Harvey, how should we do this? I don't want to appear to be moving Mr. Brown out when we all hope he returns in a few days. But I do need a place to work." He hoped this tact would make him appear agreeable and not pushy.

"Mr. Cubley, I have cleared Mr. Albert Winston Brown's desk and stored his personal items in the closet. They may be returned in short order, but for now, I think you should use the office as your own." Mrs. Harvey was all business but very cooperative in light of the circumstances. Matt was relieved to know his secretary was allowing him to use Mr. Brown's office.

No sooner had Matt hung his raincoat on his office coat rack when he saw the new chief of police and Officer Frank Younger walk into the combination waiting room and secretary's office. They had an arrest report for Mrs. Harvey to file. When Little John saw Matt, he stopped in his tracks.

"What are you doing in Mr. Albert Winston Brown's Office? Mrs. Harvey, what the hell is going on?" Little John was at first stunned, but in an instant, he had switched to anger.

"What are you doing, wearing the chief's coat?" Mrs. Harvey barked back at Little John.

"I'm the new chief of police. That's what I'm doing. What is he doing?" Little John was pointing the finger at Matt.

"Well, mister new chief of police, I guess you better meet the new acting Commonwealth's Attorney for Green Mountain County, Mr. Charles Matthew Cubley. Judge Harland appointed him yesterday afternoon. So, until the return of Mr. Albert Winston Brown, you two will be working together."

Mrs. Harvey seemed to be enjoying her role of informing Little John about something that might choke him to death.

"Like hell, I will! My daddy will hear...." Little John stormed out of the office with the arrest papers still in his hand. Frank Younger was left standing with a stunned look on his face.

Matt walked out into the outer office and stood beside Mrs. Harvey.

"Sergeant Younger, I see you also got a promotion. Congratulations. I look forward to working with everyone in your department, even the Chief."

The officer smiled, a good sign. "I agree, Mr. Cubley, but sorry, I better be going. Mrs. Harvey, I'll bring that arrest report over in a little while."

Matt noticed that Frank Younger had on an old deputy's shirt with a brand-new set of sergeant stripes sewn on the sleeve. The new sergeant wasted no time in vacating the building. He would have to run to catch up with his chief.

"Mrs. Harvey, that didn't go well, did it?" Matt commented.

"No, sir, it didn't. Now, may I pull the next docket for you? You might also want to review the recent arrest reports."

She told Matt this with a stern face, but he detected a little smile breaking through as she turned to retrieve the paperwork.

Matt spent the morning reading reports and learning Mrs. Harvey's filing system. She was very efficient.

He did notice that one of the desk drawers on the desk he was using had a padlock on it. Matt asked Mrs. Harvey about it, but she told him she didn't know what was in it because her boss had the only key. Matt tried to ignore the drawer, although it sparked his curiosity.

Noon came sooner than expected. Matt decided he would treat himself to lunch at the Black Panther. When he was seated, Carol Martin and Linda Carlisle arrived. Seeing Matt, they greeted him with smiles. Having occupied the last open table, he invited them to sit down. It was the polite thing to do.

Each had a hamburger with a side of onion rings. They laughed about ordering onions, but since they all were having them, it wouldn't matter. Matt was thankful he didn't have court that afternoon. The three enjoyed lunch as friends. Unlike the last lunch meeting, he didn't feel guilty this time. Well, not quite as guilty. Janet was in his thoughts, a comfortable presence, not as an accuser.

He passed the sheriff's office on his way back to the courthouse and decided to stop in to introduce himself. Matt could hear voices in several offices as he entered the lobby, where a deputy asked him what he wanted. Before he could explain, the sheriff stepped up to the counter.

Matt spoke up, "Sheriff Lawrence, I thought I'd stop in and officially introduce myself as the new and temporary local prosecutor."

"Mr. Cubley, the judge told me all about it. I'm looking forward to working with you. Let me know anytime my deputies can be of service," announced the sheriff.

"Same here. I'm available anytime you need me, day, or night."

"Day or night, my, my. Well, since you're here, a report was just called in that a dog has dug up some bones. They could belong to our missing person. Care to ride along?"

Matt didn't hesitate, "Sure."

The sheriff named the deputies who were to check it out. Sheriff Lawrence asked Matt to ride with him. Matt jumped at the chance to make friends with the sheriff.

The sheriff and Matt rode in the lead car, and two deputies followed in a second car. The convoy drove out to near East Gap, where they turned onto a rutted farm road until it stopped near a farm nestled at the base of a mountain. The men were approaching the northern margin of the county where East Bear Creek joined West Bear Creek. The county line ran along the top of the mountain, making it easy to figure out where the county line was located. Of course, climbing up to reach the county line was another thing altogether.

The farmer showed them two bones his dogs had brought to the house. There was a long bone and a shorter bone. One bone might have been a femur and the other an ulnar. It was hard to tell because varmints or the dogs had chewed both ends. A news reporter from the *Highland Gazette* had been tipped off about the find. She arrived to cover the story in the paper's station wagon.

"What do you think?" the sheriff asked Matt.

"I have no idea. Maybe we better call the Medical Examiner to come look," Matt suggested.

"Hey, one of you have dispatch give Doc Hill a call. If he's not busy, see if he'll run out here and take a look?" Sheriff Lawrence called out to his two deputies.

"Shoat, come tell me what you think," Lawrence called to the short fat deputy who was not on the radio. Shoat hurried over and picked up the bones.

"My guess is these bones came from a large animal, but not a human," Shoat said with some confidence after studying the bones for a few moments.

"Deputy, my name's Matt Cubley. May I ask your full name?" Matt asked the deputy called Shoat.

"Yes, sir. My name's Jeffery Baxter Lincoln, but everybody calls me Shoat. I can't imagine why," Deputy Lincoln said with a big grin on his face.

The Sheriff gave Shoat a gentle shove. "Cause we ain't sure if he's human or porcine, so we call him Shoat. He bears the resemblance of one, and he is intelligent—just like a shoat." The sheriff said this with a laugh, so Matt knew Shoat could take a ribbing in stride.

"And you are?" asked Matt to the deputy who had returned from making the radio call.

"Danny Lucas Potter but call me Danny. It's a pleasure to meet you, Mr. Cubley. I think this is the first time I've ever seen the Commonwealth's Attorney at a crime scene. Not sure this is one, but this is a first. Am I right, Sheriff?" Danny asked, but all he got was a frown from the sheriff.

"Guys, why don't you call me Matt. I feel like you're talking to my dad when you call me Mr. Cubley." Matt responded with a smile.

Fifteen minutes later, Matt was talking to the reporter from the *Gazette* when Dr. Hill drove up. He got out with his medical bag like he was going to make a house call. He walked over to the farmer, who pointed down at the two bones.

"What damned fool called me out here to see a couple of cow bones?" Doc Hill exploded and looked around for a victim.

Shoat was backing up. The sheriff was intently studying a tree over near the farmer's barn. The other deputy was bent over behind the sheriff's patrol car.

"I guess I did, Dr. Hill," Matt said, wishing he had not joined this particular field trip.

"Well, these are cow bones, plain as day, whoever you are," Doc Hill announced again, walking back to his car.

"Sorry, Doc. But if I'd known what they were, I wouldn't have bothered you. Not for the world. Thanks for driving out, and I'm...." Matt was in the process of saying more, but the doctor was driving away before he finished his sentence. The reporter was laughing and not trying to hide it.

"I think I'll keep this off the record," she said and walked back to her car, giving Matt a farewell grin. The two deputies joined in with quiet laughter, which earned them another frown from their boss.

"Sheriff, I guess there's no need for us to hang around. We'll see you back at the office," Shoat said, giving Danny a "let's get out of here" nod toward their patrol car.

"See you, boys, later," said the sheriff, softening his scowl.

The sheriff and Matt said goodbye to the farmer and rode back to town in silence. Going into the courthouse, Matt spotted the new chief of police coming out of Judge Harland's office. When he saw Matt coming up the front steps to the second floor, he turned and went down the back steps.

Matt needed to review a case that the judge was holding, so he walked into Judge Harland's office. Linda Carlisle greeted him warmly and asked how his afternoon was going. Matt told her about the case of the cow bones, which got her laughing. Judge Harland heard them and invited Matt into his chambers to find out what was so funny. Shortly, the judge was also laughing.

Matt borrowed the file he needed from the judge. Starting to leave, he was stopped when the judge asked him to close his office door and have a seat for a short conference.

He began as soon as Matt was seated. "Chief McCulloch was just in to see me. The chief's demanding I remove and replace you with someone suitable."

"Your Honor, if you need my resignation, I'll write one out and bring it right back."

The judge shook his head no and chuckled, "Chief McCulloch left here very disappointed. I'm surprised you didn't meet on your way here."

"I did see him, but he turned when he saw me and took the back stairs."

"Watch that coward closely because he'll stab you in the back," warned the judge.

"I'll be careful."

"That might be wise, but if he tries anything in my court, he'll find himself wearing a policeman's uniform without having the authority to make arrests. Big John would just love that."

The judge excused Matt, and as he left, Matt closed the door behind him. On his way past Linda's desk, she motioned for him to stop.

"I enjoyed our lunch together. I hope you did?" she said with a smile.

"Lunch was the high point of my day without a doubt," he answered as he gave her a warm smile in return.

Back in his office, he noticed the chilly fog was burning off as a beam of sunlight broke through the clouds and lit up his desk. That beam of light reminded him of Linda's smile, which had banished his dark mood. He caught himself humming *Little Things Mean a Lot* by Kitty Kallen as he returned to reading arrest reports.

CHAPTER 14

BILLY & A BIG FAMILY FIGHT
Wednesday, July 20, 1955

S cotty was in bed with me when I woke up. There must have been a storm during the night, and he's afraid of thunder. He had kicked all my covers onto the floor and was stretched out with his arms spread wide. The ankle-biter was taking up all the bed, leaving me balanced on the edge.

It was just getting light outside, so I decided to check on our bikes. They were locked in the garage, but one could never be too careful.

Scotty didn't stir when I got dressed. It took me several minutes to find my tennis shoes because they were in the trash can. He was making a habit of putting them there. So, to get even, I tossed his in—the little urchin.

I was downstairs and heard Mom and Dad moving around in their bedroom. I slipped outside and unlocked the garage with the key Dad kept in the kitchen cupboard. Our bikes were safe and sound, so I locked the door and replaced the key.

"Why are you up so early?" Dad asked, coming out of the bedroom.

"Scotty, of course. He got in bed with me last night. How could I sleep with him taking up all the room? I came down to check on the bikes," I said, opening the refrigerator door and getting out some milk.

"Are they okay?" Dad asked, starting the coffee pot.

"Yep, all secure," I replied.

Mom came into the kitchen wearing her nylon bathrobe over her nightgown. She wore that thing even though it was already warm outside. Today was going to be clear and hot. All the rain we had yesterday, and the fog last night would make it humid on top of hot.

"Billy, your mom told me about seeing Lou, Carl, and Dickie, and how they skedaddled yesterday. If you're going to work at the hotel today, you may ride your bike on one condition. When you get to the hotel, you must call your mother to let her know you arrived. Can you do that?" Dad asked with a grin.

"Heck, yes!" I said, almost spilling my milk.

"Billy, keep your voice down. You'll wake Grandma and Scotty," Mom scolded with a little frown. She didn't wrinkle her nose, so I knew it was not a serious frown.

"Can Kent ride his bike too?" I asked.

Mom answered while she was getting out stuff to fix breakfast, "Well, that's up to his mother. Anyway, I think for today, I may take the Buick to keep an eye on you. Your father thinks the bullies will leave you alone, but I'm not so sure."

"Aw, Mom. I don't need you to follow me. I can take care of myself." I could just imagine my mom driving behind me down Green Mountain Avenue. I bet every kid in my class would see it.

"Billy, you better not say another word about what your mother might or might not do. You keep talking, and you'll be riding with her to work every day this week." Dad was getting irritated. He was close to whacking me, so I knew it was time to shut up.

"Yes, sir. I won't say another word. I just hope Kent's mom will let him. Mom, can you please talk to her for me? Can you?" I asked with what I thought was a pleading look.

"Can I? I can unless I go mute or the telephone stops working. I will if you two boys behave, and you promise to call me when you're ready to come home. Is that clear?" Mom was giving me the frown and a grammar lesson. I was close to getting into a scrape this morning. I didn't want the first morning Mom and Dad let me ride my bike to Cubley's Coze to end in a fuss.

Mom did call Mrs. Clark, who said it was okay. His mom dropped Kent off to pick up his bike, and we both rode our bikes to the hotel. I noticed my mom was way back behind us, so it wasn't that bad.

Since all I had had for breakfast was a glass of milk at home, I got a real breakfast at the hotel. Kent also ate a second breakfast. Polecat was talking to Mr. Cubley about Mr. Brown being missing. We all laughed about the police finding cow bones near Bear Creek. The Highland Police officers were giving Sheriff Lawrence and his deputies a hard time about those bones. The ribbing had gotten on the nerves of one of the deputies, and harsh words had been exchanged.

Mr. Tolliver came outside and asked Mr. Cubley where he would be today.

He answered immediately, "Working on court cases and bills for the hotel. I thought I might split my time between the courthouse and the hotel."

He had a couple of meetings set up at the courthouse later that day with several deputies regarding the Brown investigation. The paper was turning up the heat, demanding to know why the police had not found the missing Commonwealth's Attorney. The state police had joined in checking out people with grudges against Mr. Albert Winston Brown—mainly suspects who had been falsely arrested in the sniper case—a long shot but necessary to cover all the bases.

Kent and I started working on a 1954 Buick Skylark convertible, which was a very rare vehicle, according to Mr. Tolliver. The guest who owned this car also owned a Buick dealership in Washington, DC. That's how he was able to get his hands on this model. It was black with white sidewall tires and chrome wheels with little spokes in them. The wheels looked like wheels off a bike but much larger. It took us over an hour to get all the scuff marks off those sidewalls. They looked new when we finished, but the cheapskate owner didn't even leave us a tip. Dad often said that's why rich people are rich; they never give their money away.

Our second car was a 1953 Chevrolet Bel Air two-door, like Mr. Cubley's car, but this one was white with a black top. It looked different from the boss's fifty-five Chevy. The grill on the fifty-three was big and ugly. I liked the fifty-five model better.

A brand-new state police car pulled into the guest lot. I knew right away that this car was assigned to Sergeant Barry Oliver. He was driving the vehicle that should have gone to Trooper Giles. I waved at the sergeant, and he waved and said hello.

When the sergeant walked around the corner of the hotel, I whispered to Kent, "I wonder if the sergeant is still mad at Mr. Cubley for rescuing us instead of letting the troopers do it?"

The office window was open; we were about to find out.

"Good morning, Matt."

"Morning, Sergeant, what's happening?"

"All the local chatter is on you. Judge Harland called me yesterday and gave me the news. Congratulations, I think. Or should I be offering you my condolences?" Sergeant Oliver was in a good mood.

What a relief!

Mr. Cubley laughed. "I hope this job works out. However, I'm afraid one agency might have some heartburn over my recent appointment."

I knew Mr. Cubley was talking about Sergeant...I mean Chief of Police McCulloch and the members of the Highland Police Department.

"Well, Matt, anything I can do to help, just let me know. My boys are looking forward to working with you. Everyone needs to get the Albert Winston Brown matter resolved. We sure didn't need his disappearance coming right on top of that sniper business. All I'm doing lately is defending my district troopers to the brass in Richmond, which is not my favorite pastime."

Sergeant Oliver was being very friendly to Mr. Cubley. The little matter of Mr. Cubley not following the sergeant's orders must have been forgiven.

"Sergeant, do you have any good leads on Mr. Brown?" Matt asked.

"Well, we're starting with the obvious. I sent Trooper Giles down to talk to the Beamis brothers. I thought if anyone could talk to them without the state police getting sued, it would be Bobby Giles. He came back convinced that they have nothing to do with Mr. Brown's disappearance."

"I agree with that. I got to know them well during the sniper investigation. Despite all they went through, they never led me to believe they were gunning for anybody—not even the town police, who had caused them so much trouble," Matt said with conviction.

"I sent Mike Quinn over to the prison to talk to Doc Hathaway, but he got nowhere. Doc isn't going to talk to the police while he's pulling time. That just isn't healthy. I know it. He knows it."

"Sergeant, I also picked up some information that Doc knows something. Have you any idea what it might be?" Matt asked in a lower voice. Lucky for us, Kent and me, er, I mean Kent and I could still hear them.

"Matt, I have no idea what he might know. He's got to have a big grudge against Brown for the payroll frame job, but how could he pull off a murder from prison? Those boys of his might hold a grudge against Brown, but I don't think they're old enough or big enough to pull off a kidnapping and murder."

It was scary to hear the sergeant say this about Skip and Barry. They were about my age and were the ones who saved me from Lou when he whacked me with that ball bat. They did do a number on Lou, but they became my friends. I wanted them to be in the clear. Kent gave me a look that told me that he, too, was surprised to hear that they might be suspects.

"Do you think Brown has been murdered? I was hoping he'd gone off with someone," Matt asked.

"Never cared much for the man, but I don't think he ran off with a skirt. I think someone grabbed him. Our problem is everyone fired at the plant has a reason to shoot him, and each is a suspect. On the other hand, why go after Brown and not Big John, Little John, or one of the local cops? They were all equally responsible for those tenant evictions, which often ended at the hospital. Finding a needle in a haystack would be easy, compared to solving this one. It would help if we could find his car or his body," Sergeant Oliver coughed and cleared his throat.

"Getting a cold?" Matt asked.

"I went over to the Beamis farm and looked around, which was a waste of time. I seem to have brought back whatever was in bloom."

Matt ordered up a pot of tea with honey from the kitchen. We listened to them clicking teacups on saucers while they talked.

Wow, a Virginia State Trooper drinking hot tea. I did not see that coming.

Mr. Cubley and Sergeant Oliver began discussing cases scheduled for court over the next several weeks. Their conversation got boring quickly, so Kent and I picked up the pace and finished our second car.

"Hey, boys, looks like you're doing a good job," Sergeant Oliver called to us. We both jumped. We were chatting and cleaning and didn't hear him come up. He laughed when he saw us jump.

"How are you two doing? Nerves bad?" he asked.

"No, sir. Doing fine," I answered.

"Fine as frog hair," joined in Superman.

Sergeant Oliver laughed and then got serious. "The troopers have been talking about how brave you were. Most kids would have been basket cases after being kidnapped by a serial killer. Are you sure, you're all right?"

"Sergeant, Superman and the BB are just fine," Kent said.

"Yeah, it would take more than a little kidnapping and a few murders to scare us. Roy and Hoppy wouldn't be scared, and neither are we." I said it, but inside, I wasn't that convinced. I doubted the sergeant bought it either. He was nice and told us we were two tough hombres.

When he left the guest lot, he turned on his red bubble-gum light and waved. We thought he was neat for a sergeant, but I still liked Trooper Giles best.

Having Mr. Cubley as the Commonwealth's Attorney was going to be fun. We might get to hear all kinds of neat stuff.

Lunchtime, and we went into the kitchen to check out what Mrs. Johnson might have ready. Boo greeted us and gave us each a poke in the ribs. Boo is so friendly like that. She also introduced us to Mrs. Hathaway, just like we were grown-ups.

"Billy, Kent, I want you to meet Mrs. Karen Hathaway, our new dining room maître d'. She's going to run things after I go back to school," Boo said with a smile.

Mrs. Hathaway was plump with a subtle smile as if she didn't want to let it out all the way. Her hair was piled up on top of her head with a row of curls across the front.

"Hello, boys. Skip and Barry were asking about you last night when they heard I was starting work here," Mrs. Hathaway said.

"Can Skip and Barry come visit us? We could show them some neat places on the mountain. Introduce them to our friends." I exclaimed. I liked Skip and Barry and wanted to be friends with them.

"They're staying with my sister in Rocky Mount for now until I can get things worked out here in Highland. I hope to get a place in town. When they start school, this fall, will you help them get acquainted?"

"Sure thing," I answered.

Mrs. Hathaway was having a hard time. Money was tight for her, with her husband in jail. Mr. Cubley had just hired her despite her husband's current problems. It would take time before she would be getting back on her feet. That's what Mom told Dad when I wasn't supposed to be listening.

Kent and I could sure use Barry and Skip living here. Four could fight off ambushes better than two.

We got our money from Mr. Tolliver, and the last guy tipped us. I remembered to call my mom to tell her we were leaving. We coasted down the hill towards town, banked through the turn at the bottom, and didn't have to pedal until halfway to the bridge. Kent spotted Carl Lockhart first. He was waiting for us. When we passed by him, he pushed off and started pedaling fast to get beside us.

"Hey, stupid man, what did you and BB do to Lou?" Carl asked as he matched his speed to ours.

"We didn't do nothing," Kent said, but I let the double negative go. We had more serious stuff going on.

"Well, BB big butt, your daddy might scare Lou, but he don't scare my brother or me. We're going to beat your asses the first chance we get. You little turds are about to get stomped," Carl bragged.

That's when I saw Mom's Buick turn onto Green Mountain Avenue from Beechwood. Carl cussed us again, turned left, and was gone.

"Kent, Dad's army buddies must have done something bad to Lou. They did more than get our bikes back."

"Uh, oh! Here comes your mom! Mum's the word about seeing Carl, or we'll be grounded again. Deal?" Kent said, keeping even with me.

"Of course, we gotta stick together. Don't say nothing about nothing," I agreed.

Kent laughed, "Nothing about nothing?"

I looked at Kent with a glare. He better not say anything about me using a double negative—not after what he had just said. He looked over at me and winked.

Mom passed us like she was going somewhere. She just waved and went on, but we both knew better. When we got home, she pulled into the garage not a minute after us.

"Boys, did you just see Carl Lockhart?" She asked.

"Uh, no, ma'am. Superman, did you see Carl?" I asked, all innocent-like.

"No, BB. I never saw him, not one time, and that's the truth." Kent was about to tip Mom off that we weren't telling the truth.

Mom gave me a funny look, but she didn't say anything. Kent and I followed her into the house.

"What's to eat?" I asked, trying to get her off the subject of Carl or bullies.

"Did they not feed you lunch at the hotel?" Mom asked me.

"Well yeah, but that was ages ago. Got any pie left?" I asked. Kent got an eager look on his face. I knew how he liked pie.

"No, boys. That's for supper. Here are the last of the cookies. You may have them with some milk. No pop, don't ask, and eat them at the table or take them outside. I don't want to see any more cookie crumbs in your bedroom, young man. I spent all morning cleaning up a mess you made last night," Mom said.

Grandma came into the kitchen with Scotty. Of course, the copycat began asking for cookies and milk. I gave him a half. He's little. Half a cookie was all I could spare and all he needed. Kent and I only had three each.

Grandma sat down at the kitchen table with us and held Scotty while he ate his half-a-cookie. "Laura Jane, I just don't like it. Not one bit," Grandma began, and it sounded like she wanted to wade into a fight with Mom. I began to eat faster. Trouble was brewing.

"Mother, I told you, it'll be fine."

"Fine? Was it fine when your little boy was almost beaten to death with a baseball bat on the Fourth in the middle of the town park? Was it fine when both Kent and Billy almost died at the hands of those three bullies behind the furniture store? Was it fine when they had their bikes stolen? How do you say it's fine?"

"Mother, the boys got their bike back. That's something," Mom argued.

"Something! I say little or nothing! The police won't act. The town's going to the dogs. How is that something?" Grandma said it with anger in her voice. It was certain that she was spoiling for a big fight with Mom. Scotty wasn't eating but frowning, which was one step away from him crying.

"Mother, John is handling it. I made sure the boys were all right today. Now please, let us handle it," Mom finished with a crinkle in her nose as she frowned. Things were not good. I sort of looked at Kent and motioned him to exit to the garage with my eyes. He got it. We both started walking towards the back door.

"I see how you handle things. I guess you won't be happy until your children are dead and buried. I guess I'll have to bury all my relatives. Then, when all of you are dead and gone, who will bury me? No one! That's who!"

Kent and I made it outside to the yard before Scotty started screaming like he was being burned alive. Mom and Grandma would be fussing for at least ten more minutes. Kent and I escaped to the garage to see if Mr. Skelton or Dad needed any help.

"What's got Grandma stirred up?" Dad asked me.

"I'm not sure." I thought it better not to answer that question with anything resembling the truth since it was my fault they were fighting. The trouble with this kind of answer, I risked getting whacked by Dad. Kent was trying to look small.

"Boy, don't you lie. Answer me!" Dad grabbed me by the shoulder and shook me. He's powerful, and it hurt.

"Grandma's mad because no one is doing anything about the bullies." I was trying not to let Dad see my eyes tear up.

Suddenly he let go of me. I lost my balance, fell, and my elbow landed on a rock. I got up without saying anything, looked at my elbow, and tried really hard not to cry in front of Kent. I failed because my elbow hurt up to my shoulder. Dad walked into the house and let the screen door slam.

I could hear screaming coming from the house—first Dad, then Grandma, and then Mom. All three were getting into it. Mr. Skelton came over and asked me if I was okay? I lied and told him I was fine, but I wasn't. My elbow was throbbing and had electric sprangles running around it, and it was all my fault. I needed to fix things! I just didn't know how.

Kent came over and put his arm around me. We went around back and sat behind some wrecked cars until things quieted down in the house. Dad came back outside, mumbling to himself, got in the Buick, and left. I knew he was going to town and wouldn't be home until late, if at all.

Kent decided it was time to go, got up, and said, "Bye." He did a running mount onto his bike and pedaled for home. He left before his mom came to follow him home. I went into the house, rubbing my arm and shoulder.

I was going to tell Mom I would fix things, but she was in her bedroom with the door closed. Grandma was in her room with Scotty, and her door was closed. The house was silent, and I was alone.

I went up to my room and started to read a comic. It was no good. I threw it at the closet and missed; it hit the wall. I just sat in my room staring at the wall. If I had a gun, I would shoot those bullies. Maybe then, my parents and Grandma wouldn't fight. I hated it when they fought over my scrapes.

I heard Mr. Skelton leave at five. I wished there was somewhere I could go. I bet he and Boo got along. It would be nice to move in with them for a couple of days.

Mom called me for supper. I told her I wasn't hungry, and she didn't make me come down to eat. That night, she ate alone. Grandma must have had something stashed in her room for her and Scotty.

I took my pillow to sleep in the closet. I wanted Dad to come home. I prayed he would. I stayed in the closet because I could hear through the furnace vents when he came home. But I fell asleep, waiting for him.

CHAPTER 15

MATT'S LITTLE VICTORY
Thursday, July 21, 1955

Matt walked down the central stairs from his second-floor apartment to the hotel lobby and found Chuck in deep conversation with Cliff Duffy, the night clerk. It was past time for Cliff to be gone, so Matt walked over to see if there was a problem.

"Good morning, Chuck, Cliff. How are things?" Matt inquired, and Chuck cheerfully responded—no nervous ticks this morning.

"Matthew, good morning. Hope you slept well?"

"I did. Rested and ready for a busy day."

"I understand this is your first day in criminal court. Perhaps justice will prevail over certain bigwigs who think they're above the law," exclaimed Chuck with a wink and soft voice so as not to be overheard.

Chuck, Cliff, and Matt were alone in the lobby, and Chuck felt free to bring up the issue of Big John's influence over court matters. It was well known that the big boss, who had the previous Commonwealth's Attorney on his payroll and in his pocket, could get all the justice money would buy.

"Well, I'll try my best."

Matt changed the subject with, "Gentlemen, I saw you talking. Is there anything I need to know about?" Matt asked the two.

Cliff spoke right up, "Mr. Cubley, I have great news! My contact at the Green Mountain Resort called me last night to tell me that Big John says I can stop spying on you. I no longer have to give him your guest lists. All his money is going toward rebuilding the plant, and he's no longer interested in buying you out, even at a bankruptcy sale. Also, his threat to fire my wife as his accountant if I didn't spy for him is over. Isn't this great?"

"That's wonderful, Cliff. Things worked out for both of us." Matt said with a pat on Cliff's shoulder.

"Mr. Cubley, I no longer have to keep this a secret from my wife, do I?"

"No, Cliff, you may tell her all about it."

"Yes, sir, I will. She needs to know that you helped both of us when you didn't fire me for spying but saved my job, my reputation, and saved her job."

"Cliff, I think you should bring your wife to dinner to celebrate. You tell Boo to reserve a table for two as my guests," Matt said and glanced at Chuck. Chuck gave Matt a thumbs up.

Cliff hurried off with a big smile on his face.

"Chuck, how did the Highland Business Owners Association meeting go last night?" Matt asked since he hadn't listened to the meeting from his secret hide on the second floor. The hidey-hole had been built by his grandfather when the hotel was erected.

"I don't think they had a meeting, just supper. Big John missed it because he's still too injured., and I noticed attendance was down. A few members came hoping they would get more details on the reconstruction of the plant or who the new plant superintendent might be. No news was discussed in the lobby, no happy faces, and everyone left right after dessert."

Matt grabbed some toast from the kitchen and walked out to see if Polecat had arrived. It was a little early for his informant, who was probably still delivering papers. The loading dock was deserted, and Matt watched a patch of mist drift across the top of the mountain. To the west, the sky was clear, which meant that the afternoon would be hot and dry.

Driving to the courthouse and thinking he would be early; Matt found the office secretary already at work. She was earning his respect.

"Good morning, Mrs. Harvey. How are you today?" Matt asked the elderly lady. Again, he noticed her hair was in a tight bun and decided it was her trademark.

"Good morning, sir. The docket for today is on your desk. I put three new arrest reports on top. The sheriff asked to have a minute as soon as you arrived. May I inform him you're here?"

"Please do." Matt was impressed at her no-nonsense manner. He was taken aback by her referring to the desk as his desk, which seemed awkward since he was a temp and not the elected Commonwealth's Attorney.

"Morning, Matt," said Sheriff Lawrence, coming in the door with a cup of coffee in his left hand. He reached out to shake hands with Matt with his right.

"Sheriff," Matt said, shaking his hand. "What can I do for you this morning?"

"We have a big problem. One that won't go away," said the sheriff with a concerned look as he sat down.

"What problem do we have?" Matt asked, knowing the problem had to be the sheriff's alone. Matt hadn't been in office long enough to have a problem.

"John Gunn came to town last night," Sheriff Lawrence reported. He paused and began looking out the window of Matt's office. He drained his cup and sighed. Matt patiently waited for him to continue.

"When John Gunn got to the pool hall, he was already half-drunk. One of the hustlers bought him two more beers, thinking he might clean John out at pool. All that did was get Gunn primed for a fight."

The sheriff paused again and turned to look at Matt.

"He gets like this from time to time. Not as much now as when he first came back from Germany. In fact, I think it's been a year since he tore up the pool hall. It took four deputies to get him in handcuffs that time."

Matt needed to get ready for court; he hadn't even started on the morning docket. He wanted to hear the sheriff's problem, just faster. So, he decided to nudge the man along.

"Do you know what set him off?" Matt asked.

"Yeah, me!" Sheriff Lawrence blurted out. He sat his empty coffee cup on the edge of Matt's desk, grabbed the arms of his chair, and rocked back.

"What's he mad at you about? Oh, I bet I know, Billy!" Matt had begun to figure out the problem.

"You got it. John's a regular guy, most of the time unless he's been drinking. When he's had a few, he gets touchy. A year ago, two guys at the pool hall made nasty comments about his wife. She is good-looking, and they complimented her figure—the caboose end. John went off like a Roman candle. After the fight ended, he'd put both men in the hospital. One of the four deputies that responded to the call came damn close to shooting him. Shoat, who gets on with John, got him calmed down. Whiskey and the war, plus two jackasses talking about his wife, almost put him in prison. Lucky for him, both men lived. All the witnesses said the two men attacked Gunn first. Judge Carlton dismissed the charges but roasted Mr. Gunn in open court. That warning and his wife have kept him from doing something stupid until last night."

"What happened last night?"

"As I said, John arrived mad, complaining about first this and that when a guy at the next table told him to shut the hell up. Lucky for everybody, Shoat was on duty and was the first deputy to arrive before things went sideways. Had it been one of the Highland Police, we might be charging John Gunn as a cop killer or be having a death by cop funeral for him."

"John didn't hurt Shoat, did he?" Matt asked.

The sheriff shook his head in the negative. "No, nothing like that. However, John was spouting off about how I wouldn't arrest that brat of Little John's and how I let shit like that get by because Big John owns me. He threatened to show Big John and me that we're not as big as we pretend to be."

"So, who did he beat up?" Matt wanted to hear the end and less about the middle of what had happened, but the sheriff was intent on telling it his way.

"No, he didn't beat up anyone. The owner of the pool hall called dispatch as soon as John started mouthing off. Shoat got there first, got John calmed down, and took him home."

"Well, it sounds like things worked out. It did, didn't it?" Matt asked.

The sheriff grinned for the first time. "Hell, no! John's wife, Laura Jane, lit into her husband like a wildcat. She slapped him—

hard—more than once. Shoat said John just took it. By the time she was done, Shoat felt sorry for John. She is usually sweet, but when John comes home drunk, she can get mighty riled. The lady has a temper like her mother. She can whip John into shape quicker than anyone else on this earth."

"Sheriff, isn't the problem solved?" Matt said, approaching his exasperation point as the office clock ticked close to the time for court.

"Heck, no, she also lit into Shoat and said if I didn't get those bullies into court, she would come down here to straighten me out. So now, the two of them are hotter than wood stove lids on a cold winter's morning. I got a problem. We got a problem."

"Sheriff, do you have enough evidence to prosecute? I know Billy and Kent, and from what I've seen, they're decent kids. But all the rumors I hear about Lou and the Lockharts are the same—three hoodlums!"

"Those three are no angels. I'll go that far."

"What did you tell John right after Billy got attacked?" Matt asked, although he was sure he knew the answer.

"I told John I would speak to Mr. Albert Winston Brown to see if he would allow me to issue warrants. That's when the man disappeared. I haven't been able to get me an answer, and I sure as heck can't go arresting Lou McCulloch and the Lockharts without permission. Besides, the evidence comes out as three against two."

"Why can't you?" Matt asked.

"Why can't I what?" the sheriff asked back.

"Arrest them," Matt answered.

"I can't go arresting Big John's grandson. Hell, an election is coming up. Besides, all three boys said they never even saw Billy or Kent—not once that day," responded the sheriff, trying to explain. It was clear he was struggling to defend himself.

"I thought a couple of girls at Green Mountain Drug saw those three come in while Kent and Billy were sitting near the door?" Matt asked, looking hard at the sheriff.

"How the hell did you know that?"

"Sheriff, Billy and Kent both work for me at Cubley's Coze, washing cars. Plus, the whole town's talking about how Lou, Carl, and Dickie are running wild, going after Kent and Billy, and killing small animals. It's almost common knowledge, and most people have made up their minds. Not making an arrest might be worse for your election than losing Big John's campaign donation," Matt countered with a wave of his hand for emphasis.

"What can I do?" asked the sheriff.

"We are missing Mr. Brown, the duly elected Commonwealth's Attorney, and I'm only the temporary one. More importantly, I'm blocked from prosecuting this case because Billy and Kent work for me at the hotel. We need to appoint a special prosecutor. A move that lets us both off the hook," Matt explained.

"I don't know about bringing in a stranger. A special prosecutor might piss off Big John."

"Yeah, it will. Sheriff, you can piss off Big John on the one hand or piss off John Gunn and a big part of the county on the other. You think about it. Let me know if you want me to go see Judge Harland. I'll be glad to talk to him. Just don't wait too long. Laura Jane may come a' calling." Matt's tone was such that it should be apparent to the sheriff that his joke was more serious than done in jest.

The sheriff rose and started for the door.

"Sheriff, don't forget your coffee mug," added Matt.

The sheriff retrieved the mug and wandered out of the office, turning left toward the courtroom, stopped, reversed, and began walking back the other way for the front steps.

"Mr. Cubley?" Mrs. Harvey called from the front waiting room.

"Yes, Mrs. Harvey," responded Matt.

"Good for you. It's about time someone stood up for the people of this county!" Mrs. Harvey's voice was loud enough to reach into the hall.

Matt was stunned by her comment. Perhaps she was loyal to Brown, as many had said, but first and foremost, she was honest. She also didn't mind voicing her opinion. This new job might turn out to be a little better than he first thought.

Matt arrived in court one minute early. He watched as several deputies and Frank Younger strolled into court at the striking of the hour. The morning docket wasn't remarkable. It began with several speeders, two drunk-in-public cases, a shoplifting from the hardware, and all the defendants pleaded guilty. Then, a domestic fight case was called. The wife and husband had made up, so Matt signed off on the *nolle prosequi* line at the bottom of the warrant. The judge endorsed the formal written request by the prosecutor for leave to have the charges dismissed without comment. After the dismissal, the couple left arm in arm.

After a ten-minute recess, things got interesting. There was a stack of skinny-dipping cases from the park. Boys from the football team swam across the lake naked during the early morning hours of the Fourth. They got caught and arrested. Matt asked the judge to admonish them and make each pick up trash in the park for twenty hours, and if they did that, the charges would be dropped. Judge Carlton went along with his recommendation, much to the relief of the boys' parents and the local coach of the football team. All in all, so far, the morning court docket had proceeded without a hitch.

Then, Little John showed up for the last case on the morning docket. This case involved a tenant of Irish descent charged with resisting a civil eviction.

After the bailiff read the charges, Little John spoke up without waiting for Matt to address the court.

"Your Honor, the evidence clearly shows that the plant fired Jack Feeney for coming to work late for the third time. Two officers and I arrived at his home two days after the firing and told him to get out. He said he needed a few more days because the baby was sick, so I grabbed him, escorted him into the yard, and one of my men hit him with a nightstick to get him under control. The tenant pushed me and tried to get away, but I held on, so my men could subdue him. Feeney fought back and hit Sergeant Younger on the ear with his fist."

The tenant blurted out, "That ain't how it happened. They beat me with clubs, and I spent three days in the hospital just for telling them the baby was sick!"

Chief McCulloch ended his testimony at this point with, "Shut your Irish mouth, boy!"

The chief was acting as if Matt, the Commonwealth's Attorney, wasn't even in the courtroom. This was more than a breach of courtroom procedure; it was a direct personal insult that Matt was not going to let pass.

"Judge, may I ask a couple of questions?" Matt asked after biding his time.

"Of course, you may, Mr. Commonwealth," responded the judge, drawing a scowl from Chief McCulloch.

Matt had the clerk swear in the tenant, so his testimony would be under oath. Chief McCulloch had missed that little procedural step.

"Mr. Feeney, do you pay rent to the landlord?" asked Matt.

"Yes, sir, I pay five dollars a month, every month on the first. I've never been late. I paid my rent the month I got fired, too," testified the tenant.

"Sir, were you served with a written notice by the landlord, McCulloch Wood Products, to leave the premises?"

"No, I never got nothing in writing. When I got fired, the foreman told me I had to get out in forty-eight hours. He just told me. I never got no papers." The man kept glancing at Little John. The defendant had moved a step away from the chief as he answered the questions.

"Your Honor, Mr. Feeney's rental was a month-to-month tenancy. The problem here is that the agents for McCulloch Wood Products only gave this man and his family forty-eight hours to get out of the house. It was an oral notice, and the law requires a thirty-day written notice. Thus, the landlord failed to follow the proper provisions under the state code." Matt paused in his remarks to the court.

Chief McCulloch looked like someone had just dropped a house on him. The chief began talking, "McCulloch Wood Products owns that house, they own it, it's their property. We get to say who lives there and who doesn't. We never had this problem before," Chief McCulloch said with finality.

Matt immediately butted in. "Chief, I'm afraid the Code of Virginia is clear on how to evict a tenant. The Highland Police

Department didn't follow the law. The tenant and his family were not given a written eviction notice and sufficient time to move."

Matt turned to face Chief McCulloch, looked him in the eye and said, "You then committed an illegal eviction. He had the right to live there for the rest of the month, sick child or not. When you grabbed him by the shirt, you committed an assault and battery on an innocent citizen. I'm very concerned that your department used unnecessary force. Even if the tenant did hit one of your officers after he was battered, this would be a case of self-defense. It's my duty to ask that this case be dismissed," Matt formally requested in closing.

Little John McCulloch became livid. The redness started on his neck, rose to his face, and over his forehead. It seemed like steam was about to shoot out of his head. An exaggeration, perhaps, but that's how the bailiff later described it.

"I don't know who you think you are. You two-bit lawyer. I'll..."

The judge slammed his gavel down on the bench. "Chief McCulloch, be quiet! I think you might want to rethink that last outburst. You are speaking to an officer of this court—my court. Let me remind you that Mr. Cubley is the Commonwealth's Attorney for Green Mountain County." Judge Carlton was shouting and frowning—never a good sign in any courtroom. Then, there was silence for ten seconds.

"Your Honor, we never had this problem when Mr. Albert Winston Brown was here," Chief McCulloch said in a much more respectful tone of voice.

Judge Carlton spoke in a normal tone of voice. "Well, this is the first time the issue of proper notice has been raised before me. The tenants never raised it, and Mr. Brown never mentioned it. Judges must remain neutral. We don't help one side or the other, but now that I know the notice was not proper, my course of action is clear—very clear!"

"But I..." started the chief of police. The judge didn't let him finish.

"Now, here is what's going to happen," stated the judge, and pointing his finger at Chief McCulloch, he said, "You will remain silent while I consider the Commonwealth's motion." Judge Carlton paused and studied the warrant as if it were telling him something he didn't already know.

He turned and pulled out one of the volumes of the Virginia Code from the shelves in the wall behind him. He read the book for a few moments. Then, he closed the book and looked at the defendant, ignoring Chief McCulloch.

"Mr. Feeney, you, and your family were removed from the residence improperly. The criminal charges against you are dismissed."

There was silence for a moment. The tenant didn't move. Chief McCulloch looked first at Matt and then the Court. He opened his mouth, but when he saw Judge Carlton slightly shake his head no, McCulloch closed it, turned, and stormed out of the courtroom. He tried to slam the big door, but the damper prevented it from slamming.

Matt turned to look at Mr. Feeney, who was still standing beside him, tugging his shirt collar with a finger.

"Do I have to go to jail?" asked the man.

"No, sir. The charges have been dropped. You are free to go," Matt explained.

"Well, I'll be. Missy ain't gonna believe this," Mr. Feeney said with a shake of his head.

"Who's Missy?" Matt asked the man.

"My wife. No, she ain't gonna believe this. Thank you, Judge. Thank you," Mr. Feeney exclaimed, and he wasted no time leaving the courtroom.

"Mr. Cubley, may I see you in chambers?" said the judge, but this was an order, not a question, although phrased as one.

Matt followed the judge into his chambers as the bailiff dismissed court. He braced himself, not sure what was coming.

The judge took a seat behind his desk with Matt standing. "Matt, I've suspected what was going on, but I strictly adhere to the premise that the court remains neutral. It's up to the tenant-defendant to bring up a defense. I hoped someday a tenant would get a lawyer or would raise the notice issue. Mr. Brown was always careful to avoid it. Thus, it was never brought out until today. Keep up the good work. You have a nice day."

Matt left the judge's chambers feeling much better. Perhaps he might be able to make positive changes within the system, after all. He heard a noise behind him and turned to see who it was. No one was there, but for some reason, he thought of Janet. She would have been pleased. He wished he could've shared this little victory with her.

CHAPTER 16
BILLY & DAD ON A TOW
Thursday, July 21, 1955

W hen my dad came home in the middle of the night, I heard because Mom was in the kitchen yelling. Then, I heard someone get slapped more than once, and that had to be my dad getting whacked.

Next, Mom fussed at the deputy everyone calls Shoat. I know because she kept calling him Deputy Lincoln. It must have been the deputy who brought Dad home. She told the deputy that the sheriff better do something, or she was coming downtown to settle his hash. I knew when Mom got angry; she was something. Dad would spank you, but I never knew Mom to slap anyone. Instead, she would talk to you and make you feel small. Last night was different and all my fault. I cried into my pillow long after the deputy left, and things got quiet.

Later, I awoke a second time after a bad dream. I crawled out of the closet and went to bed but couldn't sleep. I watched spots on the ceiling until it got light. If you stare at them long enough, they move around.

Once the sun came up, I looked at my sore elbow. It was still hurting. The joint was all swollen, and when I bent it, it hurt worse. I would have to wear long sleeves today and wash cars with my arm mostly straight.

I tiptoed into the bathroom since it was early, and I was the first one moving around. I missed the toilet when I peed. The stream went in two different directions, one in and one outside the bowl. It did that sometimes without warning, but I cleaned it up, so Mom wouldn't find out. That sometimes happens to Scotty, but he's too little to clean up after himself. Girls don't have that problem because they sit down, and that's why our teacher fusses if the boys don't lift the toilet seat. She explained all that to the class.

Shorts and a long-sleeved shirt were dumb, but perhaps no one would notice. I got some milk and went outside. Today was going to be another hot one. It was not long until I heard someone in the kitchen, so I went inside. Mom was starting a pot of coffee and asked me how I slept. I lied and said, "Okay."

Then she spotted my long sleeve shirt.

"Billy, go upstairs and change. It's too hot for long sleeves, plus you'll get the sleeves dirty washing cars. I can't afford to buy you shirts every week."

"Mom, I can roll up the sleeves. I'll be careful and not get them dirty."

"William Boyer Gunn, I have to deal with your father but not you. Now, march up those stairs and change that shirt."

So up the stairs I went, put on a clean T-shirt, and came back down. She spotted my arm before I had gotten two steps into the kitchen.

"Billy, what's wrong with your elbow?" She asked.

"Nothing, Mom, I bumped it." I felt bad about lying, but I would have felt much worse telling her that Dad had pushed me down.

"Come here and let me see it." She was both looking and sounding stern and pointed to a kitchen chair.

She examined my elbow, pushed on it, and bent it slightly. I tried not to let on that it hurt, but she saw through me pretending. She put some ice in a dishtowel and told me to hold it on my elbow for ten minutes by the clock. After ten minutes, my arm felt better.

I only ate a piece of toast and drank some milk. Since the day was clear, I would be going to the hotel to work and have one of Mrs. Johnson's' breakfasts. Guests were checking in and out regularly, giving Kent and me all the work we could handle.

Dad never got up, not even when Kent arrived. We rode our bikes up to the hotel without an escort, but I had to push my bike up the hill with one hand. I told Kent not to tell anyone how I hurt my arm. He promised, so I knew my secret was safe.

Mr. Cubley had already gone to the courthouse when we arrived, and that left Polecat, Kent, and me on the loading dock, enjoying a breakfast of sausage, eggs, and fresh biscuits. I think that Polecat knew about my dad because he asked me how my dad was feeling. I lied and said he was fine, and we moved on to other subjects, much to my relief.

He told us that the new chief of police was Little John McCulloch. Frank Younger had been promoted to sergeant, which most people had thought would happen, but it was now official. If Polecat said it, it had to be true.

We only had one car to wash because the nice weather wasn't getting the new arrivals' cars dirty. We were done by eleven, so I called Mom to tell her we were finished and were headed home. All she said was, "Fine," and hung up.

We cut back through the kitchen to get our bikes from behind the maintenance shed and ran into Mrs. Hathaway. She told us her good news. She'd found an apartment over a garage in town that had two rooms and a bath. She was going to move in tonight after work, and Skip and Barry could now come to Highland on the Greyhound from Roanoke to Lynchburg on Saturday. Richard Baker and his wife, Rose, had agreed to drive her to the bus station.

Kent and I were overjoyed to hear that Skip and Barry were coming to town, and we began to plan what the four of us could do as we got our bikes. I took it one-arm slow and easy, and even Superman was ahead of me as we coasted down the hill to Green Mountain Avenue.

Riding over the bridge, we saw Lou McCulloch riding his bike toward us from the other end. Kent and I stopped. Lou stopped, got off his bike, and stood beside it, just looking at us.

We just stared at each other for what seemed like a minute. It was near high noon, and I thought this would be the perfect time for a gunfight. Funny, the dumb stuff you think sometimes.

Lou suddenly swung his bike around and, making a running leap, jumped on and pedaled away toward town like we were chasing him. We weren't. In fact, we hadn't moved. He turned left onto Court Street and was gone.

"Wow, did you see him take off?" Kent said.

"Yeah, he acted like he was scared of us. Superman, my dad's army buddies did something bad to Lou. Promise me that you'll keep quiet about this, or my dad might get arrested," I said.

"You know me, BB, I'm a 'pillar of discretion,'" Kent said with a zipper motion to seal his lips right across his crooked grin. I knew he had picked that saying up about "pillars of discretion" from Polecat.

I had to ask, "That leaves Carl and Dickie. What should we do?"

"Who knows?" said Kent with a shrug.

A car came onto the bridge and blew its horn for us to get out of the way. We quickly moved over to the side of the bridge, and as the car passed us, the driver blew his horn a second time. We paid no attention to a jerk in a hurry.

When we got home, we saw Dad sitting in the garage, not doing anything, just sitting. It was evident that he was in one of his quiet moods. Kent and I went straight into the house, and Mom asked us what we wanted for lunch. We decided on grilled cheese sandwiches and tomato soup. Scotty, Grandma, and Mom joined us at the kitchen table, with only Dad absent. He stayed in the garage.

After lunch, Kent and I chanced going to the garage for a screwdriver to tighten a screw on my bike horn. Mr. Skelton was changing the oil in a fifty-two Olds, and he asked us about the hotel and his daughter. We told him that Boo and Mrs. Hathaway were running things well.

We fixed my horn, and Dad continued to sit, staring at the floor or his feet.

Late in the afternoon, Kent's mom drove up to follow Kent home because she was still worried about bullies. After they left, Dad roused, called to me, and I followed him over to a wrecked Ford with the front end all smashed in from hitting a tree. I could see where the out-of-town driver had busted a hole in the windshield with his head. I knew the guy was still in the Lynchburg hospital.

"Billy, have you seen Lou McCulloch recently?" Dad asked.

"Yes, sir. I just saw him on the way home." I thought I better tell Dad the truth because I didn't want to get whacked.

"Did he bother you?"

"No, sir. When he saw Kent and me, he lit out back to town. It was like he was scared of us."

"Well, that's good. You let me know if he gives you any trouble. Can you do that?" Dad said, using the wrong verb.

Mom would have given him a lecture on the difference between can and would or will. But I'm not stupid and let it slide.

"Yes, sir. I promise to tell you if he does anything," I said and hoped this was all he needed.

"Good!"

Dad turned and walked back toward the garage—our conversation was clearly over.

I was relieved that he didn't mention Carl or Dickie. I didn't want to risk telling Dad everything was fine when it wasn't. I had caused enough trouble not taking care of those bullies. Dad and Mom were mad; Grandma was angry; I was afraid my dad might go to jail, and I sure didn't need any more trouble. I needed to avoid future scrapes with Carl and Dickie. That was for sure.

After supper, the phone rang, and Dad got it on the second ring. There had been a wreck on State Route 22, just west of the Liberty Bell Gas Station. Two cars had sideswiped each other. They both would have to be towed right away to clear the road. Dad would get one, and the McCulloch Chevrolet wrecker would get the other. Dad asked me to go with him. I knew better than to say anything but, "Sure."

Mr. Skelton had gone for the evening. It was just us two men. Dad fired up Blacky, our 1941 B61 Mack tow truck, which I loved to ride in, sitting high up in the cab. You could see over the cars in front, and only big tractor-trailer trucks blocked your view when you rode in Blacky.

When we got to the wreck, Trooper Quinn, Sheriff Lawrence, Deputy Jeffery Lincoln, who everyone called Shoat, even to his face, were all gathered around a Ford sitting smack in the middle of the road. The Chevrolet Dealership wrecker had just hooked up to this car to tow it. That Ford would be an easy tow.

A second car had two wheels over a steep embankment that dropped at least twenty feet into a creek. This car was a 1950 Studebaker Champion, a two-door sedan. I could not believe it was still hanging onto the top edge of the bank. It looked like pushing it with one finger would send it over the edge, crashing into the creek below.

Dad got out with a flashlight and looked it over. The driver was a colored man who kept following Dad, asking questions. Dad ignored him.

Trooper Quinn walked up to Dad and greeted him. Dad grunted and said he guessed the Chevrolet wrecker wasn't about to tackle this tow. Trooper Quinn smiled.

Dad pulled Blacky parallel to the Studebaker in the opposite lane. They were now side by side with ten feet between them. The two vehicles sat with the front of the tow truck to the rear of the Studebaker. Dad told me to get a flashlight and hold it on the back of the car. Next, he got out the forty-foot chain. I was glad he carried it to the Studebaker and didn't ask me to take it. That chain was heavy, and with my sore elbow, I might have dropped it. I didn't want to get whacked in front of people for dropping Dad's chain. He hates weaklings.

Dad took that chain and did something with it that I had never seen before. He wrapped the chain around the rear axle behind the left rear wheel and hooked it to itself. Taking the other end of the chain, Dad attached the hook to the front of Blacky. Blacky has two iron hooks on the front bumper, and he hooked that chain to the nearest bumper hook with no slack.

"Billy, watch this and see how it's done," Dad said to me.

Now that the back end of the car was tied to the front end of Dad's tow truck, he pulled the towing cable out from the rear tow winch. He pulled it just long enough to hook it to the car's front frame and winched in the slack. That's when he made me get in Blacky's cab.

"Billy, I don't want you hit if the cable snaps," he said in a normal voice. "Stay in the cab until I tell you to get out!"

Dad then looked at several officers and bystanders who were standing around watching what he was doing. Dad put his hands up to his mouth like a speaker's megaphone and yelled to the bystanders, the sheriff, and the colored man who owned the car.

"Hey! If this cable snaps, it'll take your heads off. Y'all better move out of the way."

Not waiting to see if they moved, Dad started up the winch. The cable began to pull sideways from the pulley on the end of the arm of the tow truck. I heard metal protest and the winch whine, but the front end of that car started to move sideways from the edge of the bank and into the road. Usually, the car's rear would have shifted outwards just a little bit and being so close to the edge, that vehicle might have rolled off the edge and down the bank. My dad's so smart. He'd anchored the car's back end with the forty-foot chain, and when he pulled the front end into the road, the rear tires stayed where they were. Slick as could be, the Studebaker was out of danger. Dad unhooked the forty-foot chain and the tow cable, pulled out the fender just a little with his hands, and darn if he didn't drive it down the road and park it behind the trooper's car. The colored man walked over to see how much he owed.

Dad responded, "That'll be eight bucks."

The driver of the Ford, which was the car that the Chevrolet Dealership wrecker had towed, was still at the scene, waiting for a ride. Well, he spoke up and complained to Sheriff Lawrence.

"Sheriff, I've done been robbed! That Chevrolet wrecker driver is charging me twenty-five dollars to tow my Ford, and this here colored fella only has to pay eight. That ain't right!"

Dad smiled and said, "Next time, call me. Tell your friends." And then, he walked away.

I was helping put things back in order when a Highland police car pulled up to the scene. Out of the car stepped Chief McCulloch. Trooper Quinn, the sheriff, and Deputy Lincoln all walked over to see what was up. Chief McCulloch avoided them, never greeted them, and walked over to my dad. I noticed he stopped just out of arm's reach.

"Gunn, I'm sick and tired of you and your boy! I know the two of you are responsible for the plant trouble and hardware break-in!" Chief McCulloch was yelling, and his face was going purple. I got behind the corner of Blacky. I could hear but was putting some distance between me and the fight that I was expecting.

"Go to hell!" Dad said, and never quit putting chain into the chain locker on Blacky.

"What did you say to me?"

"I said go to hell! If you don't know the way, bend over, and I'll help you there!"

Dad finished with the chain, stood up, and slammed the door on the chain locker. He frowned, wheeled to face the chief, and I saw his hands were balled into fists. Dad took one step closer to the cop, putting him within arm's reach, and shouted, "Saturday night, my family was at Cubley's Coze having dinner! Now, get out of my face!"

I was surprised he hadn't hit Little John…yet. I knew it was coming. I just wasn't sure when.

"I don't believe you!" answered the chief.

"Well, I got about twenty witnesses, including the current Commonwealth's Attorney, you dumb, hick cop! Now back up, or I'll back you up!" Dad shouted as he drew back his right fist.

Sheriff Lawrence stepped between Dad and Little John.

I thought, *Oh, no! Dad, not the sheriff.*

The sheriff took Little John by both shoulders and looked him right in the face. "Chief, I checked. John's telling the truth. He couldn't have done either of those things. He and his boy were at the hotel in front of a dining room full of witnesses. The family didn't leave until ten o'clock. He and his boy have an ironclad alibi."

But Little John wasn't finished. "I don't care. He's responsible. I know he is!" shouted the chief, and he wasn't going to back down.

Dad had calmed a little and looked back at the door he had just slammed shut. He saw it was closed, looked back to his front, and pointed his finger at Chief McCulloch.

"Prove it, asshole," Dad said with a grin that was an invitation to set Little John off like a skyrocket.

Trooper Quinn joined the group and grabbed the chief by one arm. "Chief, this isn't the place. The sheriff says John's in the clear, so leave it be. Besides, how will you prosecute the man when the Commonwealth's Attorney is his main witness." Trooper Quinn was half trying to calm the chief but was half enjoying putting in his two cents' worth.

"Quinn, Cubley's done! He'll be gone by noon tomorrow. The shortest term of any Commonwealth in the state."

And with that, Chief McCulloch got in his patrol car and slammed the car in reverse. He spun it around in the road, backward, and came within a foot of going off the same embankment that almost got the Studebaker! Spinning his rear tires, the chief sped back to town.

Silence reigned for about ten seconds when Deputy Lincoln stated, "B, dah, b, dah, that's all, folks." He said it just like Porky Pig in the cartoons. I couldn't help it. I started to laugh. Then it seemed that everyone laughed. Even Dad cracked a smile.

Dad finished collecting his money while I took the broom off Blacky and began sweeping the glass from the broken side mirrors off the road.

That's when I heard a growling noise. I pulled out my flashlight from the pocket in my shorts and shined the light down to the creek. There were two big dogs on the creek bank pulling on something. When the light hit them, they took off, leaving something white beside a rock. It looked like a hand. I moved the light farther down the creek, and there was a car nose first in the water—a big blue car.

"Dad, I think you better come here," I said in my loudest adult voice.

"What? I'm busy." Dad answered as he took the eight dollars from the colored man and put the money in the bib pocket of his coveralls.

"I see a hand! And there's a blue car in this creek. I think it's Mister Albert Winston Brown's car. But Dad, his hand, it's all by itself," I said even louder.

That brought everyone over to the bank, shining flashlights up and down the creek. Sure enough, it was plain to see. A 1951 Cadillac Fleetwood 75 limousine, dark blue, was nose-first in the stream. There was only one like it in the county. It belonged to the Commonwealth's Attorney, Mr. Albert Winston Brown.

"Billy, what hand?" Trooper Quinn asked me.

"That one, sir, right down there." And I pointed my flashlight down to the creek bank. There was something white that looked like a hand. Also, there was a reflection on the little finger—something sparkled.

That's when Dad told me, "Billy, you go get in Blacky, right now!"

I knew not to argue. I watched as all kinds of things began to happen. *Was my magic mirror at it again?*

CHAPTER 17

BILLY & THE HAND
Thursday, July 21, 1955

By the time Mr. Cubley arrived on the scene, the Koehler Funeral Home hearse-ambulance, Blacky, several police cars, and a fire engine had the road blocked. Some drivers were impatiently waiting to get past the wreck, but others had parked and gotten out of their cars to gawk. The red lights from the hearse, fire truck, and police cars cast a ruby red pulsating glow over the area. Our big tow truck added yellow contrasts to the light show.

Doc Hill was brought to the scene by a Highland Police Officer. He met Mr. Cubley, and they pushed aside the crowd and a line of police officers to view the wrecked Fleetwood Cadillac.

I noticed Dad was busy at the back of Blacky checking his winch line, so I slipped out of the truck's cab and eased up near the group to listen. A bystander tapped my shoulder, leaned down, and asked.

"Hey, kid, who's the old geezer with the leather bag?"

"That's our town doctor, Dr. Alburtis Jonathan Hill, but everyone just calls him Doc Hill."

Doc Hill wasted no time getting down to business. "You got something for me this time, Mr. Cubley?"

I noticed Mr. Cubley winced a little. "I don't know. I just got here myself."

The sheriff heard them, turned away from the bank, and joined the two men. This time the sheriff spoke right up.

"Doc, we've found Mr. Albert Winston Brown. At least, we're fairly certain it's him," said Sheriff Lawrence, who started strong but was giving himself a little room for error if it wasn't our local prosecutor in that car.

"Not more cow bones?" asked Dr. Hill.

I couldn't tell if he was joking.

152

Trooper Quinn answered as he walked up to the other three men, "Not unless cows have started wearing pinky rings and wedding bands."

He was holding something wrapped in a piece of cloth. When he unwrapped it, I saw a swollen hand with a wedding band on the ring finger and a diamond pinky ring on the little finger. I gagged and swallowed hard to keep my supper down when I smelled the odor. I was feeling dizzy, and that's when the sheriff told them about me. I could have died!

"Doc, the Gunn boy found the car when he saw some dogs with this hand. He yelled for us, and we got the hand from the creek bank right off. The rest of the body is still in the car. What's left, that is," Sheriff Lawrence informed the medical examiner.

"Well, I'm sure as hell not climbing down there. You boys bring him on up, but I want him in one piece. Then, I'll do a look-see," Dr. Hill told Trooper Quinn and the sheriff.

Trooper Quinn turned to speak to Sam Koehler, Bill Koehler's son. I knew the father and son conducted most of the funerals in Green Mountain County. Mr. Sam Koehler was on this call and brought a canvas stretcher and a body bag. His hired man, Richard Smith, already had both items on the road's edge.

I watched from the shadows as the fire department rigged four harnesses and placed them on three firemen and Mr. Smith. To the harnesses, they attached ropes to lower the four "body recovery guys" down the embankment to the car. That's what I heard the police call them, "the body recovery guys."

Richard Smith would carry down the body bag. A fireman picked up the stretcher but almost lost it when he tripped on a rock.

A man wearing a straw hat with a round brim elbowed me and said, "I'm sure glad the colored boy's gonna get that body. Ain't no way that I'd do it!"

One of the town officers answered him with, "Richard's used to it. Won't bother him none."

I thought straw hat's comments were rude, but I didn't say a word. To make things worse, the guy wearing the straw hat was a fatty and stepped in front of me, blocking my view.

I figured Mr. Smith, and the three other firemen would have to slide the rotten body into the body bag in one piece—not an easy task nor pleasant. Doc Hill began correcting the group before they even started down the bank.

"You boys take it easy moving that body. I want this done right."

The four men were slowly lowered without incident. But after five minutes of working at the vehicle, a deputy looking over the bank announced, "Oh, Lord Jesus, two firemen just threw up. What a goldarn mess."

I got curious, leaned around the rude guy, and peeked over the bank. I was in the shadows, so no one saw me. I made sure Dad didn't. He was at the other end of the crowd. I tried, but I couldn't see the body, only the body bag with the body already inside. Three straps held the body bag on the stretcher. Everyone at the top of the bank, except Doc Hill and me, grabbed onto the four ropes. They hauled the four men and the body bag tied to the stretcher up the bank and onto the road.

Two spotlights from the firetruck were turned on to give plenty of light. That's when Dr. Hill unzipped the body bag to look. He reached in with both hands, and I think he did something with the head, looked quickly, put the head back down, and zipped the bag closed. I wanted to see better, but the straw-hat man kept moving to get a better view, and I missed seeing the body.

"Sheriff, Mr. Albert Winston Brown has been murdered. It looks like two or three shots to the back of the head. I'm sending the body to Richmond. I'll know more when I get the autopsy results."

The sheriff said something to Dr. Hill, but I couldn't hear him with everybody starting to talk. Another murder, this was terrible, and I just had to tell Kent all about it and fast.

"Trooper Quinn...where did he go? Trooper Quinn! Everybody, shut the hell up!" yelled Dr. Hill.

It got instantly quiet. The doctor pointed to the trooper and began giving him orders. "Trooper Quinn, let's get the Fleetwood towed to Appomattox. I want a complete forensic examination and get every speck of evidence to the laboratory."

Next, the doctor pointed to two deputies and a fireman when one of them laughed at a joke or something. Doc Hill shouted at them with a frown.

"Okay, I see you boys got time on your hands. You three get down that bank and find me the rest of Brown's arm. Those damn dogs took it off at the elbow. We have the hand, but I want the forearm."

Chief Danbury of the Highland Volunteer Fire Department got his two men and the deputy back down the bank on three of the ropes. They began hunting for the missing arm. Doc Hill yelled down and asked them if the driver's window was up or down. They confirmed it was down, as did Richard Smith, who said it was down when the team went down to retrieve the body.

"Well, that explains how the dogs got the arm," Doc Hill commented to no one in particular.

One more bone was found, a radius bone, but the other bone, the ulna bone, remained lost, announced Doc Hill, naming the bones. Finally, after a ten-minute search, the three searchers gave up after a copperhead, hiding under a bush, almost bit a deputy.

I jumped when someone walked up behind me and touched me on the shoulder.

"Hey, Billy, thanks for finding Brown's car. We'll have to swear you in as a trooper," said Trooper Quinn with a grin.

That's when I almost got whacked by my dad for getting out of the truck. He fussed at me some but not as much as I had expected. I think the trooper, standing there, saved me.

Trooper Quinn asked Dad if his tow truck could pull the limousine up the bank, or would he need the Chevrolet tow truck to help?

"Mike, if Blacky can't handle it, ten wreckers won't get her up that bank."

Dad put the cable over his shoulder and walked straight down that bank. He let me work the controls to keep a little tension on it, and he acted like going down that bank was easy. Me? I would have fallen for sure. All the other men had to be lowered on ropes, but not my father.

When Dad hitched up the Cadillac, I took up the slack on the big towing winch. I noticed some of the men were watching me. I felt proud my dad trusted me with such an important job.

After Dad hitched the Caddy to the winch line, I took out all the slack and made sure it was taut. Dad grabbed a rope that some firemen tossed down to him. He took a turn around his waist, tied it off, and they pulled him up the bank.

Our big wrecker was now hooked to the back of the Fleetwood. Dad took over the controls and began winching the vehicle up the bank backward.

Mr. Cubley came over and talked to me about pulling cars up steep banks. I told him how my dad was using the path the Fleetwood had followed going into the creek. The Fleetwood had already cleared the small trees and bushes out of the way, going down, so pulling it up was easy.

"Billy, I'm impressed. You're going to be one smart wrecker operator if that's what you want to do when you grow up," Mr. Cubley said, smiling.

Once the wreck was winched half over the bank's edge, Dad drove the wrecker forward, pulling the car into the road. Since Blacky and the Caddy were blocking both lanes, Dad drove down the road, so they lined up in one lane. The deputies got traffic moving because they could now open one lane.

Dad checked his rigging to be sure it was good and tight. After putting a blinking light on the dash of the Cadillac to warn any cars that might follow us, he went back to talk to Trooper Quinn. I eased up to listen.

Trooper Quinn told Dad he would follow him over to headquarters. I asked the trooper if I could ride with him. I thought Dad would say no at first, but he said I could go with the trooper if I behaved. How was I going to misbehave, sitting next to a Virginia State Trooper?

I hopped in the front seat with Trooper Quinn. We followed Dad, who was towing the Fleetwood backward. I saw Dad's little yellow warning light flashing on the dash. Trooper Quinn made my night. He told me to switch on the red light on the roof of his patrol car. I could see the reflection bouncing off the Cadillac and Blacky. Then things got even better. Once or twice, on deserted sections of the road, Trooper Quinn let me blow the siren. Dad slowed down the first time I did it, but Trooper Quinn stuck his arm out the window to Dad on. He figured out what was happening and waved back at me. I was having a fantastic time.

Superman was going to be so jealous. First, me seeing another dead body, well, only a hand, but I was the one to find it. Then, getting to ride in the trooper's car, running the lights and siren would blow Kent's mind.

When we got to state police headquarters in Appomattox, Dad backed the Cadillac into the state police impoundment lot. Trooper Quinn took me inside the new offices. I got a tour while we waited for Sergeant Oliver and Trooper Giles. Dad finished unhooking Blacky and came into the building to take me home. Tonight, he was nice and waited for me to get the whole tour.

I wished I could have stayed to watch the three troopers process the car, but it was getting late. I had seen so much that I was okay with going home.

Dad drove halfway back to the garage without saying anything. Then he surprised me.

"Billy, are you okay?" Dad asked me.

"Yes, sir. My elbow hardly hurts at all."

"Your elbow? No, I didn't mean that. What's wrong with your elbow?" he asked.

"I bumped it, but it's fine. It'll be healed by tomorrow," I said, but I could feel it throbbing. I hoped the swelling would be down in a few days. I just didn't want Dad to worry. I didn't think he knew he'd hurt me, and I would leave it that way.

"Son, seeing those dogs with that hand, it's not good for you to see such things. That's why I told you not to get out of the truck. When you don't mind me, that's when you see things that you shouldn't. Now, are you okay?" Dad asked me, and I noticed his speed had slowed.

"I'm fine, Dad. Heck, I'm getting used to seeing dead bodies. I have dreams about the sniper, but not scary ones. He never hurt Kent or me. Those people he killed, sure I feel bad about them, but I ain't scared. The only blood I ever saw was the sniper's. The deputy and Mr. Beamis were all covered up."

After I said it, I knew I had used the word "ain't," but Dad didn't mention it.

"Son, if any of this stuff starts to bother you, will you tell me?"

"Yes, sir. But it won't. Kent and I have seen a bunch of dead people watching Roy and the other cowboys. We're tough," I said, feeling all big.

"Well, you come talk to me if it does. It might take a while, so remember what I'm telling you." Dad got quiet and sped back up. He had slowed to about twenty while we were talking.

When we got home, all the lights were on downstairs. Mom and Grandma were up, wearing bathrobes, and both came to the back door when we pulled in. We walked into the kitchen right at midnight. This was way past my bedtime. Grandma was frowning and tapping her right toe with her arms crossed.

"John Gunn, where have you been with my grandson? Keeping him out all hours of the night and working him like a coal miner's mule!"

Mom was also mad at Dad for keeping me out late, but after Grandma got ahead of her fussing at Dad, her anger switched from Dad to Grandma. It was easy to figure out adults on some things.

"Mother, please hush! John, where have you been?"

"Laura Jane, you know that I got called out on a simple tow, but things went in a whole different direction. The state police gave me a second job. I had to do it. I had no choice. Billy here was my man and a big help, but if I'd known we would be out this late, I wouldn't have taken him." Dad explained, tried to explain, and he was calm about it.

I didn't understand him being so calm unless—that was it—he wasn't going to tell them about me finding the body—not tonight—maybe not for days. But when Mom did find out, boy, would she be mad. But it wasn't Dad's fault. It was my fault for finding that hand.

Looking back on that summer when I was twelve, I just kept stepping into messes. I wasn't even trying. They just happened for no reason.

Grandma bought his explanation but didn't like it. "Well, you should be more careful with Billy. I've always stayed out of your family affairs, and I'm steering clear of this one tonight. But you should not have taken the boy. I'm going to bed." And then, Grandma went to her room.

"Billy, you go on to bed. We'll see if you feel like going to work tomorrow, or it might be better if you sleep late. I'll call Kent's mom and Mr. Cubley in the morning and let them know what's happened. Goodnight," Mom said.

I went upstairs and got ready for bed. I also moved the clothes off the vent in the bedroom closet to hear Mom and Dad talking. This might be the perfect night to listen, and I was right.

"John, what really made you so late?" Mom asked.

She didn't waste any time. She could read Dad's moods better than anyone, and she knew he wasn't telling her something.

"Laura Jane, I wouldn't have taken Billy had I known how this was going to turn out. I'm so sorry. I feel awful about what we ran into," Dad was softly talking. I was afraid that this might lead to an even bigger fight. Bigger than the one they had already had.

"John, what happened?" Mom asked.

He told her about the first tow job and then what happened. I thought Mom was going to start screaming, but she didn't. She just said, "Oh, John, not again. He didn't see another body, did he?"

"Laura Jane, no. He saw two dogs with a hand. Billy saw the hand, that's all. And he only saw it from a distance. Billy found Albert Winston Brown's Cadillac over the embankment. I put him in the truck just as soon as I knew what we had. I swear, he never saw the body—not up close."

"John, thank the Lord my mother didn't hear this. She would have gone off the deep end for sure. Can we keep it from her?" Mom asked.

"I doubt it. Half the fire department knows. The firemen were all talking about Billy, finding the hand, the Caddy, and solving the case of the missing county prosecutor."

"I guess it's out. No way to keep it from Mother."

"It'll be all over town by breakfast. It might even make the papers. I talked to Billy coming home from the state police area office. That's why we were so late. Billy rode over with Trooper Quinn, and Quinn let him run his red lights and blow the siren. I think that made a bigger impression on Billy than the body. I hope so. He said he would talk to me if it ever bothered him."

Mom groaned, "Why Billy? My poor little Billy."

"Our boy's too smart. That kid noticed those two dogs when no one else paid any attention. I think, hope, he can handle all this." Dad finished, and I heard the bed squeak several times. They both had made it into bed.

"We sure seem to be living in Sodom and Gomorrah," Mom said, and I knew that story from the Bible. I hoped God didn't burn down the place. Actually, after the sniper burned down the plant, a big part of the place had already burned down.

Dad added, "I agree this town's a sorry mess. Oh, Little John showed up, spouting off again. I almost punched him in the face."

"What did he want now?" Mom asked.

"Oh, he was just being Little John. Nothing to worry about. Sheriff Lawrence told him I was at Cubley's Coze all evening. I'm clear. It should die down, given a little more time."

Dad was only telling Mom part of what happened. I heard it all, and I didn't think Dad was in the clear. I would have to be sure nobody other than Kent ever found out about Dad's army buddies. I had to make sure of that.

Things got quiet for a while, and I decided to go to sleep. I heard a giggle from downstairs, and the bed squeaked. Mom said, "John, stop that. I'm sleepy."

I looked over at Scotty. He had tossed all the covers off his bed, and he had one arm and one leg hanging off the bed. I got up, scooted him back into the middle of his bed, and put the covers back over him. He made a snorting sound but went back to sleep. I crawled into bed and drifted off, thinking about how much fun it would be to drive around, blowing a siren and running red lights up and down the highway.

CHAPTER 18

BILLY, THE LOCAL HERO
Friday, July 22, 1955

Scotty was sitting in the middle of his bed, looking at his left big toe. He bent over, which he could do, and licked the end of it.

"Scotty, what are you doing?" I cried out when I realized what he was doing.

"Toe hurts. Making it better," Scotty informed me, leaning in closer for another lick.

"Scotty, licking your toe will get it infected. It sure won't make it better," I scoffed, getting out of bed.

"Will too. Mom says so." Scotty had changed his focus from his toe to picking his nose. This kid was a mess!

"Mom would never tell you that licking a sore makes it better." I tried to figure out what he could be talking about.

"Brad's puppy, Lucky, had a hurt foot and was licking it. Momma told me that's how dogs make it all better. So there."

"Scotty, you're hopeless. Dogs might do that, but people don't. What's wrong with your foot?" I asked and bent over it to look.

"I got a boo-boo. See."

He picked up his foot with both hands and tried to turn it over to show me. That worked about as well as him licking it.

"Here, put it down on the covers. Yeah, you scraped it on something. Let me put some medicine on it and a bandage."

"No-No-Oooh. *Medercine* hurts. Don't want no *medercine*. Licking it makes it feel better," Scotty said, getting louder and louder.

"Billy, what's wrong with your brother?" Mom called from the foot of the stairs.

"He's got a scrape on his big toe, but he won't let me put any medicine on it," I called back.

"Well, bring him down here," Mom said.

Scotty was still fussing about not wanting any medicine. It was no use trying to correct what he was calling it. The dope wouldn't change.

He was in for it. I knew when the iodine hit his sore that he was going to go into a screaming fit. He would learn, as he got older, to keep quiet about his sores. That was how kids avoided medicine. Mom was going to use either iodine or Mercurochrome; both were awful.

Once, when I had a bike wreck and Mom wasn't home, Dad put turpentine on me. He called it turps, but I called it liquid fire. I never want to see that stuff again, not near a sore, anyway.

Scotty followed me to the kitchen, and Mom gave us our breakfasts. I went upstairs to my room after breakfast because I knew what was coming. It was bad enough listening to yelling and screaming from upstairs in my bedroom. I was not about to go back downstairs until the yelling was over. My little brother didn't disappoint, and I was sure the neighbors would probably call the police to report a child being murdered. It all ended with the little brat getting a Dreamsicle when it should have been a swat on his butt.

Kent arrived on his bike for our ride to the hotel and missed the screaming. He told me that his mom was still not comfortable with either of us riding our bikes alone. She followed him, but he was so embarrassed that he waved for her to go on before either of them turned into the garage lot. She spoiled it by blowing her horn as she drove past.

I told Kent all about finding Mr. Albert Winston Brown in his car. Like me, he was more interested in me riding with Trooper Quinn and getting to blow the siren. He made me promise that the very next time I found a body, I had to find a telephone and call him.

We rode our bikes to the hotel with Mom playing tail gunner. We were lucky; none of our friends saw her.

Entering the hotel kitchen, Boo greeted us with a poke in our ribs, which made us feel better. Mrs. Johnson gave us plates of pancakes with bacon. We were enjoying the food when Mr. Cubley came out and sat down beside us with his plate of pancakes. Polecat rode up on his bike, and soon the four of us were eating and talking.

Then, Polecat started the ribbing with, "Master Clark, it would seem that you are in the company of a celebrity. A luminary of spectacular achievement. A personage worthy of being awarded the golden key to this metropolis." Polecat ended with a flourish of his right hand. The fork that he was holding made it look like he was conducting an orchestra with a baton.

"Mr. Smith, who would that be? Did Mr. Cubley save someone else?" Kent countered.

"Master Clark, 'tis not Mr. Cubley of whom I speak. It is your compatriot, Master William Boyer Gunn, sleuth extraordinaire. He solved the case of the missing public official. By doing so, he has achieved notoriety in our local periodical." Polecat was "waxing eloquent," his phrase, not mine, as he reached down into his bag of papers. He pulled one out and tossed it with accuracy at Kent's feet.

The newspaper landed with the front page up, and I could read the bold headline.

"Local Boy Solves Disappearance."

The smaller caption by my picture said, "William Boyer Gunn finds the body of local Commonwealth's Attorney. Police suspect foul play."

I read the article over Kent's shoulder. It gave me all the credit for locating Mr. Brown and his car. Then, I guess to fill up space, it repeated the sniper story about Kent and me being kidnapped and rescued.

I knew immediately that my life was over. I was going to be the target of every kid in my class. Heck, every kid in the county, maybe the state, would be gunning for me. I figured that I would have to move to Alaska and hide out in the Yukon. One of my favorite radio shows was *The Challenge of the Yukon* with Sergeant Preston of the Royal Canadian Mounted Police. People on the run often fled to the Yukon. The show came to us on a Chicago station. So, Chicago could be my second place to hide out. I could hop a freight to Chicago, pal around with gangsters, and haul whiskey for the mob.

I knew all this but couldn't think of a good way to catch the train out of town since the nearest train depot was in Waynesboro. That's when Superman interrupted my planning.

"BB, you know what this means?" Kent said.

"Yeah, I need to hide out for six months, maybe a year," I said with a sad look.

Kent pointed a finger at me like firing a pistol. "Lou, Carl, and Dickie will be after you for sure. Barry and Skip better hurry up and get here."

Mr. Cubley was listening to us and spoke. "Boys, I talked with the sheriff. I told him he needs to ask for a special prosecutor to handle your problem with those bullies. I think I might just give him a follow-up call and hurry him along."

"What? Kent asked. "Why can't you handle it? I would feel a lot better if you were helping Billy and me," Kent requested, and I was surprised he spoke up.

"Wish I could. You boys work for me, so that requires me to step aside. A special prosecutor from another county will not be biased for or against anyone. It must be that way to be fair. I hope you understand?" Mr. Cubley explained.

I began to study on what he had said.

What he suggested would be fair to everyone. But fair was never how things worked before. Those bullies had Big John and now Chief McCulloch on their side. I knew they wouldn't step aside or be fair.

My thoughts were interrupted this time by Polecat speaking.

"...the recipient of several rumors that our newly appointed chief of police went to see his daddy. Their new stratagem may result in another attempt to embroil the governor's office into local matters. Big John will petition the governor to intervene and have our illustrious chief judicial officer remove you from your high office, Mr. Cubley."

That man could pick up more information from hanging around our local police department in five minutes than all the top reporters in Richmond in five months. At least, that's what I had heard Mr. Tolliver say to Mr. Cubley one morning when the sniper was causing all the trouble.

Mr. Cubley wiped his napkin over his mouth and said, "So that's what Chief McCulloch meant last night at the wreck. Several deputies and a couple of firemen told me what Chief McCulloch said to John Gunn. I figured he was just spouting off. Heck, getting fired wouldn't hurt my feelings all that much. In fact, it would suit me fine to be let off the hook."

Mr. Cubley grinned and looked irritated at the same time. Anyway, it was a funny look that he had. He gathered up the newspapers and his dirty dishes, ready to depart.

"Boys," he said. "Come by the office on your way over to the wash area. I think it's time I gave Sheriff Lawrence a call, and I want you to know what's up."

After Mr. Cubley left, I gave Kent a look towards the kitchen. He caught on right away. We finished our breakfasts, left the dishes on the sink to be washed, and went straight into the lobby. We told Mr. Tolliver that Mr. Cubley wanted to talk to us.

"Boys, he's on the phone, but he should be finished in a minute. Will you watch the desk while I go get a cup of tea?" Mr. Tolliver asked us.

"Sure we will," I said.

"We know how you check in guests, and I can run the switchboard," Kent spoke up with confidence. I was not so sure that he could handle all those phone lines.

When Mr. Tolliver left for the kitchen, I went behind the front desk and cracked open the outer door of the passthrough and heard Mr. Cubley on the phone.

"Sheriff, if that's what you heard, nothing would make me happier. I'm not sure who they would get to replace me, but if that's what the judge wants, I'm good with it."

There was a pause, and then, "So, you heard it directly from Little John. Well, I'll give the judge a call. Thanks for telling me."

Mr. Cubley finished and hung up the phone, and then we could hear him dialing a second number.

"Good morning, Mrs. Carlisle. This is Matt. It's nice for me too. Is the judge in and not busy?"

Mr. Cubley, I knew, was sweet on Mrs. Carlisle, but I guess this was official court business. He was calling her Mrs. Carlisle and not Linda. I knew he called her Linda when she came to dine at the hotel. If I was older...well, she's a doll!

"Judge Harland, Matt Cubley here.... Yes, sir, and a good morning to you.... I got the call last night. I'm sad it turned out that way. I was hoping for a better result.... Yes, Your Honor. I even went out there last night. Doc Hill.... It was. He said murder.... The same.... That little guy sure seems to find himself in the wrong places at the worst times.... Yes, I've seen the paper. Billy's talking about leaving town until things blow over."

Mr. Cubley paused, and then he laughed at something the judge said to him.

"Well, I hope his friends aren't too rough on him. The history of those three and Billy has been something.... That's part of what I need to talk to you about. Sheriff Lawrence says I may be getting my walking papers this morning. That the governor is all fired up over local events."

Mr. Cubley paused as he listened to the judge, and that's when Mr. Tolliver came back with his cup of tea. He shooed us from behind the front desk, closed the passthrough door, and frowned. Next, he pointed to chairs on the other side of the lobby where we wouldn't be able to listen.

We waited for five minutes, and then Mr. Cubley opened the door to his office. He looked to the side, saw us, and invited us in. Once we all were seated, he began.

"Well, it looks like I'm stuck being the Commonwealth's Attorney for the near future. When the governor called Judge Harland, apparently Big John forgot to tell him that the vacancy was filled. The governor asked that Ben Southwall serve as the temporary Commonwealth's Attorney. Mr. Southwall is a member of the governor's former law firm, which does all the major legal work for Big John."

Mr. Cubley told Mr. Tolliver to come on inside the office that he needed him to hear this as well. He had noticed the passthrough was closed.

"I'm afraid Judge Harland wasn't very accommodating to our governor. He informed him he had already made the appointment, and it was me. The judge reminded the governor that the last time the governor interfered in Green Mountain County business on the Beamis case, it got him bad press in every newspaper in the state. He told him that firing me after all the news about me rescuing two little boys from a serial killer would expose the court to criticism.

166

The governor decided to withdraw his request. I guess I'm stuck," Mr. Cubley said with a chuckle.

Mr. Tolliver exclaimed, "It's about time somebody did something right!"

Mr. Cubley grinned and continued, "So boys, I'm going to call the sheriff and urge him to request a special prosecutor. Those boys need to be held accountable. Now, unless you insist on staying to listen in on my next phone call like you did on my last one, how about getting started on Mr. C. W. Tyler's Plymouth."

Kent and I jumped for the door so quickly that we bumped into each other. We sort of knew that he wasn't mad, but we also knew that we had been caught and needed to get out of there…fast!

Later in the morning, Mr. Cubley let us know that a special prosecutor from the Amherst County Commonwealth's Attorney Office would be appointed. Our boss asked us, again, if we knew who returned our bikes. We both told him no; they just turned up.

"Well, perhaps it's best you don't know," he announced.

Mr. Cubley went back into the hotel. Kent and I looked at each other, but neither of us said anything. Keeping secrets was becoming harder than I thought it would be. It was necessary, but I wished it wasn't, and I felt guilty about it.

Kent and I finished work around four o'clock. I remembered to call Mom to tell her we were leaving. This time it was Mr. Cubley who followed us into town. He turned left onto Court Street, leaving Kent and me to continue to the garage.

Tim Hodges, a classmate of ours, was walking his dog, Smooch, along the sidewalk on Green Mountain Avenue. He spotted us and waved us over.

"Superman, BB, how's it going?" he asked as we pulled up and stopped astraddle our bikes.

"Doing great," said Kent.

"Just fine," I replied.

"BB, I guess you saw the paper. They made you out to be a real hero, finding a dead body and solving the Brown mystery. I guess that makes you important," Tim said with a grin. I knew what was coming.

"No, it just happened. Could have happened to anybody," I tried to explain. I hoped this was the end of it.

"Finding a body could happen to anybody. That's a good one. Body, get it?" laughed Tim.

"Tim, come on. It could have been you, Kent, or anyone."

I would never say the word, anybody, nope, never again.

"Aw, BB. I'm just funning you. Don't get your drawers in a bunch." Now I realized that Tim wasn't going to be a big butthead about it.

"You know all the kids are going to give you a rough time. Heck, first you get whacked with a ball bat at the Fourth of July celebration, then kidnapped by a sniper who killed important people at the plant, and now, you find a dead body. You must admit that all that happening to one kid is strange." Just then, the sun went behind a cloud. "See! Here comes your black cloud."

Tim was getting to me, but he wasn't being that mean about it.

"Well, Kent helped," I stated, trying to share the blame.

"Hey, don't get me involved. All I did was get kidnapped. The other stuff was all your doing."

My buddy Kent wasn't backing me up. No, he was just backing up. Some friend he was! I needed to change the subject.

"What's wrong with Smooch?" I inquired.

"He has the mange. The vet shaved all his hair off, and he's not liking it. I think the ointment burns a little, so he licked it, and it made him sick. He threw up on Mom's new rug. That's why I'm walking him. Mom's mad, Smooch is miserable, and I got to stay out of the house until things cool off—poor dog."

I knew about the mange. "Tim, my dad gave one of his customers burnt motor oil to put on his dog for mange. That dog was smeared with dirty thirty-weight for several weeks. He looked awful and smelled to high heaven, even worse than Smooch," I reported.

"Speaking of looking awful. What did you two do to Lou McCulloch?" Tim asked Kent and me.

"I didn't do nothing to him. You, Kent?" I said, giving Kent "the look."

"No, we didn't do nothing to him." Kent responded, giving me "the look" back.

"I was over to the park with some kids. Lou came up to Karla Carson to ask her who she had for a teacher this fall. Carl and Dickie rode up on their bikes and started giving Lou junk about being yellow. He got mad, and I thought they were gonna fight. Karla told them to stop, and that's when Carl called Lou a chicken. Dickie said something about Lou better hide or big bad BB Gunn would come and blow his house down. Lou told him to shut up, turned tail, and walked off toward home."

"Don't look at me. I have no idea what's going on," I said and tried to make it sound like the truth.

Tim looked puzzled. "I thought Carl and Dickie were part of Lou's gang. Something must have happened. I figured it had something to do with you," Tim said.

"I have no idea what you're talking about. The last time I saw Lou was when I got kicked in the head the day our bikes were stolen." I wished I had left the bike part off.

"I see you got them back. How'd that happen?" Tim asked.

"We don't know. They just turned up," Kent jumped in, trying to help me out.

"You guys don't know much, do you?"

"Kent replied, "I guess not."

"Well, I'm glad you got them back. Mum's the word. Hope you didn't hurt Lou too bad, but he deserved whatever you two dished out to him." Tim laughed and walked off with Smooch. That dog smelled worse than Polecat on a rainy day.

I started to say something else to Tim, but Kent put his hand on my arm. We both knew it was useless. He wasn't buying what we were selling.

Kent and I rode on to the garage in silence. Now, I was really worried for my dad. What if people began putting two and two together?

CHAPTER 19

BILLY AND LOU
Saturday, July 23, 1955

S aturday was a beautiful day. The clouds were big and made neat shapes as Kent and I raced each other down Green Mountain Avenue to the hotel. But best of all, the Top Hat Movie Theater had a cowboy double feature this afternoon with Randolph Scott. We were in a hurry to finish our work in time for the first show.

We flew across the bridge and cut left into the entrance to Cubley's Coze. A third of the way up the hill, we jumped off to push. Then, topping the rise in a fast walk, we jumped back on our bikes and rode them behind the hotel. I beat Kent by twenty feet.

Stashing our bikes behind the maintenance shed, we wasted no time collecting our breakfasts. Teresa Long greeted us because both Mrs. Hathaway and Boo had the day off. I could hardly wait for Mrs. Hathaway to pick up Skip and Barry. We had important business to discuss.

Mr. Cubley joined us on the loading dock, and Polecat arrived five minutes later. The chair of honor was always downwind of the rest of us.

Mr. Cubley began the morning questions to Polecat. "Mr. Smith, I hope your morning is going well?"

We were dining on scrambled eggs and bacon with a double order of raisin toast. As far as I was concerned, the day couldn't get any better.

"Well, very well. Thank you for asking," mumbled Polecat with his mouth full of food.

"Are you aware of the failed effort to have me removed from office almost before the ink on my appointment certificate was dry?" asked Mr. Cubley to get to the heart of the information session.

"Big John McCulloch better beware of silent dogs, still water, and honest judges," he responded. Then he took two large spoonfuls of scrambled eggs, dropped them on a slice of raisin toast,

170

and capped it with a second slice to make a sandwich. He picked it up, held it in his left hand, took a big bite, and continued.

"I'm fully aware of the total failure of the conspiratorial efforts of Big John and the governor regarding your impeachment. Our local judiciary obliterated the governor's plan, and Judge Harland, by his brief but powerful argument, seems to have permanently quashed the threat. The governor and his minions have retreated into the dark recesses of the Governor's Mansion." Polecat gave his report while eating his unusual sandwich.

"How did that set with the Highland Police Department?" Mr. Cubley asked Polecat.

"My good Sir, I cannot fathom how you were not cognizant of the recent explosions and shock waves emanating from the bowels of the Highland Police Department. A political mushroom cloud still hangs over that station house, and the extent of the fallout is yet to be determined. However, other police authorities rejoice. The high sheriff and most of his deputies are elated that you retain the reins of the prosecutorial wagon." Polecat spoke with the voice of authority, and upon most subjects, he was infallible. Another one of his big words.

"Any gossip about who might have killed my predecessor?" Mr. Cubley asked Polecat.

"Sir, the tittle-tattle grapevine has withered and died. There is not a bud of information regarding that homicide. One might conclude the man shot himself three times in the occipital region of his cranium, after which he swerved his conveyance into the creek." Polecat rose and went into the kitchen with his dirty dishes, so sure of his report that he failed to wait for comments from his audience.

My mouth dropped open.

A shocked Kent asked, "Mr. Cubley, did he just say that Mr. Albert Winston Brown shot himself in the head three times and then swerved into the creek?"

I knew the answer to that question. "Superman, he said it, but he's joking. He is joking, isn't he, Mr. Cubley?" I questioned my boss.

"Yes, Billy. No one can shoot themselves in the back of the head twice, let alone three times. That's impossible. Mr. Smith is pulling our legs, which I think he enjoys doing from time to time."

"Yeah, that's what I thought," said Kent, trying to make a recovery.

Polecat came out of the kitchen, left his papers, and rode off to the Green Mountain Resort. That resort barely tolerated him and never gave him so much as a crumb or crust of bread from their kitchen. Polecat, eating a meal there, would have made front-page news!

Kent and I gathered our buckets, rags, and supplies and carried them to the wash area. Our first car was a 1952 Ford Crestline, V8, Victoria, hardtop. It was a beauty. Dad once told me this model Ford was fast. I told Kent all the details that I knew, and we spent a little extra time polishing it.

Halfway through working on this car, Trooper Giles stopped in to talk to Mr. Cubley. The window to Mr. Cubley's office was open, and when he failed to close it, Kent and I had an invitation to listen.

"Matt, it sounds like you and the governor locked horns," Trooper Giles said upon entering Mr. Cubley's office.

"Bobby, I never even talked to the governor. Judge Harland blocked that maneuver before it got any momentum."

"Well, all the troopers in the division and our sergeant are happy."

"Thanks. Is that why you're here? To boost my spirits?"

"No. This is an official visit. I need a search warrant, and the sergeant wants you, not me, to write it. Getting it through the county court will be tough and cause ripples back to the governor," said Trooper Giles, who normally would sweet-talk people into what he wanted. This time was different.

"Bobby, sure to heavens, you're not going to search Big John's house!" replied Mr. Cubley.

"No, but almost as bad. We need to search Mr. Brown's home office. We asked his wife, but Big John had already called and told her not to let anyone in until his new attorney, Mr. Ben Southwall, had removed all the business files."

I whispered to Superman. "Kent, Big John has a new attorney already? At least this guy doesn't use all three of his names."

Kent whispered back, "Big John sure isn't wasting any time finding replacements for his murdered employees ."

Mr. Cubley and Trooper Giles worked on the search warrant for almost an hour. They had to make some phone calls for information, and Kent and I quit listening; it was too dull. We got busy on our Ford because there was a double feature to make.

Trooper Giles left with whatever Mr. Cubley had typed for him. I never knew a man who could type, but Mr. Cubley typed up that search warrant just as slick as frog snot on a log.

Next, Mr. Tolliver told Mr. Cubley that the Hartford group would arrive on Sunday for their two-week stay at the hunting lodge. I remembered Dr. Hartford was the biology professor from the University of Virginia who had rented the hunting lodge for two whole weeks to do research on forest animals. He was bringing his family and two graduate students. Mr. Tolliver assured Mr. Cubley that the lodge was almost ready. Connell Washington would be taking up the final load of groceries later today because Richard Baker was picking up Barry and Skip in Lynchburg.

Kent and I did our last car. We could hear thunder in the distance, so I called Mom. She told me to tell Kent to come home with me, eat lunch, and Mom would drive us to the movies because a bad storm was coming. Mrs. Clark had to pick up some alterations in Waynesboro and would pick us up after the film on her way home from the city.

We hopped on our bikes and took off for the garage. Mom met us at the kitchen door and relieved us of the college portion of our earnings. She put Kent's part of his college money in an envelope to give to his mom.

When my mom drove us to the movies, we couldn't stop at the five and dime for our peashooters. We also missed out on our Charm suckers that could last for an entire film and two cartoons. Times were hard on us kids because of all the recent trouble, which meant not many of our friends would be at the movies.

Superman and I were lucky and had money from our jobs at the hotel, despite our moms keeping half for college. We felt sad the other kids were not so fortunate. Their parents weren't sure how soon they would be back on the payroll and were "playing it safe." "Playing it safe" was another way of saying no money for movies.

We did see Tim Hodges and asked him how Smooch was doing. "Better, " he said.

While getting our tickets, popcorn, and drinks, Lou, Carl, and Dickie arrived. Tim whispered, "Watch out, BB, I think a storm's brewing."

Kent and I, to be safe, entered the theater and sat halfway back in the middle of a row. The three bullies went down front, clearing the front row of smaller kids. They didn't take just three seats, not on your life—no—they cleaned out the whole row. The youngsters moved, but not fast enough. One third grader came by us, sniffling and holding his ear.

The first movie was *A Lawless Street,* which meant the second feature was *Rage at Dawn.* Everything was quiet throughout the first movie. Mr. Stone, the owner, didn't have to come into the theater once because cowboy movies have lots of shooting, fast horses, and all kinds of action.

I had seen the second cartoon, so I went to the bathroom. I was finishing when in walked Lou, Carl, and Dickie.

Carl began with an evil grin, "Well, look who we have here. If it isn't our old friend, BB big butt."

Dickie followed with, "I bet you think you're big stuff, Gunn, getting written up in the paper. I bet when you saw that hand, you wet your pants like a little baby."

Carl kept ribbing me. "I bet your mommy had to wash your pants, or did she burn them? Do you pee your pants often? I bet you do, even more than your snot-nosed baby brother. Let's check, Dickie. Pull his pants off! I bet he even wears diapers!"

I noticed Lou wasn't joining in on the teasing. He was just standing and staring, not saying a word.

Dickie moved closer and started again with another threat. "BB, you're a dead meat treat—rotten, rank, and rancid. I wasn't finished riding your bike, and Lou tells me you took it back. Well, I guess I'll just have to borrow it again."

That's when Dickie gave me a shove into the wall. I tucked my head down with my chin on my chest. That saved my head from banging the wall. Pain shot through both of my shoulders. I tried to leave around him but only got about two steps to the door. Dickie grabbed me by the collar of my shirt. I had to stop or risk tearing off the buttons.

"Lou, hold him while I demonstrate a couple of punches he needs to see up close. I guess he didn't learn his lesson behind the furniture store. BB, you're one stupid-slow learner," Carl snarled at me while balling up his fist.

"No!" Lou shouted to Carl, and that surprised everyone.

"No? What do you mean, 'no'?" Carl asked in surprise, and without any warning, Dickie grabbed me from behind. He held me by both arms so Carl could get in free blows. I guess they wanted to be sure I couldn't punch their noses.

"Leave him alone! You haven't tangled with the Brotherhood like I have. It ain't worth it. Leave him alone!" Lou begged.

"I thought we got that settled," Dickie said to Lou.

"You better leave him alone! They'll cut you open with a knife while you watch. As I said, it ain't worth it. Let's go back and watch the movie…you coming?" Lou asked. He turned towards the door without waiting, just as it started to open. Someone was coming into the bathroom.

Dickie whispered, "We aren't afraid of you, your old man, or the Brotherhood. Lou may be a chicken, but not us. Today, you die!"

Then, Carl punched me hard in the stomach.

That was when Mr. Stone stuck his head in the door and asked, "What's going on in here?"

Dickie let me go. I dropped to one knee, trying to catch my breath. I saw Kent behind Mr. Stone, looking around him.

Mr. Stone's face changed from curious to angry. "You three are nothing but trouble. All right, that's it! You three are banned for the rest of the summer! You come to see me when school starts. After that, I'll decide if I want to give you a trial period to come back."

When the bullies moved away from me, Mr. Stone asked, "Are you all right, son?"

"Yes…I'm fine. Uh, Mr. Stone…Lou wasn't…causing trouble," I said, still breathless.

"Billy, you're telling me Lou McCulloch was not in on this?" he asked me wide-eyed.

"No, sir. Lou was trying…to make them…stop," I told him as I continued to catch my breath. Carl could sure punch hard.

"Well, in that case, Lou, you can go on in and watch the rest of the movie. You two, come with me!" Mr. Stone ushered Carl and Dickie out to the lobby. I knew he would banish them for the summer. He never played around with troublemakers who hit someone.

"Why did you tell him that?" Lou asked me.

"Because it's the truth. You tried to help me," I said.

"Are you going to tell the Brotherhood what I did?"

"Lou, I've never heard of the Brotherhood."

"Yeah, right," Lou said, turned, and left the bathroom, brushing past Kent in the hall.

I slipped out as Kent held the door and said, "I saw them follow you into the bathroom."

"Thanks for watching out for me. That could have been bad," I replied as we returned to our seats. I told Kent we needed to talk after the show. *Rage at Dawn* was just starting, so we settled down to watch the movie.

I missed a couple of good scenes, thinking about what Lou had said. Something about the Brotherhood might use a knife. Dad's buddies didn't play around. The town gossips were saying that Lou was having bad dreams; no wonder. One thing was sure; whatever they did to Lou, it had stopped him from bullying me. At least for the present.

After the movie, we let Lou leave first, then we followed. Kent's mom was waiting for us, and it was raining, raining hard with thunder and lightning. The streets had water across them, and the gutters were overflowing in two different places. Kent's mom had to drive slowly to see the road.

I ate supper with Kent since he ate lunch at my house. That was great because Mrs. Clark fixed hamburgers. She even put cheese on mine, just the way I liked it.

After supper, Kent told his mom we were going to his room to check out a new comic book. He really didn't have a new comic book. He just wanted to know the details about my bathroom scrape. I told him all about it but made him swear to keep the Brotherhood part a secret. Even if they burned him alive and then shot him three times and then burned him again, I made him promise.

We talked about Dad's phone calls and how his buddies had made such a difference in Lou. However, we decided we still needed to get Barry and Skip on our side, but I made Kent double-die swear not to tell them about the Brotherhood. That was our secret that no one else could ever know about.

I heard a horn toot and knew it had to be Mom. It was. I ran as fast as possible to the car, but I still got all wet because of the pouring rain. However, since it was hot, I didn't much care. Mom made me sit on a towel to keep the upholstery dry.

Dad was gone to tow in a car that some goof had driven through deep water and stalled out the engine. When he got back to the garage, he got another call from a hotel guest stuck at Cubley's Coze. He let me go with him on that job.

The guest was stuck in the mud in a slight depression. To make things worse, the idiot had spun his tires to get out. If he had eased out slowly, he might have made it. Dad pulled him out in a flash and charged him the special Cubley Coze rate of half price, even though we were both soaked. We were just alike, muddy and wet.

We drove back to the garage, talking about different cars and which ones got stuck the easiest. Dad was being friendly, and I liked being with him in Blacky.

Scotty was already asleep when I went upstairs to take a bath. I thought some more about what Lou had said. He was mean, but I still felt terrible about what Dad's buddies did to him. Something so bad that Lou couldn't sleep. I knew how strong my dad was and how it hurt when he whacked me. If Dad's buddies were like that, no wonder Lou was having nightmares.

I was about to drift off when it sounded like we were about to have another storm. The next thing I knew, Scotty was in bed with me, snuggled up, and was asleep before I hardly knew he was there. Well, that's a little brother for you.

I went to sleep thinking about how it would be nice to be Randolph Scott. If I were Randolph Scott, I wouldn't need any army buddies to scare off bullies.

CHAPTER 20

BILLY HOPES HE'S BUBBLE STRAIGHT
Sunday, July 24, 1955

S cotty woke up at about five a.m. with a sore throat. That was bad enough, but he also had wet the bed. My pajama back was wet, and this had been the wrong night for him not to be wearing a diaper. I jumped up and started to whack him one, but he looked pitiful. I touched his forehead, he had a fever, and his face was red.

When I started to fill the tub to bathe him, Mom knew something was wrong. She hurried upstairs, took over, and got Scotty cleaned up and into clean pajamas. Then she put him back to bed in his bed. I knew Scotty would be allowed to stay home from church with Grandma.

While Mom was changing my bed—the mattress cover saved it—I took a bath. I thought I might have a chance, so I put in my request.

"Mom, can I stay home with Scotty?" I pleaded.

"William, you may not! I'm not raising you to be a backslider. You should go to church and pray for the Lord's blessing on this family. We need his help," Mom stated.

No getting out of church for me.

It was raining a cold, steady rain and few people were in church. The preacher's sermon was about the Battle of Jericho. Rahab, a prostitute, was a big sinner because she traded sex for money. It got worse when she betrayed her city and lied to the police about hiding several spies from Israel, the enemy of her people. Despite all those sins, she and her family were saved when the walls came tumbling down. The preacher praised her for her horrible deeds.

If I had even committed one of Rahab's sins, my dad would have whipped me with his belt until either his arm or the belt wore out. Church stuff is so hard to understand. It depends on who the pastor needs to be wearing a white hat and who a black one. Preachers call things good or bad to fit a particular sermon.

Speaking of miracles, like walls falling down for no reason, I began to think that if this town would ever get back to normal, it needed a miracle. One from God, not from a mirror that might take off like a runaway horse pulling a buckboard.

We went home for lunch. Mom had a pot roast in the oven with all kinds of stuff in the pot with it. I love carrots when she cooks them with pot roast. The potatoes were not bad, either. Scotty was fussy, and Grandma fed him ice cream in front of the TV while we ate lunch. We were just finishing lunch when the phone rang.

"Gunn's Garage," Dad said, getting it on the third ring. "Good afternoon, Mr. Rosser. Sure, I'll hold."

I saw Mom turn and frown at Dad at the mention of Mr. Rosser's name. He was a gangster who worked for Mr. MacDonald, an evil bootlegger, according to Mom.

"I'm not working on any at the moment. I just finished one for Trooper Giles, and Trooper Quinn might be bringing me his car, but not right away. When do you need it finished? I could work you in this week. How much do you want done?"

There was a long pause while someone told Dad a long list of things.

"That much? Why don't you let me see it first, then I can order the parts, and when they arrive, you can drop it off. I should be able to get it in and out in about a week. Are you sure you want all that done on a 54? Okay. Yeah, this time, I would need some upfront. Me paying for that many parts would run me short. Okay, I'll see you in a while." Dad finished and hung up the phone.

"John, please don't get involved with that man again," said Mom, using her scolding voice. Her tone was cross, and the look on her face left no doubt about her mood.

"Laura Jane, the man wants me to work on his pickup. Just that and nothing more. Plus, he's going to advance me five hundred dollars for parts. The whole job will earn us more than we normally make in a month, maybe two. He wants a lot of work done and fast." Dad was headed for a collision with Mom, and he knew it.

"John, I heard you say this was a 1954 pickup. I bet it's almost new, never been wrecked, but he wants a lot of work done on it. You keep this up, and you will end up in jail with Doc Hathaway." Mom meant business because the top of her nose had those funny crinkles. A fuss was about to explode into a fight in our kitchen.

Dad turned on Mom. "Laura Jane, don't you dare mention Doc's name when Angus MacDonald's here! You keep quiet about such stuff! Besides, I'm not going to get into trouble for only working on his pickup. You hear me?" Dad ordered, sitting back down at the table.

"Who was that on the phone?" Grandma Harris asked, holding Scotty as she prepared to take him upstairs for a nap on her bed.

"Just a customer, Mother. He wanted to book some work. How's Scotty's fever?" Mom asked, changing the subject.

She and Grandma went upstairs into Grandma's bedroom with Scotty, and the kitchen got quiet.

Dad and I had talked about working on bootlegger's cars last month, and I even heard some of the troopers agree that what Dad was doing was okay. Everyone knew Doc Hathaway, Skip and Barry's dad, had been the driver for Mr. Angus MacDonald. Mr. MacDonald lived in Waynesboro and ran bootleg from Franklin County up here to Green Mountain County, Waynesboro, and several other places nearby. Trooper Giles finally caught Doc Hathaway and wrecked him, but it totaled his trooper's car as well as the pickup full of bootleg. So, I guess Mr. MacDonald was replacing the pickup that had been wrecked.

There was a steady rain all afternoon, with not much for me to do. Several cars pulled into the lot at about four o'clock. I went outside with Dad to see if it was Mr. MacDonald. It was.

Dad opened the garage doors, and Mr. Rosser, the bodyguard, drove the pickup into the garage. Mr. MacDonald was in the backseat of a Cadillac driven by another employee, a Mr. Chill Dawson. All I knew about this guy was his nickname, Chill, and his last name. Everyone called him Chill, but I knew I better call him Mr. Dawson.

"John, a bonny day not to be on the moors." Mr. MacDonald made it a point to shake Dad's hand. "Moors" was a word I would have to ask Polecat to explain.

"I agree with you there, Mr. MacDonald. A good day to spend indoors," Dad said, trying to be friendly, but I could tell he was not comfortable with Mr. MacDonald or his two employees.

Dad walked over to the pickup, popped the hood, bent over, and it looked like he might crawl into the engine compartment. He tugged on a couple of things, got a crawler, and went under the truck. When he finished, he stood up and was the first to speak. No one said a word while Dad checked out the pickup truck.

"Mr. MacDonald, you brought me more to work with this time. This 1954 Chevrolet 3100 is going to be fast and stable in the curves. I'll need to redo the front suspension and put truck springs on the back. The transmission let's leave alone. I want to rebore the cylinders for a little extra power because the block has room to make the change. I can get you hot-rod parts that will improve performance and definitely replace this radiator. That's the weakest part of this whole setup. We need to beef up the front and rear bumpers with one-inch steel. If it were me, I'd put in a new carburetor and toss this one. The clutch might need adjusting to handle the extra weight, but not much. You do need different tires. These are street tires and no good for the speed you'll need. Also, a new paint job of flat black or dull gray? So, does that suit you?" Dad finished and looked at Mr. MacDonald for an answer.

"Black is fine, and the rest is acceptable if the price is not a wee too high."

"Well, you know my rates. I try to be fair and give you what you pay for. I have a new man, and I can let him work on it to save you a little," Dad said.

Mr. MacDonald looked at me and laughed, "The bairn may be good for coloreds and crackers, but I want no laddies on this job."

"Mr. MacDonald, I wasn't talking about Billy. No, I have a top-notch mechanic helping me now," Dad responded, and he was smiling.

I wasn't smiling. I could pull my weight; at twelve years old, I was almost full-grown.

"Who might that be?" Mr. MacDonald asked.

"Dan Skelton," Dad informed him.

"I thought he worked for Big John at the Chevrolet Dealership?"

"He got fired, and I picked him up. He's a good man, but it's up to you. I'll be glad to do all the work, or I can get him to help me. You know I stand behind what I put out," Dad said.

"I'll give it some thought. You go ahead, write down what parts you'll need, and Chill here will give you five hundred cash to start. Call me when the parts come in."

Mr. MacDonald walked over to me and asked me about school. I answered about last year, the grades I had earned, and knew to be very respectful, or Dad would whack me. Mr. MacDonald gave me a quarter and pinched my earlobe. I thanked him without wincing from the pinch and maintained eye contact with him.

I could have tipped the old Scot a dollar since I was a working man, but that would have gotten me whacked for sure. Only an idiot would insult a bootlegger. I was no idiot.

Dad finished up the list of parts he would need and priced them. He had a fish on the line, and I knew he was going to reel him in.

"Mr. MacDonald, I can throw in a couple of tricks for a few dollars more."

"Faith, me boy, what might they be?" the Scot asked.

"I can put in a switch that kills both taillights, the one taillight on the left or the one on the right. Anyone following at night would think they got behind the wrong pickup and lost the one they were after. I can do the same on the front."

"The back, I can see, but why in the front?" asked the bootlegger.

"If you're meeting someone at night, you might want to fool them into thinking you're not the pickup truck they're looking for," Dad said with a smile.

"I like that, a cleverness that suits me style," Mr. MacDonald said and broke into a smile that was sneaky looking.

He began talking to Mr. Rosser while Dad finished up his parts order.

The man that scared me the most was Mr. Thomas Pinkard Rosser, the man whose full name I knew. He was mean-looking and reminded me of Pinkerton Detective Agency detectives in some of my cowboy comics. I remembered his full name after only hearing it once because of the Pinkard part. He never smiled and always looked like he would love to whack little kids just for fun.

All the men said a formal goodbye to my dad and shook hands with him again. Mr. Rosser took the pickup, and Mr. Chill Dawson drove Mr. MacDonald's Caddy with the boss in the back. Both vehicles had big motors that rumbled.

"Dad, that Mr. Rosser gives me the creeps," I said when Dad began to close the garage. That was all the work he was going to do this Sunday.

"Billy, they all three give me the creeps, but I can't afford to turn down a job that pays like this one will. You were smart to answer Mr. MacDonald the way you did. It earned you a quarter," Dad said.

"Dad, I know how to answer people like him. Can I tell you something, and you won't get mad at me?" I asked.

"All right, what?" Dad returned the question with a question, plus he added a curious look.

"I wanted to tip him a dollar to see what he would do. Tipping me a quarter, how cheap is that?" I joked, hoping Dad would take it as a joke and not whack me.

"What? Tip him a dollar." Dad started to smile, then chuckled, and then he laughed out loud. "Billy, as tight as that old Scot is, he would have taken it. But mark me, boy, don't you ever tease or mouth off to any of those men. They're dangerous. Also, don't you dare tell your mom what you just told me about tipping that gangster. She would skin us both. Tip him a dollar. That's rich."

No sooner had we gotten stuff put away, and Dad was about to turn off the lights when Trooper Giles pulled into the garage lot. He threw up his hand at Dad and waved at me. Then he flashed on his red roof light. I waved back.

"John, Billy, nice day for ducks," Trooper Giles called out and patted me on the top of my head. It was okay for him to do that, but anyone else who tried, I might have to show them what could happen.

"Bobby, what brings you into town?" Dad asked.

"Running down leads on the Brown case. The sergeant has Mike and me working with Sheriff Lawrence to figure out who has the worst grudge against Mr. Albert Winston Brown. We have plenty of candidates and few ways to narrow the list. But that's not the reason I stopped," said Trooper Giles.

"Okay, you here to arrest Billy? He's been looking guilty all day." Dad smiled as he said it.

"No, unless he's ready to confess to something. Are you, boy?"

Today was a gloomy day, but with a lot of joking going on. So, I joked right back with, "I ain't spilling the beans for no copper, see!"

The trooper smiled and shook his head.

"Actually, Billy's not even on my list. No, I just passed Chill, Angus MacDonald, and his man Rosser. Rosser was driving a 1954 pickup. I figured they'd come by to ask you to soup her up. Right?" Trooper Giles asked.

"Bobby, I swear I think you and I must share a party line. You got to stop eavesdropping on my calls. Yeah, they wanted some work done on that 1954 Chevy. They also wanted to be sure I wasn't working on one of the state cars right now. I guess they want to keep it quiet and not cross paths with any of you troopers."

"Richmond pays us to disappoint people like MacDonald. I plan on crossing his path often."

"If you do, it might cost me a month's pay," Dad said with a frown, but I knew he wouldn't hide stuff from Trooper Giles. He wouldn't tell him stuff unless he asked hard questions, but he wouldn't lie.

"John, I think you're safe," said Trooper Giles. "I just hope my visit doesn't mess you up. I don't think they saw me. I came out from a side street after they'd passed."

"Well, I'm not going to worry about it. Want to come in for some cake and coffee?" Dad asked.

"I guess I could go 10-7 for a few minutes. I did miss lunch."

I knew 10-7 was police radio talk for going out of service, like for a meal or bathroom break. I learned a lot of the ten codes from the troopers talking to me. We all went into the kitchen, and Mom greeted Trooper Giles. She liked his visits a lot better than Mr. MacDonald's visits. That was obvious enough for a blind man to see.

"Mrs. Gunn, how are you?" asked Trooper Giles.

"Better, now that you're here. I wish you had arrived in time to run off the riffraff that was here earlier. Please tell my husband he will get into trouble working for that bootlegger."

"Ma'am, as long as John just does garage work, he should be fine. I think John is smart enough not to get into something that could cause him trouble with the law. He has always been bubble straight with me," said the trooper.

"Bubble straight? What is that? I never heard of that before," Mom asked, which was good. The trooper had diverted her from talking about bootleggers.

"That's what my dad used to say about someone he thought was a good person. Dad was a finish carpenter and a good one. He measured three times before he cut, and he used a level every way you could use a level. His corners were square, and his level was always right on the bubble. A job that was bubble straight was done right in every plane. Thus, people who were straight and honest, he referred to as bubble straight. That was his highest compliment. Mine too. Your husband is bubble straight in my book," Trooper Giles said with a grin at Dad.

"Laura Jane, think we could offer Trooper Giles some cake and coffee before the afternoon is plum gone?" Dad asked, pushing it just a little. Mom was not in a great mood after a visit from Mr. MacDonald and his gang, but Trooper Giles had helped improve her disposition.

"I just made a pot, and the cake's in the cake holder."

That was a big round tin that Mom kept her cakes and pies in to keep the flies off. Only Trooper Giles got cake because it was too close to supper time for kids and husbands to have a slice. Oh, well, I asked; I tried; I failed.

Trooper Giles and Dad switched to talking about progress on the Brown murder case. The trooper told Dad how Big John had held up a search warrant the police had tried to get from Judge Carlton. Mr. Southwall had blocked it with a circuit court injunction on the grounds that it dealt with privileged information between the plant attorney, Mr. Albert Winston Brown, and the McCulloch Company Board of Directors. The circuit court judge would rule on

Monday if the state police could search after both sides had a chance to present their arguments. The troopers figured by then, what they were looking for, would be long gone and stored in the office safe of Mr. Ben Southwall. Good luck getting it, then!

Since all of this was now in a court filing that the press had access to and would be published soon, the trooper could tell Dad about it. We just got it one day before it would be in the newspaper.

Trooper Giles left with a second piece of cake and a ham sandwich for his supper wrapped in wax paper and in a paper sack. I thought about what the trooper had said about Dad. I hoped he thought I was just like my dad—bubble straight. Then, I wondered if someone had to tell a lie for a good reason, like keeping certain army buddies' visit a secret, if that meant you were no longer bubble straight?

I wondered about that for the rest of the evening.

CHAPTER 21
A FISH CABIN OR FISHY CABIN?
Monday, July 25, 1955

The Honorable John Winston Harland, III, judge of the Green Mountain County Circuit Court, began the hearing on the injunction against the search warrant for Albert Winston Brown's office promptly at nine o'clock. Matt had arrived ten minutes earlier to meet and confer with Sheriff Lawrence and Sergeant Oliver, but when the three walked into the courtroom, they were astonished to see who was seated at the defendant's table.

Big John McCulloch was in a wheelchair in the center seat and to his right was a male nurse. Chief McCulloch sat beside the nurse. To the left of Big John sat Mr. Ben Southwall, the new attorney for McCulloch Wood Products, and the fifth man was the surprise of the morning. He introduced himself as an assistant attorney general but announced that he was not appearing for the prosecution but for the McCulloch corporation. Matt was shocked that a big gun from the Virginia Attorney General's Office was even aware of this local search warrant.

Judge Harland announced that he had read Matt's affidavit for the search warrant and found sufficient probable cause thus far. He asked the McCulloch Wood Products Company attorneys to explain their objection.

First, Mr. Southwall stood and began with the standard, "May it please the court."

Then things got interesting.

"I find no justification for the issuance of this search warrant because there is no evidence of criminal activity or evidence pointing to any criminal actor within the corporation. The company documents are all civil in nature. However, these files contain proprietary information that would irreparably harm the financial health and ability of McCulloch Wood Products to compete in the marketplace. Furthermore, it's obvious that this is a fishing expedition from an inexperienced Commonwealth's Attorney on his first venture into the waters of his office."

Matt was furious at the condescending tone of Mr. Southwall. But what rubbed salt into the wound was when the assistant attorney general repeated the allegation of his inexperience and added that this matter should have been presented to his office for approval before it was filed with the court. A procedure that was never done in local criminal cases.

Matt took a deep breath, let it out slowly, then recited his prior experience as a prosecutor. He gave the approximate number of the many search warrants he had written and the numerous criminal jury trials he had conducted in Roanoke. He directed his next questions to both the assistant attorney general and Mr. Southwall.

"Gentlemen, might I inquire as to how many search warrants you have drafted? How many felony jury trials have you tried?"

Matt knew the answer was probably zero to both questions. Assistant Attorney Generals wrote briefs, seldom tried cases, and a corporate attorney would have tried none. Not waiting for an answer, he explained the need to search the files.

"Your Honor, we are not searching for corporate crimes currently. We are looking for the names of employees and vendors that might have a grudge against Mr. Brown. Frequently, when a family was evicted after the breadwinner was fired, trouble occurred. These evictions were under the direction of Mr. Brown, and the process often resulted in the hospitalization of the tenant or other family members. Unfair and heavy-handed treatment is a strong motivation for revenge."

Matt also argued the sheriff and state police needed to be allowed to search for possible suspects with grudges against Brown due to certain sharp business contracts written by Brown. Then, Matt pointed to Mr. Southwall.

"Mr. Southwall would not be able to draw the same connections, not being privy to the evidence known only to the investigators," argued Matt.

He went on to say, "This case is about the murder of a state official. Also, Mr. Brown was an officer of this very court. This requires the broadest investigative effort possible, and I'm shocked that the attorney general's office wants to block this investigation."

Matt concluded, "I understand the necessary balance between the right of a corporation to keep proprietary matters private versus the right of the state to solve murder cases. However, we need to bring to justice the murderer of a state prosecutor. The needs of this company should yield to the needs of the people. I will see that safeguards are put in place to protect the case files. That should be sufficient to protect the civil interests of this business."

Judge Harland began his concluding remarks by stating it was highly unusual for the state's attorney general to appear on behalf of a citizen in opposition to a local prosecutor in a criminal case. Recognizing the state's necessity to solve this murder, he ordered Mr. Southwall to immediately inspect the files. Then, he was to turn over to the Commonwealth all files that would not harm the corporation or reveal any production secrets.

Matt left the courtroom with the sheriff and the sergeant of the state police, and all three knew what would happen. Time proved them correct. After lunch, Mr. Southwall delivered only one hundred and fifteen files to Matt's office out of a thousand or more. Mr. Southwall claimed the other files held critical company secrets.

Matt quickly divided the files into equal shares for himself, the sheriff, and the state police sergeant. They would read them tonight and meet the next day to discuss them.

After the officers left, Matt put his feet on top of the desk and closed his eyes, trying to cool his temper. Then, he had just begun shooting rubber bands at the light fixture when in walked Mrs. Harvey.

"Mr. Cubley, does that help?" she asked.

"Yes, ma'am, it does. When I imagine the faces of Mr. Southwall and Big John up there, it helps some. I don't know how we're going to solve this murder with our hands tied. There's something certain people don't want us to find out, and those people are well connected."

"Mr. Cubley, you could be right."

Matt continued to vent. "It's bad enough for Big John to attempt to block our efforts, but then, calling in the attorney general's office...I'm glad I was able to hold my temper this morning."

Matt took his feet off the desk and stuffed the files he needed to take home into his briefcase. Mrs. Harvey remained to tell him some other news.

"Mr. Cubley, Trooper Quinn dropped off the autopsy report and the forensic expert's findings while you were in court. I took the liberty of reading them. Mr. Albert Winston Brown always insisted I read them before I gave them to him. If you want to change that procedure, just let me know," she said with a questioning look.

"No, ma'am. Your local knowledge might shed some light on things."

"I'll be happy to help when I can."

"Did you notice anything I should know?" Matt asked, just starting to read the first of the two reports.

"The autopsy report agrees with the forensic report. Albert Winston Brown wasn't shot in his car but somewhere else, and bloodstains found in the trunk indicated the corpse was moved in his vehicle. Then, it was placed in the front seat, and the car went down the bank and into the creek."

"Are they certain?" Matt stopped reading and asked.

"Yes. The forensic team didn't find blood spatters in the front passenger compartment of the car, despite Mr. Brown being shot three times in the back of his head. If the murder had occurred in the front seat, blood spatters would have been present."

"Okay, now we're starting to get somewhere. Anything else?" inquired Matt.

"Yes, sir. The Medical Examiner found that the body had been horizontal for some time after death and not upright. The blood had pooled in the posterior plane of the torso and the lateral side of the right leg."

Matt knew that these two items, agreeing, were of great importance. The body had been transported on its back after death. Probably transported in the trunk with the legs bent at the waist, right leg down, and left leg on top. This was how a body would fit when jammed into the trunk of a car.

"Mrs. Harvey, I want you to continue to read these reports. You spotted all the important points," Matt said with a smile.

"That comes from doing it for a long, long time. Well, not too long," she concluded, correcting herself.

"I'm sure you were a fast learner," Matt remarked and looked down to finish reading the two reports. However, his secretary wasn't done yet.

"Mr. Cubley, did you know Mr. Albert Winston Brown leased a fishing cabin on West Bear Creek? He kept it quiet so only a few people knew. Fewer still know who owns the property," Mrs. Harvey suggested.

"West Bear Creek. Where is that?" Matt asked.

"West Bear Creek joins East Bear Creek to make Bear Creek. That creek flows under Route 22, then continues south beside the McCulloch Wood Products plant. Close by, where the two creeks join, is where the sniper hid to fire on Chief Smith and Big John McCulloch. Understand?" she asked.

"I sure do. That's not too far from where we found Brown's body. You know that fishing cabin might be where the murder took place. I think our next move will be to search that cabin. Finding where the murder took place would be valuable. My goodness, I don't suppose you could produce the killer, could you?" Matt joked, but that was a mistake.

"No, Mr. Cubley, if I could do that, I would have done so already."

Mrs. Harvey looked irritated. Matt could kick himself for his last remark.

"I'm sorry. I never knew an office secretary who could locate a murder scene so quickly. Please call the sheriff and Sergeant Oliver to come back here," Matt requested, looking at Mrs. Harvey in a new light. She might take second place only to the gold mine he had in Polecat. Today, which had started badly, was quickly improving.

The sheriff and Sergeant Oliver were still talking over the case in the sheriff's office, so they were back within minutes. Matt then told the sheriff and Sergeant Oliver about the fishing cabin and asked if they thought a search warrant might be good.

"That won't be necessary," Sheriff Lawrence said after Matt's question.

"Why won't it be necessary?" Matt asked in confusion.

"That cabin's on county property. The county owns forty acres on West Bear Creek. That fishing cabin sits smack in the middle of it near some great fishing holes. The land was donated to the county by the widow of a past county court clerk. She donated the property if the county would name it after her husband. The county tried, but everyone in the county always knew the place as Bear Creek. While there's a nice plaque on the wall of the fishing cabin that says it's called the William Drake Strongmire Fishing and Hunting Camp, that never seemed to take. Everyone calls it the Bear Creek Cabin."

"Okay, sheriff, I get the name. Why don't we need a search warrant?" asked Matt.

"The property is…no, was leased to Mr. Albert Winston Brown for a dollar a year after McCulloch Wood Products built the cabin. Mr. Brown maintained the cabin, but a few of us knew Big John's company was footing the bills. It's a private retreat for the plant supervisors and special guests. It's been their poker, hunting, fishing, and other things cabin for as long as I can recall."

"Well, I'll be skunk sprayed and smell like lilacs. That means the county now holds full title since the tenant is deceased," Matt declared and looked at Sergeant Oliver, who was staying quiet for the moment but smiling.

Sheriff Lawrence added that he had a spare set of keys in his office.

Sergeant Oliver spoke up. "So, I bet Big John won't let it remain county property for long, will he?"

The sheriff shook his head no. "Not likely. Big John will get the county to lease it back to someone he controls, right quick. He just doesn't want his name on the place because of what goes on there. Certain conduct is not quite what one would want in the local paper."

"Was Mr. Albert Winston Brown a party regular?" Matt wanted to know.

The sheriff answered him in detail. "No, he hardly set foot on the place unless he needed to have something repaired or handle some company legal business there. Anytime things got interesting, usually of the female variety, he went home."

"He was honest?" asked an incredulous Matt.

"Hell, no! The man was crooked as a bent nail. I'm just telling you what little gossip I've heard. You see, Brown was the frontman. He took care of things for Big John, but he was a good husband, just not an honest lawyer. When his name got mentioned in connection with the cabin, it was for a shady contract or unscrupulous business deal. When the entertainment started, it was said that he never stayed. He was the guy who was paid to keep Big John protected if someone went too far with a skirt for hire. That's why Big John made him sign the lease."

"This company is a den of snakes," Matt said.

The sheriff concluded with, "Now, gentlemen, I suggest we hurry before the county assigns the lease to the next frontman for Big John. We might just find something."

Sheriff Lawrence was surprising Matt. Giving them this information was one thing, but would he stay the course if Big John started putting pressure on him?

"So, what do we need to do?" asked Sergeant Oliver.

The office door opened, and Mrs. Harvey walked in unannounced. She placed a file on Matt's desk. "You might want this copy for your files, Mr. Cubley." She then turned and walked out of the room, quietly closing the door behind her.

Matt looked inside the file folder. There was a copy of the lease for the fishing cabin. He quickly found the clauses that read just as reported by the sheriff. He handed it to the state police sergeant to read and said, "I guess we're ready to go. Let's see what we can find."

Sheriff Lawrence informed Matt that he had an appointment that he must attend, but Shoat was working and would drive Matt out to the cabin. Shoat soon arrived with the keys to the gate and the cabin. Sergeant Oliver called his dispatcher to ask Trooper Giles and Trooper Franklin to drop what they were doing and meet him at the McCulloch Wood Products Plant with a camera and a forensic kit.

Deputy Lincoln, better known as Shoat, drove Matt to the McCulloch Wood Products Plant, where the state police waited. The group left the plant, turned left, drove over the bridge that spanned Bear Creek, and turned right into West Bear Lane. Coming to a fork in the road, they went right until a metal gate stopped them. The gate was hung on big telephone-pole-sized posts set between high banks on both sides, a practical choke point. Shoat opened the gate, and the caravan of cars proceeded to the cabin.

The cabin was built of 10″ x 10″ square, not round, logs. It resembled a log cabin, only nicer. Inside were six bedrooms, a kitchen that would make a mining camp cook smile, a large living room, and a couple of storerooms. One was full of gambling paraphernalia. There was even a Las Vegas roulette table with a velvet cover and folding legs for storage. Not that Matt had ever been to Las Vegas, but he had read about it and had seen photographs of the Dunes and the Stardust in the Roanoke paper.

There was no evidence of a recent party. All the gambling paraphernalia was packed in the storeroom, but they found a table and six chairs in the main room. One chair had a cracked backrest, and the table was turned at an odd angle. Someone had used bleach on the stains because the wood beside the table was lighter than the rest of the floor.

The state police began taking pictures and cutting out slivers of wood from the floor. The chair was bagged and placed in one of the patrol cars. Trooper Franklin went back to his car for a tape measure to make a scale drawing of the crime scene.

He returned and reported, "Gentlemen, a Highland police car started up the drive, stopped, and then backed out. I think it was Chief McCulloch."

The men continued their work. Shoat searched and found the kitchen stocked with canned food, paper plates, and cooking supplies. There was no evidence of garbage or food left to spoil. Everything in each of the bedrooms was in order. Trooper Giles didn't find any bullet holes in the main room. Someone had sanitized the place except for a cracked chair back and some residual stains on the floor. There was not much to go on.

"Matt, this could be where Mr. Brown was shot—plugged three times in the back of the head. Entrance wounds but no exit wounds, thus no bullet holes in any of the walls. Only slight evidence of a scuffle. If this is the place, it tells me he met someone here he knew. We'll know more once the lab analyses the bits of wood and the chair. Gentlemen, let's search outside," said Sergeant Oliver to his troopers.

Matt stood with Shoat on the cabin porch and watched the troopers proceed with their outdoors search. When the search party had arrived, everyone parked away from the cabin so as not to disturb any evidence. However, the road was gravel and left no tracks except for one old tire impression found in the soil near the walk.

No footprints were found because of the flagstone walk. However, Trooper Franklin found a cigarette butt, and Trooper Giles found an old Indian Head penny in the grass beside the walk. These were collected and preserved. An impression of the tire tread was made, but it was so old and degraded that it was of little use other than showing the tire's width.

A car was heard driving in from the road. Everyone turned toward the sound as a Highland Police car stopped forty yards from the cabin. Matt noticed that the driver was Chief McCulloch, not his favorite person, and one passenger.

After a pause, the chief drove right up to the walk, ignoring the first rule of entering a crime scene. Don't trample the evidence, or in this case, drive over it. Thankfully, the troopers had collected it all, but Chief McCulloch didn't know that.

Ben Southwall stepped out of the passenger side of the police car. Chief McCulloch got out of the driver's side, hitched up his gun belt, and pointed at Matt.

"What are you people doing on McCulloch property? I thought you were put in your place in court this morning, but I guess not. Now you've gone and done it...." Chief McCulloch was trying his best to finish, but Ben Southwall interrupted with a tug on his elbow.

"Chief, let me handle this!" barked the attorney. "Now, I advise each of you to cease and desist this trespass. Furthermore, you will turn over to me any evidence you have recovered. Who's in charge?"

"That would be me," Matt spoke up, much to the relief of Shoat and possibly the sergeant.

"Now, being an attorney, one would think you'd know better," said Mr. Southwall.

"I do know better. It's a shame, being an attorney, you don't," Matt said with a smile that wasn't a smile at all.

"What? You look here, Cubley. I represent McCulloch Wood…"

"Products, yes, I know. Trouble is, they have no interest in this land. None! The people of Green Mountain County own this property. This is public land."

"You are wrong," retorted Mr. Southwall.

"No! I'm afraid Mr. Albert Winston Brown only held a tenancy under a lease, which ended at his death. Here's a duplicate original, if you would care to read it, Mr. Southwall," Matt responded in a less than civil tone. He handed Mr. Southwall the lease that Mrs. Harvey had provided him. The plant attorney must have read the lease twice based on the time it took him.

"Chief, they're correct. I thought you told me McCulloch Wood Products held the title to this cabin. That's not what this lease says. My apologies, Mr. Cubley, I was grossly misinformed," spat out Mr. Southwall, using the formal Mister Cubley this time. The plant lawyer turned in anger, strode back to the car, and as they left, he was seen shaking his fist at the chief.

Generalized laughter broke out.

"One for our side, Mister Matthew Cubley, Esquire, sir," remarked Shoat, who enjoyed having the last word.

"I just hope our efforts here mean something," Matt said, looking at the cabin. "This case isn't going to be easy with so little evidence, and the people with the answers won't cooperate."

Matt returned to the courthouse and grabbed his briefcase with the McCulloch files. Then, he walked over to see if Linda was still in the courthouse, and she was.

"Hey. I wanted to say hi. Things have been crazy, and I miss our little talks," Matt said as Linda packed up her things. She was also taking work home.

"Matt, if things slow down, perhaps we can do lunch again?" she asked with that smile that Matt could never resist.

"Sounds good."

"Mr. Cubley, are you staring at me?" she teased.

"Yes, ma'am, I am. So may I walk you to your car?" he asked.

"You may," she responded with a giggle.

When they left the courthouse, it was evident to one of the deputies coming into work that Matt Cubley and Mrs. Carlisle were walking out together, chatting. The deputy smiled as he passed them.

CHAPTER 22

BILLY, KNIVES, AND BASKETBALLS
Monday, July 25, 1955

Monday, nothing was going on for a change. Nothing was okay. Nothing was good. Kent and I rode our bikes to work without seeing Lou, Dickie, or Carl. Nothing was great.

We missed Mr. Cubley for breakfast because he had to go to the courthouse for a hearing on a search warrant. Polecat was a little late, and when he arrived, he brought only news we knew already.

After Kent and I cleaned two cars, we were done for the day. It wasn't even lunchtime, so we decided to check out the park on the sly. As we were getting our bikes, Mrs. Hathaway arrived for work, and Skip and Barry were with her. Well, that called for a reunion. And the four of us needed to form a pact.

"Hey, Barry, hey, Skip, how have you guys been?" I called out when the two hopped out of the hotel wagon. Mr. Cubley had given permission for Mr. Baker to pick up Mrs. Hathaway for work and take her home until she could get her own transportation.

"We've been okay. How about you two? Mom told us about your bikes getting stolen. I see they're back," Skip said, walking up to us with his younger brother following.

We exchanged stories about our summer but left out how our bikes got returned. We told them that Lou was not being as big a bully but warned them that Carl and Dickie were worse.

"Skip, Barry, thanks again for helping me out at the park on the Fourth of July. You saved me from Lou and his baseball bat, that's for sure," I told them for the umpteenth time.

"Let it slide. Glad we happened by," Skip insisted.

"I just wish I had gotten in one or two more good kicks to Lou's family jewels," bragged Barry.

Kent moved to another subject and asked, "How did you like Rocky Mount?"

"Okay, not great, just okay. We would much rather be with our mom," said Barry.

"Yeah, Mom needs us with Dad being away," added Skip.

Kent and I always tried to avoid the subject of their dad, him being in prison, but we sure let them know how glad we were that they were in town.

Skip told us some good news. "Guys, Mr. Cubley's going to let me work at the hotel, helping Richard Baker. He's gonna teach me how to fix things and do yard work. When Mr. Baker doesn't need me, I can work for his wife, Rose."

Barry blurted out, "Yeah, but it's not fair. Mr. Cubley told me I'm too young. Horse hockey!" complained the nine-year-old.

Kent tried to help, "Hey, I bet you can get a job here, easy, when you're older."

He asked, "Like, how much older?"

We told him twelve.

"No way, I'm waiting that long. I'd be half growed up."

Skip then put his hand on my shoulder and leaned nearer. "BB, tell me about finding Brown's body."

I told him the facts. I watched his face grow angry.

"Guys, I'm glad the bastard's dead."

"I don't blame you much for saying that. The whole town knows he framed your dad for stealing the plant payroll. How's your dad's pardon coming?" I asked.

"Trooper Giles is getting some good evidence, but no one knows what our crooked governor might decide. My guess is that Big John will tell him what to do. I'm afraid Dad may have to serve out his whole sentence."

I thought I could avoid the topic about Skip and Barry's dad, but we kind of fell into that mudhole without trying.

Since Mr. Cubley was gone and no one knew when he might return, Mrs. Hathaway told Barry and Skip they could go to the park with Kent and me. We all had to be back at the hotel by four o'clock, which suited us.

Skip and Barry borrowed a couple of the bikes the hotel kept for guests, and we all four rode down to the park. Several of our classmates were in the park playing basketball. Now we had enough for a proper game.

I heard Roger Younger ask Skip a question that scared me.

"Hey, haven't we met somewhere? You look familiar."

Skip looked at me, and I shook my head no, but just enough for him to see and no one else.

Skip answered, "No, we just moved to town today."

I added, "That's right, they're new in town. Their mom just got hired at Cubley's Coze."

That seemed to satisfy Roger, and nothing more was said about it.

Roger, Kent, and I were on one team. Skip, Barry, and Frank Varner were on the other. Since Barry was only nine, my team had to score four baskets over the other team in our game of twenty-one. That made Barry pout since, once again, he was reminded of his age. But darn, if he didn't score five baskets, and his team won. That made him feel a lot better.

We took a break in the shade. That's when I heard someone call my name.

It was the pretty desk clerk from the Green Mountain Resort. She was the one who had been nice to Kent and me when the three bullies jumped us at that other resort.

Kent and I walked over to see her while the other guys headed for the lake to skip stones.

"Well, if it isn't the two tough hombres," she said. "So, how is the famous duo doing? I've been reading all about the exploits of William Boyer Gunn and Kent Farnsworth Clark in the papers."

I thought Kent was going to die when she used his middle name. His middle name, the one he wanted to keep secret, had been in all the papers. I told her not to believe everything she read in the Highland Gazette.

"Well, how have you two been? I understand, in addition to being kidnapped, beat up, and robbed, BB recently found the body of Mr. Brown. What do you boys do, hunt up adventures, or schedule them?" she laughed.

"Actually, I've been trying to avoid scrapes," said Kent. "But BB here keeps getting me into trouble."

"Thanks a lot, Superman. Why don't you drop me in a hole and cover me up?" I said with a frown. "Say, you know our names, but we never found out yours."

"Misty. Misty Sue Johnson, but just call me Misty. No one else around here is named Misty—only me. I really don't need my last name."

"That's a pretty name," Kent said, then blushed red.

"Well, thank you for saying so," she said, smiling at Kent.

"I've never heard the name Misty before. How did you get it? Some relative?" I asked.

"Not exactly. I think it's the name of a horse—a horse in a book. Just a story my mom was reading when she was about to have me. Funny how those things work out." Misty smiled at me. I think my face was starting to get red.

"Do you still work at Green Mountain?" Kent asked.

"I do, still on the desk. But I'm hoping to find a job in Lynchburg, Waynesboro, or even Charlottesville. However, so far, no luck," she answered. But, this time, she wasn't smiling.

"Don't you like working for Green Mountain Resort?" I asked.

"Oh, it's okay. Some of the guests frighten me. The hotel has these private parties, and the party guests sometimes get rude. The Highland Police are there a lot, but they seem more interested in making the guests happy than helping the staff when a guest gets out of hand," Misty was whispering and then stopped, almost like she was afraid she might have said too much.

"Are the police partying with the guests?" I asked.

"Oh, nothing like that. No, they sometimes deliver stuff for the parties or give the drunks a ride home."

"What would the police be delivering for a party?" Kent asked, which was the question I was about to ask.

"Boxes of something—plain cardboard boxes that are heavy. They carry heavy boxes in and then bring them back out empty. I have no idea what's in them. Only certain staff are allowed on the party floor, and I'm not one of them, thank goodness," Misty said and started to move away. "You boys stay out of trouble and avoid those three friends of yours."

"Those bullies are no friends of ours!" Kent said.

"Kent, I think she was being funny," I told him and gave him a poke in the ribs.

"Oh!" Kent looked at me. "I knew that."

Kent and I walked over to the bathhouse and met Skip, Barry, and Frank, returning from the lake. A Highland Police Car was sitting in the parking lot, and Roger's uncle, Sergeant Frank Younger, was talking to Roger. When the officer saw us approaching, he started his engine to leave, but I heard his final words to Roger.

"I mean, what I say."

Roger walked over to the gang and joined us.

"My Uncle is a soda jerk," Roger said to no one in particular.

"What did he want?" asked Frank Varner for the group.

"He said I was hanging out with undesirables and threatened to have a word with my father. He warned me that he better not catch me doing it again." Roger watched the police car as it backed out of its parking space.

"Come on, Barry, I guess we better be going," Skip said to Barry.

He wasn't talking about you two. He was talking about BB and Superman." Roger was not one to hold back when he was mad.

"Well, BB, I guess we had better be going. I would sure hate to contaminate the fine youth of Highland by letting them associate with us undesirables," Kent said with his typical sarcasm.

"Hey, guys. The only undesirable just left. I hate to say that about my uncle, but he can be a donkey's rear end. Let's finish our game," Roger said with a dribble of the basketball and a bounce off the bathhouse wall a few feet away.

"Sounds good to me," said Frank Varner, trying to take the ball away from Roger.

Skip, Barry, let's play some ball," Kent said with his crooked grin.

The game resumed with a switching around of players. This time there was no handicap because Barry was beating the pants off the rest of us. He was fast, even if he was short. No one noticed Carl and Dickie Lockhart until it was too late. They snagged our ball when it bounced out of bounds.

"Dickie, look what I found," Carl said with a smirk.

"Yeah. Finders keepers, losers weepers. That's what I always say," responded Dickie.

Roger walked over to the two and invited them to join the game. Their refusal was a little less than pleasant. I noticed Kent was looking at where we had left our bikes to ensure they were still there. They were.

"Come on, guys. Either join us or give us back our ball," said Frank. He was getting worried. It was his basketball.

"Hey Carl, toss me that ball. I need to check to see if it's regulation size," Dickie said and caught the ball when Carl threw it over Frank's head to his brother.

Dickie caught the ball and examined it carefully.

"Hey Carl, this ball is overinflated. I need to take out a little air."

And with that, Dickie pulled a knife, flipped open the blade with one hand, and jabbed it into the side of the basketball. There was a pop, a hiss, and he threw the ball back to Frank.

"Wow, that's much better," laughed Carl, enjoying what Dickie had done.

"Dickie, you owe me a new basketball," Frank said, throwing down the ball. It landed with a thunk and didn't bounce. But, of course, it wouldn't being deflated.

"Yeah, well, come and collect," taunted Dickie, not putting away his knife but holding it as I've seen in the movies. "You a chicken? Come on and do something about it. I think I'll gut you like a chicken!"

Frank just stood there. He wasn't about to risk getting stabbed.

Dickie and Carl turned and strolled off toward town, making rooster sounds. Kent sighed in relief when he saw they weren't headed toward our bikes.

"Gosh, darn, they make me so mad. That was almost a new ball," Frank said, looking at his ruined ball.

"I think we ought to go over to Highland Hardware, tell Mr. Lockhart what happened, and ask him to replace your basketball," Kent said.

"Well, it was his boy who ruined it. Okay, let's go," Frank said, and that surprised me, but I guess Kent's optimism was infectious.

We picked up our bikes, walked them over to the hardware, and asked to see Mr. Lockhart. He raised up to look down on us from his office. His office was on the little balcony at the rear of the store. That's where he had his desk and watched over the store. He came down to see what we wanted.

"What can I do for you, boys?"

Frank Varner launched into the explanation, showed him his ruined ball, and Kent added a couple of points. When they were all finished, we all said that was what happened. Frank asked him politely for a new ball.

Mr. Lockhart stared at Frank for a moment, then yelled, "You get out of here and don't come back!"

Then he turned to Roger. "Roger, you take these boys and get out of my store! I'm tired of the lies being told on my sons by the white trash of this town. Get out! And you better believe that your father will hear about this. It's time he took you in hand if he wants to keep his job."

Mr. Lockhart just stared at us all red in the face, and it gave me the creeps. We all turned and walked out of the store with as much dignity as we could muster. When we got outside and around the corner, we just looked at each other.

"I better get on home," Roger finally said. We all knew his dad was not going to be happy after the call from Mr. Lockhart. I feared Roger was going to get whacked. It might be as bad as my beating, which resulted in my scars.

"This is something," said Frank. "They knife my ball, and we get in trouble. This whole town is full of soda jerks."

Our group split up and headed in our respective directions. Skip, Barry, Kent, and I rode back to the hotel. Frank and Roger walked toward their homes.

"BB, we need to stick together," Skip said.

"Yeah, Kent and I have been sticking like glue since they jumped us and took our bikes. Did you notice that Lou wasn't with them? Kent and I think those two are the ones we better worry about. If we four stick together, we should be okay," I said with some confidence.

Barry then spoke up, "He pulled a knife. Maybe we better get some of our own," he looked at Skip to see what he would say.

Skip thought for a moment and responded, "Dad never thought carrying one was good. He told me once that they got you into more trouble than they got you out of." Skip patted his little brother on the shoulder to emphasize their dad's feelings on the subject.

"We better keep this quiet, or our parents won't let us ride our bikes," Kent said.

"Good idea, Superman," I readily agreed.

When we got back to Cubley's Coze, Mrs. Hathaway asked us how things went. We all four said, "Fine." No mention of the Lockharts or knives or anything.

Looking back on that day, my friends and I changed. Learning to be like adults wasn't easy at first, but it was necessary, and the more we did it, the easier it got.

CHAPTER 23

BILLY PLAYS IT SAFE
Tuesday, July 26, 1955

Tuesday was terrific, with a clear blue sky. As we rode our bikes to work, Kent and I talked about how we could get even with the Lockhart brothers for slashing Frank's basketball. But getting even would have to include replacing our friend's ball.

We were also worried about what Roger's dad might do to him. Both his uncle and Mr. Lockhart were sure to call Mr. Younger, and we feared a lousy outcome.

When we turned into the hotel entrance on our bikes, we saw Polecat ahead. We caught up to him at the crest, and we three quickly rode to the hotel and hid our three bikes behind the maintenance shed.

Skip was inside the kitchen door at the time clock when Mr. Cubley invited him to have a free breakfast before he started work. So, Skip joined our group on the loading dock. Mr. Cubley came onto the loading dock, but all the chairs were taken. Kent gave him his seat and brought out an extra. When Mr. Cubley thanked Kent, he called him Jack, but no one said anything. Our boss often called Kent by the name of his dead boy. Odd, but we were getting used to it.

Polecat immediately began telling us the big news.

"My compatriots, 'tis a certainty that Big John McCulloch has hired a new plant superintendent, a Mr. William Thomas Grant. He's the second son of L. F. Grant of Grant Furniture. The Grant family operates factories around Martinsville, and it's rumored that the other captains of industry were shocked by the news."

"Why a surprise, Mr. Smith?" inquired Mr. Cubley.

"My goodness, because of him being the son of L. F. Grant and leaving the family furniture business. He was a company vice president of sales. Henceforth, the Grants may refer to their second son as Benedict Arnold Grant," added Polecat with a wide grin.

"If that's the case, why did he come to work for the McCulloch family?" inquired Kent in a follow-up question. The same one I wanted to ask, but I had remained silent.

"Being the second son, he was forced to work for his older brother, the general manager of the corporate empire. Their dad, the president and CEO, favored the eldest son. It seems the brothers have never gotten along. Relations have recently grown worse because each wanted to expand sales in a different direction."

"Mr. Smith, once again, you astonish me. How do you know about the inside workings of a plant in Martinsville?" asked our boss.

"My sources are local plant workers, who have relatives working for Grant Furniture," ended Polecat with a pause as he lit a smoke, reared back in his seat, and blew a giant smoke ring that drifted slowly over the dock.

I watched the smoke ring and was convinced that Little John McCulloch would remain the chief of police. He was too proud to take a position as a mere plant supervisor under this outsider.

The conversation moved onto the topic of what the workers were thinking. Some of the workers were thankful, but many remained afraid that Little John, as the chief of police, could be more dangerous for everybody. Our muse of news wisely said, "Only time will tell."

Polecat excused himself to the kitchen, poured himself a second cup of coffee, and returned to his seat. There, he lit up a second Camel off the butt of the first.

"Mr. Smith, what kind of guy is this Grant fellow?" Matt asked, leaning forward and setting his empty plate on the dock.

"My good sir, speculation is rife regarding this new appointee. It is reported he's ruthless and is known for cutting costs on the backs of the workers. History shows that anyone who complains is fired on the spot." No one questioned Polecat's sources this time.

Mr. Cubley started to rise but stopped and settled back in his chair.

"Mr. Smith, what are your thoughts about how Mr. Grant will get along with Big John? I've heard of this William Grant but never met him. I did pick up one thing from a City of Martinsville officer I met on a case. Mr. Grant enjoys whiskey and rum. Thus, in college, he earned the nickname of "Wild Bill" Grant."

"Mr. Cubley, you have just added to my repertoire of information, for which I am most grateful. I shall depart, being in your debt."

Polecat drifted off to deliver his papers to the other resort. Skip went in search of Mr. Baker to get his first assignment. Mr. Cubley asked Kent and me to come to his office after finishing our pancakes and eggs.

We finished straight away because we thought our boss might need to leave for the courthouse, but we hurried for no reason. Today, he was working at the hotel.

We knocked, entered from the kitchen, and stood waiting. He motioned for us to have a seat.

"Billy, Kent, Judge Harland has appointed a special prosecutor from Amherst County to handle what the bullies did to you two. If he can gather enough evidence, he'll have Sheriff Lawrence issue arrest warrants for Carl, Dickie, and Lou."

Kent immediately spoke. "Can't you do it? Bend the rules for us, just this time?" He knew the answer but asked anyway.

"No. I told you I couldn't. I must recuse myself because you both work for me. Also, I'll call your parents and let them know. So, how have things been since you got your bikes back?" Mr. Cubley looked first at Kent and then at me.

"No problems," I said. "Lou has been okay." My statement was almost correct. I wasn't about to tell our boss why Lou had changed.

Kent spoke next. "Carl and Dickie are going after the other kids and may leave BB and me alone." He played down the bully problem because we had two more to help us—well, one Hathaway and a half, to be precise.

"If you have any problems, let me know. I'm here to help," Mr. Cubley said. I knew he meant it, but he was an adult, and they always made things worse.

"Sure, no problem," I said, and Kent followed up with something similar.

Mr. Cubley started talking, but at first, I wasn't sure if he was thinking aloud or talking to Kent and me.

"I was hoping local crime would slow down, but now we have the infamous Brown case to solve. Billy, I'm sure glad you were observant. We might have lost more evidence if you hadn't spotted those dogs. Thanks for being on the ball."

"Well, they were hard to miss. Come to think of it, I don't think Roy or the Lone Ranger ever found a hand to help solve a murder," I replied.

"Is it bothering you?" Mr. Cubley asked me.

"No. I'm okay. I just wish you could solve the Brown case. Do you have any leads?" Since he asked me about it, I figured I would try to get some useful information from our boss.

"Oh, so you want to be an investigator? How about you, Kent? Do you want in on this as well?"

"Yes, sir," Kent said right away, "Could we?"

"We could look for clues and stuff," I said.

"That's what I was afraid you boys might say. The answer is no."

We had walked into that one. Mr. Cubley wasn't finished, either.

"You have gotten into enough trouble because of your curiosity. You two stay away from crime scenes and suspects. No more detective work from either of you. Got it?" Mr. Cubley said and didn't smile.

"We didn't mean to get kidnapped or that other stuff. It wasn't our fault," Kent tried to argue.

Mr. Cubley surprised us with a laugh. "I know. Things come to you without you even trying. Just don't go looking for trouble. That's an order!"

"Yes, sir," we both said at the same time.

"Good! I'll hold you to it," Mr. Cubley announced.

I decided I would offer up one item we already knew. "Sir, if a person hears something, is it okay to pass it on to you?"

Mr. Cubley groaned, "Okay, what did you hear?"

"It's something strange about the Green Mountain Resort and the Highland Police Department."

"Okay, tell me."

"I was talking to a lady who works there. She said the Highland Police were making deliveries of heavy boxes to the hotel for special parties. They carry these boxes to the basement, which she thought was odd because most employees aren't allowed down there. It's like off-limits. I thought what she told me sounded strange. She also said she was afraid of some of the guests when they got drunk at those parties and acted rudely." I was going to finish, but Kent butted in.

"She's really nice, Mr. Cubley. I believe she's telling the truth," Kent said, adding his two cents' worth.

"Well, boys, I'll keep that in mind. You may let me know anything else you overhear by accident. But don't you go near the place, or your moms will skin me alive."

We both promised.

Mr. Cubley stood and stretched. "Now scoot. You have cars to wash."

"Yes, sir. We'll get right on them," I said, and Kent joined in with, "Anything we hear, we'll report, just like G-men."

We walked around to the wash area, where we found several cars waiting for us. Kent went to get the bucket, soap, and rags, while I hooked up the hose and checked for leaks.

I was sitting under the window, waiting for Kent to return with the supplies, when I heard Mr. Cubley on the phone.

"Sergeant Oliver, good morning. I need a favor. Would you have one of the men take that Indian Head Penny out to Mrs. Brown and ask her if it belonged to her husband? They're out of circulation and finding it strikes me as odd. Also, I talked to Kent and Billy this morning, and they found out from one of the Green Mountain workers that the Highland Police have been making deliveries of heavy boxes to the hotel for parties. Do you know why policemen would be doing that? Really…that is interesting. Any proof, or just gossip? Okay, let me know about the coin. You have a nice day."

Mr. Cubley hung up the phone as Kent came around the corner, banging the bucket. I filled him in on what I had just learned and whispered what might be in those boxes.

"I bet it's booze. That's why the guests were rude to Misty. The guests got drunk. Liquor can make even nice people mean," I said, all satisfied.

"Why have the police bring it? They could just have it delivered," Kent whispered.

"Because it's bootleg, dummy. It's illegal whiskey," I said.

"Cops don't haul bootleg. They pour it out. I saw it on TV. They do, don't they?" Kent said.

"Honest cops do. These Highland boys…it's bootleg," I said it almost without thinking.

But was I right? I suddenly wasn't sure!

"Kent, do you think I'm right?" I asked, needing convincing.

"We could ask Skip about it. His dad ran the stuff for that guy over in Waynesboro," Kent suggested.

"I don't know. It might be better not to ask him. Let's think about it first," I said, not wanting to make Skip mad or hurt his feelings. We needed him.

While we were washing our first car, I heard the rattling noise of the reel mower coming around the corner of the hotel. Skip was pushing it with his shirt off and was all sweaty. He had a hot job but seemed to be enjoying it. When he saw us, he waved.

I waved back and pointed to our hose. He came over and asked Kent to run the water over his head. Then, Skip held the hose to take a long drink by letting it run into the side of his mouth.

"Thanks, Superman. You guys working hard?" Skip asked.

"Not as hard as you," I replied.

"Yeah, Mr. Baker has me mowing, but it's not so bad. The pay is good. Mom needs it," Skip confided in us.

"Where's Barry today?" Kent asked.

"Oh, Mom farmed him out to a neighbor, but he has to help her with her kids. He's mad because I got the best deal," Skip said, laughing.

"I can believe that," I said, joining him with a chuckle. "Taking care of my brother Scotty would be my worst nightmare."

"Well, better get a move on. I don't want to get fired my first day," Skip joked as he started off with a rattle and a whirr.

The hotel was nearly full. Cars to wash kept Kent and me busy until late afternoon. Near quitting time, Kent and I heard the phone ring in Mr. Cubley's office.

"Sergeant, good to hear from you. What did you find out?" There was a pause, then I heard, "She did. So, the penny was his. How sure is she? Two Indian Head pennies? And he carried them as good luck charms—both the same date—finding the one is helpful, now we need to find its mate. What? There's a nick on each penny below the date. Indian Heads with nicks in the exact same place… better believe it."

We could hear papers rustling, and after a few moments, I heard Mr. Cubley. "I just checked. It was not on the body. We need to find who has the other one. This is fantastic news! Thanks. You, too." Mr. Cubley's chair creaked, and we heard him walk across the floor.

"You boys about finished up?" he asked us through the window.

"Yes, sir. We're almost done," Kent responded.

We finished up, put the hose away, and we both checked to be sure the spigot was turned off. Tight. No leaks.

We got our pay, rode our bikes down the hill toward Green Mountain Avenue, and caught up with Skip, who was walking home. We were just at the bridge, pushing our bikes while Skip walked beside us when Chief McCulloch passed us. We watched him turn into the Green Mountain Resort.

"Kent, let's go check it out," I suggested, despite having promised the opposite.

"I don't know," he replied.

"Where are you guys going?" asked Skip.

It was my idea, so I answered him. "We thought we would tail the chief. See what he's up to. We hear the cops have been making funny deliveries to the Green Mountain Hotel."

"Don't you do it!" Skip cautioned, frowning.

"Why not? We're just gonna take a quick peek," I replied.

"Listen, if it's the delivery I think it is, you stay clear. Spying on their deliveries might get you killed. Leave it be!"

"How do you know?" Kent asked, and I was afraid he had just pushed it over the line.

Skip gave him a stern look.

"BB, Kent, you know how I know. Don't ask! It could cost my dad his life. Swear you won't say nothing?" Skip was waiting for an answer.

"I swear. I won't say nothing," Kent said, holding up his right hand just like Mr. Cubley had taught us.

"Skip, I won't tell anyone, but what if it gets out? We heard it from someone else. Gossip gets spread in this town quicker than jam on bread," I warned as we began walking toward home.

"Just as long as it doesn't get back to certain people that it's my dad or his family doing the blabbing, it's okay. Being in prison, he wouldn't last a day," Skip ended with a sigh, stopping at the turn to his house.

"We'll keep quiet. You can trust us," Kent promised as Skip walked toward his house.

We hopped on our bikes and rode down to the turn to Kent's house, where we stopped once again to talk.

"BB, did we lie to Skip? We told him we wouldn't tell, but we already told Mr. Cubley," Kent asked me.

"Superman, we didn't lie. We ain't gonna tell what Skip told us. We told what Misty told us. That makes it okay. We just gotta be careful that we don't get Misty in trouble. They might hurt her," I explained.

"BB, this is starting to get too confusing. What goes on in this town is bad enough, but now, trying to keep track of all the secrets that need to be secret is giving me a headache. Roy and the boys never had this kind of trouble," announced Kent.

"They did too. Don't you remember the show with the little girl who had the funny name of Toss Up? She had to keep quiet about the secret gold mine. But Roy finally got the two feuding families back together, and that little girl, Toss Up, no longer had to keep the mine a secret from half her relatives," I reminded Kent.

"But BB, I don't think these bootleggers are ever going to be friends with each other, like Toss Up's relatives," Kent said with a frown.

"Well, Roy Rogers did have it easier. Toss Up was related to both families, and they both loved her. Here, I don't think the McCullochs have much love for anyone. I think Skip is right. If certain people think Mr. Hathaway is talking, they just might kill him," I stated in a low voice.

"Nobody won't hear nothing from me...see ya," Kent shouted, and pulled a wheelie on his bike, headed towards home.

I walked my bike home because I needed some time to think. How were two kids gonna get the goods on a bootlegger's gang and the McCulloch family when saying the wrong thing could get someone killed? I started to think about all the scrapes Kent and I could get into and decided it was better to leave the dangerous stuff to Mr. Cubley, the sheriff, and the local troopers. Kent and I needed to play it safe. How could we get into scrapes if we played it safe?

CHAPTER 24

SILENCE, NOT GOLDEN
Wednesday, July 27, 1955

R ichard Baker and Matt drove to the hunting lodge to take the professor's party fresh provisions and remove the trash. The morning drive was more enjoyable when they spied a doe and two spotted fawns in the bushes beside the road. First, the fawns froze in place, giving the men a close-up view. Then, the doe ran up the road for a distance as a diversion.

Arriving at the lodge, Matt learned that the professor and his two graduate students were off collecting samples of ferns, but the professor's wife and children were enjoying a game of croquet in front of the lodge. Matt noticed the sniper's bloodstains were only slightly visible on the front porch, and only if one knew where to look. He avoided the topic, and Mrs. Hartford didn't ask or complain. He hoped the stains would remain unnoticed, and it appeared all was peaceful on Green Mountain.

The trip back to the hotel was also uneventful. The two men were silent, each lost in personal thoughts. Matt retired to his office and was looking over some hotel invoices when the phone rang. Chuck informed him that it was the medical examiner.

"Dr. Hill, good morning. Any new information on the Brown matter?" Matt pulled the case file out of his briefcase and grabbed a pen and legal pad to take notes.

"Mr. Cubley, I'm afraid I don't have much to add. Richmond sent me their final report, and after studying it, here is what I concluded. The date of death was sometime on the eleventh of July or perhaps the twelfth. My preliminary finding matched the full autopsy report, confirming that the body was supine for at least an hour, based on the pooled blood posteriorly."

Matt, being curious, asked about the missing ulna bone.

Doc Hill gave a short answer. "Not important."

"No evidence value at all?" asked Matt.

"Animal gnaw marks were evident at the point of detachment of the proximal portion of the hand, both ends of the radius, and the distal end of the humerus. Unfortunately, I have always found it difficult to get animals to testify."

Matt wasn't sure if the doctor was attempting a joke or just being Doc Hill. He let it pass.

The doctor did add one item of information. "Insects were present, which aided in determining the time of death."

"Doc, any idea how far the body may have been transported in the car? If we knew the distance, that would be helpful," asked Matt.

"No way to tell. We know how long it was horizontal, and that's it," replied the doctor. "I do know the body was finally propped up in the car, and the car went over the edge into the creek. I'm sure of that point because that's how we found it, and the body had some injuries that occurred after death. There were blunt force trauma injuries to the face and anterior torso, most probably caused when the vehicle crashed nose-first into the creek. Richmond and I noted tissue damage where the corpse hit the steering wheel and windshield with great force."

"Anything more on the gun?"

"Three bullets were recovered from the brain. Two were intact. They have good striations, which will be useful if we find the gun. One bullet was fragmented, nearly useless for comparison purposes. All three are thirty-eight calibers. The firearms expert suspects these rounds were loaded by hand and not commercially purchased. That part of his report is a probable determination, not conclusive."

"Thanks, doctor. That helps. Oh, any indication if alcohol was involved?" Matt asked, drawing on what information Billy and Kent had provided about parties at Green Mountain Resort.

"Advanced decomposition ruled out a determination of ingested alcohol in the body. The toxicology screen for other drugs was negative. You should receive the toxicology report in the mail," concluded Dr. Hill.

The doctor immediately hung up, and Matt was left with his thoughts. He rewrote his notes, called the sheriff and the state police sergeant, and filled them in on Dr. Hill's call. He also brought up the topic of the party room at the Green Mountain Resort. Both officers had heard rumors of such a place, but neither had any concrete evidence that it existed.

Matt took a chance and suggested, "Gentlemen, let's go talk to Big John McCulloch about the party room."

The sheriff laughed. "Waste of time."

Sergeant Oliver indicated, "Big John will never admit such a place exists."

Matt insisted that the question be asked if only to get the man's negative response.

The sheriff firmly declined. However, Sergeant Oliver gave in and reluctantly said he would inquire.

Matt had been thinking about Polecat's comment regarding Doc Hathaway. Should he approach Doc about the Brown murder? Matt finally decided he would ask Doc's wife, Karen.

Matt found Mrs. Hathaway in the kitchen and asked her to step into his office. When they were settled, and he was sure the window and passthrough were closed, he began cautiously.

"Mrs. Hathaway, how are things going in the dining room?"

"I'm trying to master it. Have there been complaints, Mr. Cubley?"

"Oh, no. I'm hearing things are progressing nicely. No, I didn't ask you here because there was a problem. I was curious about how you and Skip were making out working here. Is there anything I can do to help? Anything to help you fit in? Our little hotel is like a family."

"No. Everything's fine. I'm so thankful my family's back together. Well, at least most of it, anyway."

This last comment gave Matt the "in" he was hoping to get. He jumped on the implied reference to Doc with his next question.

"I can only imagine how hard it is being separated from your husband. How is Doc?" Matt asked, trying to be concerned but not overly nosey.

"My Doc is tough. He'll do what he must. I just wish his sentence could be over soon. Trooper Giles is trying to clear him from the phony embezzlement charge, but my husband will have to pull his time for running that load of liquor and smashing up a patrol car."

"Does Doc ever talk about who he ran the liquor for?" Matt asked and waited for a response from Doc's wife.

"Mr. Cubley, everyone knows who he worked for. I expect half the state knows, but he won't tell, and I never asked."

"Too dangerous?" Matt asked, knowing what her answer would be.

"He always kept the boys and me out of it. Those men would not hesitate to hurt us if Doc so much as breathed a word about that operation."

"Would Doc ever consider talking to someone? Not about the liquor, but maybe about something else?" Matt was intentionally vague, but he knew Mrs. Hathaway was afraid of where this conversation was going.

"Mr. Cubley, I appreciate your current position, but I can't risk my boys. It's just too dangerous. So if this is going to mean my job with the hotel, I'll get Skip, and we'll leave right now."

"No. No! Mrs. Hathaway, I would never dream of putting you, your husband, and especially your boys in danger. Forget I asked, and forgive me for bringing it up."

When Mrs. Hathaway left his office, he reassured her again that her job was safe. Matt felt terrible about putting the lady on the spot, even though Doc might have information helpful to the Commonwealth.

Trooper Quinn had previously gotten nowhere with Doc. Matt now knew he should have listened to Polecat. His informant told him that while Doc was in prison, he would never talk. Even when Doc was released from prison, his lips still might remain sealed.

Late in the afternoon, Matt heard a knock on his office door. Chuck stuck his head in to announce Sergeant Oliver. Matt invited the sergeant to have a seat.

"Matt, this won't take but a minute. I went by to see Big John. I politely asked him about certain rumors of a party room at the Green Mountain Resort. I suggested that Albert Winston Brown may have been shot there, and the body moved to prevent him from finding out."

"How did your diplomacy work?" Matt asked, expecting the worst. He was not disappointed.

"Big John told me I needed to try working on facts and stop chasing gossip. He assured me there was no party room at his resort, and Albert Winston Brown was nowhere near Green Mountain Resort the day he went missing. He told his wife to see me out with some quite colorful language."

"Sergeant, this case is turning ice cold. Doc remains silent, and based on what I now know, he'll remain that way. Us putting pressure on him might only get him killed or put his family in jeopardy. The autopsy and firearms reports aren't much help unless we find the gun. If there are any witnesses other than the killer or killers, I'm not hopeful they'll talk. So, what do we do now?"

"I don't know," said the sergeant, and that was the end of the discussion. Sergeant Oliver left the hotel, signed off duty, and went home. Matt closed the file and put it back in the old leather briefcase his Uncle TJ had left him.

Matt walked into the kitchen to check on things. He had a conversation with Boo and Mrs. Hathaway over the dinner count. Mrs. Johnson told him what she planned for tomorrow's menu.

Things seemed normal between himself and all his staff, even Mrs. Hathaway. He decided his best course of action was to proceed as if their afternoon conversation had never happened.

Billy and Kent had come and gone. Those two were now the center of much of this town's gossip. He wanted to help them with their bullying problem, but like the Brown case, all his pathways were blocked.

Just when Matt thought things were at a low point, Carol Martin and Linda Carlisle came into the lobby laughing about some man. Matt hoped this wasn't about him. He tried to listen without appearing to listen, but Carol caught him.

"Matthew, are you eavesdropping on our private conversation?" Carol asked Matt with a sly grin.

"What? No. What were you saying?" Matt responded, trying to cover himself.

Linda smiled and added, "We were talking about men—one in particular. I was telling Carol what a fool he made of himself today."

Linda gave Matt a smile that always grabbed his attention. Matt knew he hadn't been in the judge's office today, so he was safe this time.

"What did this gentleman do?" Matt asked Linda.

"An out-of-town attorney came in to file a brief. That man lingered and kept staring at me. When he left, he looked back, a long look, not paying any attention to where he was walking. He took a fall down the stairs. Luckily, he wasn't seriously hurt. More bruised ego than anything." Linda gave Carol a glance and a wink. They both started laughing.

"It's good to know that present company would never do anything like that. Right?" Carol said and smiled at Linda.

"Yeah, right. Thanks," Matt said and suddenly realized he was staring at Linda; he blushed and looked away at the wall, bringing more laughter from the ladies.

"Why, Mr. Cubley, are you in danger of being a victim of a tumble?" asked Carol, which caused Linda to break up.

Matt responded and joined in the fun. "Uh, why no. No stairs in the vicinity, but I might as well admit to admiring the view. One might fall victim to you two beautiful ladies in more ways than one," countered Matt, and this caused all three to start laughing.

Boo peeked into the lobby to see what was causing all the merriment. She looked confused until she saw who the three were. Chuck, however, gave the three a frown since he tried to maintain a quiet lobby. He would have been a perfect librarian.

Matt's depression evaporated like fog in the sunshine. He seated the ladies in the dining room and, upon their request, joined them for supper. The problems of the day were forgotten. They conversed with no thought of time, and they were among the final guests to leave the dining room.

The only argument that evening was over who would pay. Each insisted, but Matt finally won by merely canceling the bill for the table. Of course, he would pay it later, but as far as his guests knew, there was no bill.

Matt got a goodbye hug from each of the ladies, which brought another blush to his face. Linda suddenly leaned over and kissed him on the cheek. She whispered, "I believe you are blushing, Mr. Cubley."

Thankfully, he escorted them to Carol's car without a mishap as they descended the veranda steps.

Returning to the lobby, Chuck and Matt went over the day's receipts until Cliff Duffy came on duty. Upon concluding the bookwork, Matt and Chuck went up to Matt's apartment for a nightcap of Scotch. While sipping their drinks, they discussed a problem that Rose was having with one of her new maids. Both men decided to let Rose handle it, and Chuck retired to his apartment, drink in hand.

The hotel finally settled down for the night. All the guests had retired for the evening. Matt had just downed his last dram of Scotch when he thought of something.

Doc might not be of any help, but there was Angus MacDonald, the man who had reported his truck stolen. The locals knew that Doc had been hired to drive bootleg for Angus. He took the fall for auto theft to clear his boss of any blame for the liquor charge. Perhaps it was time to put a tail on MacDonald's truck. It wouldn't be easy. The last time they tried to follow his hooch truck, it outran everyone except Trooper Giles. Both vehicles ended up on the scrap heap. But secretly following the bootlegger's man on deliveries might turn up something. If nothing else, it would provide the police with information on the local illegal-whiskey business.

Matt decided he would talk to Sergeant Oliver about how best to track MacDonald's shipments. It would have to be done without the driver knowing he was being followed, which would be very difficult. But finding out about the bootleg operation might result in some leads on the Brown murder. Polecat thought there was a connection, and his informer was usually right.

Matt went to bed and quickly fell asleep, but he had a bad dream starring Doc Hathaway. When Matt finally drifted off, another nightmare involving Big John woke him. He decided to refrain from bedtime Scotch.

It was close to four in the morning before he finally settled into a troubled sleep. He would find out the following day that he was not the only one having a bad night.

CHAPTER 25

FRANKLIN COUNTY SHINE
Thursday, July 28, 1955

M att decided he needed to relax. Distressing dreams the previous night had left him tired and irritable, but the end of the month was upon him. There were financial items he had to complete so Chuck could close the books for July.

To help his mood, he decided to enjoy his breakfast on the loading dock with Polecat, Billy, and Jack…Kent.

Why do I keep doing that? He scolded himself.

Matt had just settled down on the dock with his food when Billy, Kent, and Polecat rode up on their bikes. The three arrivals trooped into the kitchen and returned with breakfast plates of omelets, fried ham, hash browns, and grits to match what Matt was enjoying.

"Mr. Smith, what's happening in town?" Matt asked between bites. While Matt stopped eating to talk, Polecat was not so inclined.

"Chief McCulloch has filled the ranks of his department. His new sergeant is, of course, Frank Younger."

A large spoonful of omelet went into Polecat's mouth, but he continued his discourse.

"Frank's brother, Roger, remains on the day shift. There was consternation by the Highland Town Council when the last chief didn't fire Roger after the bills for the two patrol cars he recently damaged were submitted. Shooting through the fender of one's own patrol car was considered unpardonable by the town fathers when that damage followed the backing of his cruiser into a tree," reported Polecat as Billy and Kent broke out laughing.

Billy blurted out, "Mr. Smith, I think the patrol car's bumper is still at the base of that tree. I saw it there when Dad and I towed in the stolen car that Officer Younger had been chasing."

"Master Gunn, may I continue with my revelations?" Polecat then stabbed half a slice of ham, deftly snatched it off the tip of the knife with his teeth, and chewed.

"Sure, sorry," Billy said as a blush rose from his neck to his forehead.

"Where was I? Oh, yes. Officer Zeke Barnes, Ed Barnes' cousin, has been moved to the day shift, and he should provide some refreshing fairness and justice within the ranks of the scoundrels, rogues, and miscreants that the town fathers call the Highland Police Department."

After the group discussed Little John's hiring policies, Polecat was first to finish his meal, arose, and took his empty plate into the kitchen. There, he handed his dishes to a waitress who gave them to Toby the Cleaner at his washing station.

Seeing the paper man was finished, Maddie called out, "You boys, hurry up. I need them dishes. We hain't got's all day. Stop your prattling and eat up."

She was letting everyone know who presided over this part of the hotel. However, in direct contradiction to acting like "the boss," Maddie Johnson was speaking like a dollar-a-day field hand when she could teach English or French at any national university. Maddie was being, well, Maddie.

The other three finished quickly and rose as one to take their empty plates into the kitchen. However, they returned to the dock with fresh coffee or juice, suspecting Polecat had more news.

Their informant had returned to his seat and began again as soon as everyone was present. "One of the plant guards was hired for the day shift. His name is Oscar Little, and he is one very dangerous bloke. Never let him get behind you," warned Polecat.

"Is this personal knowledge?" asked Matt.

"No, but I was told on good authority. Now gentlemen, prick up your ears for this next bulletin. Officer Roscoe Taylor has finally escaped his jailor's job, the one he was so bad at performing. Sheriff Lawrence is glad to see him depart, and it's reported that when the prisoners heard the news, a celebration erupted. However, woe be to future town drunks because Chief McCulloch placed Taylor on the night shift," Polecat reported with a yellow-toothed grin to punctuate his report.

Matt announced his displeasure. "This sounds like the members of the Highland Police Department, except for Zeke

Barnes, are going to be one sorry bunch. Is there any good news other than Zeke's promotion?"

Matt was concerned about how this bunch would affect the community and his job as the temporary Commonwealth's Attorney. It did not look good for anyone.

Polecat confirmed his fears with his next statement. "Alas, poor Yorick, I fear that what I tell you next will not bring you cheer. The appointment that fills the last slot on the roster of vacancies goes to Tommy Reynolds, age twenty. He just flunked out of Lynchburg College after one semester of only attending a portion of his classes."

"Just great," lamented Matt.

"Alas, it gets better. His fellow officers are teasing him because he bought a Colt 357 magnum with a six-inch barrel to carry as his service revolver. He also purchased a gun belt and holster that looks like something a cowboy would wear to a gunfight."

"Does it have places for extra bullets?" asked Kent.

"Young sir, mind your elders and be silent," Polecat warned and made a shushing noise. Then he told them, "The first-time young Reynolds shot the gun, he learned the definition of the word *recoil*. The powerful weapon flew backward, and now he has a goose egg on his forehead. He's lucky to be alive, according to several of the sheriff's deputies who saw the incident."

Polecat was most amused. He was snorting and showing his full set of yellowed teeth for a second time. Then, his news report done, he immediately made this request. "Mr. Cubley, I'm in dire need of two dollars until payday next. I shall happily reimburse you with interest on that date."

Matt pulled eight quarters out of the pocket where he kept his stash of coins dedicated to fulfilling Polecat's loan requests. He knew repayment would never happen.

The newscast having ended, all the silver pieces paid, Polecat departed, smoking a Camel. Off he rode on his bike with smoke trailing him as if from a railroad steam engine.

Matt sent the boys off to work and retired to his office to complete his part of the books. He had enjoyed thirty minutes to himself when Chuck knocked.

"Matthew, there's a Henry Watkins here to see you. He's the special prosecutor from Amherst," Chuck informed Matt.

Matt closed his work, rose, and walked to the door to greet the visitor.

"Mr. Watkins, Matt Cubley, come in and have a seat. Would you like some coffee or tea?" Matt asked the middle-aged man.

"Coffee would be nice. This is one fine office for a prosecutor. My office is a lot smaller with no hotel amenities," remarked Mr. Watkins with a smile.

Matt asked Teresa Long if she would bring in a service of coffee for two. Henry and Matt got on a first-name basis and shared small talk while waiting for the coffee. When Teresa delivered it, Matt noticed Henry sat up a little straighter in his chair and tried to watch the pretty waitress without appearing to do so. When Teresa left the office and closed the door, Matt didn't comment on Henry's longing stare as she left the room.

"Henry, what news?" Matt asked after the two had taken a sip of coffee.

"Not what you want to hear, I'm afraid. I interviewed Lou McCulloch and the two Lockhart brothers. Lou refused to speak to me on the advice of his father. The Lockhart boys talked but said they were at work and never saw Billy or Kent that day. I know they're lying. Their statements sounded like a couple of low-grade actors reading lines to audition for a play. I believe Kent Clark and Billy Gunn, but this case has turned into a he-said versus he-said case," reported Henry.

"Didn't the two young ladies from the drugstore help?" Matt asked.

"Laura Akers saw Lou grab Dickie by the arm and push him back out the drugstore door as soon as they entered. Carl was behind the first two, and when they backed out the door, they pushed Carl backward. Judy Peterson missed seeing some of it because she was facing away from the door. She is sure that she heard Carl yell, 'stupid' and 'big butt.'" Henry paused, and it looked like he might be finished because he settled back in his seat and took several sips of coffee.

Matt spoke up with his thoughts. "Well, the two girls prove that the bullies were present. That evidence should support Kent and Billy's version, but will you place a charge?"

"If it ended there, I might try it on for size. However, I spoke to the parents of the three boys. Guess what they said?"

"Henry, are you telling me they covered for them?" asked Matt with a sick feeling.

"Yes, and there's more. I asked Chief McCulloch if he would please ask Lou to tell me the truth. In exchange, I would be lenient on his boy. The chief refused. He told me Lou spent the afternoon with his grandfather. I went over and got five minutes with Mr. McCulloch, the one they call Big John. That old man verified Lou was with him from noon until suppertime."

Matt banged his fist on the desk so hard some of his coffee splashed out. "That lying, arrogant sack of manure. That boy was no more at his house that afternoon than I was," exclaimed Matt, approaching his boiling point.

"Matt, it gets much worse. I spoke to Richard Lockhart, who not only told me his two boys worked in the hardware all afternoon but even showed me their timecards. He had them ready before I arrived or asked for them. He hand-wrote those timecards, claiming the hardware time clock was temporarily out of service. I can't take this case to a judge with these two pillars of the community being star witnesses for the defense. I feel like I've let you down, but what can I do?" asked Henry.

"You aren't letting me down. Certain adults are letting down Billy and Jack...K-Kent," Matt responded, stuttering over Kent's name. "Those fathers are letting everyone down, including their sons!"

"I know, so true," responded the prosecutor from Amherst.

"All right, how about Lou hitting Billy in the head with a baseball bat at the Fourth of July Celebration? A son of one of the Highland Police Officers saw it," Matt said, changing the subject to the older attack on Billy.

"Well, again, Lou refused to talk to me. Billy gave me a clear account of what happened, and I read over the doctor's report from the hospital. It matches Billy's version."

"So far, so good," muttered Matt.

"What was weird, when I spoke to Roger Younger, his dad insisted on being present. I told his dad that Roger Junior was a witness and in no danger of getting into trouble. It made no difference."

"The boy's dad works for Big John, through and through," exclaimed Matt.

"Matt, young Roger kept glancing at his dad after each answer. The boy said he saw Billy and Lou in the distance near the bleachers, but he looked away at a barking dog. When he turned back, Billy and Lou were on the ground some distance from each other. Two boys that he had never seen before were beating on Lou."

"That's not what he told John and Laura Gunn right after it happened. He said he saw Lou rush Billy and hit him with a baseball bat," Matt indicated.

Henry frowned. "Matt, I went back to Billy. I asked him who those two other boys were in the fight, but he wouldn't tell me. He apologized but said he didn't want them to get into trouble."

Silence hung over the room. Matt was now on the horns of a dilemma himself. He knew with the state of affairs in Highland, if Little John McCulloch or Richard Lockhart found out about Skip and Barry, not only might those boys be harmed for trying to do a good deed, but their father could pay an even higher price. Matt decided to remain silent. He felt guilty because he was now no better than the rest of the liars in this town. He was lost in thought when Henry startled him.

"Matt, when I reported lies blocked this case, Mrs. Clark reacted as I expected. She was furious. The lady was civil, but I knew she was on the verge of an explosion. When I told Billy's family, his grandma started yelling all kinds of crazy stuff about dogs and killers and leaving town on the next train. Billy's mom had to take her out of the room, and Billy's mom looked as mad as Mrs. Clark. Then, the strangest thing happened," Henry paused and took another sip.

"What? So far, that's what I expected," stated Matt with a curious look. Under the surface, he was glad Henry was off the subject of Skip and Barry.

"No, Billy's dad, John Gunn, surprised me. He took it like he didn't care. Like prosecuting those three, who had attacked his son and stolen his boy's bike, didn't matter to him one way or the other.

He was gracious, thanked me for my efforts, showed no emotion, and walked me to my car."

"Henry, you know the boys got their bikes back. No one knows how or by whom, but they got them back. I think John got them back...somehow, but he's as silent as the Sphinx on that subject."

Matt also told Henry that when the hardware was burglarized, John Gunn and his whole family were with him at the hotel all evening. "Henry, over twenty witnesses will swear to his alibi. He may know who retrieved the bikes, but for sure, it wasn't him!"

Matt and Henry talked for a few minutes more about how best to tell Kent and Billy that no charges would be filed. Then, Matt went out to the wash area and brought the two boys into the office. The window had been closed during his meeting with Henry; thus, the outcome of the investigation was news to the boys. They also took it better than Henry or Matt expected. They either knew more than they were revealing or because they had gotten their bikes returned, the prosecution of the bullies was no longer very important.

When it came to the Fourth of July attack on Billy, he was too calm about the case not going forward. He gave Matt a glance that confirmed to Matt that Billy was not going to tell Mr. Watkins about Skip and Barry Hathaway. If Mr. Watkins didn't talk to Trooper Giles, the secret would remain a secret.

Billy spoke up toward the end of the meeting, "Mr. Watkins, sir, kids getting into scrapes with other kids is not unusual in this town, that's for sure. Us kids know we have to look out for each other and leave the adults out of it."

Kent and Billy thanked Mr. Watkins for trying to help them. Then, the two boys left and went back to work.

"Matt, I guess that's it. I'll close out these cases and go back to Amherst. You have a strange town here. I'm glad I'm in Amherst, not here. Good luck handling your new job. You'll need it," Henry said and meant it. He wasted no time in departing. He wanted to write his report for the judge and put these cases behind him.

Matt returned to his hotel paperwork but felt uncomfortable about what he had not revealed during his conversation with Henry

Watkins. He was just getting back into the hotel's financials when Chuck interrupted him again with a knock.

"Sorry, Matt, you have another visitor. Shoat Lincoln is here to see you. He says it's urgent, or I wouldn't have bothered you."

"Chuck, I think I've done all I can with these figures. I'm giving up. Look them over, and if I need to work on them some more, give them back. Tell Shoat to come on in," Matt said, trying to keep the exasperation out of his voice.

"Mr. Cubley, I'm so sorry to bother you," said Deputy Lincoln, coming into Matt's office.

"Shoat, if you call me Mr. Cubley one more time, I might have to throw you right out of my office window. So, unless we're in court, call me Matt."

"Okay, Matt. I'm still sorry to bother you," said the deputy.

"What can I help you with?" asked Matt, noticing blood on the deputy's uniform.

"I was on graveyard last night and ran into something near the plant. I spotted a car half on, half off the road, and stuck in a ditch. I checked it and found the driver had been shot in the shoulder. He was bleeding and in a lot of pain, but he should live. After the Koehler ambulance took him to the Waynesboro Hospital, I grilled him for an hour. However, he won't tell me who shot him or why. He refused to give me his name, so I drove over to the impound lot, searched, and found the car's registration. The car belongs to a Jenkins Landon Perry," reported Shoat.

"May I see that registration?" asked Matt.

Shoat handed Matt the registration. Matt looked it over, and when he read the address, he responded with, "Well, well, well. This is interesting. Do you know who this is?" Matt asked Shoat.

"I have no idea."

"Jenkins Landon Perry is one of the biggest bootleggers in Franklin County. What age is the guy you found shot?" Matt asked, handing back the registration to the deputy.

"Young fellow. Mid-twenties or so. He had a scar over one eye and dark hair. Slim, and he looked like a hard case to me."

"Sounds to me like Sam Perry, Jenkins' boy. His boy getting shot way up here in Green Mountain County isn't good. Was there liquor in the car?" asked Matt.

"No, but that car was rigged out to run shine. It had a beefed-up suspension and a souped-up motor, but not a drop of whiskey anywhere," answered Shoat.

"Well, if he was here, it was about moonshine," Matt said with the voice of authority.

"How do you know the Perry family?" asked Shoat.

"Everyone in the Roanoke Commonwealth's Attorney's office knows them. They live near Ferrum on Shoot'n Creek. The family runs five stills all the time and hauls their own liquor. If you aren't family, you don't get near their operation or deliver their moonshine. Using only family has kept them out of prison. We tried and tried to catch them when I worked in the Roanoke prosecutor's office, but they beat us at every turn. It's unusual for them to run their moonshine this far north. They sell all they can make around Roanoke, Blacksburg, Martinsville, and Danville. I'm not sure what's with him being here." Matt concluded without any reasonable explanation coming to mind.

"I know it's a trooper's case…but if you can tell me…who was Doc Hathaway working for?" asked Shoat.

"We suspect Doc was working for Angus MacDonald as a new hire, a 'pickup' driver. It was MacDonald's truck hauling the liquor. The old fox reported it stolen, and Doc took the fall for auto larceny."

"You mean a 'pickup' driver like he drove pickup trucks?" asked Shoat

"No, I mean a temporary driver or driver who is paid by the run and will take a fall for his boss if caught. Everyone knows that Angus doesn't make the liquor. No, he just delivers it."

"For whom?"

"There are several still owners that might supply Angus. My guess is he was running shine for the Woody family. They're also from Franklin County, but they hire anyone to haul for them. And they supply customers clear to Harrisonburg," concluded Matt, and it was becoming clear that Matt knew about this business.

"You went after both families when you were in Roanoke?" Shoat asked Matt.

"Sure did. The Woody and Perry families supply a lot of liquor to Roanoke and all the cities and towns in that part of the state. We traced big shipments of sugar to these families. A grocery store in Ferrum buys a boxcar load of sugar every other month. This little grocery sells more sugar than some of the big chains. If they gave Green Stamps for sugar, there would be more toasters in Franklin County than the rest of the state combined," Matt laughed.

"How much liquor would come from a boxcar load of sugar?"

"Shoat, I bet you could float a battleship in the liquor that comes out of Franklin County in one year. Most of the shine is good stuff. There's only a small amount from small still operators that's of poor quality. The bad shine can eat a hole right through the steel plates of that floating battleship. I know of a few citizens who bought the bad stuff, and it ate up their stomachs—several went blind."

"What quality would Perry and Woody make?" asked Shoat

"Those two families have a reputation for only making good-grade whiskey. I know the stuff Doc had in his truck was very high quality, blue flame stuff. Sergeant Oliver lit some off. It must have come from the Woody bunch because Angus MacDonald would never be allowed to haul Perry shine. He's not family."

"I've heard about how you can burn good hooch and get a blue flame. I wonder what Sam Perry was doing up here to get himself shot?" asked Shoat.

"I wish I knew. I really do," Matt said, glancing out his office window.

After promising to keep Matt up to date, Shoat left, and things got quiet again. It was after four when Matt decided he would stroll outside for a short walk around the grounds.

Walking through the kitchen, he was going to leave by the back door to pick up a hiking trail in the woods when Maddie called to him from behind the counter. She was seated in a chair, which was strange because Maddie was always on the move in the kitchen.

"Mr. Cubley, may I talk with you,' said the chief cook.

"Yes, of course. Would you like to talk to me here or in my office?" responded Matt.

"Your office, please," said Maddie.

When they got into the office, it was clear to Matt that Maddie was distraught over something. When he asked her what was wrong, she began in French, stopped, and began again in English.

"Mr. Cubley, I hate to bother you with this, but my pastor, Tobias Helms, was arrested and is in jail. From reliable accounts, he's hurt seriously."

Maddie was using refined English, which was not normal for her. She was wringing a dishtowel with her hands and moving slightly backward and forward in her seat.

"I'm sorry to hear it. Do you know why he was arrested?" Matt asked, needing more information.

"I do! McCulloch Wood Products began hiring back workers to clean up the mess from the big fire. They put up posters downtown signed by the new plant superintendent, Mr. William Grant. At the bottom, it said, 'no coloreds need to apply.' Pastor Helms went out to the plant to talk to Mr. Grant.

Maddie paused, so Matt asked, "What happened?"

"The plant has recently hired security guards from the James Baldwin Detective Agency. Virginia coal mine owners used the same agency during the coal strike of April of '46. Many of the miners were killed or injured during that strike." Maddie paused again.

Matt decided to coax more from her. "Yes, ma'am. I read about those guards and that company during the mine strike. I'm surprised that Big John would hire them. What happened to your pastor?"

"The guards refused to let Pastor Helms in to see Mr. Grant. When he insisted, they set upon him with ax handles. He was taken to jail, unconscious. The congregation is worried those guards might have killed him." Maddie broke into sobs.

Matt immediately called Sheriff Lawrence at home. The sheriff came right on the line and told Matt when Pastor Helms was checked into the jail by Chief McCulloch, his head jailer called him. A short conversation ensued between Matt and the sheriff, with the sheriff doing the talking.

Matt hung up and reported to Maddie that Doc Hill had treated her pastor on orders of the sheriff. Pastor Helms had stitches over one eye, a broken arm, and bruised ribs. He was currently resting in a cell by himself and was being checked on four times an hour. He was hurt but alive.

"Maddie, I have court in the morning, and I'll investigate this to find out what happened," promised Matt to his chief cook.

"Matthew, I thank you. I'll get on the phone to some deacons to spread the word that Pastor Helms is alive. The congregation will be relieved to know he's been treated. Thank goodness Sheriff Lawrence is a Christian man," responded Maddie with relief, at which point she smiled at Matt. Then, rising, she went back to the kitchen, an abnormally quiet kitchen.

Matt was thinking today was just full of news and surprises.

Big John had hired some private guards for the factory. Matt wasn't surprised that a much better security force had been employed to protect the plant. But these guards were adding to the town's problems.

To make matters worse, one race was being excluded. He knew this detective agency had supplied guards to break up the union strike and guard the mines. The miners called these guards "bulls." Many a miner had suffered a broken head at the hands of these brutes. A few had died from the beatings. Ax handles were their trademark, with shotguns close at hand.

Matt got a light supper from the kitchen and took it to his room. He was going to turn in early because tomorrow would be a challenge. Matt was wrong. It was going to be much worse.

CHAPTER 26

A PASTOR'S TRIALS
Friday, July 29, 1955

M att awoke to Uncle TJ's windup alarm clock that he had set for six o'clock. Getting an early start to finish the end of the month's payroll would allow him time for Polecat and get to court.

Coming into the kitchen after checking the payroll sheets, Maddie greeted Matt with a bright smile. She handed him a plate overloaded with two eggs over easy, four pancakes, a biscuit with sausage gravy, and a bowl of fresh fruit. He made his way out to the loading dock and carefully placed his dishes on the seat of one of the chairs. Before he could return to the kitchen, Boo came out with fresh-squeezed orange juice and a mug of coffee, fixed the way he liked it.

"Boo, tell Mrs. Johnson this isn't necessary, and it's illegal to bribe a prosecutor. She's in danger of eroding my prosecutorial independence," Matt joked.

"Sir, I told her she might be joining Pastor Helms in the calaboose, but when she's in her kitchen, Mrs. Johnson rules, her decisions are final, and there are no appeals. If you would like to file a formal complaint, I'll see if she'll grant you an audience. I wouldn't hold my breath because Madam Maddie is busy," Boo joked.

Polecat arrived next, followed by Billy and Kent. When the other three were settled and enjoying their food, Matt inquired if Polecat knew something of the arrest of Pastor Helms.

Mr. Smith sat up straight and began as if addressing a university class. "A front-page story has been censored into obscurity by my editor. A travesty of justice was perpetrated upon this holy man, but my paper will not cover it."

Polecat paused to gather his thoughts and then reported, "Pastor Helms was merely requesting an appointment to speak to

Mr. William Thomas Grant, the plant superintendent, when a guard denied him entry with near-deadly force."

Matt interrupted with, "Mrs. Johnson says her pastor worked there for years. So why was he barred?"

"In short, racial prejudice. Mr. Grant has posted flyers at the plant and in town that read, 'Construction workers needed. Members of the Negro race need not apply.' Rumors have spread that no coloreds will be hired for construction projects at the plant. When the factory re-opens, future jobs for coloreds are for log and lumber yard positions only."

"That's terrible," proclaimed Matt.

"Oh, there's more. The pay for coloreds will be two-thirds that of whites."

"Mr. Smith, this will divide the community!" lamented Matt.

"It will, and more changes are coming because Big John has put Mr. Grant in charge with full authority. The boys at the fire station claim that coloreds will not be allowed inside the new plant to work or use the bathrooms. Inside bathrooms will be for whites only, and the coloreds will have a two-hole privy in the log yard."

Billy could restrain himself no longer. "Why is the plant singling out the coloreds? They never did before, and it was a white man who burned down the plant and shot Big John!"

Polecat nodded and smiled at Billy. "A good question, my young student of society. However, social injustice is coming for all employees, and they better keep their mouths shut. Mr. Grant will see that the James Baldwin Detective Agency deals with complaints and resistance. The same agency that dealt so effectively with the miners during their strikes in 1946."

"Mr. Smith, did your paper carry articles about the miners' strike?" questioned Matt. "I might need to review a little history concerning these detectives."

"Sir, the *Highland Gazette* has at least fifteen lengthy articles on those strikes and their bloodbath aftermath. According to Sergeant Frank Younger, Pastor Helms is quite fortunate he was so lightly disciplined."

"I'm confused over why they attacked the pastor?" asked Matt.

"I'm not sure, Mr. Cubley, but I heard Little John tell several officers last night that Pastor Helms got a little dose of the way things were going to be. Getting shot was a wake-up call for his old man. Orders from Big John to Mr. Grant are to make an example of the next few men who step out of line. The coddling of employees has ended, and troublemakers, like Pastor Helms, will know to do the quickstep next time they're told to move along."

Based on Polecat's remarkable memory, Matt was sure that Polecat was reporting direct quotes. He thought it was time to change topics.

"Any news on the man Shoat found shot on the side of the road?" asked Matt. He noticed Billy and Kent suddenly got interested.

"Someone got shot?" asked Billy.

"Do we have another sniper in the county?" Kent asked second, but only because a mouthful of pancakes slowed him.

"I hope not!" exclaimed Matt.

Polecat suddenly laughed, then addressed the two boys. "Masters Clark and Gunn, I believe the possibility of you being seized and transported to a secure location against your will for a second time is remote. However, after reflecting upon your recent history of calamities, perhaps I am premature in my prognostication. Mr. Cubley, perhaps we had better secure them within the confines of Sheriff Lawrence's penal institution for their protection."

Neither Kent nor Billy favored that safeguard once they figured out what Polecat had said.

Matt came to their rescue. "Boys, I think you're safe. This time it was the shooting of an out-of-town bootlegger. I doubt the Franklin County bootleggers even know you exist. You boys haven't been running hooch on your bikes, have you?"

"No, sir, we would never do that," Kent replied before seeing Billy giggle.

"Superman, you fell for that one, slick as a monkey on a greased pole," Billy said and grinned at Mr. Cubley.

Polecat's expression turned serious. "I speculate that ambush involves a turf war between two factions vying to control the local beverage market. The boys down at the pool hall were whispering rumors about Angus MacDonald and his enforcer, Chill Dawson, protecting their territory. This gossip, I fear, is correct."

Polecat's thinking was right in line with Matt's on the subject. Knowing it and proving it would be a whole other matter.

Matt glanced at his watch, rose quickly from his seat, and asked the boys to clean up his dishes. He was late. Picking up his briefcase from inside the kitchen door where he had left it, he drove to the courthouse, parked in his reserved spot, and hurried up the stairs to his office.

Mrs. Harvey greeted him with a stern look, making him feel like a tardy schoolboy.

Matt found the cases for this morning's docket neatly stacked on the corner of his desk. He called the clerk and asked for the Helms arraignment to be called first. She advised him the judge had already ordered it and that Sheriff Lawrence would be in court this morning as bailiff.

When Matt arrived, the courtroom was crowded. Ten or fifteen whites were jammed into the front two rows of the courtroom, and then, there were two pews without anyone sitting in them. The back four rows were filled with colored men and women dressed in their Sunday finest. Matt presumed that they were most of the congregation of the Clear Vision Gospel Church.

Such a crowd was rare because almost no one came to an arraignment. Today was going to be interesting.

Sheriff Lawrence opened court promptly at nine o'clock, and the first matter was the arraignment of the Commonwealth of Virginia versus Tobias Washington Helms. Judge Carlton called the case himself, which was unusual. Typically, he let the bailiff call the cases.

Sheriff Lawrence walked over to the door, which admitted prisoners to the courtroom from the jail. He cracked it open and called for the prisoner by name. He waited. The sheriff apologized to the judge but advised the court the defendant was having trouble getting up the stairs. When Pastor Helms entered the courtroom, it was obvious why there had been a delay. Several shocked gasps came from the people in the back of the courtroom.

One of the pastor's eyes was closed because the upper eyelid was twice its normal size. He also had stitches over that eye, still oozing blood. His arm was in a cast. He was having difficulty breathing. His shirt was not buttoned in front because of the bulky bandages across his chest to support his ribs, which were badly bruised, if not broken. Talking and whispering going on in the back of the courtroom got louder and louder.

Sheriff Lawrence called for silence. The courtroom got instantly quiet.

"Pastor Helms, can you continue?" asked Judge Carlton.

"Your...Honor...I find it...hard...to breathe...but...I will do...my...best. I...would like...to find out...my charges," said the Pastor. It was obvious he was doing the best he could manage.

"Very well, the charges filed against you by Chief McCulloch are as follows. First, one charge of trespassing on the property of McCulloch Wood Products; second, a charge of resisting arrest; third, damaging the property of the Baldwin Detective Agency; and finally, damaging a local patrol car. Do you understand the charges as I have read them to you?" questioned the judge.

"I understand them...but I can't see...how they would be possible," said Pastor Helms, who had partially caught his breath from climbing the stairs to the second floor of the courthouse. He was able to finish half-sentences this time.

Matt rose from his chair. "Your Honor, I'm curious as to what facts caused the police to use such force in this arrest. *Abjudicatio* of the charges might be required if unnecessary force was used."

His comments caused whispering in both the front and rear of the courtroom.

"Mr. Cubley, your request to ask permission to look into the facts for a possible dismissal of criminal charges is rare at this stage of the proceedings, but considering the pastor's appearance, I'll allow it. Chief McCulloch is present as the arresting officer. Would you like to call him as a witness?" asked the judge.

But before Matt could answer, Chief McCulloch spoke up.

"So what is this? I brought this colored boy in to have his charges read. What's this abju-whatever nonsense," complained Chief McCulloch.

The chief looked down at the meanest-looking security guard Matt had ever seen for support. The guard didn't notice his boss because the man was glaring at Matt.

Judge Carlton pointed to Matt and gave him the nod to handle this. The judge sat back to listen.

Matt had the clerk swear in the witness.

"Chief McCulloch, I notice your name is on the warrant. Did you make the arrest?"

"I got the warrant. Mr. Denkins made the arrest," said Chief McCulloch. He again looked at Mr. Denkins, the mean-looking plant guard.

"What authority does Mr. Denkins have to make arrests in Green Mountain County?" asked Matt, fearing the answer.

"Mr. Buster Brown Denkins oversees the detail of detectives that Mr. Grant hired to protect the plant. Judge Harland made all James Baldwin Detective Agency men special police officers. That's his authority," testified Chief McCulloch with almost a sneer at Matt.

"Your Honor, in that case, the Commonwealth would like to call Mr. Buster Brown Denkins to the stand for several questions."

The witness came forward and was sworn. He took his seat on the witness stand and sat perched on the front of the oak chair because the chair arms were too small for his girth. The man was large, not fat, just enormous. He made Little John look small.

"Please state your name and occupation for the court."

"Buster Brown Denkins, but I go by Bulldog. I work for the James Baldwin Detective Agency and have for fifteen years. I'm boss of the McCulloch plant unit."

"Are you a sworn officer of this county?" inquired Matt.

"I was sworn in last Monday."

"Why did you arrest Pastor Helms?" asked Matt in short order.

"He was at the plant, so I arrested him," responded the detective.

"Was the property posted with no trespassing signs?" asked Matt.

"No, not exactly," was the answer of the detective.

"Didn't Mr. Helms work at the plant?" asked Matt.

"Don't know. Don't care," responded Mr. Denkins, who shifted in his chair, and it gave a groan of protest.

"Detective Denkins, why are you making this so hard? Again, why *did* you arrest Pastor Helms?"

"The nigger came up …

Wham! The gavel banged on the judge's bench. "Sir, do not use that word in my courtroom. You use the defendant's name or use the word defendant, but not what you just said," scolded the judge.

"The *defendant* came up to one of my men and asked to speak to Mr. Grant. My man told him that Mr. Grant was not hiring people like him and told him to leave. He mouthed off that he had worked at the plant for ten years and needed to speak to the man in charge about his job. Since the defendant wasn't on his way off the property, I tapped him with my ax handle. When he hit the ground, I placed him under arrest," said Bulldog Denkins.

"Did you warn him that if he didn't leave, he would be arrested?" inquired Matt.

"I figured if the ax handle wasn't sufficient, telling him wouldn't do no good."

"So, when you hit him, he fell to the ground?" asked Matt.

"Yeah, they always do. Never know'd but one man to stay on his feet, but my shotgun put him down in short order," announced Bulldog Denkins while smiling at Matt and enjoying the opportunity to brag.

"If Pastor Helms was on the ground, how did he resist arrest?" Matt asked the security guard.

"When we got him up, the defendant fell against my assistant, Luke Tannersly. He got blood on the front of Tannersly's shirt— ruined it!"

Matt responded. "Why is that the fault of Pastor Helms?"

The crowd in the rear of the courtroom was whispering, "Amen, yes, why?" until the sheriff called for silence.

Bulldog waited a moment for quiet and then answered Matt's question. "He got blood on a uniform shirt, which will cost the agency three dollars and fifty cents to replace. We'll want restitution when this case comes to trial," the detective said in a demanding tone as he looked toward the judge.

"How did Pastor Helms manage to damage a patrol car?"

"Same way, he got blood all over the back seat."

"Was the pastor conscious or unconscious when he got blood on your man's shirt and the back seat of the patrol car?" Matt asked, growing angry but trying not to show it.

"When I tap them, they don't move. How am I supposed to know if they are conscious or unconscious? Besides, what difference does that make? He's gonna pay for what he did, one way or t'other," said Mr. Denkins, now growing angry at Matt's line of questioning and not trying to hide it.

"How do you define a tap?"

"A tap is worth four stitches, sometimes more." And Bulldog grinned at Matt.

"Sir, thank you for your cooperation. You may step down."

Matt went over to his desk and picked up the arrest warrant copies Mrs. Harvey had given him.

"Your Honor. Pastor Helms has been a good citizen of this county all his life. He's the Clear Vision Gospel Church pastor and has been a good worker at McCulloch Wood Products for many years. He's been the religious counselor to many souls and raised a nice family. His family and his congregation often come to the aid of whites and colored families when times are hard, or death visits."

Matt paused for a moment. He gave Detective Denkins a long cold look, then continued. "The employee went to the plant to speak to his employer—a reasonable request. Unfortunately, a brand-new guard at the plant refused his request, so he repeated it and tried to explain how long he had worked there. Then, without warning, he was brutally attacked by the newly appointed head of security. Severely injured, probably unconscious, and bleeding, he was taken to jail. Because he bled on another security guard when he was knocked senseless and on the backseat of the police car, he now faces these spurious charges. I move the court to dismiss all charges."

After a pause, the judge announced, "Granted!"

The courtroom erupted with two types of shouting—from the back with surprise and relief—down front, angry shouts by Chief McCulloch and Bulldog Denkins. Matt was not sure that the security guard might not attack him in the courtroom. The man's face was changing from a flushed pink to purple.

Chief McCulloch lost it and began to yell. "What the hell kind of Commonwealth's Attorney are you? First, you throw out tenant charges, and now this! You better watch your *p*'s and *q*'s because you done pissed off the wrong people!"

Turning, he and Detective Denkins stormed out of the courtroom, knocking down one of the ladies of Pastor Helm's congregation in the process. She shrieked as she fell, adding to the commotion.

Judge Carlton called a ten-minute recess for the sheriff to get the courtroom into some semblance of order. Several of Pastor Helm's congregation came forward and thanked Matt. Then, the church group departed in a babble of voices. Sheriff Lawrence made no effort to silence them as they left but shook hands with several of the congregation.

When the court was called back into session, three of the ten scheduled cases were dismissed because Chief McCulloch had left the courtroom and could not be found. One case was tried on a not-guilty plea involving charges by a sheriff's deputy, but that case ended with a conviction. The other defendants pled guilty, and the court was over by ten o'clock.

Matt returned to his office, battle-weary, drained by a war not of his choosing but one where he had been forced by the facts to pick a side. Perhaps the losing side. He described his morning to Mrs. Harvey, feeling compelled to include her. When he finished, her face flashed a quick smile, and then it was gone. She returned to her typing without comment.

Matt spent the next half-hour talking on the telephone with Trooper Bobby Giles. They tried to figure out how they might put a tail on the newly registered MacDonald pickup. Giles indicated it would be difficult to follow the truck and not be seen, but he suggested that if they tailed the pickup in short intervals on different nights, they might be able to piece together a route without tipping off the driver. Giles would get with his sergeant and see what they might work out. Putting puzzle pieces together would take manpower, which was in short supply. Matt thanked him for his efforts and wished him good hunting.

After the phone call, Mrs. Harvey brought Matt a cup of coffee from the break room down the hall. He didn't fully appreciate the small gesture was a considerable accommodation. This was the first coffee that she had ever delivered to any boss.

After the first sip of the hot beverage, the phone rang. Matt answered it before Mrs. Harvey could get it and instantly recognized the caller. Linda Carlisle needed an answer on a case coming up. The two worked out the conflict that a witness was having. Business concluded; they did not immediately hang up. He asked her how she was doing, and they traded small talk. He had an impulse to ask her out. He began to form the words when a metallic click came from the next room, and a picture flashed in front of his mind's eyes.

In the church in Roanoke, the morning of Janet and Jack's funeral, he looked down on them in that single casket. Finally, the funeral director whispered three words, "Matthew, it's time."

When the lid of that casket closed, there was a metallic click—a sound he would never forget. His loss became real with that sound.

"Matt, are you still there?" Linda asked, not hearing anything for several moments.

"Uh, sorry, Janet, where was I?"

She detected a quiver in his voice and immediately recognized he had called her by his wife's name.

Linda responded in a soft voice. "Off somewhere," said she, knowing where he was, a familiar place also known to her.

"Do you think it's all right if we're friends?" he asked suddenly.

She immediately picked up on Matt's state of mind. "I understand from my husband's death three years ago that I'm now ready to move on. Is it too soon for you?"

Matt hesitated with his answer, but Linda didn't wait. She knew.

"I'm here when you need to talk. Talking will help, but until you're ready, it won't work. So, you call me when you're ready." And she hung up the phone.

It took him a moment, and then he hung up his receiver. Matt continued staring at the office bookcase, looking for answers that weren't there.

CHAPTER 27

BILLY JOINS A GANG
Saturday, July 30, 1955

S omething was wrong. I couldn't move my legs. I popped open one eye to see my sheet balled up around my chin, and I saw why my legs were stuck.

Scotty was sound asleep across the end of my bed. He must have been there most of the night because both my legs were numb. I jerked one out from under him and then the other. He didn't wake or even move.

I tossed my sheet over him and swung my feet onto the floor. Slowly I stood and remained still until the little electric shocks stopped—what I call the "sprangles"—and the feeling partially returned. I carefully clumped to the bedroom door with a thump, thump and held on for the feeling to return to normal. That's when I heard him stir.

"Billy, where are you going?" asked Scotty.

"Getting up. I gotta pee. Why are you awake?" I asked him back.

"I'm hot, and I gotta pee, too," he said as he rolled off the end of my bed and dropped onto the floor on his hands and knees. Of course, little kids can do that, but for me, that would have hurt.

After taking care of the necessities, we dressed and arrived in the kitchen together. Grandma lifted Scotty and hugged him.

I said, "Hi, Grandma. Where's Mom?"

"Your mom left early for the farmer's market. We're going to make pickles, and she wanted the pick of the baby cucumbers."

Grandma was bouncing Scotty on her knee as she talked.

"I don't want pickles. I want oatmeal," whined Scotty.

Why that kid liked oatmeal was a total mystery to me. I hated oatmeal, and he loved it. I don't know what happened to him as a baby, but something damaged his taste buds. We learned about taste buds in fifth grade, but Scotty must not have any.

"Billy, your mother left your breakfast warming in the oven. Slow down! Get a potholder, don't burn yourself, and be sure to turn the oven off. Pour yourself some milk."

Grandma was good at telling folks what to do, mostly when they didn't need it. Of course, I knew to turn off the oven, and only an idiot would burn themselves on a plate straight out of a hot oven. However, my plate was just warm.

The ham was good, but the eggs were hard since Mom had scrambled them earlier. It helped to take a small bite of egg, a sip of milk, hold everything in your mouth to soak, chew a couple of times, then swallow. Scotty was both eating and playing in his oatmeal.

I hurried breakfast because I had to make it to an important meeting in the park. Something had to be done about those Lockhart brothers, so my class decided to gather for a secret meeting. We told our parents there was a softball game at ten, but that was a spoofer.

I finished breakfast, went out to the garage, and learned Dad had gone out on a tow. He was bringing back a wreck from Lynchburg. Mr. Skelton, to my relief, said there was nothing for me to do. He was tuning up a car and changing the oil, a one-person job. So, I was free to have fun because no guests at the hotel needed any vehicles washed.

I told Grandma I was going to the park for a ball game. I almost ran into trouble with her because she told me not to go; the park was too dangerous.

"Grandma, Kent and I will be fine. All my school friends are meeting at the baseball field for a game. If those bullies show up, there'll be a bunch of us, and they won't try anything. Besides, after the game, Kent and I will eat lunch at the Black Panther with Laura and Judy. From there, we're going to the Top Hat for two neat westerns."

"You're too young to be dating," Grandma announced to the world, well, to Scotty. It took me a moment to decide what to say to her.

"Grandma, Laura and Judy are just friends. It ain't a date. We're too young. I'm only twelve, you know? And it's the middle of the day, and dates are at night."

I laid it on a little thick.

"The language you use. If you were my child, I'd keep you home and teach you some sense," fussed Grandma. She smiled, and I knew she was only half-serious.

I went into the garage for my green Schwinn. I'd been keeping it inside the garage, safe from bullies. Back outside, I ran beside it, jumped, and landed on the seat. I got my feet on the pedals and flew left out of the gate and down Main Street to Beechwood Lane, where Kent was waiting. He was riding circles in the street on his red Columbia. We joined up and rode hard to the ballpark.

Flying at top speed into the parking lot, I pulled off a back-wheel slide to a stop. It was a beauty that threw dirt and gravel ten feet. When the dust cleared, I saw we were not the first to arrive.

Kent and I stashed our bikes under the bleachers and walked onto the infield. Frank Varner had organized this meeting, and almost the entire class had come.

I yelled at Frank, "Hey, nice roundup."

Roger Younger was talking to him, and they both walked over to Kent and me.

However, Roger hung back behind Frank and spoke, "BB, I know you're gonna hate me. But honest, I didn't have a choice. Dad made me say I didn't see Lou bean you with that bat," Roger wouldn't look me in the eye. I knew he felt terrible.

Kent was not going to give him any slack. "Roger, I thought you would tell the truth, but you didn't. We were counting on you."

"Superman, you don't know what he did. My dad was crazy mad at me. He said I was going to get him fired."

"But you said!" Kent stated harshly.

"Superman, he beat me bloody! My dad told me I better tell them that BB started it, or my next beating would be worse. I did the best I could. I said I didn't see how it got started. My dad drew back his fist in front of that special prosecutor guy. The guy saved me from Dad punching me a good one. He told my dad to back off. Now, dad is so sore that he won't look at me!"

Kent started to say something else, but I put my hand on his arm and shook my head no. "Roger, I ain't mad at you. I know about grown-ups. Forget about it. I'm sorry he beat on you."

All the gang saw us make up. Only then did everybody gather in a big circle. Frank looked around and began calling names like he was calling the class roll.

"Will Arnold, Bernard Carter, Mike Carson...." We all answered, just like in school. He continued talking.

"Thanks for showing up. I guess you all know by now that we got us a problem. Lou, Carl, and Dickie are doing bad things. Not just to Superman and BB, but they knifed my basketball, and we're sure they've been setting cats on fire in the woods. Two of the cats were kittens that belonged to Tim and Nancy Hodges. Tim found the bodies, and a neighbor told Nancy that she saw smoke, and then those three came out of the woods, laughing. That was ten minutes before Tim found the kittens burned," concluded Frank.

Laura had a big frown and spoke over the others. "Judy and I thought that special lawyer and the sheriff were going to do something, but they told Kent and BB there wasn't enough evidence. The adults won't help regardless of what we tell them, so it's up to us."

Frank couldn't hold back anymore. "Yeah! And when I told Mr. Lockhart that Carl and Dickie had knifed my basketball, he called me a liar and threw me out of the hardware. Told me not to come back, like I was to blame." Frank was steamed, and his fists were balled up.

"We need to do something, but what?" asked Nancy, who was furious over her little kittens.

"Carl and Dickie need to be taught a lesson," I said, hoping that I could divert the gang away from Lou. Dad and his buddies had taught him his lesson, and I didn't want Lou hurt worse. That's when things turned against me.

"What about Lou?" asked Danny Mason. "He stole my baseball glove last year."

Kent jumped into the conversation. "Yeah, he stole my tennis shoes last year, but something's up. When Carl and Dickie recently jumped BB at the movies, Lou tried to talk them out of it. He's changed. I don't think he's a problem anymore," said Kent, knowing what I was thinking.

I saw my chance.

"I agree. Let's leave him be for now. We need to get Frank a new ball and teach Carl and Dickie a lesson. The main thing—we all got to stick together. Are you willing to lie and cover for each other? That's what the adults do. I guess we better learn how to do it too!"

I felt terrible about asking everyone to start lying—a bad thing. It was a sin, even, but what else could we do?

"BB's right. If we do this, we got to cover for each other," Mike Carson agreed. He was the one person I thought would argue against not telling the truth. He said grace at every meal.

"Okay, so what are we going to do?" asked Bernard Carter.

We discussed plans to get Frank a basketball and get Carl and Dickie to leave us alone. Some ideas were okay, but some were dumb. For example, Tommy Russel wanted to rob the hardware store and steal a basketball. We voted that idea down right off.

Sheila Martin lived near the Lockhart family and told us that Carl and Dickie often left their basketball on their driveway beside their goal. She offered, "We don't need to break in anywhere because we can just take it."

One of the boys said, "That gets Frank a replacement, but they will just take it back, and those two bullies need a dose of their own medicine."

Nancy then spoke up, "Guys, why don't you take their ball and leave them a note? Tell them if they want their stupid ball back to come to a certain place. That way, all you boys can teach those two bullies a lesson. A good one."

Tommy agreed, "That will bring those brothers to a spot where we can ambush them."

Nancy spoke up with her next idea, which shocked us. "Let's set them on fire. Do to them what they did to Snowball and Snuggles." She looked around and saw the horrified look on our faces. Then, she quickly said, "I know we can't do that, but you get them good. Promise?"

No one answered until Sheila came back with, "All us girls will swear you were with us somewhere else. We will!"

Therefore, the girls and not the boys came up with the ambush plan. We had the how, so now, we were only missing the where. That's when one of the girls shouted the solution. "How about the woods behind the school?"

Nancy looked at Lucy Scarlett, who nodded and exclaimed. "That's perfect—it's summertime and no teachers or adults are around. The clearing in the woods behind the school will be a good place to hide and spring the ambush!"

Lucy voiced one flaw in our plan that concerned her.

"If they see a bunch of seventh-grade boys, they might not stick around. I think Nancy and I should be the ones holding their basketball. All you boys hide in the woods around the clearing. When they come at us to take back their ball, you jump out and surround them. That way, they can't get away."

"I like that," said Superman, and we all agreed.

"That sounds pretty good, but how does that get my ball back? They'll know the ball we have is their ball." Frank wanted his ball back.

Will Arnold gave Frank his answer. "You take their ball, and we give them back Frank's messed-up ball—the one they knifed. We can take a knife and cut it some more. They'll think you got even by cutting up their ball worse than yours."

"Where'd you buy your basketball, Frank?" asked Superman.

"I bought it at the hardware. It looks just like Dickie and Carl's. When I get their ball, I could write my name on it. That way, if anyone asks, you guys can swear I bought it last year. I can claim I had two, and both were marked with my name. The one they cut up and this other one is my good one. If we all stick to the same story, what will the adults do?" Frank was warming up to this idea. It was interesting to see how easy it was for my class to agree to lie. We were beginning to think it wasn't such a big deal.

Kent spoke up next. "Okay, let's swipe their ball first chance." Kent wanted in on the "get even" part more than I did.

Danny told Sheila, "You call Frank when you see the basketball left on their drive. Frank can steal it and leave the note." Danny Hodges was liking this idea more and more.

"When do we get them in the woods?" asked a girl.

Frank took back over the planning. "How many of you can show up either Monday, Tuesday, or Wednesday, say around four o'clock in the afternoon?" asked Frank, and almost everyone said they could make it. Some of the girls wanted to join in, but that was discouraged. An argument resulted, so the boys told them they could come, hide, and watch. Except for Nancy and Lucy, everyone would make hoods for their faces and cloaks over their clothes from burlap sacks. The burlap sacks were easy since several of the fathers were farmers.

Kent and I told them we knew how to make sniper suits for hiding in the woods. "We can attach bits of green cloth and real leaves to the burlap cloaks and make Ghillie suits. That way, the Lockhart brothers won't suspect a thing. They'll just think it's only Lucy and Nancy returning their ball. Superman and I learned about snipers using Ghillie suits from listening to Trooper Lusk and Mr. Cubley talking about them during the sniper murders."

Kent gave them a quick lesson on how to make them. The girls agreed to help the boys who couldn't sew.

Everyone promised to get ready and to show up when called. Members of our class, who were not at the meeting, would be told of our plan, but first, they had to take an oath to lie. If they didn't take the oath, we wouldn't let them in on the ambush.

Kent asked me to swear in everyone, which I did, just like Mr. Cubley had taught us. We all swore we would not betray the group and would lie for each other. Tim Hodges said he would be loyal even if they burned him at a stake. It was obvious the gang was all bothered about those kittens. The talk kept mentioning fire.

The meeting broke up with our friends going in all directions. Kent and I rode our bikes to the five and dime to get ready for the movies at the Top Hat. We decided not to buy peashooters because Judy and Laura might think a peashooter fight was childish, but we did buy four Charm suckers—two for us and two for the girls—since it was a double feature.

Right on time, we met Laura and Judy at the Black Panther for cheeseburgers, fries, and chocolate shakes. Kent and I treated the girls to lunch. We talked about stuff with no mention of our plans for the bullies—too many adult ears around.

After lunch, we walked to the theater. I paid for Laura, and Kent paid for Judy. We all bought popcorn and drinks on our own to prove we weren't dating. After we sat down, Kent and I slipped our dates...er...friends the Charm suckers. Mr. Stone would confiscate smuggled-in suckers if he spotted them.

The four of us sat down front for *The Nevadan* with Randolph Scott and Forrest Tucker. Randolph Scott was a United States Marshall by the name of Andrew Barclay. He was one tough cowboy who rounded up a gang of outlaws.

We moved halfway back to get away from some third-grade brats for the five cartoons, the one serial, and Gene Autry in *The Blazing Sun*. In one of the scenes, Gene Autry gets thrown in jail. That made me feel better about our plan. If Gene Autry could go to jail, it must not be all that bad. I wondered if they let kids out of jail on Saturday to catch a good movie. I hoped so.

Kent and I thought the movies were great. Judy and Laura complained they should make westerns where the girls save the cowboys. Kent and I thought that was funny, but we hid our smiles. Judy's mom was waiting when we left, which made it clear this was no date.

Kent and I walked to the alley where we had stashed our bikes, talking about our local jail. He said he had never heard of a kid being locked up by our sheriff, but I replied that I knew two local cops who would love to lock us up.

We pulled out our bikes from under some cardboard boxes and rode hard for leather to my house. When we got there, Mom told Kent that his mom wanted him to come straight home, which ended our afternoon together.

In the kitchen, Mom and Grandma were arguing over how to get Scotty to stop sucking his thumb. Mom wanted to use hot sauce, but Grandma said tying a ribbon around it was enough to remind him. Dad rolled his eyes and kept quiet.

That night when I went to bed, I found Scotty in my bed again. His bed was all torn up, with the sheets in a jumble on the floor. I fixed his bed and dumped him back in it. It took me some time to fall asleep that night. I kept thinking about cowboys, baseball bats, and if prisoners were allowed to have sheets and soda pop.

CHAPTER 28

A TURTLE & DEAD ENDS
Saturday, July 30, 1955

T rooper Giles arrived right on time to take Matt to Waynesboro for an interview with Sam Perry. Normally, Matt would have waited until Monday, but there was a strong possibility the bootlegger would be released from the hospital and go home today or tomorrow. Matt needed to speak with him before he got with his kin. He just hoped Sam would talk.

The drive to Waynesboro was pleasant, and the hospital parking lot was nearly empty. Visiting hours would not start for several hours, which suited the pair. They wanted Perry alone with no distractions. They ran through a gauntlet of clipboard-armed nurses but finally got to the patient.

Sam Perry was in a private room dining on a breakfast that could only have come from the General Wayne Hotel. The hospital kitchen was not the source of eggs Benedict, bacon, French toast, a fruit medley, coffee in a silver urn, and two large linen napkins. Matt noticed an untouched hospital breakfast tray on the floor by the door.

"Mr. Perry, I'm Matthew Cubley, the Commonwealth's Attorney for Green Mountain County, and with me is Trooper Bobby Giles. May we ask you a few questions?"

"Ask away. Don't know nothing, but feel free to ask me whatever you want," said Sam as he continued to dine.

The questions were typical, and the answers were disappointing.

"Do you know who shot you?"

"No, didn't see."

"Were you robbed?"

"Nope."

"Do you know the reason or motive someone might have had to shoot you?"

"Not a clue."

"Where did it happen?"

"I don't know the area. Somewhere on Route 22."

On and on, the questions were asked, and the answers were all the same.

"No," or "I don't know."

They were able to dig out the following facts. After Perry got shot, the other car drove off. The victim didn't see the make, model, or license plate of the shooter's vehicle. Perry had tried to drive away to get help, but before he found anyone, he passed out and woke up in the hospital.

When asked how his car was rigged, he denied knowing anything about moonshine. Matt almost laughed when Perry explained that he used his vehicle to carry heavy farm parts for the family farm. They had beefed up the springs so it wouldn't drag over old rutted-out farm roads. Matt knew the Perry family had a big trailer for hauling the farm tractors and other equipment to Rocky Mount to the Massey Ferguson tractor dealership. No need for a family car to transport anything heavy.

"Mr. Perry, if we have more questions, would it be okay to visit you at your farm?" asked Matt, and he winked at the trooper on the sly.

"No! Sorry. Been having trouble with people stealing our cattle. If you need me, I'll come to you," advised the patient.

Matt knew the Perry family would never allow anyone, not family, to set foot on the farm. Tales were told of a lime pit reserved for burying dead cows, horses, and the rare trespasser. Hunters knew to stay off the Perry farm. When a hound would chase prey onto the farm, no one went after the dog. Custom would allow it, but hunters knew to lose a dog was better than not coming home at the end of the hunt.

The interview ended when Sam Perry seemed to recognize Matt.

"Say, I know you from somewhere. Your face is familiar," stated Sam.

Matt did not shy from his answer. "I used to work in the Roanoke office."

"Now, I remember. You tried to bring my dad up on conspiracy charges. I thought it right funny how he beat your ass in court," stated Sam with a smirk.

Sam Perry indicated he was done talking. Matt tried one more question and got a cold stare in return. He thanked Mr. Perry for his cooperation. They left the hospital, none the wiser about what really had happened.

Driving back to Highland, Trooper Giles heard about a chase coming north out of Amherst County on his police radio. Once again, the pursuit was on State Route 22, but this time, Trooper Franklin and two Amherst County deputies were chasing a vehicle. Trooper Giles turned on his red lights and siren, climbed Afton Mountain, then raced down the steep road on the other side to pick up State Route 22. Based on the radio traffic, they were several miles ahead of the pursuit group. Traveling west towards Highland on Route 22, Trooper Giles stopped at the end of a long straight stretch.

"Matt, I don't know if you're good luck or bad, but you sure know when to ride with us to pick up a chase," joked Trooper Giles.

"Bobby, I hope this one turns out better than the last one. Richmond might put you on foot patrol if you bang up another car."

"Don't I know it! You notice that I'm blocking the road after a long sight distance. I'll be as careful with this cruiser as the little old lady driving to Sunday church in her brand-new Packard Clipper."

Suddenly, the lead police car of the pursuit came roaring out of the curve on the far end of the straight stretch. No other vehicle was in sight.

"What happened to the car they were chasing?" Matt asked as the two Amherst cars with Trooper Franklin in the rear slowed and stopped near Trooper Giles' vehicle.

"Franklin," Trooper Giles greeted the other trooper.

"Bobby," said Trooper Jayce Franklin.

"Looks like you lost him," said Giles.

That's when a deputy joined the conversation. "We were right on him until we hit the straights into Hidden Valley. Then, that boy took off like his tail was on fire, and his pockets were full of gasoline," exclaimed one of the Amherst deputies.

"Guess he must have turned off. No way he could have outrun you," advised Giles, giving a little wink at Matt.

"Beats me," said Trooper Franklin.

"Think we should check the side roads we passed?" asked the other deputy from Amherst.

Trooper Giles put his arm around the deputy's shoulder and confided, "Well, it wouldn't hurt, but if I were a betting man, I'd bet that old boy ducked into a side road, let you fellas pass, and he lit off back in the other direction. I bet he's halfway to Vesuvius on the Carlisle Falls Road or caught the Tye River Turnpike and is blazing past Crabtree Falls by now. What do you think, Trooper Franklin?" asked Giles.

"I think I'm going over to the Black Panther Restaurant and get me a late breakfast or an early lunch. Anybody want to join me?" asked Trooper Franklin.

The party split up in different directions. Two going to eat, one deputy returned to duty, and Trooper Giles left, taking Matt back to Cubley's Coze.

"When I get back to the office, the boys will have a good time ribbing Jayce, 'the Turtle,' Franklin about how he lost another one."

"Bobby, is that what they call Trooper Franklin, the Turtle?" asked Matt.

"Yep. And a well-deserved nickname it is. The boy rarely catches what he's chasing, but I do have to give him credit for one thing," said Trooper Giles, but Bobby paused without finishing his sentence.

Matt just had to ask, "What would you give him credit for?"

"He's never wrecked a state car," said the trooper with a little laugh.

"Well, I guess that's something. You know the fable of the race between the turtle and the hare?" asked Matt.

"Yes, but if I'm not mistaken, the turtle was not a sworn officer of the Virginia State Police, whose duty it is to catch criminals and traffic violators," Giles concluded.

Matt arrived back at the hotel without any additional excitement. He waved goodbye to Trooper Giles, went into the lobby, and found Chuck putting the finishing touches on a large flower arrangement for the central lobby table. The special arrangement had become a weekend custom for the hotel.

Matt stopped at the kitchen to check on Boo, Maddie, and Karen Hathaway. He was doing his best to smooth over that darn awkward meeting regarding Mrs. Hathaway's husband.

Business done; Matt returned to his office to think.

He was getting nowhere with the Brown murder, and now he was getting nowhere with the shooting of Sam Perry. It also appeared that bootlegging operations were growing and not decreasing in Green Mountain County because of the recent pursuits. Of course, some cases might be speeders running from a citation. However, the speed, the specially rigged vehicles, and the professional way the drivers could evade the police led Matt to conclude that bootlegging was booming.

The murder of the Commonwealth's Attorney might be tied to it or might not. He was at a dead end on the most important murder case ever committed in this county, and Big John and his people were doing everything in their power to block the investigation. Even Mrs. Brown, the victim's wife, was not helping. It was like searching for someone in a liars fog.

Matt's thoughts were interrupted when Chuck knocked on his office and told him that Professor Hartford would like to see him. Matt said, "Sure," and Chuck showed the educator into his office.

"Mr. Cubley, thanks for seeing me. Hope your day is going well?" said the professor with a smile and warm handshake.

"Things are fine here. Is there a problem at the lodge?" Matt asked.

"Oh, no. One of my graduate students forgot to pack a piece of equipment we needed. So, I had to run back to the university to pick it up. Everything's fine at the lodge. We just had something odd happen, and I thought I'd better tell you about it."

"Not a problem. What was it?"

"This morning, just after dawn, we were out on one of the game trails near the lodge, and we ran into a young lady. She looked like she'd spent the night on the mountain. She was alone and had nothing with her but a light jacket and a purse. When we asked, she said she wasn't lost, but she did ask us for help," said Hartford.

"That is odd. Where had she come from?" asked Matt.

"I don't know. The young lady avoided telling us who she was or from where she had come. She did ask for water from our canteen. We insisted she come back to the lodge for breakfast, which the young lass consumed with gusto. She was very appreciative. When she found out we were going to drive into Charlottesville, she asked for a ride," advised the professor.

"I doubt she's staying here. If one of our guests had not returned last night, a member of her party would have reported it. We don't have any single females staying with us at the moment."

"I tried to find out what was going on with her but got nowhere. I asked if the police might be of some help. She instantly refused, but she didn't appear to me to be a criminal. No, my impression is that she's a nice young lady—well-dressed and very respectful. But she didn't want any part of the local police," reported the professor.

"What became of her?" asked Matt, who was now curious about the mysterious young lady.

"We dropped her at the train station in Charlottesville. She had funds with her because I asked her if she needed to borrow some money. She said, 'Goodness, no. I have money. I'm just going to stay with a relative in Maryland.' She even offered me money for gasoline."

I left her at the station but thought I'd better tell someone. One never knows about these things. Being a university professor involved with young men and women, I'm cautious and insisted my wife ride with us to Charlottesville. The grad students are looking after our children, so my wife wants me to hurry back. I just wanted to let you know in case questions were asked."

Professor Hartford said his goodbyes to Matt and proceeded to the car where his wife was waiting.

Matt asked Chuck if he had overheard the conversation. Chuck pointed to the partly opened passthrough door to indicate he had heard it all. Matt looked at the lobby clock and bolted for the stairs. He was about to be late for the funeral of Mr. Albert Winston Brown. The first one since the death of his family. He hoped he could make it through the service.

Matt came right back down the stairs wearing his dark suit for the funeral, which was being held at the First Baptist Church of Highland. The burial would take place in the Highland Cemetery.

He felt compelled to attend the funeral because he now held the man's office. Therefore, it would be disrespectful not to attend.

When Matt neared the church, he noticed men in dark uniforms around the church building, at the entrances to the parking lot, and even a group lined up across the street. When Matt pulled up to enter the church lot, a large man in uniform stopped him. The guard demanded his name, checked his clipboard, and told Matt he was not on the list.

"What does that mean? I'm not on the list?" asked Matt.

"It means you're not going to the funeral, Bud. This is a closed funeral for family and friends. Move along!" ordered the security guard in a gruff voice. Matt saw other church members being turned around. As Matt departed, he noticed Big John's Cadillac driving down the street with a Highland Police Department escort in front and to the rear. The Cadillac was waved right into the parking lot without being checked. The boss had arrived, and the first person who got out of the Cadillac was Bulldog Denkins.

Matt drove back to the hotel and parked. He went into the kitchen and saw Chuck helping himself to a cup of tea and a piece of cake.

"Matt, did you forget something?" asked Chuck.

"There were security guards at all the entrances to the church, and unless they had your name on some list, you were turned away," answered Matt.

"Did you tell them who you were?" asked Chuck, with Maddie and the kitchen staff stopping their work to listen.

"No. I didn't want to make a scene, not at a funeral. They were turning away other members of the congregation as well. I saw Big John drive up with a full police escort. I think the man's become paranoid. Guards around a church in little old Highland at a funeral, for Pete's sake. What's next?"

CHAPTER 29

BILLY JOINS THE AMBUSH
Monday, August 1, 1955

W e planned things on Saturday, got ready on Sunday, and by Monday, it seemed like a week had passed because so much had been done and happened. Sheila spotted the basketball on Saturday evening. She called Frank, who snatched the ball at sunrise on Sunday. He left a note in place of the basketball with a rock on top to hold it down.

Sheila checked on her way to church, and the note was gone. After Sunday service, phone calls went out to all my classmates. The ambush was set for Monday at four-thirty. Everyone was to be hidden by four o'clock. Sticks and bats were optional, but we agreed on no knives or guns.

Kent and I made our Ghillie suits from burlap feed sacks after church. We tied tiny branches and leaves on them for camouflage, avoiding poison oak or poison ivy leaves. While the suits were itchy and hot, it was hard to spot us when we hid in the woods.

All the guys would hide, so it would look like just the two girls had come for the meeting. The other girls were going to wait in a clearing deeper in the woods, but only a short distance away. All the girls had decided that crawling around in the weeds with snakes, ticks, and chiggers was not for them, but they wanted to come to watch the bullies get their punishment.

When the bullies arrived, Nancy and Lucy would hold up the mutilated basketball. The guys were impressed that they were willing to be the bait. When the trap was sprung, Nancy and Lucy would run deeper into the woods to a clearing where the other girls were in hiding. Then, with the bullies busy, all the girls would return to watch.

Monday afternoon, Kent and I finished our last car just before two. While we put away our cleaning materials, we talked about the funeral of Mr. Albert Winston Brown.

"BB, did the ladies at your church get mad about the funeral?" asked Kent.

"Mad? No, they were furious. They always put out refreshments after a funeral. Those dumb guards wouldn't let them into the church to set them out. They'd gone to all that trouble to make refreshments for nothing. Several of the women called the Board of Deacons to complain. Dad says the women were idiots to think the deacons would do anything. All but one works for Big John," I told Kent.

"Yeah, it was all the talk at the Methodist Church. Mom couldn't say much because she works at the bank, but she told me it was the worst, most rude thing she had ever heard of," responded Kent.

"Are you going to bring a bat this afternoon?" I asked Kent, changing the subject.

"No, I don't want to mess up my only bat. I'm bringing an old cowboy belt with horses stamped on it. It's thick and hurts but won't do any major damage. How about you?" Kent wanted to know.

"I've been giving it some serious thought. Like you, I only have one good bat. I found an old chair that Dad broke when he got mad one day. I think I'll bring the leg as a club. After it's over, I can toss it in the woods. I don't want to get caught with anything that looks like a weapon," I said to Superman.

"That's a good idea. I'll wear my belt, and when the rough stuff is over, I'll just wear it home. No one will be the wiser."

"Do you think some of the guys will chicken out when they arrest us?" I asked.

"What? Do you think we will get arrested, scout's honor?"

"Kent, just because the police didn't arrest Lou, Carl, and Dickie when they beat us up, do you believe they'll think twice before they throw us in the hoosegow?"

"I hope we get a cell together. I don't want to be in jail alone. Not that I'm scared or anything. I just want someone to talk to. You know, to pass the time." Kent's voice was strong, but his face had that worried look.

We rode our bikes home, avoided our parents, picked up our stuff, and rode out to the school. That afternoon, the Highland

Elementary School was deserted. No cars were in the parking lot, and no adults were around.

Roger Younger and Tommy Russel got there before Kent and me. After that, the rest of the gang arrived in twos and threes. The last to arrive was Danny Mason, who was late because his mom had given him a haircut just as he was about to leave.

A little after four, we all hid in the woods. Lucy and Nancy, wearing hoods but no cloaks, stood in the back part of the clearing with the slashed basketball.

Suddenly, there was a whistle, which was the signal that the Lockharts were coming. They were early by twenty minutes. We all went to ground under our Ghillie suits, holding our breaths.

The two bullies appeared, coming down the path at a fast walk. "Hey, you girls! Did you steal our basketball?" called out Dickie, just as he entered the clearing.

"Yeah, we did. You burned my kittens, you poor excuse for a person," yelled Nancy. We all knew why she was there. She loved kittens and would never forgive Carl or Dickie for their evil deed.

"Yeah, you should have heard them scream. Those furballs screamed like little girls. Now give me my basketball," demanded Carl.

"You want your ball. Here it is," called out Lucy. She threw Carl the deflated basketball. When it hit the ground, it made a thumping sound—no bounce.

"What is this shit?" Dickie said to Nancy. She and Lucy started slowly backing away from the two bullies.

"I don't normally beat the pulp out of skirts, but whoever you two are, I'll make it an exception," Dickie said and started toward the two girls.

Nancy and Lucy turned and ran into the path on the other side of the clearing. Dickie and Carl were about twenty feet behind, chasing them. Then, suddenly, bushes began to rise from the forest floor.

"What the...?" exclaimed Carl, stopping all at once. Dickie collided with him.

"You don't scare me," said Dickie to the four boys who had risen in front of him. They were blocking the path that the girls had taken. Lucy and Nancy were now farther down it and being joined by other hooded girls coming to watch.

Then, Dickie and Carl heard a noise behind them. They looked and saw they were now surrounded by ten seventh-grade boys, all wearing hoods. The hooded boys began shedding their burlap cloaks with the branches, leaves, and weeds stuck to them.

Kent and I were standing side-by-side. Me with my chair leg club, and Kent with his belt. Large eyeholes had been cut in all our hoods so we could see, but our faces were covered. We closed in on the bullies, and the other boys with bats and I began to work on the two brothers. Down they went.

I got in two good licks with my club, the second one harder than the first. Kent was swinging wild with his belt. Darn if he didn't hit me once on the arm, and it hurt.

Ten boys kicked, hit, whipped, and stomped on the two brothers. They were screaming for help, trying as best as they could to cover their heads.

Will Arnold finally yelled, "Stop!"

A hesitation swept over us. And it was suddenly clear; we had gone too far!

The Lockhart brothers were still alive but badly hurt. Both were moaning and not getting up because Carl and Dickie had received some severe injuries. First, Carl tried to get up onto all fours but fell over. Dickie wasn't moving at all. I began to worry we had killed them. We all just stood there, staring at the two beaten bullies, and fear of what we had done spread over the group.

After three minutes, with only a little movement and only moans, we finally heard, "You sixth-grade punks, we'll kill you," snarled Carl as he wiped blood from his mouth. Someone, I don't know who, whacked him hard with a stick, which shut him up. He began a low moan as he held his ribs with one arm over the other.

"No, you won't," I answered. My voice surprised me as if someone else was speaking.

Next, Frank threatened him. "We're seventh graders, you moron, and we're a gang. You touch one of us, and this will be nothing compared to what we'll do to you next time. There are twenty of us today,"—which was nearly correct, counting the girls.

"We have promises from two other grades to help us if we need them," concluded Frank, trying to disguise his voice. Of course, what he'd said about the other grades wasn't true, but I thought Frank had thrown in a nice touch.

"If we ever catch you burning any more animals, we might set you on fire and watch you run in circles and scream. See how funny you think that will be," said Tim Hodges with a chorused shout by half the kids standing around.

Nancy pushed Danny aside and stepped into the circle. "We're all for one and one for all, just like in the book. You're on notice to be nice to kittens, or things will get scary-bad for you!" It was clear there was hate in Nancy's voice.

I read in a book once that the Sioux turned prisoners over to the squaws when they wanted the enemy to suffer horribly. I could believe it. Nancy wanted to get her hands on the brothers in the worst way. They were lucky she didn't.

Carl and Dickie slowly helped each other up to limp and stagger over to their bikes. They couldn't ride them but pushed them back toward the street, wiping blood from their faces every few seconds. I saw the cut-up basketball was left and forgotten.

It was time to cover our tracks. I called out, "Gather round! Take all the Ghillie suits and hoods, pile them up, and burn them! Let's check our bats for blood. Make sure they're clean. Yeah, if not, burn them, too! Come on. Hurry up before the cops come!"

Everyone got busy. I thought of a few more things, "Now, it's going to get difficult. We must stick to our plan and our story." It was like I was teaching a class. When you are doing something dull, like washing cars, you can get in some good thinking time. I had thought all this out at my job.

The other kids must have thought my instructions were pretty good because they followed them to the letter. First, we burned all the suits. Next, we pulled our bikes out of the woods and washed at the school's water fountain. We washed shoes, hands, bloody clothes, bats, belts, and anything that could tie us to the ambush. One bat had to go on the fire because it had bloodstains that wouldn't wash off.

The girls helped get the stains out of our clothes. If the stains were too bad to remove with water, the girls took grass, balled it up, and rubbed it until the grass stains covered up the bloodstains.

Each of us took a solemn blood oath never to tell what we had done. We skipped pricking our fingers, but we did give our solemn promise, one at a time—even the girls. Next, Kent gave a little speech.

"Beware the police. If the cops say someone squealed, don't believe it. Cops do that all the time on TV to get crooks to talk. Our story has got to be that we were all fishing over at Smith River. The bullies lied about what they did to BB and me, and even the bullies' parents lied. Now, for this to work, we must lie better," instructed Kent. I knew he had picked that trick about one suspect being told other suspects had confessed from listening to *Dragnet.*

After checking each other over one last time for bloodstains, we rode our bikes back to First Street. Walking in single file, we took the shortcut down the path to the fishing hole near "Big Rock." This Smith River fishing hole was widely known because there was a big rock in the riverbank. The older kids would tell first graders that Big Rock was where witches cut up first graders to make potions and spells. This story was old as the hills, but every first grader believed it.

We made tracks in the mud with our shoes to make it look like a bunch of kids had been fishing. Getting our tennis shoes muddy would make our moms mad, but this was part of making our lie more believable. Karla Carson had even thought of having her brother, Mike, dig worms. She left them in two soup cans down by the river for the cops to find.

When the group split up, Kent and I hurried over to the garage. I had burned my chair leg club with my Ghillie suit and hood. Kent's belt looked normal, except it was still wet. Neither of us had bloodstains on our clothes. I told Kent to follow my lead.

I walked into Mom's kitchen, tracking mud on her kitchen floor. Kent was right behind me. Of course, she spotted it right away. Both Kent and I got a bawling out that would have caused Roy or Gene to ride for the hills. We apologized and told her we must have gotten mud on our shoes at Big Rock while fishing. Kent even complained about the one that got off his hook. Sometimes, he doesn't know when to stop.

We retreated to the garage, where Dad didn't much care about mud, and we made a big deal about telling him how the fish weren't biting. We were lucky he hadn't noticed my fishing pole had never left the closet.

We played in the garage until it was time for Kent to ride his bike home for supper. No ruckus so far, but we knew things were about to change. I was trying to act normal. So, that's when I struck up a conversation with Dad.

"Whose car is that with a tarp over it?" I asked.

Dad stopped what he was doing and gave me a stern look. "Boy, you keep quiet about Angus MacDonald's Chevrolet 3100."

"You got the parts in this fast?"

"Got enough to get started. I want to finish it and get it out of here."

"You afraid of the cops?" I asked, unsure if he would get mad at me for asking a dumb question.

"Cops? You know better! It's your mom. She's on the warpath. Worse than the last time," he warned.

"Yeah, I just found out."

I told him that Kent and I had gotten fussed at the worst ever, just for tracking a little mud into the kitchen.

"You tracked mud on your momma's kitchen floor? Boy, you're lucky to be alive."

The way he said it, I wasn't sure if he was joking or not. Then, Dad told me how things would be while that pickup was in the garage.

"Billy, you listen up! I want the garage doors closed when I'm working on that pickup. You're not to mention it's here to anybody. That includes your buddy, Kent. You keep your mouth shut around your mother, too!"

I told him no problem. I was thinking to myself that I was getting a lot of practice keeping secrets. So many, I might have to start writing them all down.

Supper was tense. I finished in record time and went straight up to my room. Mom didn't say two words to Dad all evening, and she went into their bedroom early. Dad worked on bills for customers on the kitchen table without Mom helping, which wasn't normal. Grandma and Scotty retreated to the living room to watch television.

I heard a car pull into the lot at eight-fifteen. I peeked out of my bedroom window and saw it was a police car.

This was it. I knew I better put on a convincing show, or my goose was going to jail. I hated to lie in front of Mom and Dad, but I'd given my word.

There was a loud banging on the kitchen door. I heard Dad tell whoever was banging to shut up before they woke the baby. I knew Scotty was still up, but I wasn't about to correct him.

Sergeant Frank Younger and his brother Roger Younger told Dad they were there to talk to me. He asked them what about, but they refused to answer other than I was in big trouble. I thought Dad might hit one of them, but then I heard Mom barge into the conversation. Mom told them to sit down at the kitchen table and that she would call me.

When I walked into the kitchen, the two Highland Police Officers were seated. Dad was leaning against the counter by the sink, and Mom was in her bathrobe, holding Scotty. Grandma was in the living room, listening for all she was worth, but not at the television.

"Billy, come over here and sit down. We need to talk," Officer Frank Younger advised me. I knew he would be the one asking the questions because he was a sergeant and the brighter of the two.

I sat down and looked at them but didn't say a word.

"Where were you this afternoon about four or four-thirty?" asked Sergeant Younger.

"Fishing at Big Rock with Kent and a bunch of us kids."

"No, you were not! You were at the school beating up Carl and Dickie Lockhart!"

"Frank, are you nuts? Those two bullies attacked Billy behind Dalton's office and put him in the hospital! Now you claim my boy beat them up. You have got to be crazy! They're twice his size!" Dad was doing all the talking. I saw Mom start to say something, but she let Dad have this round. I kept quiet about the "twice his size" stuff.

Sergeant Frank Younger puffed out his chest and claimed, "Carl and Dickie were set upon by a gang of kids and beaten badly. They're both in the hospital. Their dad says Carl claims your boy was one of them. He's demanding we charge Billy."

Dad took one step closer to look down on the deputy. "Go to hell, Frank. When those two beat my boy two different times, what was done about it? Not a damn thing. Y'all said it was Kent's and his word against three. Billy says he was fishing. End of story. Now get out of my house before I show you what a beating is!" threatened my dad. He was madder than when he hurt me that time with his belt.

"Now, John, don't make me take you in for assault on an officer."

Then things got nasty; Mom sounded off. "You touch Billy or John, and I'll show you assault on a police officer! You'll have more trouble than you ever thought possible!" Mom was even madder than Dad. I had never seen her quite like this. She was shaking; she was so angry.

Grandma Harris got up and came to the door, at which point Mom handed Scotty to her. Grandma was looking fierce, as well. The only one not looking like they wanted to fight was Scotty. He was grinning at the grown-ups at first, but when he saw Mom and Dad so angry, his face clouded over.

The two policemen decided they could finish this interview another time. That's what they told Mom and Dad. They would be back in the morning when tempers had cooled.

But Mom wasn't finished. "You boys come on back right after you bring charges against those three bullies for hurting my Billy. Goodnight!"

"Mrs. Gunn, the only case we're working on tonight is the Lockhart case. We'll be back," announced Roger Younger, who remained out of Dad's reach.

"In that case, the Gunn family has nothing to say to you. Now, you get out of my kitchen!" Mom shouted.

They did leave. When Mom followed them to the kitchen door, I thought she might pick up the butcher knife drying on a dishtowel on the counter. She left it, thank goodness.

Grandma was bouncing Scotty to keep him quiet. Scotty figured it was time to wake the neighborhood. He had been too startled by Mom to cry at first. He now made up for lost time.

I sat still, studying the saltshaker. Dad watched the police leave. Once they were out of sight, he jerked me out of the chair by my shirt. My feet were off the floor. Dad was about to whack me good when Mom told him to put me down. He took one look at her face and did. More like he dropped me, but it didn't hurt much.

"Billy, what did you do?" Mom asked, studying my face carefully. My resolve started to weaken.

"Honest, Kent and I were fishing. We got muddy at Big Rock. There was a bunch of us fishing. We didn't do nothing."

I hated telling Mom a whopper, but I had no choice. I had taken the oath, and it was too late to back out now.

"Billy, go upstairs and don't come out of your room! I'll deal with you in a minute!" Dad told me in no uncertain terms. I ran up the stairs and went straight to my closet to put my ear to the vent. I knew I better listen because I was about to get the worst whipping ever. I needed to know how bad. If he beat me worse than that one time...now, I was scared, no... terrified!

"Laura Jane, come into the bedroom," Dad said to Mom, and they closed the door. I could still hear just fine—my closet vent connected to the kitchen and their bedroom. Only Grandma was cut off from listening.

"That boy isn't telling us the truth. I'm going to wear him out. He won't sit down for a month," threatened Dad. I knew this one was going to be the worst yet. I started to cry. Some things you can't help.

"John, you wait just a minute. I know you got your army buddies to do something to Lou McCulloch. I think Billy found out or figured out what you did. Lou stopped bullying Billy all of a sudden, so I think Billy decided to get his friends to do the same thing to the Lockhart brothers."

"What? There's no way he would know about that little midnight formation. We were careful. You don't even know much about it."

"You big lunk, Billy's too smart for his own good and yours. It's obvious. He copied you. You got your buddies, and Billy got his. What I hate, he lied to us," Mom said, then sobbed, and I felt terrible hearing her. She was hurt, and that hurt me. Now, both Mom and I were balling.

"Laura Jane, that can't be right. Please don't cry. No way, Billy found out what I did. It's this town. Between the McCullochs and the Lockharts, the town thugs are ruining everything. They ganged up on Billy and then lied. I agree that Billy is a fast learner. I think he just figured how this place works. No way he knows what I did. The kids of this town are doing the same thing the bullies are doing, doing it right back at them because the law in this town is crooked."

"Well, now what do we do? We must protect him from those town cops. Sergeant Younger said a bunch of kids beat up Carl and Dickie. This problem involves more than Kent and Billy. We need to find out who all is involved. I wonder just how many there were. How do we find out?" asked Mom.

"I know how," said Dad.

"John, you are not going to whip Billy. Do you hear me? No!" ordered Mom.

"Laura Jane, that boy deserves a whipping."

"Not while I'm alive," insisted Mom, "besides, I have a better idea. I will handle Billy."

Both Mom and Dad talked for five or ten minutes, but they were whispering, and I couldn't hear what they were saying. That's when I heard footsteps coming upstairs, but I was able to hop onto my bed before they could catch me in my closet. I wiped my eyes and blew my nose on my sheet.

"Billy?" Mom called to me outside my door, which was closed.

"Yes, ma'am."

"Open the door," she demanded.

I jumped out of bed and opened the door. She was standing there by herself, just looking at me. That made me feel worse than if Dad had whacked me one.

"Billy, I need to know something, and you have to tell the truth," said Mom with a look I had never seen her have before. I had seen this look when she talked to Dad about very private stuff, but not ever with me.

"Yes, ma'am?"

"Tell me all the kids who went fishing with you," she said in a gentle voice.

I couldn't believe it. I could tell her this and not break my oath. I told her it was a bunch from Miss Jones's class. She made me write down every name. I did.

Mom took the list, and without saying anything else, she started down the stairs but stopped after descending three steps. She turned, came back up to my room, and stood for a moment, looking at me. When she spoke, it was in a soft voice.

"Billy, I'm disappointed in you, and you know why. But you may come downstairs and watch TV with Grandma and Scotty. Your father and I are going out. You mind your grandma." And when Mom finished, darn if she didn't lean over and kiss me on the forehead.

I had braced for a beating, but that kiss struck my soul far worse than any belt on my back. Tears ran down my cheeks. Mom went on down the stairs and didn't see me wiping them away.

That's how my day ended. I wanted to tell Mom and Dad the truth, but if I told the truth to my parents, I would break my oath to my friends. Either way, I was a terrible sinner, going to hell. I watched some shows with Grandma, but I don't remember anything about them.

CHAPTER 30
TWO CAMPS
Tuesday, August 2, 1955

Matt was thinking about how things were a little better. But, of course, his depression over losing his wife and son was still with him, especially when he was alone in his apartment. Those moments were still agony. He thought of his loss first thing when he awoke, and it was always with him when he tried to fall asleep each night. That loss was a constant in his life, a mantle of grief he could not remove. But work and new friends were helping.

Hotel reservations were better since the public believed the sniper scare had passed, improving his outlook. A diversion that helped the most during daytime hours was created by those two scamps, Billy and Kent.

Following his morning ritual, Matt picked up his breakfast and was the first of the group to enjoy the morning air on the loading dock. Richard, his maintenance man, cleaned the loading dock like it was part of the hotel kitchen. Matt appreciated Richard's work because it kept the bugs at bay and rid the area of unpleasant orders except for one.

Polecat had just arrived with the morning papers and joined him. Matt was watching for Billy and Kent to come next, but they were unusually late.

"Mr. Smith, how are you this morning?" asked Matt.

"The corpus is well and wants to partake of another glorious meal prepared by your kitchen staff. However, my mind is full of concern."

"Is something the matter?" inquired Matt.

"Yesterday, it appears the rising seventh-grade class retaliated in response to the past malicious conduct of Carl Lockhart and his brother, Dickie. The two bullies became the victims of an ambuscade in the woods behind the elementary school. Payback included a full measure of personal damage with interest compounded at an exorbitant rate. They were treated by the Waynesboro Hospital's emergency department physician and several Florence Nightingales of medicine. Fortunately, by dawn, both boys could be discharged into the tender care of their mother. Unfortunately, their father is demanding that the entire seventh-grade class be charged with attempted murder. As we dine, the constabulary is rounding up the young suspects for a rigorous interrogation," reported Polecat.

"Would that be why Billy and Kent are not dining with us this morning?" asked Matt.

"Your supposition is correct. The boys and their class members are at the Highland Police Department. Parents, townspeople, and a certain teacher are about to storm the Highland Bastille, armed with anger and expletives in lieu of pitchforks and clubs. According to the local gossip guillotine, heads are about to roll," opined Polecat with the satisfaction of knowing his opinion was one hundred percent correct.

"Excuse me, Mr. Smith. I'd better get to town," Matt exclaimed. He ran from the loading dock, through the kitchen, and to his apartment to change into a suit. Ten minutes later, he was drove to the courthouse slightly above the speed limit.

Seeing the crowd in the street, Matt decided his first stop would be to gather some neutral assistance. He went to his office and called the state police. Explaining things to Sergeant Oliver, Matt asked him to send all available troopers to the Highland Police Department. He requested they avoid using red lights and sirens once they arrived near town. Matt wanted to calm down, not incite matters.

He found Sheriff Lawrence in his office, calling in more deputies. Both men agreed that the crowd was about to become a mob. Matt observed Officer Lincoln unlocking the department's gun cabinet, which was not good.

"Sheriff, Shoat, looks like we have a mess," said Matt to the two officers.

"More than a mess. Hell, we got moms and a sixth-grade teacher about to lynch the chief of police. That dummy promised to let the parents stay with the kids, but when he got them inside the police station, he and his men tossed the parents out. We may need the state police here before this is over," replied Sheriff Lawrence.

Matt looked sheepish and announced, "I've already called them, but I told them to arrive quietly without red lights and sirens. I'm praying Trooper Giles comes with them. He can calm things down if anyone can."

The sheriff nodded. "Probably not a bad idea. I was just about to do the same. Let's go on over to the PD and see what's going on. I just hope we aren't too late."

It was evident that the sheriff was worried. However, Matt was relieved to see that he had not caused a rift between himself and the sheriff by asking for troopers.

Matt, Sheriff Lawrence, and Shoat walked down the street to the Highland Police Department, where thirty agitated people were in front of the building. Two plant security guards were blocking the door, keeping the parents and others from entering. Many parents were demanding entrance, and others their children's release. When they saw the sheriff, they began calling to him to bring out their children.

"Folks, let me see what's going on. I promise I'll be sure your children aren't being harmed. Give me a minute. I'll come back out and let you know the situation," yelled Sheriff Lawrence with his hands high.

It got a little quieter, but threats were still being yelled, especially by some men in the rear. When the sheriff, Matt, and Officer Lincoln tried to enter the front door, the two guards blocked their way. Each had a twelve-gauge shotgun at port arms.

"Gentlemen, I'm the sheriff of Green Mountain County, and this is the Commonwealth's Attorney. Move aside!" ordered the sheriff.

"We got orders from the chief. No one comes in until Chief McCulloch tells us it's okay," said one of the guards.

This was a standoff of the worst order. Matt saw several men run across the street to the parking lot behind the furniture store. He was sure they weren't leaving. He figured that within moments, there would be shotguns and rifles in the hands of some outraged parents.

"Let us enter, or I'll arrest you!" demanded the sheriff.

The two guards pointed their shotguns at the sheriff, and a hush fell over the crown.

That's when a voice behind Matt spoke. "Lower your shotguns. Place them carefully on the ground!"

Matt turned his head to see Sergeant Oliver, Trooper Giles, Trooper Quinn, and Trooper Lusk. They had their pistols aimed at the foreheads of the two guards. The crowd began moving back. Several men had returned with shotguns, but they were just standing in the street holding them, watching the confrontation between the Virginia State Police versus the McCulloch plant guards.

The two security guards did as they were told. They quickly found themselves searched, and their sidearms were taken. Sheriff Lawrence had Shoat escort them to the jail in handcuffs. Trooper Quinn went with Deputy Lincoln as additional help.

The sheriff then stood on the steps and addressed the crowd. "You, men, do me a favor and put those guns up." Those men with weapons started back to their vehicles.

Sheriff Lawrence added, "We'll handle this, folks. Now give us a minute and let us help you."

Three more deputies arrived. The sheriff posted two of his men at the front door of the police station. They didn't have shotguns or stand with weapons. In fact, the deputies began talking with members of the crowd in a friendly manner, calling people by name. One deputy wore a sports shirt and jeans with his gun belt over his civilian clothes. He had remembered to pin his badge to his shirt pocket.

Sergeant Oliver, two troopers, Sheriff Lawrence, and Matt all walked into the Highland Police Department, where there was bedlam. Sixth graders were in the lobby, and children were being interrogated in every space available. Several students were crying, which didn't help the noise level. Kent was in the chief's office; Billy was in the weight room; Danny Mason was in the drunk cell with Officer Roger Younger, and so on. When Sheriff Lawrence's group walked into the lobby, things got quiet by degrees as the kids and officers noticed them. Then, Chief McCulloch came storming out of his office to confront the group.

"What the hell is this?" he demanded.

"Chief, you're about to cause a riot. I don't know if you've looked outside lately, but you have a mob of parents who are about to take this police department apart," said Sheriff Lawrence in a very calm voice. It was soft, just above a whisper, which was more effective than yelling.

"My security detail can handle a bunch of parents and townies," responded the chief.

"Your security detail is in my jail. My men, not yours, are outside, and I need some answers. That mob is getting armed, and things might get nasty if we don't calm some tempers."

"Parents can wait. The first order of business is to arrest these sixth-grade hooligans. They beat up Carl and Dickie Lockhart. Mr. Lockhart's on his way over here right now to press charges," responded Chief McCulloch.

Matt decided it was time for him to get involved. "You're going to arrest the entire sixth-grade class? Have they confessed?"

"Not yet. But we'll break the little shits before this day is out," declared the chief of police.

The sheriff walked a little closer to the chief. "Chief, do I need to remind you that when the shoe was on the other foot, you warned me to do nothing. You claimed it was the word of three against two. As I remember, no charges were brought against your son and the Lockhart boys because the evidence was conflicted. Now, you say no one has confessed. So how is this different, other than it's two versus ten or more?" asked Sheriff Lawrence.

Billy and Kent, along with everyone else, had come out into the lobby to listen.

"Mr. Cubley, BB, and the rest of us were fishing over at Big Rock. You can ask everybody."

Matt turned to see who was speaking. It was Kent, which was a shocker.

Suddenly, all the kids started saying the same thing in different ways. "Yeah, we were fishing. We were all together, fishing. Ask anybody."

Matt was about to say something else when the front door of the police department slammed open. Richard Lockhart had arrived—angry.

"Little John, why aren't these little monsters in jail? Just what in Sam Hill's going on?" Richard Lockhart demanded to know.

All the kids began to yell. Yelling how they were fishing, and they were innocent and wanted to go home.

"Shut up!" yelled Chief McCulloch. "By God, we'll get you to talk, and I'm going to charge every last one of you. Now let's get back to it."

Chief McCulloch yelled so loudly that he began to cough. When the chief of police stopped coughing, there was a moment of silence.

That's when a voice was heard from behind Mr. Lockhart. "It's true. We were all fishing." This voice belonged to Roger Younger, Jr., who had arrived behind Mr. Lockhart.

"Boy, you shut up and get back to the house, or I'll tan your hide," yelled Roger's father, whose face was beet red.

"Dad, you made me change my story when Lou hit Billy with the bat, but I'm not changing it anymore. Besides, now there's a conflict of interest because I'm in Miss Jones's class," said Roger Junior.

"Shut your mouth, boy!" again yelled his father.

"Let the boy speak, or I'll have you in jail for interfering with a witness," said Matt. He asked Roger to explain why it would be a conflict of interest. Matt knew the reason, but he wanted the other to hear it from a student.

"Mr. Cubley, Billy explained to me how you said a relative or your boss needs to step aside from a criminal case. That's what the law calls a conflict of interest. The law requires the court to get a special person to handle things so everything is fair. Isn't that right?" asked Roger. He went on to add, "Besides, it took place on school property."

"Sheriff, what the boy says does change things. I recused myself as Commonwealth's Attorney when the two boys who work for me were victims of a crime. Now, I don't see how the Highland Police Department can investigate this matter since Roger is a classmate," Matt said, walking up to young Roger Younger and putting his hand on Roger's shoulder.

The sheriff took up the argument. "If Roger might be involved, it would be better for another department to handle this. And he's right about the other point, too!" agreed Sheriff Lawrence.

It was clear from the look on his face that Chief McCulloch was missing the second point.

"Chief, where did the Lockhart boys say this alleged assault and battery took place?" asked Matt.

"No alleged to it. It's crystal clear. It was attempted murder behind the Highland Elementary School. Am I not correct, Mr. Lockhart?" the chief asked Richard.

"You are, Chief. Now, can we get on with writing up the criminal charges?" asked Mr. Lockhart.

Matt called out, "Sheriff, my Uncle TJ served on the school board for many years. He told me that the county school board asked the Highland Police Department to help provide officers to manage traffic and law enforcement at the local schools. They refused. So, a contract was signed with the sheriff's department to handle school matters like traffic control and criminal investigations. Therefore, Sheriff Lawrence, not Chief McCulloch, should be conducting this investigation under that school board contract."

Matt finished his speech and looked at Sheriff Lawrence.

The sheriff added more fuel to Matt's fire. "Mr. Cubley, we sure don't want Mr. Lockhart's sons to be shortchanged on an investigation as important as this one. Besides, we might have to bring charges against Lou McCulloch for certain crimes recently alleged that he committed. His dad would have a conflict of interest in those cases for certain. We must be fair to everyone, correct, Chief?" asked the sheriff. He got no answer and expected none.

"Now, all of you sixth graders, who are ...." The sheriff got interrupted by a voice near Chief McCulloch. It was Kent, again.

"Sheriff, we're seventh graders. We finished sixth grade and will start seventh grade at the end of August. Just so everyone knows," said Superman, and his classmates giggled, just a little. Many were afraid to laugh. Trooper Giles and Deputy Lincoln coughed into their hands to hide a chuckle. Billy gave Kent a pop on the arm and a frown to be quiet.

"I stand corrected, Mr. Clark. Now, with your permission, may I continue?"

Kent never said a word, but his face flushed bright red.

"I want all of you seventh graders to follow me outside. My men and I will be sure you get with your parents or get a ride home. In a day or two, I'll need you to come down to my office to tell me your side of things," said the sheriff. A mass exodus of children left the Highland Police Department, out the front door, and into the street.

When the students began to appear, a cheer went up from the crowd. Moms and dads pushed forward to grab a child or children. Sheriff Lawrence explained to the group that he was taking over the investigation. Parents could stay with their children during any future interviews, which would begin in a day or two.

Just when it looked like things were over and the crowd would disperse, two trucks and a van drove up. Ten plant security men jumped out, holding shotguns with ax handles hung on their gun belts by rope loops.

Matt noticed Linda Carlisle standing on the steps in front of the courthouse. She was watching the activity. That's when Miss Jones, the schoolteacher, walked right up to Buster Brown Denkins, also called Bulldog, and pointed a finger at his face.

"You go back to the plant where you belong and put those stupid shotguns and ax handles up. You should be ashamed, scaring people." She ended her speech by saying, "Now git!"

When two of the guards grabbed her, Sheriff Lawrence and Sergeant Oliver told them to let the teacher go. There was a sort of growl coming from the crowd. Men were drifting back to their cars and pickups again.

The security guards focused all their attention on Sheriff Lawrence and Sergeant Oliver. Miss Jones was released, but one guard after another racked his shotgun to load a round. The guards made no effort to leave.

Matt glanced at the courthouse, but Linda wasn't there. He was relieved that she had gone back inside and was out of harm's way. He was expecting things to get ugly quickly.

Bulldog Denkins, the head of this group of James Baldwin Detective Agency guards, walked up to the sheriff and Sergeant Oliver. He paid no attention to Matt, who wasn't in uniform.

"My men are special police of Green Mountain County. Now get out of my way. We're here to clear the street and secure the Highland Police Department," said Bulldog to Lawrence and Oliver.

"The street was about to be cleared when you showed up. It's you who needs to leave. I have things under control," said Sheriff Lawrence.

"We'll handle this our way," said Bulldog, turning to the crowd. "You have five seconds to leave, or my men will make you wish you were never born. Get in your cars and move. One…Two… Three…

That's when a voice cried out, "Sheriff Lawrence, I'm revoking the Baldwin Detective Agency appointments as special officers right now. You, sir, remove your men at once," shouted Judge John Winston Harland, III. He was still wearing his robe. "You are disturbing the peace, and you just disrupted a civil trial in my court. If I don't see the last of you in less than a minute, I'll hold every one of you in contempt of court. Sheriff, Sergeant Oliver, see my orders are carried out, forthwith!"

The security guards began to look around them. They saw eight men with deer rifles and shotguns to their rear, deputies and troopers to their front, a red-faced judge to their left, and a schoolteacher who was livid and about to tangle with their boss. Moms on every side looked like they might just enter the fray along with their husbands.

Chief McCulloch and his officers had remained in their building. They were watching through the front windows.

The crowd parted, allowing the security men to leave. Things went from boiling to calm in a minute. Parents departed with their children, and peace returned.

Matt and Sheriff Lawrence made sure Roger Younger was outside with them, and he was. The sheriff had one of his deputies drive Roger home. The deputy explained to Roger's mom that Roger was not to be punished, and the sheriff wanted to know the first moment it looked like Roger Senior might give the boy a whipping. He hoped she would do as asked.

Billy and Kent were standing with Billy's mom and dad. Kent's mom was at the bank and not allowed to leave. The bank doors were locked with the shades drawn. The bank manager was so afraid of the mob that he was shaking.

Mr. Cubley walked over to Billy and Kent. "Boys, you ask your parents if you should stay home or come to work. Your choice," said Mr. Cubley.

"Matt, I think I'm going to leave that up to Billy's mom," John Gunn wisely said. Laura Jane sent Kent and Billy up to the hotel to work. She told her husband she thought they would be safer there—more out of sight of certain town officers.

Matt knew that the parents of the rising seventh graders needed to talk this out. The sheriff was wise to give them a day or two because some fundamental changes would be required for the health of the community.

The town was tearing itself apart. One camp involved the workers and the middle class. The other camp consisted of the bigwigs, town police, and now these plant guards. If things exploded, neither side would win. Three bullies and most of the seventh graders were right in the middle of what might turn into a class war.

CHAPTER 31
LIES WRAPPED IN LIES
Friday, August 5, 1955

Matt felt anxious as he drove to the courthouse for a nine o'clock meeting. The Amherst Special Prosecutor, Henry Watkins, had agreed to return and conduct the investigation into the attack on Carl and Dickie Lockhart. After two days of inquiry, Henry would give a preliminary report to Matt and Sheriff Lawrence. Police Chief McCulloch had not been invited to the meeting.

Polecat had kept Matt informed about the town's ill feelings regarding the roundup of the seventh-grade class. The *Highland Gazette* made no mention of the attempted interrogation of the class but published an article about the brutal attack on the Lockhart boys. The vague identity of their attackers referenced local hooligans, but no names were printed.

Matt recalled that the attacks on Billy and Kent never made the local paper. In this week's edition, the article was silent on the Highland Police Department's standoff, with no mention of Judge Harland retracting the Baldwin detectives' power to make arrests. After reading today's article, Matt angrily threw the Friday morning paper into the trash can.

Special Prosecutor Watkins had tried to calm the parents by honoring the sheriff's commitment to allow them to come with their children for interviews. Thankfully, most parents and children had shown up for questioning, with only a few fathers grumbling about the inconvenience.

Today, Matt and the sheriff would learn who Special Prosecutor Watkins wanted arrested. Matt was worried that Billy and Kent might be at the top of the list.

Henry Watkins, Sheriff Lawrence, and his chief deputy, Ed Barnes, arrived promptly at nine o'clock. After a short greeting, Mr. Watkins started to speak but was interrupted by Police Chief

McCulloch barging into Matt's office. Mrs. Harvey was following on his coattails in protest.

"Chief McCulloch, is there some emergency?" asked Sheriff Lawrence.

"Damn right there is! Why was I not told about this conference?" demanded Little John.

"Chief, there's a conflict of interest in your department. You know that. Why would you think you should be at this meeting?" responded Mr. Watkins, rising to his feet. Mrs. Harvey was standing behind the chief, looking like she was ready to toss him into the hall.

"This is my town, and I want to know what you are going to do about these delinquents. You've delayed long enough. My officers stand ready to start serving warrants," growled Chief McCulloch, and he looked almost as angry as Mrs. Harvey.

That's when Matt stood. "Mr. Watkins, while this is my office, I'll defer to you on who stays and who leaves," announced Matt.

Watkins paused and said, "Chief, I don't have strong feelings on the matter. Get a chair from the other room if you want to stay, but this meeting will remain orderly. Is that clear?"

Chief McCulloch didn't respond but brought in a chair from the next room. Mrs. Harvey left with a lingering cold look at the chief. The meeting started a second time with a bang when Matt's door was closed by an angry Mrs. Harvey. Matt was confident that someday, Little John would pay for ignoring Mrs. Harvey, the keeper of the inner sanctum.

Once everyone was seated and the atmosphere had returned to a ceasefire climate, Henry Watkins reported he first interviewed the two girls, Lucy Scarlett and Nancy Hodges. Both had stuck to the fishing expedition story. Nancy was angry over losing her two kittens and blamed Carl and Dickie. Despite Mr. Watkins trying to keep her testimony centered on the attack, she kept returning to that event. Lucy confirmed that the boys had fished with worms. And the police found two cans of them discarded by the river. Each described how everyone had gotten muddy, which claim was supported by several mothers.

Chief McCulloch muttered the word *liar* several times until Mr. Watkins warned him what would happen if he kept interrupting. The chief, after that, kept his comments to under-his-breath mutterings.

All the boys, except one, insisted the class went fishing and had nothing to do with any attack on Carl and Dickie. The stories were alike in detail, too much so, commented the prosecutor.

The boy, who admitted the attack and implicated the children, was Roger Younger. His dad had escorted him to the interview room. When the boy entered the room, his dad shoved him toward a chair so violently that he fell over it.

"I'm staying here," the father had announced. He then pointed his finger at Roger and said, "Boy, you better tell the truth!"

"Well, now we're getting somewhere," muttered Chief McCulloch, loud enough to be heard.

Mr. Watkins ignored the comment and told the group how Roger Younger identified who laid out the plan, stole the basketball from the Lockhart's drive, wrote and left the note, and what happened to Carl and Dickie behind the school. Roger said he couldn't remember what each child had done during the attack.

"We all had hoods," Henry quoted the boy, then added, "At that point in the interview, Roger's dad moved toward his son, and the boy flinched as if he feared that he might be struck. I told his dad to back off."

Roger told me how the group cleaned up at the school, burned the weapons, and moved to the fishing hole to create their alibi.

Chief McCulloch's chair creaked as he shifted his weight to the front edge of his seat.

"There you have it. Let's get started on the arrest warrants. My men want to be finished before dark," stated Chief McCulloch, who stood as if the meeting were over.

"Chief, I'm not satisfied who's telling the truth," Mr. Watkins declared.

"What! What kind of Tom foolishness are you putting out? You got two victims and now an independent witness to corroborate their testimony. Any jackass could win this case," Chief McCulloch had raised his voice almost to a shout.

Henry said nothing for a long moment.

"Roger Younger, I'm certain, was forced by his dad to repeat a certain version. This is not the first time he's done it, either. When Billy Gunn was hit in the head at the park, Roger Younger announced in public that your boy struck first without provocation. Then, when I interviewed Roger, he said he didn't see what had happened."

Chief McCulloch gave Matt an icy look. "That's because the Gunn boy's a liar!"

Henry looked pained. "Chief, when I had the word of Billy against your boy, no warrants were issued because the evidence was almost even. I wasn't close to the bar of proof beyond a reasonable doubt."

Chief McCulloch sat back down, "So what?"

Now, Henry stood to speak. "When Billy and Kent were attacked behind Dalton's law office, Lou, Carl, and Dickie denied doing it. I didn't believe them, but Lou's grandfather swore Lou was at his house all day. Likewise, Richard Lockhart said Carl and Dickie were working at the hardware. No warrants were issued".

"What has that got to do with anything?" asked the chief.

"Quite a lot. I have sworn statements from nine boys and two girls that they had nothing to do with the Lockhart attack but were fishing. Such testimony will be nearly impossible to overcome in a trial."

"Give those little snots to me. My men will make them tell the truth!" growled Little John.

"No judge will buy into such a fouled-up mess. Lies on lies are all I'm finding. Regarding the attack on Billy and Kent when their bikes were stolen, I believe that Lou, Carl, and Dickie lied to me."

"You better watch your mouth. You go calling Big John and Mr. Lockhart liars, and you might find yourself, ..." began Chief McCulloch.

"Chief, I'm not finished. If you want to stay, you better let me finish. I'm not from here, and I don't much care what your daddy or Mr. Lockhart thinks or doesn't think. Now, be silent," shouted Mr. Watkins, and his face was moving into a shade of red.

Chief McCulloch glared at the prosecutor but remained quiet.

"Gentlemen, my star witness is a boy who's changed his story several times. When Roger got up to leave at the end of this last interview, I put my hand on his shoulder. He winced. I asked him to take off his shirt because I suspected he'd been beaten. His dad grabbed him, jerked him out the door, and told me to 'go to hell.' I never got to see the boy's back. I won't go to trial on the testimony of a boy I think was abused. I don't know how this town will survive on a foundation of liars. So, I'm halting my investigation," concluded Mr. Watkins.

The room was silent, but only for a moment.

Chief McCulloch blurted out, "By gosh, we'll handle this the old-fashioned way, with or without warrants!"

Sheriff Lawrence stood up and faced the chief.

"Chief, have you not been listening? The town officials must start setting a proper example. Otherwise, our children will turn out worse than the adults, if that's possible.

"Well, things are going to change. That's for sure!" replied Chief McCulloch, and he opened Matt's door so hard it banged on the wall. Then, he stormed out of the office without even looking at Mrs. Harvey.

"Have a nice day, chief," Mrs. Harvey called out as the chief was halfway through the outer office door.

The lady has guts, thought Matt.

"Guess I would have been better off not letting the chief stay," remarked Mr. Watkins.

Sheriff Lawrence shook his head, no. "Wouldn't have mattered none. Nope, I think Little John was destined to detonate. I wish I could be a fly on the wall when Little John tells Big John about this meeting. The shock might kill the old bastard," said Sheriff Lawrence.

Ed Barnes paled. "Sheriff, I know you don't mean that. Uh, gentlemen, could we keep that last comment to ourselves?" requested Barnes, trying to protect his sheriff.

"Ed, Big John's going to be so mad that it won't matter what I just said. And he is an old bastard, and I'm probably off his Christmas card list for good," said Sheriff Lawrence.

Matt asked Mr. Watkins to write a report for the press and the public.

The special prosecutor smiled and spoke, "Matt, I'll be happy to write that the evidence of the witnesses is conflicted, and the investigation will not continue for now. I will, of course, omit the sheriff's colorful description of a local factory owner. The statement was incorrect—much too restrained."

That broke the tension, and even Ed Barnes smiled.

When his visitors left, Matt asked Mrs. Harvey into his office for her thoughts.

"Mr. Cubley, I've only worked for you a short time, but I judge you, to be honest. I'm not sure how much help that will be in this town, but I'm glad you are. However, I do have a suggestion. You need to go to Miss Jones. That teacher's the key to dealing with the children. She'll help you, but only if you assure her all efforts are directed to helping the children and not locking them up," advised Mrs. Harvey.

Just as Matt picked up the phone to call the teacher, Sergeant Oliver arrived and asked Mrs. Harvey if he might have a word with her boss.

Matt called out, "Sergeant, come on in."

They exchanged greetings, and Matt gave the sergeant a brief report on the meeting with the special prosecutor. He left out the colorful language but did warn him of Chief McCulloch's reaction.

"I would expect no less from Chief McCulloch," said Sergeant Oliver.

"What brings you into town, Sergeant?" asked Matt.

"I wanted to report our progress on tailing the MacDonald bootleggers. We have had limited luck. We know MacDonald changes the route from Franklin County every time his man runs a load. His driver uses portions of the Blue Ridge Parkway from Roanoke to Afton Mountain. He doesn't use it much because he wants to avoid the Feds, but he uses parts to connect to back roads. Angus's man is good at avoiding us, especially near the end of his run," stated the sergeant.

"How so?" asked Matt.

"When he gets near Waynesboro, this bootlegger uses blocking cars. He's smart. We even got an unmarked ghost car out of Richmond, and darned if his people didn't block it with up to three blocking cars. We never get close enough to know where his storehouse is located. This is getting very frustrating," complained the sergeant.

"Are no loads going over to the cabin on Bear Creek?" asked Matt.

"Not a one since we started tailing him. He's avoiding Green Mountain County like the plague."

"Sergeant, we may be on to something. Angus MacDonald may be using a delivery system we can't detect," suggested Matt.

"Matt, I'm thinking the same thing. If the Highland Police are running the liquor over to the hotel from Waynesboro, that'll make it darn difficult for us. Are we chasing our tails?"

"I hope not," responded Matt, but with Polecat's hint about Doc, Matt was sure they were on the right track.

The sergeant then asked, "Is this effort helping with who killed Mr. Albert Winston Brown?" stated the sergeant with a question, not entirely a question but a doubt.

"I hope so. Bootleggers, the McCulloch operation, and this murder sure seem connected. Can we get someone inside that hotel?" asked Matt.

"We tried several years ago, but Chief Smith knew about it within days. We had to pull our man out. I think Big John may have a contact high up in Richmond. We need a local who already works at the hotel that we can flip—a stool pigeon. But even if someone flips, will that lead us to who killed Brown?"

Matt shrugged his shoulders. "I don't know, but it looks like it might."

The two men shook hands and promised to keep plugging along, but so far, no breaks other than that Indian Head Penny.

Matt tried to call Miss Jones, but there was no answer. He made himself a mental note to keep trying. While Matt was glad no arrest warrants had been issued for the kids, especially Kent and Billy, he feared for the children's future. What would a city populated with McCullochs be like? Matt was sure he wouldn't want to live in such a place. The adults were spinning lies wrapped in lies, and the kids were starting to get better at it than the adults.

CHAPTER 32
A YOUNGSTER SHOT
Saturday, August 6, 1955

Matt was talking to Maddie when Polecat arrived for breakfast. They waited while Maddie filled two plates with biscuits and gravy, bacon, and scrambled eggs. Then, along with a cup of hot coffee, they moved to the loading dock.

"Mr. Smith, what news this morning? I want something cheerful. The boys are being kept at home. I miss their company and need a bit of merriment."

"My good sir, merriment has fled the shire for parts unbeknownst to me. 'Tis no joy to which I'm privy. Our spirits will profit not from the gyre of malcontented dispatches being set to ink at the *Highland Gazette*. Sunday's periodical will confirm the worst. The young prince, the heir to the throne, has been laid low, and it bodes not well for his recovery. The only offspring of a patrolman has absconded. The boy is lost within the mists of obscure travel. A hue and cry have been raised for the capture of the assassin," announced Polecat, but Matt had only an idea of what Polecat had just said.

"I don't understand," replied Matt.

Suddenly, Chuck Tolliver rushed onto the loading dock. He was agitated, with one eye twitching. The slamming of the kitchen's screen door accented his arrival with a bang.

"Matthew, the sheriff just called! Lou McCulloch has been shot! His mother found him on the family tennis court at dusk after hearing the shot. A gun was recovered, but it didn't belong to his father or grandfather. The youngster is in the hospital in critical condition with a gunshot wound to his head," Chuck blurted out, then paused for a breath.

"Oh, no, that's awful!" exclaimed Matt. "Mr. Smith, is that what you meant?"

"Isn't that what I just told you?" proclaimed Polecat.

"Do they know who shot him?" Matt.

Polecat spoke before Chuck. "I just told you. It was Roger Younger, the son. The only offspring of one of the day-shift officers. One should be able to deduce the facts without these extraneous and redundant questions. Plus, Roger has fled the county. His father reported him missing last night at midnight. I expect by now the entire state is searching for him," responded Polecat to Matt's question.

"Why in the world would Roger shoot Lou?" Matt asked and looked first at Chuck, who shrugged, and then at a stoic Polecat.

"The injured animal bites the one responsible for the injury without hesitation or remorse," said Polecat.

Mr. Tolliver interrupted with, "Matthew, the sheriff did tell me that Officer Younger admitted that the gun found at the scene was one of his house guns."

Matt had hoped for merriment but found disaster. Now, there was a manhunt out for a twelve-year-old boy who might have just killed the grandson of Big John McCulloch.

"Mr. Smith, where might the boy have gone?" wondered Matt, knowing if anyone had a good guess, it would be Polecat.

"I know not! The only certainty is that if Chief McCulloch locates the boy first, well, a trial will be unlikely. But, if Roger's father finds him first, the adolescent may wish Chief McCulloch had found him—for a less painful and quicker end. Either way, a bad result ranks paramount for the future of Master Younger," said Polecat, and with that statement, silence fell over the loading dock.

Matt picked up his plate with food still on it and returned it to the kitchen. Then, knowing his duty waited, he drove to town.

Upon arriving at the sheriff's office, he found that the place was a beehive of activity. Sergeant Oliver at the front counter greeted Matt. When the sheriff heard Matt's name, he came out into the lobby. The three men went into the sheriff's office, and Matt was given an up-to-date report on the search for the youngster. Roger was partially safe for the present because Chief McCulloch and the rest of the family were at the hospital. Lou was in a coma, but the bullet had not penetrated the skull. Instead, it had passed underneath the scalp, following the bony surface in a curve until it exited. That was the good news. The bad, he suffered a severe concussion. Prayers were being offered for his recovery because the doctors were saying only time and nature would decide Lou's fate.

Now, Roger's father was missing and presumed to be looking for Roger Junior. Everyone was concerned that he might find him.

The sheriff called Henry Watkins at home to tell him the news. Henry voiced what the others were thinking. Roger Junior shot Lou because of the beatings that forced him to support Lou's version of events.

After an hour with no other news, Matt returned to the hotel. When he parked, he noticed a familiar blue 1938 Buick Special in one of the check-in spaces. He knew either John or Laura Jane Gunn was at the hotel. When Matt walked into the hotel lobby, Billy's mom rose from a chair and approached.

"Mr. Cubley, may we talk?" Laura Jane asked.

"Of course. Would you like some coffee or tea?" asked Matt.

Laura Jane chose tea. She was shocked to hear of Lou being shot and even more surprised to learn that Roger Younger may have been responsible.

Also, she believed Roger Senior was an abusive father. She immediately asked Matt to join her in praying that his dad wouldn't locate Roger Junior. Then she did something that Matt wasn't expecting.

Laura Jane began to cry.

In between sobs, she told Matt how her husband had whipped Billy with a belt for damaging one of the customer's cars with a rock. This had happened last summer, and since then, she wouldn't let her husband keep Scotty by himself. Also, she was more guarded when John and Billy were together.

She ended with, "While my husband suffers from things that happened to him in the war, I don't think John will ever hurt Scotty or Billy. He learned his lesson because he suffered so much after scarring Billy with his belt."

Laura Jane wiped away a tear, blew into a tissue, and recovered her composure.

"Mr. Cubley, Billy has been so happy working for you."

"Is that why you wanted to speak to me, to talk about Billy's attitude?" Matt asked Billy's mom.

"Yes! No! I'm worried about all the children. Things are not what we mothers want. Recently, many of the mothers have been meeting. We're fed up with what's going on. Things need to change, but we don't know how to change them. We need help!" said Laura Jane, and her eyes were starting to fill with tears again.

"I'll help, but where should I start?" asked Matt.

"We want you to stop the bullies from hurting our children. This situation is turning our children into worse than bullies. The children are banding together, taking the law into their own hands, and someone may end up dead. If Lou McCulloch dies, we're too late!"

"I know. It's terrible about poor Lou. I didn't know Roger hated him so."

"I can't believe it. Neither Kent's mother nor I ever saw that side of Roger Junior," stated Laura Jane.

"It's strange that he could hide his true feelings so well," agreed Matt.

Laura Jane wiped her eyes with her soggy tissue and then whispered, "The main reason I'm here is that my boy has never lied to me about something important. With this attack on the Lockhart boys, Billy lied to me. I know he was one of the attackers, and it's breaking my heart. What can I do? Can you help me?"

"Mrs. Gunn, I want to help. Here, have a clean tissue," Matt said as he handed Laura Jane the box of tissues off his desk. Matt sat, thinking, while Laura Jane was drying her tears.

"Let's think this through together. Now that we have a special prosecutor looking into the cases involving the bullies, I'm out of that investigation and free to do other things—legal things as a private attorney."

"What does that mean?" asked Laura Jane.

"Since I'm a part-time prosecutor, I'm free to serve other clients, private clients. I just can't take clients that would conflict with an active criminal case I'm prosecuting. So being recused from taking part in Billy's cases, I'm free to help you. My fee is one dollar. How does that sound?" asked Matt.

"How can you charge a dollar?" asked Laura Jane.

"I can charge whatever I want. One dollar is sufficient for you to be my client," stated Matt.

"I want my boy to tell me the truth, but I don't want him to be the only one punished," explained Laura Jane.

"I think the answer is to get Billy to talk to someone not connected to law enforcement. Someone that he trusts. Who would you pick?" asked Matt.

Laura Jane sat perfectly still for thirty seconds. She looked at Matt several times but then would look away and out of the window. Finally, she turned to Matt and said, "I think Billy would talk to Miss Jones. Billy and Kent think Miss Jones hung the moon and stars."

Matt smiled. "You're the second person to tell me I should call on her."

"Did another parent tell you to call Miss Jones?"

"No, it was my secretary, Mrs. Harvey. She told me Miss Jones knows the kids of this town better than anyone. She urged me to contact her," said Matt.

"Well, your secretary's smart," confirmed Laura Jane.

"Okay, let's start there. Why don't we have a meeting with Miss Jones? I will hire her as my investigator so my attorney-client privilege will cover her."

Laura Jane asked, "And no one can make her testify against Billy?"

"That's correct. You tell her what you know, and I'll do the same. Armed with as much information as we can give her, you can set up a meeting between Billy and Miss Jones. I don't think either of us should be there—just Miss Jones and Billy. What do you think?" asked Matt.

"I'm willing," responded Laura Jane.

"Does that make you feel better?"

"It does. Kent's coming to visit Billy this morning, and the boys are begging to go to the movies. Do you think it's safe to let them?"

Matt nodded his head to signal yes. "Not making light of a tragedy, but Lou's in the hospital, the bullies are at their grandparents' house, and all the cops are looking for Roger. The town children should be safe today."

"Mr. Cubley, there's one other matter that worries me. It involves my husband. I'm afraid he might go to prison if certain people find out something he's done. John has me as worried as Billy, and I need to talk to someone before I bust wide open!"

Matt hesitated but finally decided he would help her, regardless of this being a potential ethical problem if he didn't handle things just right. Any case involving John Gunn could fall into a gray area. He felt he would be doing it for Janet and Jack as much as for Laura Jane and Billy. He was risking his law license, but he decided the risk was worth it.

"Laura Jane, I don't want you to say anything because I might have to reveal what you said if asked by certain officials. But let me tell you what I suspect. I don't have any proof. I'm just speculating. Your husband didn't break into the hardware to recover the two stolen bikes, but he knows who did."

Laura Jane's eyes blinked in surprise, but she remained quiet.

Matt continued. "Someone went to Lou's house, scared him, and after that night, Lou stopped bothering Kent and Billy. I overheard your son and Kent talking about Lou no longer being a threat. I also heard them say what happened to Lou must remain a secret."

Billy's mom said nothing, but as Matt made these statements, her eyes grew larger in wonderment, and she put her hand over her mouth.

Matt continued. "Now, when Kent, Billy, and the other kids saw the bullies getting off scot-free by lying, they figured they would do the same. They got their friends, many of whom had also suffered injuries at the hands of the bullies, and they launched their big attack. However, there's a difference between the bullies and these kids. The parents of the bullies helped them to lie, but the parents of the seventh graders want to do what's right. I just hope we can correct the situation but not get your children punished while those bullies go free," Matt concluded.

"Do you think it's too late for our children?" asked Billy's mom after she got over all that Matt had guessed.

"I don't. I've gotten to know Billy and Kent. They are basically good kids. It's the adults in this town that need to grow a conscience. Some of the leaders, the normal role models, have done terrible things. We need to stop the bad conduct, and it won't be easy, but we need to try."

Laura Jane smiled. "I agree one hundred percent. We need to try. I'll call Miss Jones today. I'll tell her about our meeting and set up a time for us to talk with her."

And with that, Laura Jane stood, handed Matt a one-dollar bill, and thanked him. They set up several possible meeting times, and Laura Jane left his office.

While Billy's mom might have felt better, Matt's concerns had deepened, and he was way out on a fragile legal and ethical limb. If Lou died, things would get worse. If Roger Younger died, things would get worse. If the kids continued to get into fights, things would get worse. Unfortunately, everything was pointing to things getting worse!

CHAPTER 33

BILLY AND TWO FUGITIVES
Saturday, August 6, 1955

"Hey, Superman, over here!" I yelled as Kent rode past me on his bike. Kent's mom had followed a block behind him in her car but turned left toward town on Main Street.

"BB, what are you doing in the bushes?"

"Come here and get down!" I urged.

Kent hurried his bike into the bushes across the street from the garage and squatted beside me. As he crouched, he asked, "Well?"

I checked up and down the road and then answered. "Can't be too careful. I was watching for you when I saw one of the Highland police cars coming down the road, and he was looking for someone."

"And you know that how?" asked Kent.

"Easy. He would slow down, look down a side street and then speed up and slow down at the next street. The cop did that all the way up Main. He's hunting for a kid to push around. I didn't want it to be me, so I hid here in the bushes."

Kent peeked up and down the street. "We better be careful. I bet the cops are furious because all our friends are sticking to the plan. The Lockhart investigation is stuck in the mud," proclaimed Kent in good spirits.

"Yeah, my mom told me the same thing last night, but then, she asked me for the hundredth time if I helped beat up the Lockharts. I told her no, but I knew she didn't believe me. When I got up, she was on the phone talking about children not telling the truth. I feel awful," I whispered. If the look on my face was as sad as I felt, I could pass for Sad Sack in the comics.

"I feel the same, but we made an oath to our friends. So, what can we do?"

"Nothing. Not a thing, but I don't like it," said I with a shrug of my shoulders.

"What can we do for fun?" asked Kent.

"I know we're supposed to be grounded, but here's the deal. Dad's towing a wreck to Roanoke, which will take most of the day. Mom left a note on the kitchen table and won't be home until noon. Scotty had Grandma and Mom up most of the night. He was throwing up gobs of yellow stuff."

"Yuck! That could be catching," Kent said as he screwed up his face.

"Okay. Now, Grandma and Scotty are fast asleep in Grandma's room, and we should be able to sneak off and have fun until lunchtime," I said, trying to put a better light on things.

Kent frowned at first but then said, "Mom thinks I'm at your house. But I guess we can have a little fun if we don't get caught. Let's go chuck rocks in the lake," suggested Superman.

"Naw, too close to the Highland Police Department. Let's cruise the back streets to Mountain Drug. I heard the drugstore has some new comics, and I need a dog and Dr. Pepper for breakfast." I was hungry. Mom hadn't left anything in the oven for me, and I didn't want cereal. Heck, she left the house without even saying goodbye.

"Okay, I'll race you," Kent challenged.

We tore down side streets and across parking lots to the drugstore, where we were careful to stash our bikes in the basement entryway of Mr. Dalton's law office. We figured that was about as safe a place as we could find.

Entering the drugstore, we saw two of our buddies in a booth with drinks, reading comics. I was right, and some new comics were in. Our friends looked up and invited us over when they heard the bell over the door ring.

"Hey, Danny, Tim, how are things?" asked Kent.

"Terrible. Haven't you heard?" responded Tim Hodges.

"No, we just got here. What's going on?" I asked with a feeling of dread.

"The cops are after Roger because he shot Lou. The whole town's talking about it," Danny Mason whispered.

Tim closed his comic, pointed a wrapped drink straw at me, and spoke.

"You guys been under a rock. Lou's in the Waynesboro Hospital, and the Lockhart brothers have been shipped off to their grandparents by their mother. Every cop in the state is hunting for Roger. Talk is, if they find him, they'll shoot faster than a farmer bangs a rabid dog in August," said Tim in a whisper.

"Why would Roger shoot Lou? They aren't the best of friends, but Lou hasn't done anything to Roger," Kent said in a low voice.

The waitress came to the table and asked Kent and me for our order. We both said, "One hot dog, shoot the works, and a cold Dr. Pepper in the bottle with a straw."

I was hungry and added, "Also, an order of fries to split—two forks, please."

She left, and Tim leaned over the table, "My dad heard from a neighbor, who overheard some cops, that Roger got one beating too many from his old man. Everyone knows his dad beat him when he squealed on Lou for bopping you in the head with that baseball bat. Then, he got a worse beating when he lied about us going fishing." Tim was talking softly so we all could hear, but no one around us could.

Kent leaned in close. "I was afraid that might happen. That deputy sheriff telling Roger's mom she had to tell on her husband if he whipped Roger only made it worse. But, heck, everyone knows she would never squeal—too afraid," exclaimed Superman.

Danny butted in with, "Yeah, I heard Mom on the party line with a neighbor of the Younger family. Roger's dad was mad as a bull in a room of red flags when he discovered it was his gun that shot Lou. Roger running is all that kept his dad from killing him."

Tim added, "My mom heard from two women that several neighbors are saying they heard his dad yelling, breaking stuff, and smacking his mom around for letting Roger leave. And Mom found out that Mrs. Younger canceled her beauty shop appointment this morning."

"How bad is she?" I asked Danny.

"No one knows. She's hold up inside their house and won't answer the door," reported Danny.

"How did Roger get his dad's gun?" asked Kent. I was going with that question next, but he beat me.

Danny looked around to make sure no one was listening and then said, "My dad knows one of the cops, so he called him. It was a spare gun that Roger Senior bought for his wife to have when he worked nights. The police figured Roger swiped it and shot Lou to get even for the beatings. Anyway, all the cops and some plant goons are looking for Roger. Those Baldwin guys are bad news on a good day. If they were after me, I would leave the country and never look back," stated Danny.

Shush, someone's going to hear you," cautioned Kent when Danny got a little louder than a whisper.

Our food and Dr. Peppers arrived. When the waitress left, we began to whisper among ourselves again. We agreed it was strange that Roger tried to kill Lou. Although, we four also thought Roger had a good reason.

Thinking it through left me with this thought, so I told my friends. "At the Fourth of July Celebration, Roger got in trouble for standing up for me when Lou hit me with the ball bat. If Roger doesn't hold a grudge against me, why would he hold one against Lou? Lou's mean, but he hasn't done that much to Roger."

Round and round went our conversation, and Kent and I gave up on the comics. We were hungry and thirsty, so we rushed to finish our dogs and drinks. Since reading the comics was off-limits unless you were drinking or eating something, we had to tell Tim and Danny goodbye and leave.

Getting our bikes and not seeing any cops, we rode to the park to check it out and maybe skip some stones. Hopping off and pushing our bikes across the grass, we were deep in conversation when someone called our names.

"Billy, Kent, hi," said a voice coming from behind us. Turning, we saw Misty, the clerk from the Green Mountain Resort Hotel.

"Hi, Misty. What's up?" I called out to her. Kent gave me "the look" since I beat him, saying hi to Misty. It was evident that Kent couldn't figure out something to say. He's bashful like that.

"I guess you boys heard the news about Lou McCulloch," said Misty.

"We heard he got shot. Do you know how he's doing?" asked Kent. He got ahead of me on that one.

"No. He's alive, but no real word on his condition. How about you?" asked Misty.

"Just the same. The cops think Roger Younger shot him. Kent and I think that's not right," I said.

"It does seem odd for Roger to shoot Lou. I don't know him well, but he seemed like an okay kid. I do know his dad. Can you keep a secret?"

"Sure," we both answered her.

"I can't say I like his dad very much," Misty replied softly.

"We don't like him either. I don't know many who do," said Kent, sneezing.

"God bless," responded Misty.

"So, what are you doing out today? Anything fun going on?" I asked.

"A friend of mine disappeared, and I'm worried about her. She works with me at the hotel. I just came from her dad's house, but he claims he doesn't know where she is. I asked if he had called the police, and he told me no. Then, he asked me to leave things be," she told us with a frown.

I could see that she was worried, so I spoke up. "He's right. Calling the local police would be a mistake. I'd talk to Trooper Quinn or Giles. You might get some help from them," I said.

"I would trust those two as well," Kent added.

"Do you know them? I mean, really?" she asked.

I knew it was time to convince her. "Yeah, we know them. We see them at Cubley's Coze all the time, and we're...uh.... friends. They even let us turn on their red lights and blow their sirens, sometimes."

"How would I get in touch with them? I can't let anyone from Green Mountain Resort know," she asked us, just like we were adults.

"Well, Billy and I could arrange it. Mr. Cubley's our boss. We could ask him," Kent said.

"No, I don't want anyone else to know that it's me asking. All the cops around here are in cahoots with Big John. I could get fired or something worse," she was almost pleading. "Just forget what I said. I'll look for her on my own," she concluded.

"What if we talk to Trooper Giles and not you? I know he's not in cahoots with Big John or any of the Highland Police officers. I double swear and hope to die," I said.

"Billy's right. Trooper Giles is bubble straight," said Kent, and I knew Misty had no clue what he was telling her. We then had to go into the story about Trooper Giles' dad, the carpenter, and being on the level. Then, she got it.

"Okay, can you tell just one trooper that Cindy is missing without giving him my name?" she asked.

"I guess so. What's Cindy's last name? What does she look like?" I asked.

Misty wrote out Cindy's full name, home address (not that she was home), and her description. I took it and put it in my pocket for safekeeping.

Misty thanked us and left, walking in one direction while we rode off the other way.

We decided that we still had enough time to ride to the hotel and ask Mr. Cubley to tell Trooper Giles to meet us on the sly. It was Saturday, and we knew he wouldn't be at the courthouse. Since this was so important, we decided to get right on it.

I had just ridden onto the bridge when I saw Mom driving our 1938 Buick in our direction. We were caught, and when she got even with us, she stopped. It looked like she'd been crying, which was better than her being angry.

"Boys, why aren't you at the garage?" she asked.

I thought fast!

"Dad went on a tow, Grandma and Scotty are asleep, you weren't home, and we didn't want to catch whatever Scotty has. So, Kent and I grabbed hotdogs at the drugstore for lunch. We just came from there."

"Where are you going now?" she asked.

"Cubley's Coze to check on things. Where have you been?" I asked, turning things around, which sometimes works on adults.

"I just came from there. I wanted to ask Mr. Cubley about you boys working this week. You come straight home after you leave the hotel," she ordered.

"Mom, do you know about Lou?"

"I do. Why?"

"Okay, Lou's in the hospital, the Lockhart brothers are at their grandparents' house three counties over, and the cops are busy looking for Roger. Things are safe. May Kent and I go straight to the Top Hat? We've had lunch. We promise no side trips. Is that okay?" I asked in a rush. Kent stayed quiet, not saying a word...the chicken.

I was a little surprised by Mom's answer.

"I guess so. Mr. Cubley also thinks the streets are safe, at least for today. Just don't be late for supper. You're not to go anywhere after the movie. You hear?"

"Yes, ma'am. I won't be late," I promised.

Mom drove off, and I looked at Kent. "That was weird. I thought for sure that we were in for it. She didn't even insist on driving us to the show. Let's go before she comes back," I said to Kent.

"Up, up, and away," yelled Superman. We made it almost halfway up the hill to the hotel and pushed our bikes the rest of the way. Mr. Cubley was in his office, and we asked Mr. Tolliver if we could see him. Mr. Cubley heard us and called for us to come in.

We talked for a little bit about hotel stuff and the movies at the Top Hat, and he was nice. He never mentioned the Lockhart fight, which was a relief. I saw things were almost normal. That's when I asked him about Trooper Giles.

"Mr. Cubley, if a fellow needed to talk to a trooper, and it was really important, how would someone set it up?" I asked.

"Can you tell me what you want to talk to a trooper about?" asked Mr. Cubley.

"Uh, it's not us. We have a friend that needs to talk to a trooper," Kent chimed in.

"Any particular trooper, or would any trooper do?" Mr. Cubley asked, looking at Kent and then at me with one eyebrow raised.

"Trooper Giles," I requested.

"I'm sure that could be arranged. Here or at the garage?" asked Mr. Cubley.

I knew then that he knew it would be Kent or me asking to talk to the trooper. I figured he knew, so there was no point in making him think I was being devious. I had done enough of that lately.

"Either place is okay. We have something important to tell him," I said it, giving up any pretense that it was not Kent and me.

"How about tomorrow after church? If he's on duty, I'll have him drop by your house, Billy. You three can have a chat. Make sense?" Mr. Cubley told us.

"Yes, sir, perfect. Thanks for the help," I said.

Kent decided I had talked enough. "Billy's mom said you needed us to work this week. Do you need us on Monday? Is that okay?" Kent asked

Mr. Cubley at first hesitated, he looked slightly surprised, but then he answered.

"It is, boys—Monday, bright and early. Now, you two scoot. Have some fun. No bullies to worry about today, and the police are occupied." Then he shooed us out of the office.

"Kent, that's why Mom wasn't mad at us. Mr. Cubley assured her we were safe."

"We're in luck. Let's ride."

Our bikes were where we left them, so down the drive we rode. I looked back. Mr. Cubley was watching us from the veranda. When he saw me look back, he waved. I waved back.

"How come you told him it was us?" asked Kent.

"Because he knew, stupid. He knew. I'm getting tired of not telling the truth. I've decided from now on, I need to tell it like it is. This summer has gotten things all wronged-up." I knew I had just invented a word.

"Billy, do you think something bad happened to Misty's friend? Do you think she's dead like Mr. Albert Winston Brown?" asked Kent.

"I know Misty wouldn't be worried over nothing. I hope her friend just ran off. We don't need any more dead people around here," I said with a frown.

Coasting slowly down the hill, our brakes on the whole way, Kent and I talked back and forth.

Kent agreed with me, "Maybe you're right. She just ran off."

I thought of something. "Roger took off because he's a fugitive. Maybe Cindy makes two fugitives."

Then, we both rode in silence as I prayed.

Lord, please bring Cindy back safe! We don't need any more dead people because we've had too many!"

CHAPTER 34

BILLY HEARS ONE'S CAPTURED
Sunday, August 7, 1955

F lower arrangements filled our church. There were orchids, daylilies, chrysanthemums, and flowers I'd never seen before. They smelled nice, but people were crying. Miss Jones was wiping tears from her eyes. Lou McCulloch was dead. The doctors couldn't save him, and I was at his funeral with Mom, Dad, Scotty, and Grandma.

After the choir finished Amazing Grace, it had gotten very quiet. Then, a bee buzzed in one window and out another.

Suddenly, people began screaming. I looked at the front of the church, and my heart stopped. Lou's corpse was sitting up in his walnut casket. His face was pasty white as he turned and slowly looked over the congregation. Scotty let out a yell. And that's when Lou pointed at me. "Billy Gunn, you're going to burn in hell for all eternity. My death is your fault!"

I began to fall!

Bam!

Pain shot through my left leg and arm. I awoke crumpled on the hard floor because I had just fallen out of bed.

Scotty bolted upright in his bed and looked at me, which gave me the creeps.

"Billy, why are you on the floor?" But before I could answer, he continued. "I'm hungry. I want oatmeal."

We got up, and he raced me to the toilet. I beat the little bugger but let him go first. I had learned that sometimes he couldn't hold it. Cleaning up his mess was not on my list of fun things to do this morning. We finished in the bathroom, and while I got dressed, he went downstairs in his pajamas.

I pulled on a t-shirt and jeans from the floor. These were the same clothes I'd worn for three days, but there were no stains. I skipped putting on my shoes and saved that chore for after breakfast.

This morning, I was the last one to the table, except for Grandma, and the first thing I saw was a big black headline on Dad's newspaper—**Attempted Murder in Highland!** The article told about Lou McCulloch being shot down in the yard of his grandfather's house. The paper had it wrong because Lou had been found unconscious on the tennis court, not in the yard. I knew without reading the article that the police were searching for my friend Roger for the attempted murder.

Grandma arrived at the table just as Mom handed me a plate of eggs, toast, and bacon. Last night the adults had received several phone calls about Lou, and Grandma had had all night to prepare a breakfast tirade.

"Laura Jane, it's time. Time to pack and go to my sister's house in West Virginia. This place is too dangerous for decent folks. We'll all be in our graves by Labor Day. Mark my words, by Labor Day. You and John had better listen to some common sense for once!" ranted Grandma. I knew this Sunday was going to be unpleasant.

Mom's response was predictable.

"Mother, the McCulloch boy is injured, not dead. And this has nothing to do with our family. We need to pray for that little boy and not go off the deep end."

Dad continued to read his paper and ignored the women.

Grandma's voice got louder. "Are you telling me you want me to pray for one of the meanest children ever born? I feel bad saying it, but after what he did to Billy, well, being a Christian woman, this is God's vengeance working. No doubt about it."

"Mother, you forget that Lou's still a child."

"Well, he's one sorry excuse for one, bless his little heart," proclaimed Grandma.

To speak or not to speak? Well, that was the question. I usually stayed silent during one of Grandma's rants, but not this time.

"Grandma, Lou was nice to me at the movies. Carl and Dickie weren't, but Lou stood up for me. Please, don't talk bad about him." I asked her as nicely as I knew how. I saw Dad look at me over his newspaper. It turned into more than a look. He was staring at me. It got uncomfortable until Mom came to my rescue.

"See there, Mother. Lou was trying to help Billy. So, we need to pray for him. Goodness knows there's been too much evil in this town," Mom said, and that's when Dad shifted his gaze to Mom. I was glad he was done looking at me.

"Laura Jane, children attacked, snipers killing grown-ups, people trying to burn the place down around our heads, how can you live here? We need to move. I won't listen to anyone who says otherwise," Grandma countered.

Dad got up, threw down his paper, and went into the bedroom. He closed the door, didn't slam it, didn't even close it hard, just shut it. Grandma and Mom kept at it, so I finished my breakfast and went upstairs to get dressed for church. Mom had my stuff laid out over my desk chair. Mom would dress Scotty, the wiggle worm, just prior to us leaving, which was often fun to watch.

Later, while working on my hair, I heard voices getting louder until someone slammed a door. I figured it was Grandma, who wouldn't be going to church with us today, and I was correct.

It was just Mom, Scotty, and me in church. Dad had begged off because he wanted to finish a certain pickup. We all knew Mom's mood would improve once that truck was gone. So, Dad stayed home from church, called Angus MacDonald, and told him his pickup could be picked up that afternoon.

When we got home from church, I was in a panic. I remembered during the last hymn that I was meeting Trooper Giles today. Mr. Cubley set up the meeting for Kent and me, but Kent's mom made him go with her to see a relative. He couldn't make our meeting with Trooper Giles. If the trooper arrived with that MacDonald gang here, no telling what might happen. There might even be a shootout.

I tried twice to tell Mom or Dad, but each time, they were in a spat. I had to do something and was afraid to tell Dad, so I slipped inside and told Mom. She smiled, leaned close, and whispered, "I hope your trooper runs that bunch of bootleggers off the property." This was not what I wanted to hear, and Trooper Giles wasn't my trooper.

Luckily, the trooper arrived at one-fifteen and before Dad's customer. When Dad saw Trooper Giles pull into the lot, he quickly threw the tarp back over the pickup. Then, he came out to see what the trooper wanted.

"Bobby, what brings you here on a Sunday?" asked Dad.

"Is this a bad time, John?" asked Trooper Giles, who was good at picking up on what people were thinking from their tone of voice and posture.

"Not the best. I got someone due to arrive that would prefer not to see a trooper hanging around. If you get my drift?" said Dad, who was nicer than I expected.

"Well, I promised Billy a ride in my patrol car. If we took a little jaunt for about an hour, would that be okay? I could stop and call before I bring him back," offered the trooper.

Mom walked up and put her arm on my shoulder. "That would be very nice of you. I know Billy would enjoy a ride in your police car," said Mom, not giving Dad a chance to give his permission. I could tell Dad was starting to get steamed, but he wanted the trooper out of there more than he wanted to pick a fight over Mom ignoring him.

"Billy, let's go," said the trooper.

"Just a second. I got to get something."

I ran up to my room and got the piece of paper with Cindy's information. I came flying down the stairs and almost fell, trying to hurry. I let the screen door slam, but no one fussed. Then, I got in the front seat and sat up all straight, just like I was another trooper.

We pulled onto the road, and I could see Mr. MacDonald's car coming. We had just made it. Trooper Giles also spotted him and turned into First Street to let him pass.

Trooper Giles and I rode all over. I got to blow the siren and run the red lights when no other traffic was around. Mostly though, we talked man to man.

I told him about Misty but never used her name or revealed anything about her. Trooper Giles didn't seem to mind. I guess troopers were used to secrets.

He asked me questions on several topics. We talked about bullies, baseball, and how I liked working at Cubley's Coze. Before

I knew it, the hour was up. I told him about boxes and deliveries and mean people who scared girls. I gave the trooper the paper that Misty had written. Trooper Giles promised he would do his best to find Cindy and make sure she was safe.

We stopped at the Liberty Bell Gas Station, and Trooper Giles bought me a Dr. Pepper and called Mom. She said it was okay for him to bring me home. Kent was going to die because, once again, he had missed out.

When we got home, Dad and Trooper Giles began to talk about cars and motors. I thought things were getting dull until the trooper asked Dad about a particular pickup truck. I moved closer to listen.

"John, I notice your tarp is folded. Does that mean that the special project is gone?"

"Picked up, paid for, and gone. Sorry I was a little testy. That job was worth two months' pay. With the plant closed, and few customers, I needed the income."

"I know how it is," said the trooper. "I am a bit curious. Can I catch him?"

"I don't see why not. He'll give you a run for your money, and depending on the driver, he might get away. But he won't be faster. Knowing both vehicles, it'll be close to an even match when he's light. But when he's loaded, you still have the advantage. He might use a new trick that I gave him," Dad revealed. I knew he was starting to let the trooper know this pickup was not your average truck.

"Something I need to worry about?" asked the trooper.

"No, nothing that will hurt anyone. Just a little magic. First, you think you see him, and then you don't. Something that works best at night," explained my dad.

"A light trick?"

"Could be, Bobby. Could be. A good mechanic, like a good magician, never tells his secrets," Dad ended with a little laugh. I knew he was playing with the trooper.

"I might need that magic on my patrol car. A headlight trick might help on a night tail. What would it cost?" asked the trooper.

"Parts run eight and three to fix her up, but that's both front and rear," quoted Dad.

"Sounds good. Do you need the money up front?"

"Not this time. I got cash going in the bank tomorrow. I'll call you when I have the parts, and it'll take about two hours to install them."

Just then, the trooper got a call on his radio. I was always amazed how the trooper could be doing something, even talking, and when his call sign came over the radio, he picked up on it right away.

He answered the radio call but came back from his car to tell us something.

"They just caught Roger Younger. A railroad dick pulled him off a freight train in Roanoke. This detective happens to be a friend of mine. May I radio him your number so he can call me by landline?"

I knew he meant a telephone call. Trooper Quinn told me all about calling telephones "landlines."

"Sure, after you do, come on in the house to wait for your call. Let's get a drink," said Dad, and we all ended up in the kitchen. I wanted to hear this conversation, so I tried to stand behind Dad and not be noticed.

When the phone rang, Dad answered it but handed it to the trooper. Trooper Giles and the detective talked for about two minutes. When he hung up, Trooper Giles shook his head.

My Dad asked, "How's the Younger boy?"

"Okay—not hurt, but something's not right. The Younger boy denies shooting Lou. The kid claims Lou begged him for a gun because some gang called the Brotherhood was after him. Roger let Lou borrow the gun two days ago, thinking his dad wouldn't miss a house gun that he never carried to work."

When Trooper Giles mentioned the Brotherhood, I got scared—scared for Dad, but also for my friends and me. The local cops might try to pin what had happened at the plant on our seventh-grade class. Dad's army buddies had made it look like teens had done it.

"Billy, any of the kids in town ever start up a gang called the Brotherhood?" Trooper Giles asked me.

"No, sir. None of the kids I know have ever mentioned a gang called the Brotherhood."

That part was true, as much as I was telling. My friends had formed a gang, but we never called it the Brotherhood. Then I began to worry if this could be considered a lie—not telling the whole truth.

I noticed Dad kept quiet. But he never took his eyes off me. I felt like a watched bug just before it got stomped.

"John, gotta go. I have to meet a Roanoke deputy in Lynchburg. I'm bringing the Younger boy back to Highland."

"He got a good distance, trying to run away," Dad added.

"Yeah, he did. You know, he started a fistfight with a jailer when he learned they were sending him back here. He begged them to charge him with assault on a police officer and keep him in Roanoke. And that's when they discovered blood seeping through his shirt. That boy had been beaten recently. He had scars from an old beating and wounds from a recent one. He finally broke down and admitted his father had done it," Trooper Giles told us with a stern face.

I noticed Dad never said anything. My scars were almost gone, and I didn't blame him. It was my fault because I knew better than to throw rocks around a customer's car.

"Will they put Roger in jail when you bring him back to town?" I asked. I knew if they turned him over to his dad, things would not go well for Roger.

"No, Billy, we don't put youngsters in jail. I don't know where he'll go. Usually, the justice of the peace turns someone that young over to the parents. In this case, I don't know. Judge Carlton left word with my dispatcher for me to call him when I get back. He wanted to handle this one personally. The justice of the peace will be relieved when he hears he's off the hook," responded Trooper Giles to my question, just like I was another trooper. He's nice like that.

The trooper put his empty glass of tea in the sink. "Well, better be going. Don't want to be late. I hope you enjoyed our little ride, Billy?" the trooper asked, but he didn't need to.

"It was swell, Trooper Giles. Anytime you need a partner, give me a call," I said, trying to sound big.

"I will, Billy. I will do just that," said Trooper Giles, laughing as he climbed into his blue and grey. He backed around and waved as he drove out of the garage lot.

Dad touched me on the back, and I turned to face him as he spoke. "Billy, there are some things in this family that need to stay in this family."

"Yes, sir. I know all about secrets. I can swear an oath just like I do with Mr. Cubley on hotel secrets. Me and Kent know all about that," I responded.

"Kent and I, not me and Kent," Mom said, sneaking up on me when I wasn't looking. "I wish you would remember your grammar rules," Mom complained, walking out to where Dad and I were standing.

"Yes, ma'am, Kent and I will try to listen better. I promise," I told her, and I meant it.

"Billy, you know you can talk to us about anything, don't you?" Mom spoke to me as she looked me in the eyes.

"Uh, sure, I guess so," I said with hesitation. I had no idea where this was going, but it didn't sound good.

"Billy, who would you pick if I asked you to talk to someone?" asked Mom.

"Laura Jane, what are you saying?" asked Dad, frowning.

"John, hush. I need to know something from Billy, and you keep quiet," Mom said with a matching frown, and this time her frown had little crinkles. I knew this was a serious conversation. Dad knew it too. He got quiet, but his eyes stayed on me.

"Well? Who in this town do you trust the most?" Mom asked again with an intense look.

"You and Dad, I guess," I said, trying to get out of this one as quickly as possible.

"No, your dad and I don't count. Name someone outside the family. Someone you would feel comfortable talking to," she asked.

After giving this one some thought, I came up with Kent, but I knew she was asking about an adult. I finally came up with two names. I hoped this would end it before Mom and Dad got into a real fuss—a fuss that was my fault.

"Mom, other than you and Dad, I would pick Mr. Cubley or Miss Jones. Okay? Can I go now?"

I said it, but I knew I had messed up just as it came out. "I mean, may I go now?" I changed my grammar, hoping this would end things.

"Yes, you may. Run along," Mom said, and I skedaddled. I saw Mom and Dad go into the garage, and I was afraid this might turn into a big fight. I wish I could learn not to cause trouble.

CHAPTER 35
BILLY MEETS WITH MISS JONES
Monday, August 8, 1955

Superman exploded when I told him about my afternoon ride with Trooper Giles. First, he accused me of taking his turn. Then, Kent said mean things about his mom and her dumb Afton Mountain relative. After he calmed down, we rode our bikes to work but in silence. It wasn't until we neared the hotel that he spoke.

"My mother making me go to my stupid aunt's house for Sunday dinner is a sin. Afton died when the railroad closed the depot. Excitement is watching the weeds grow. It'll take a gazillion years for me to get over you taking my turn."

I didn't say one word. It was no use.

Entering the hotel kitchen, Mrs. Johnson and Boo were glad to see us, which helped Superman's mood. It got even better when Boo set out a jar of honey butter for our biscuits.

The usual group ate breakfast on the loading dock. Today, we all had a ton of news to share. I started with, "Guys, Roger's back." I filled them in on Trooper Giles bringing Roger back to town but skipped over about my police car ride."

Mr. Cubley already knew my news, but he told us that the local judge had sent Roger to his grandfather's house in Piney River. He added that the court had ordered Roger's father to stay away from the boy. Since this grandfather was on his mother's side of the family and the two men didn't get along, the judge thought Roger should be safe.

Polecat was next and reported how he overheard Sergeant Younger tell Officer Zeke Barnes that Lou remained in a coma. The doctors could only wait. We all agreed that Roger needed Lou to wake up to verify Roger's version of what happened.

The talk at the police department was also about Lou's dad and the sheriff getting into an argument over how Lou's case was being handled. Then, they got into a second argument over the

Lockhart case. Polecat predicted that Sheriff Lawrence would not get a significant campaign contribution from Big John for this year's election. We all thought Polecat picked an easy one to predict.

Polecat then dropped a news bomb. "My good sirs, the following news came in too late last night to make the *Gazette's* morning edition. There's been a shoot-out with several dead near the town of Ferrum."

Mr. Cubley leaned closer to Polecat, "Tell me the details, Mr. Smith. I'm all ears."

Polecat paused to collect his thoughts and unloaded. "Well, a frenzy of felonies between two feuding families fighting in Franklin County forecasts a financial fissure within that industry. The trouble has resulted in numerous fatalities involving the farm families, and I forecast more fights. Finally, I conclude that the 'water of life' is the catalyst."

"Mr. Smith, your alliteration is shocking," responded Mr. Cubley. Then, the two adults began laughing, leaving Kent and me wondering what they were talking about.

"Please speak English," I requested.

"Yeah, what happened in Franklin County?" asked Superman.

"Two bootleg groups in Franklin County had a shoot-out. Two dead and one wounded so far. I predict that no one will talk to the authorities, meaning no one alive is conversing," reported Polecat to our little group.

"I can guess which families are shooting at each other," announced Mr. Cubley.

Polecat responded, "Sketchy reports insinuate that the Perry family visited a Woody family still and shot it up, killed two, and wounded one. The wounded shiner escaped after he winged one of the Perry cousins."

Mr. Cubley and Polecat agreed that the raid was to get back at the Woody family for Sam Perry getting shot here in Green Mountain County. Mr. Cubley suspected Angus MacDonald's people shot Sam Perry because Angus was protecting his business interests from a Perry intrusion. Plus, the two families had never gotten along.

"I guess we're lucky these murders are in Franklin County, not here. We already have had our fair share of shootings," lamented Mr. Cubley

Mr. Tolliver strolled out onto the loading dock and spotted Superman and me. "Boys, if you plan on doing any work today, you might stop jabbering and get on with it."

None of us had food on our plates. Kent and I had been lingering to listen to the news and were guilty of being late for work.

"Yes, sir," we both said and rushed into the kitchen, dropped off our plates with "Toby the Cleaner," and told him we would see him at lunchtime. Four cars waited for us, and we worked hard to make up for our late start.

I thought that afternoon, Mr. Cubley came to the wash area to check on us. Therefore, I was shocked when he asked me to stop working and join him in his office. When I sat down in front of his desk, he got up and closed the window, the door to the kitchen, the lobby door, and the passthrough door. I started to worry.

"Billy, your mother came to see me. She believes the grown-ups have not been behaving, and it's affecting you. I agree with her. We think something must be done, but we'll need your help. Would you be willing to help us?" asked Mr. Cubley.

"I guess so," I answered, figuring this was as close to a promise as I wanted to get. At least until I knew what the heck Mr. Cubley wanted.

He began with, "Mrs. Clark and your mother called Miss Jones and asked her to talk with you and Kent. Will you talk to her?" Mr. Cubley asked me.

"I guess so. What about?" I wanted to know and was sticking to my same response about making promises.

"She'll explain, and she's waiting for you in the private banquet room. You first, then, she'll talk to Kent. Okay?" Mr. Cubley ended with a question that I didn't answer.

"And Billy, Miss Jones has an ice-cold Dr. Pepper for you. Don't keep her waiting, but this is all up to you. You may leave anytime."

Like I would walk out on Miss Jones.

When I reached the second floor, Miss Jones was waiting for me wearing a blue dress, and her arms were bare. This was not something she would wear to school, and she was smiling. I relaxed a little and took a sip of my Dr. Pepper. She had one too.

"Billy, I think you're so nice to help me. I need ideas, and I think you are just the one to give them to me," Miss Jones began. It didn't sound like I was in trouble...not yet, anyway.

I soon found out it was about everything going on in town. She began way back when Kent and I got jumped at the Green Mountain Resort. Miss Jones knew all about it. She talked about our friends and what happened to me at the Fourth of July Celebration in the park. She acted like she believed my version of Lou attacking me with the baseball bat. I told her about the attack behind the furniture store and how my bike got stolen. Things went smoothly until she began to ask me how I got my bike back.

I sat silent, and she picked up at once that I didn't want to answer her. She held up her hand like you would to stop a car, and that's when she dropped a house on me.

"Billy, I know your dad told you never to reveal family secrets. But I already know what he got his friends to do. Let's talk about that," she said.

"Do I have to?" I asked.

"Don't worry! Your mom told me what happened, and I don't need to hear it from you. But you may keep your promise to your father. I want to know how you feel about it."

"How I feel?"

"Yes, Billy. How do you feel about what was done to Lou?" she asked me.

I sat, looking first at her, then at the floor, and then back to see what was on her face. She smiled at me, and I had to tell her.

"Miss Jones, I feel rotten about it. When my bike was stolen, I wanted to kill Lou or beat him up. I wanted my bike back more than anything in the world. Later, I realized that I would never really kill him. Looking back on all that's happened, I really didn't want Dad's army buddies, the Brotherhood, to do anything to Lou. I hate what they did to him," I professed.

"So, you know that your dad got some army buddies to punish and scare Lou, and get your bike back?"

"Well, yes. I thought you said Mom already told you that," I said, not quite understanding.

"She did. However, I needed to know if you would be honest with me," said Miss Jones with a smile. "And I believe you. Also, I agree that Lou needed to be punished, but not like that. Revenge isn't justice."

Once we got that behind us, I began to talk about all the stuff that had happened. When I got to the part where we started to talk about Frank Varner's basketball and how we tried to get Mr. Lockhart to fix things, I confessed to the attack in the woods behind the school. I told her I'd been wrong to attack the Lockharts. I concluded by telling her that I was going to hell because I'd just violated my oath to all my classmates.

Miss Jones took my hand and said, "Do you think telling the truth is good or bad?"

"Miss Jones, it's both. And breaking my oath and telling on my classmates makes me a terrible person!" Then, I asked the question that worried me most of all. "How long will I have to go to prison?"

She smiled, patted my hand several times, leaned back, and said, "Billy, I don't think you're a terrible person at all, and children your age don't go to prison. But together, we need to fix a few things."

We talked about taking vows of silence and how some secrets were okay and some were not. Miss Jones said she understood why the members of her class had attacked those bullies. She never once said we were terrible. She said the attack was wrong, but since the adults were helping the bullies, she understood why we were driven to do bad things. Then, we spoke about how to improve things and how she could help.

Some stuff, I didn't reveal. I never told her about my dad hurting me or the secrets between Kent and me. I kept quiet about Misty and Cindy.

When we were done, I felt better. She promised to help all my friends if they would let her. She told me she had given Mom her word to keep all this confidential.

"Billy, it's time for you young people to set the example for the adults in this town. Please tell the truth from this point forward. Promise?"

"Yes. I guess so," I promised, sort of.

"I started with you because you've been hurt more times than anyone. If you help me, your friends will also think it's a good idea. We need to start being honest, so when someone asks us an important question, everyone will know we are telling the truth if we say *on my honor*."

She asked me to think about everything that we had discussed. Then, we would talk again from time to time. No one would know what we talked about unless I told them or gave her permission to speak to someone.

"Will you tell Mr. Cubley?" I asked.

"Only if you tell me, it's okay."

"You can tell him, but what about the Brotherhood stuff? Will my dad go to prison if that gets out?" I asked her.

"I don't plan on telling anyone about that. I'm bound by a legal privilege not to reveal certain things. Also, your dad has never mentioned anything about a Brotherhood to me. Mr. Cubley and I have no first-hand knowledge about what they did or didn't do. All we know are rumors."

"Okay," I said with relief. I knew that I could trust Miss Jones to keep her word.

I had one final question. "What happens next?"

I saw her face cloud over, and she spoke almost in a whisper, "I'm afraid that Mr. Watkins will have to decide whether to prosecute some or all of you for the attack on the Lockhart boys. He prefers to fix things, but he's a prosecutor and must follow the law. You shouldn't worry. You leave that problem to the adults and be certain that all the mothers are with you. Okay?" she asked.

"Yes, ma'am."

When we parted, she said she was looking forward to this school year and having me in her classroom. She sent me back to Mr. Cubley's office with instructions for me to send Kent to talk with her.

I finished washing one car and was halfway through a second one when Kent showed back up. We cleaned the last car of the day, telling each other about our secret meeting with Miss Jones when a voice startled us.

"Boys, what has you so wound up?"

When we turned around, Trooper Giles was standing with his hands on his gun belt, grinning at us.

"Trooper Giles, you owe me a ride," Kent blurted out.

"I do. You have my word that I'll take you on a ride and let you blow the siren and run the red lights, just like I did for Billy."

"Wow, can we go now?" asked Kent.

"Can't do it today, pardner. Besides, I must ask your mom. If she says okay, I'll do it the first chance I get. Deal?"

"Yes, sir, deal!" Kent said and turned to give me the okay sign.

Trooper Giles motioned for us to come closer and softly said, "Boys, could you help me with our little matter of the missing lady? I need the address of Samuel Hairston, Cindy's relative. I think she might be hiding out on his tobacco farm in Pittsylvania County. I know Cindy's family moved here from that county, and a fishing buddy of mine heard talk of a girl named Cindy who was working for her grandfather, a Sam Hairston. My problem is that there are twelve Sam Hairstons in that county, and six are farmers. My buddy isn't sure which farmer was her grandfather. I don't want to go knocking on doors. Would your secret friend tell you or find out for us?" Trooper Giles asked us.

"We'll see what we can do," said Kent.

"I'm not sure Cindy's family will tell our friend, but we'll try," I responded, not wanting Kent to have all the say.

The trooper shrugged and said, "Well, there's the problem. Cindy's father is concerned because a man who claimed he was from the Green Mountain Resort asked him about Cindy. Her dad didn't know the man, had never seen him at the resort, and the man had a hard look about him. So, Cindy's father told him she'd run away and good riddance. When I showed up, he told me about the man from the resort, but he wouldn't tell me where she'd gone. Let's see what else your friend can find out," said a perplexed trooper.

"I'll go see her, er, I mean, I'll go see him," I said, trying to cover up my slip.

"Trooper Giles, how's Roger?" Kent asked to help me out, and he was way ahead of me today.

"Kent, that boy's hurt. I saw his back, and no one should do that to an animal, let alone a child. No wonder he ran."

"Is he going to be okay?" I asked.

"His grandfather seems like a nice old gentleman, and Roger was happy to be with him. Pray that Lou pulls through and can tell us what happened," reported Trooper Giles, and he talked to Kent and me like we were adults.

I saw my chance and added a question on a new topic. "I guess you heard about the recent bootlegger shooting in Franklin County?"

"You boys know more about stuff than most troopers in the area. Where do you get your information?"

"We hear stuff around the hotel," I responded.

"Official police stuff?" asked the trooper.

"Oh, gosh, no, sir! Mr. Cubley don't tell us nothing! Sorry, Mr. Cubley doesn't tell us anything!" I corrected myself, and Mom would have been proud of me.

"We hear it from visitors and reporters who stay at the hotel—honest. Mr. Cubley was surprised to hear the news, too. He knows those people from his work in Roanoke, but he doesn't tell us anything confidential—honest Injun," Kent said, and I knew he got that one from the Lone Ranger. The honest Injun stuff, I mean.

"The boys are right, Trooper. Nothing confidential comes from me."

"Matt, I didn't mean to imply you were doing anything wrong. I stand amazed at how much these boys pick up on the sly. I may visit here more often to stay current on local crimes."

"Bobby, you're welcome anytime." Mr. Cubley said to the trooper and smiled.

Trooper Giles said goodbye, and Mr. Cubley went back into his office as Kent and I finished our work. I used the hotel phone to call the Green Mountain Resort and asked to speak to Misty. They said she'd just left, so Kent and I hightailed it down the hill because we knew Misty walked to work on pretty days.

We caught up with her near Court Street. We hopped off our bikes, pushed them beside her, and told her about our meeting with Trooper Giles. When we asked her for Samuel Hairston's address, she said she had it at home. Two summers ago, Cindy had spent tobacco-picking time with a relative named Sam, and Cindy had written Misty a funny card. Misty kept the card, and it had a return address. She would see that we got that address.

Finally, we were getting somewhere!

CHAPTER 36

A FARM VISIT
Wednesday, August 10, 1955

Matt awoke, feeling that he had made some progress this week. He prayed it was in the correct direction. Monday, he had arranged for Miss Jones to meet with Kent and Billy. More meetings followed on Tuesday, and several youths were scheduled for today. Where Henry Watkins had gotten nowhere with them, Miss Jones had been successful. The local moms had helped, but Miss Jones was the key to success.

Matt knew he might find himself far out on a legal limb if Henry took these cases to court and seventh graders were punished. Matt feared that the parents would riot.

Matt decided to put the matter aside when he joined Polecat, Kent, and Billy on the loading dock for their Wednesday morning breakfast. This morning, the local paper reported nothing about the children except an update on Lou McCulloch, who was still hospitalized. The poor boy had not regained consciousness, and there was no mention of Roger Younger.

Matt was surprised to see Trooper Giles at the front desk. He explained he was picking up an address from Billy and Kent on a missing girl. The description matched the girl who had caught the ride to Charlottesville with the professor.

Next, the trooper asked a question that Matt was not expecting. "Matt, I need a favor. Would you mind going with me? I may need a prosecutor to give her immunity to convince her to talk to me."

Matt agreed for three reasons. First, he had been cooped up for several days doing paperwork and wanted to get outside. Second, being frustrated about the lack of progress on the Brown murder, this witness might know something about the criminal activity at the Green Mountain Resort. Finally, Trooper Giles was an engaging conversationalist, and it would give him a chance to get to know the trooper better.

Giles walked outside and found Billy and Kent working hard, washing a car. They handed over the address that he needed. Then, the boys were surprised when Mr. Cubley rode away with the trooper.

The ride south to Chatham took about two hours. The trooper turned onto State Route 58 and went east into tobacco and corn country. There were several turns on back roads until they crossed a creek. Giles was reasonably sure they were near their destination when the men heard a shot, followed by two more.

"Little early in the season for deer," remarked Trooper Giles.

"If it's deer they're after, someone's a terrible shot," commented Matt.

Four more shots rang out. By the sounds, it was clear that different weapons were firing. The trooper eased his car nose-first into the entrance of a tobacco field.

"I hope this is just target practice," stated Matt.

"Or, we may be walking into the middle of a gunfight," said Trooper Giles as he got out of the car.

Giles opened the trunk, loaded a twelve-gauge, and slung a bandoleer of shells over his shoulder. Then, he pulled out a 30-30 with a scope, which he handed Matt along with a box of cartridges. Matt pulled out two handfuls of bullets, dropped them into the front pockets of his pants, checked, and loaded the rifle.

"Is she sighted in?" he asked Giles.

"Should be close if not right on the money. I better call in our position and let dispatch know what we might have here. Let's work our way through the trees. The open field or this road may not be a good approach," suggested Trooper Giles.

"I agree with that," commented Matt, still looking over the rifle and scope.

Trooper Giles called the division dispatcher, gave his location and a few details, and requested the area office at Chatham be notified. Then, he signed off, turned off his car, and locked it.

He and Matt started making a slow approach to where they heard more shooting. The trooper went first. Matt stayed back about thirty feet to provide backup and cover fire if the trooper walked into something unexpected.

Keeping behind a slight rise, the two crawled to a hillcrest at the edge of the woods. From the top of the little hill, they saw two black 1953 Kaiser Manhattan two-door sedans parked on the farm road. Matt noted the cars were out of sight of the house. Both vehicles had their trunks up with no one around them. Shots were being fired from a fence line past a big red barn.

Working their way above and closer to the farmhouse, they could hear return fire coming from the house. Someone was putting up a good defense with a deer rifle. The trouble was that whoever was in the place was outmanned and outgunned. For each shot fired by the defender, three to five shots were fired by the attackers. Then, someone fired a shotgun at the rear of the farmhouse. Was it being fired from the house or into it? They couldn't tell from the sound alone.

Matt spotted three men dressed in dark clothing firing high-powered rifles into the front of the farmhouse. There were at least two shooters at the rear of the house, out of Matt's sight. He could hear the weapons but couldn't tell the exact number or location.

Trooper Giles motioned for Matt to stay put on the rise at the edge of the trees. He began to sneak down through a field of grass that was several feet high. It provided cover but no protection.

Matt settled in and took up a firing position a hundred yards from the men shooting into the house. He had a clear sight picture, an easy shot for each target, but the odds were against him—one against three, not counting Giles. If he fired first, he feared what might happen. He could take out one, maybe two, but that third man remained a danger to Trooper Giles.

There was a lull in the shooting from the farmhouse. One of the men in front shouted, "Give it up. All we want is the girl. Don't be stupid."

The response was two more shots from the farmhouse.

Suddenly, the shouting man turned, and Matt almost fired. He thought the gunman might have seen Giles, who was in a crouch, slowly creeping down the hillside of tall grass. Instead, the man bent over and was working with something.

The first gunman shouted at his two companions, but Matt couldn't make out what he said. Then, number one stood as his two companions fired round after round into the farmhouse. Matt now saw the man holding a bottle with a rag in it. He was lighting the rag to throw a Molotov cocktail at the farmhouse.

Just as the arsonist drew back to throw, there was a boom. The thrower was flung forward as he exploded in flames. Trooper Giles had unloaded his twelve-gauge into the man's back, striking the man and the firebomb with deadly force. Matt hoped the man was dead instantly and wasn't burning to death. His concern, however, ended almost as quickly as the first flash of flame.

Matt switched his aim to the man farthest from Trooper Giles. This gunman was aiming at the trooper. Matt put two rounds into his chest and aimed a third at the man's head. Round three caught him just under the chin as he fell, taking out half his throat. He was dead before he struck the ground.

The third man jumped over the fence away from Trooper Giles and landed in the yard of the house. Before the trooper or Matt could get a clear shot, the man was struck down by fire coming from the farmhouse.

Then, Matt spotted movement on the far side of the farmhouse. Three more men broke for the barn, firing as they ran. Trooper Giles called for them to halt, but they kept running and shooting. Matt fired one round, dropping one of the runners. The other two made it behind the barn. Matt's view was now blocked.

Trooper Giles called to the house, "You folks in the house. I'm a Virginia State Trooper. Hold your fire! I'm going to check around back. I also have a sniper with me. Don't shoot. Do not come out of the house. I'll tell you when it's safe!"

A male voice from inside the house called out, "We won't fire. This better not be a trick, or you'll be sorry!"

Before the trooper could make his way around the house, the two Kaisers cranked up and sped away. Matt prayed they would not shoot up Trooper Giles' police car on their way out, or Sergeant Oliver would have a heart attack.

Matt heard no additional shots as the two cars sped off in the distance.

Thank goodness, Matt thought.

Trooper Giles checked the area around the farmhouse and the barn and went back to where he parked his patrol car. He got in it, started it, hit the lights and siren, and drove up to the house. Matt knew this was to assure the occupants that he really was a trooper.

When Matt walked down to the patrol car, keeping an eye on the farmhouse, he heard the trooper giving a detailed description of the fleeing vehicles to the state police dispatcher. The dispatcher told Giles she had help on the way.

A bit late for that, Matt thought.

The front door of the farmhouse opened, and an elderly farmer came out. Since there was a blue and gray parked in front, he was all smiles. He wisely left his rifle in the house.

"Mr. Sam Hairston?" called Trooper Giles, getting out of his patrol car.

"Yep. That's me," answered the farmer, who had on bib overalls and a long sleeve flannel shirt, despite the heat. His shirt sleeves were rolled up with long johns visible. His face was weathered, and his smile was missing one tooth in front.

"Mr. Hairston, I'm Trooper Bobby Giles of the Virginia State Police. This is Mr. Matthew Cubley, the Commonwealth's Attorney for Green Mountain County. Do you have anyone injured in the house?" asked Giles.

"My wife got some glass in her face when those scalawags shot out the front windows. Cindy's looking after her. Say, you boys sure happened by at the right time. What brings y'all clear down here from Green Mountain County?" he asked, and his tone turned from "glad to see ya" to a little suspicious.

"A friend of Cindy's was plumb worried and asked us to check on her. Glad we showed up before things got serious," answered Bobby Giles in his down-home way.

A young lady came out of the house and put her left hand over her eyes to block the sun. She was of sturdy stock, not fat, but built for hard work. Her face was friendly, with warm brown eyes. When she saw the remains in the front yard, especially the man whose corpse was still smoldering, she moved her hand from her forehead to her mouth. Matt noticed she continued walking toward her grandfather with determination. She didn't scream or run back into the house.

"Pete, hey Pete," yelled Mr. Hairston. There was no answer.

"Who's Pete, your dog?" asked Bobby Giles.

"Pete's my hired hand. Good man, he yelled us a warning. That's how we knew to hold up in the house. We need to find him," said Mr. Hairston as he started toward the barn.

"I checked around the barn but didn't check inside it," responded the trooper.

Cindy went back into the house to be with her grandmother. Matt, Trooper Giles, and Sam Hairston walked to the barn. When they opened the main sliding door, they found Pete. He was tied to a support post in the barn and very fortunate not to have been hit by a stray bullet or silenced by the assassins.

After cutting Pete loose, the entourage walked back to the front yard of the house. Sirens could be heard in the distance, and within a few minutes, two Pittsylvania County sheriff's deputies pulled up. They parked around Trooper Giles' car.

While they were looking at the four dead bodies, Sam Hairston walked over to a pump in the side yard and pumped two buckets of water. He carried them over to the body that was still smoking, doused the fire, and ended the smoke. The odd, sweet smell was still prevalent, however.

Trooper Giles filled in the deputies on what he knew. Then, they began to collect evidence.

None of the bodies had any identification on them. The clothing was dark, almost black, and all the clothing tags had been removed. The uniforms looked like those worn by Baldwin Detective Agency guards, except these displayed no insignias or markings.

More police and a medical examiner from Chatham arrived. After checking the bodies and talking to Trooper Giles and Matt, the doctor told the local sheriff to take the bodies to Danville for autopsies. Their local Commonwealth's Attorney would review the evidence and give Matt a call.

A trooper and an area sergeant arrived to conduct the state police investigation. Trooper Giles would have to justify each round he had fired. Matt would also have to explain why he fired a state police weapon.

The local area sergeant started to give Trooper Giles a rough time until Sam Hairston and Pete provided plenty of justification for both his rescuers' actions. After a heated response from the victims and a quick tour of the shot-to-pieces farmhouse, the local sergeant got a lot friendlier.

Trooper Giles and Matt only reported they were there to interview Sam Hairston about a case in their home county. Neither man mentioned Cindy. Several hours later, the local authorities completed their investigation. The area sergeant told Matt and Trooper Giles that they were free to leave as he and the local trooper drove away.

Sam Hairston invited Matt and Giles into the house for some sweet tea. They couldn't help but notice that Sam's wife and Cindy were cleaning up broken glass in almost every room. Bullet holes were visible throughout the house. Swiss cheese had fewer holes. Pete, the hired man, was nailing plywood over the broken windows. It grew dark inside the house with the windows covered, so the lights were turned on. It was a miracle they worked.

Cindy came into the parlor, the one room without a broken window. It was on the side away from the barn and had escaped damage.

Trooper Giles decided it was time to reveal their true purpose. "Cindy, you have a friend who is very worried about you. She got two boys to ask us to find you. Your friend wouldn't let those little boys tell us who she was, but she did give them this address to pass on to us. Who's your friend? She may be in danger as well." Advised Trooper Giles, who then paused, hoping she would answer him.

"Trooper, thank the Lord for Misty. It had to be Misty Johnson. We work together at the Green Mountain Resort Hotel," Cindy revealed.

"Your friend saved your life. Tell me what happened. What was so bad it made you come live with your grandfather? Not even your father would tell me where you were," exclaimed Trooper Giles.

Cindy, Matt, and Trooper Giles talked for over an hour. She spoke very little at first, but then, she opened up about what she knew of the criminal activity at the Green Mountain Resort.

The conversation finally got around to where Cindy could now go to live. Her grandparents' farm was no longer secret or safe.

Matt suggested that the best place to hide might be in Highland. Her response was, "Mr. Cubley, my dad's house isn't safe, everyone knows us, and I don't want to risk him getting hurt."

Matt agreed with her but had an idea. "There's my old attic room at the hotel. My uncle built it for me when I was a teenager. You may use it as a temporary hide."

Matt needed to ask the state police to provide someone to help guard her. For the short term, the attic hideaway was available; no one would suspect she was hiding there, it was on a floor to itself, and access was limited to one inside stairway—a place easy to secure.

It took another hour for Sam Hairston and his wife to come around to the idea. They finally agreed that the farm was no longer viable for Cindy. After more discussion, Trooper Giles, Matt, and Cindy left in the trooper's car.

When they arrived at Cubley's Coze, it was late. So, just to be extra careful so no one would notice Cindy, Matt had the trooper park next to the loading dock.

Matt and Trooper Giles now knew that Cindy had positive information about criminal activity at the Green Mountain Resort and that it might help with the Brown murder.

All the hotel staff knew parties were being conducted at the fish camp cabin and in the hotel's basement Casino Room. Big John had lied. While most of those parties were furnished with tax-paid whiskey, some were stocked with bootleg. She discovered this after being promoted to assistant bookkeeper in the accounting department. Mr. Albert Winston Brown purchased all the legal alcohol for the resort and the cabin at Bear Creek, as indicated in the books. He personally handled the orders and payments.

The young lady also discovered by accident that Mr. Brown had kept two sets of books. One set at the resort for the legal whiskey and one set in his briefcase for the bootleg. She had seen the secret set by accident.

Recently, she also overheard Chief McCulloch accuse Mr. Brown of skimming money from the bootleg accounts. Working in the office next door, she overheard them. Things got tense when the Chief bumped into her in the hallway after that meeting. She knew he was suspicious about what she might have heard.

When her boss went missing, and Chief McCulloch called her to meet with him at his office, she sensed that she was in danger and ran. Events had proved her fears were well-founded. Someone wanted her dead, but who? Was it the McCulloch family or Angus MacDonald, or some unknown party?

CHAPTER 37

BILLY AND KENT GROUNDED AGAIN
Thursday, August 11, 1955

Kent and I were on the loading dock wondering if Trooper Giles had located Cindy when Mr. Cubley joined us.

"Morning Kent, Billy, how are you boys this morning?" he asked.

"Fine, Mr. Cubley," replied Kent.

"Fine as frog hair," I countered. "May we ask you something?" I added.

"You may ask. I might even answer," he bantered back. I could tell he was in a good mood.

"Kent and I saw you leave with Trooper Giles yesterday. Did he mention anything about finding a girl?" I asked.

"As a matter of fact, we found her safe and sound," announced Mr. Cubley.

"Yes!" I hollered.

"Great Caesar's ghost!" came back Kent with a line from *Superman*.

Mr. Cubley smiled and then asked, "Trooper Giles told me there might be someone else worried about her, but you boys wouldn't reveal who she might be. Is this secret friend of yours real or make-believe?"

"No, she's real," Kent responded. "We need to let her know her friend's A-OK right away!"

"We do! Mr. Cubley," I joined in with Superman.

Mr. Cubley held up his hand like he was stopping traffic. "She needs to talk to Trooper Giles. There could be some bad people after her!"

"May we use the hotel telephone?" I asked.

"Slow down, Billy. Trooper Giles will be here shortly. You talk to him before you call her. He may need to arrange protection for her."

What Mr. Cubley was telling us made sense. We both promised not to say anything until we talked to Trooper Giles. We didn't take an oath or anything, but we knew this was important police business.

Mr. Cubley informed us that he was meeting with several police officers, and we were to wash cars quietly with no horseplay.

He ate quickly, retired to his hotel office, and missed Polecat's morning news report. However, we were still eating when Polecat rode up on his bike.

"Mr. Smith, good morning," Kent called out.

"Masters Clark and Gunn, how fare ye this morn?" asked Polecat.

We knew he was being "flamboyant." That was a word he had taught us—flamboyant, which meant something exaggerated. Superman called it, talking goofy.

When he passed by us on the way to the kitchen, we noticed his odor was more pungent than usual. "Pungent" was another Polecat-ism.

Upon his return, Kent and I breathed a sigh of relief when he sat downwind of us. However, we were glad he had joined us because he was almost bouncing on his chair. We knew there was something newsworthy that he was itching to tell us.

"I don't suppose there's any news this morning?" I asked, baiting him.

"Yeah, I expect yesterday was quiet, calm, and boring," said Kent, playing along. He had picked up on Polecat's excitement as well.

Polecat immediately reported details that Mr. Cubley had omitted about the big shootout in Pittsylvania County. Reports had arrived on the news wire too late to make the morning paper, but it had spread across town and reached the Highland Police Department in a flash.

Mr. Smith announced, "Regarding Chief McCulloch, *cave canem.*"

Superman had a blank look.

"Mr. Smith, what has a cave got to do with the Pittsylvania County gunbattle?" I asked because I was curious.

Polecat raised his fork high with his right hand and swung it down to point it at Kent and me. "My young sirs, *cave canem* is Latin for beware of the dog, or in your case Chief McCulloch. What has become of our educational system? I fear the foundation has crumbled." He immediately went back to eating.

After several large bites of breakfast, Polecat furnished us with choice details of the event. Finally, he finished with gory tidbits from a member of the pool hall gang who had a relative in the Pittsylvania County Sheriff's Office. We could not believe Mr. Cubley acted like it was no big deal. He didn't even mention four dead, a body on fire, a big shootout, and he was right in the middle of it with Trooper Giles.

"Masters Gunn and Clark, according to the weather report, a tropical storm named Connie is fast approaching our conurbation. Downpours are expected, but the worst should pass to the east of Charlottesville. It's recommended that foul weather gear be kept close at hand."

I had to ask, "Mr. Smith, what is a corn-bation thing?"

"C-o-n-u-r-b-a-t-i-o-n, my young scholar, is a geographical area consisting of a city, suburbs, and surrounding smaller towns. Why do we waste money on a school system that fails to teach the basics?" he answered by asking a question.

We continued to ask questions about the shooting and the storm until Polecat became irritated and said he had to go. That's also when Mrs. Johnson began yelling for us to bring her our dishes.

While we were washing our first car of the day, Trooper Giles arrived. He gave us the official version of what happened at the farm. Like Mr. Cubley's version, it wasn't as exciting as the Polecat version. Trooper Giles even thanked us and bragged about how we were helping solve important cases. However, he made us promise not to mention the names of Cindy Hairston or Misty Johnson to anyone.

"Where is Cindy?" Kent inquired.

"Somewhere safe," answered the trooper. That was all he would say.

He asked us to try and convince Misty to let the police provide her with protection. Again, he stressed that she was in great danger and told us no one must know that we helped him find Cindy or where she was.

"We can't tell what we don't know," responded Kent.

"Exactly," was all Trooper Giles would say, and he put his pointer finger in front of his mouth to shush us.

Around mid-morning, we saw Sheriff Lawrence and Sergeant Oliver arrive. They joined the trooper and Mr. Cubley in the hotel office, and Mr. Cubley closed his office window, keeping Kent and me in the dark. I figured it must be about Cindy because of all the secrecy.

Skip Hathaway dropped over to the wash area on his noon break, talking about the big storm coming. No rain yet, but the sky looked odd. The clouds were light gray and were glowing like pearls in candlelight.

Skip then told us Miss Jones had asked his mom if she could talk to him. His mom told the teacher, "No."

Kent and I explained that Miss Jones was our teacher and friend and that he could trust her.

"Don't make no difference. My mom doesn't trust people she doesn't know."

He was going to stick to the fishing story, and that was that. I didn't argue with him, and neither did Kent. We did tell Skip that Miss Jones was only trying to help, not get anyone in trouble.

Kent and I took a break at two o'clock. We got some cake and a couple of Dr. Peppers from the kitchen. That's when I saw Boo fix a plate of cake with a pot of hot tea for one of the guest rooms.

The only reason I noticed was that usually, she'd have a waitress take it up, but this time, she took it herself. I thought it was odd but forgot all about it when Kent asked if I had seen *Dragnet* the previous night on TV. We got to talking about suspects and how devious they could be.

Mr. Baker and Skip loaded up the hotel's Ford Club Wagon to begin the clean-up of the lodge. They also needed to secure it for the storm that was coming. I knew that Professor Hartford and his family, plus the two graduate students, had left on Monday, and no one would be renting the lodge until after the storm.

When Mr. Baker asked us to help, we said sure. It would be fun to see the lodge again and learn how to put up storm shutters. We might even spot a bear.

The ride up was easy, without any bears or even a bobcat. It didn't take the four of us long to clean out the lodge and burn all the trash in the trash barrel. The empty tin cans we put in sacks and loaded them in the back of the Ford.

The storm shutters were stored in the stone bunker beside the lodge. Superman and I named it from war movies we had seen. The shutters had big hooks that attached to eyebolts screwed into the tops of the lodge windows. A latch made of iron secured them to the bottom of the windows.

It took no time to put them on the back and side windows. Then, with two ladders, Mr. Baker and Skip got the second-floor windows done. We were about to finish on the front when a man wearing a hunting outfit without a gun stopped by. He said he was a hiker from the Green Mountain Resort and asked all kinds of questions about the lodge, like what it would cost for a week and if it was rented. Mr. Baker answered all his questions while we hung the last of the shutters.

We thought the stranger would continue his hike, but he fooled us. He said he might want to rent the lodge and asked to see inside. Mr. Baker showed him all the rooms, and he still stayed. He chatted with Mr. Baker even while we removed some leftover frozen meat and all the linens. I thought he had overstayed his welcome and was becoming a pest, but I kept it to myself since he was an adult.

We had special instructions to secure the lodge for the approaching hurricane, and it was clear to anyone with eyes that's what we were doing. When we locked the lodge's front door, the man thanked Mr. Baker and finally left.

We made sure the fire was out in the fire barrel and locked up the bunker with a big key. It was time to hurry because it was getting late.

Skip, Kent, and I argued over who would get the shotgun seat. Skip won. Kent and I climbed in the back seat, and as we started to drive down the mountain, I turned and looked out the back of the van. The hiker stepped out from between some trees. He had been watching us. He gave the lodge one last look, then turned into the path that led down the mountain's west side. He would have to hurry back to his hotel before dark and ahead of the rain. The guy could have caught a ride with us, but he never asked.

Mr. Cubley was still at the hotel when we returned. Mr. Baker told him about the hiker, and Mr. Cubley got very interested. He asked a lot of questions about the man—more than normal. While they talked about the strange hiker, the storm we had been expecting arrived with a crash of thunder and steady rain.

Kent and I left our bikes in the maintenance shed, and Mr. Baker gave us a ride home in the hotel wagon. On the way, we met two Highland Police patrol cars with red lights flashing, escorting Big John's Cadillac. When the Cadillac passed us, I saw several people in the back. However, the rear windows were tinted, making it hard to tell who they were. No one waved.

We dropped Kent at his house, and Mr. Baker took me to mine. Grandma was putting a milk container in the refrigerator as Dad let me in the kitchen. He didn't greet me but pointed to the telephone.

"Boy, some girl's been calling. She sounds older than you. Don't you be doing anything dumb," he said.

"No, sir. I try to avoid dumb and leave it to others."

Grandma left for the living room, and Dad frowned because what I just said hadn't come out right. I was afraid Dad would whack me. This time, I was lucky. He went out to the garage, mumbling. I saw him checking customers' cars to ensure the windows were closed tight.

Mom came into the kitchen and gave me the actual message. "Billy, Misty something or other, called you twice today. She wants you to call her at home, and I wrote the number on Dad's work pad. Don't stay on the phone. You know how people need a wrecker when it rains."

"Yes, ma'am."

Now, when I called Misty, she answered right away. It was like she was sitting on top of the telephone.

"Hello," she said.

"Misty, it's Billy. Mom said you called."

"Oh, Billy! This morning, I heard Chief McCulloch call Big John on the hotel phone. He told his dad that Cindy's been found, and they were both furious. I couldn't tell if she was hurt or not by what they were saying. I'm worried, sick. Have you heard anything?" she asked.

"Are you where you can talk?" I asked—not thinking. She was at home, and I was the dummy.

"Yeah, I'm home alone. What's happened?" she was begging and almost in tears.

I told her that Cindy was fine, and I filled her in about the shooting at the farm. When she asked me where Cindy was now, I had to tell her I had no idea.

"Misty, Trooper Giles wants to meet with you. He says you're in danger. Will you?" I asked.

"No, Billy, I won't. I think I'm safer here if you haven't told anyone about me." She said this last sentence with a little quiver in her voice.

"No! Of course not. Me and Kent have been as quiet as church mice."

"Billy, Kent, and I. It's Kent and I," Mom called from the kitchen.

"Who was that?" immediately asked Misty.

"That was my mom fussing at me for not using proper English. Sorry, Kent and I," I said louder to satisfy Mom.

"Well, let me know if you hear where she might be staying. I need to talk to her. And thanks for getting your friend, the policeman, to find her. You're my hero!" she told me out of the clear blue.

I felt all proud and stuff.

"Misty, please be careful. If you let me, I'll ask Trooper Giles to help you. He is bubble straight. I mean it. He really is a good person."

Just before she hung up, she whispered, "Billy, never call me at the hotel, only here at home. And Billy, thanks again!"

"What was all that about?" asked Grandma as Dad came in dripping from outside.

"Grandma, just some police work. Nothing important," I answered, not thinking.

"Oh, my Lord in heaven! They have babies doing police work in this awful, awful town. It's not bad enough you got yourself kidnapped, shot at, almost killed, and beaten on a regular basis. Oh, no! Now the police are working little children, doing Lord knows what. Laura Jane, I never thought I'd see the day a child of mine would allow a twelve-year-old to get mixed up with older women and cops. How do you live with yourself?" Grandma was almost yelling.

No matter how hard I tried, I kept getting Mom and Dad into fights with Grandma. I just couldn't seem to stay out of trouble.

"Oh, Mother. Billy's not doing police work. That was the little clerk who was nice to him when those bullies punched Kent and Billy at Green Mountain. There's nothing going on. Here's your plate. Sit yourself down, and please, let's have a meal in peace," Mom was pleading, trying to avoid a fight at suppertime.

I thought I was safe, but Mom gave me a look that made me change my mind. I was not off the hook. She was just trying to calm Grandma. I also saw Dad giving me the look he often used just before he whacked me. The next time I took a secret call, I needed to do it from the payphone at the drugstore. I was causing too much trouble here at home.

Mom handed me my plate with fried chicken, mashed potatoes, and green beans—not my favorite. I'm talking about the green beans because the rest was great. However, I wasn't about to complain about green beans—not that night. I wasn't going to say another word about anything. I knew Dad was right on the edge.

My wonderful brother took that moment to turn over his milk. I thought I might give him a great big hug later when we went to bed. I changed my mind because he might start yelling that I was trying to strangle him. I would have to thank him after he grew up.

Both Mom and Grandma were trying to clean up the mess before it ran off the table onto the floor. Scotty could not have picked a better time to mess up. Dad's gaze had shifted to him from me.

I quickly finished my supper, cleared my dishes, and retreated to my room. I was hoping not to see Mom or Dad until breakfast. No such luck.

Grandma had Scotty in the living room, watching television. Then, Mom and Dad came upstairs together—an awful sign.

"Billy, your father and I are concerned about you getting into so much trouble in town. We want you to park your bike until we say otherwise. Hurricane Connie is coming with lots of rain, so you won't be able to ride it for a few days anyway. You boys will be driven to work until further notice."

I must have frowned. I don't think I did, but I must have.

"Don't you give me that look, young man! Today, your dad heard that Chief McCulloch is back in town, saying bad things about you, Kent, and the other children in Miss Jones's class. Several of our friends have warned us that he's out to get you. Kent's mom has also heard the same thing. So, we're going to drive you, and that's that. Is that clear?" Mom was using her meanest tone of voice. The way Dad was looking at me, I was sure he wanted half a reason to whack me.

I just said, "Yes, ma'am. If you think that's best, I understand."

"Mr. Cubley wants you to come to work tomorrow. He needs you to help Richard Baker paint guest rooms, so wear old clothes. I don't want you getting paint on your good ones."

When Mom and Dad left, I kicked Scotty's teddy bear clear across the room.

Kent and I were right back in prison. I thought when Mr. Cubley killed the sniper, I would have a normal summer, but my summer kept getting worse. The more Kent and I tried to help. The more things got messed up.

The police weren't helping. Grandma had it right. Our town was going to the dogs. That's when I heard another crash of thunder, and the lights blinked and went out. Then, I heard it start to rain harder, and I thought to myself, *my life is over*.

CHAPTER 38

THE RAID
Thursday and Friday, August 11-12, 1955

W hile sitting in his hotel office, Matt's thoughts were on his rival, Big John McCulloch. Cindy had told him of the business practices employed by McCulloch Wood Products and the Green Mountain Hotel and Resort. He was now familiar with the legal and illegal work that Mr. Albert Winston Brown performed for the two businesses.

Matt was not surprised to learn that Mr. Brown had chosen Cindy to keep the two companies' legitimate ledgers. There was a head bookkeeper for Big John's entire operation, and Mrs. Duffy, Cliff's wife, handled the smaller businesses. But Mr. Brown was responsible for certain entertainment expenses. They were limited in scope but involved many transactions each month.

Cindy was talented in math and made straight A's in high school and business school. Her talent earned her a position with the head bookkeeper as his assistant. Later, Albert Winston Brown learned of her talent and switched her to keep his entertainment accounts. However, only he could approve the invoices and bills.

She informed Matt that Mr. Brown had kept a secret ledger. One day, Cindy noticed an unfamiliar ledger open on his desk. At first, she thought it was only a duplicate. However, blessed with an almost photographic memory, Cindy remembered all that month's entries. So, when she compared the secret ledger against her memory, they were different.

Three months later, she saw another month's entries in the secret book of accounts. Again, the entries were different from her set. The discrepancies were sufficiently large for her to conclude the differences were not mere mistakes.

One fraudulent line item was titled "special whiskey" in one book and "bootleg (AWB)" in the other. She guessed "AWB" stood for Albert Winston Brown, who was paying less for the bootleg whiskey than he was billing the company for reimbursement. Mr. Albert Winston Brown had a nice income off the difference.

Based on the delivery dates, Cindy concluded that Thursday night was a big night at the hotel for those "special parties." Today, being Thursday, Matt decided to raid the place.

The raid wouldn't be easy. Cindy had reported that most hotel employees, except a select few, were prohibited from entering this basement area known as the "Casino." Thus, the raiding party would not have a floor plan for the Casino.

Also, two steel doors secured the Casino—one in front and one in back. The rear door was serviced by a freight elevator, which carried supplies to the lower level.

Guards, or sometimes local cops, admitted all the guests from the front or main lobby of the hotel to a special elevator, which only served the lower level. Exiting this elevator, the guests then passed through a vestibule to the final steel entry door. This door was more ornate than the rear door but was equally secure.

Cindy had recently dated one of the Casino guards. She learned about the elevators when he drank too much.

She broke off their relationship when he put a waiter in the hospital. He refused to tell her why, but rumors among the staff indicated that the employee was caught snooping around the lower level. Whispered gossip blamed Mr. Brown for ordering the object lesson, leaving Cindy afraid to report her findings to anyone.

After the employee ended up in the hospital, Mr. Albert Winston Brown grew more suspicious. He questioned her on ledger entries about which she was not supposed to know. She pretended to only know about the books kept in the hotel office. Her memory kept her safe on what to say and when to claim ignorance.

She was retained but often detected clicks on her phone line during her conversations. She was sure Mr. Brown or someone else was listening in on her calls.

After Mr. Brown disappeared, Cindy noticed someone had moved all the items on her desk and in her employee locker. When Mr. Brown was found dead, she really got nervous. Then, Sam Perry got shot. She knew Mr. Brown had recently talked with him on the phone.

She discussed her concerns with her parents, who told her it was time for her to go live with her grandfather until she could find another job out of town. When the gunmen showed up at the farm, she knew they were after her.

Matt felt he had sufficient facts to get a search warrant to raid the Green Mountain Resort. But Cindy's information would go stale quickly since she no longer worked at the hotel. Thus, Matt decided to raid the hotel that day and got busy typing the affidavit for the search warrant.

Sergeant Oliver agreed to swear to the search warrant, so when Oliver arrived, Matt had Cindy tell Oliver all she knew. Then, the sergeant swore to the warrant, not Cindy. Cindy was listed as an unnamed informant in the search document to keep her identity secret until she appeared in court.

When Sheriff Lawrence arrived, he had a concern. "Matt, I hope this works. Being forced to use an unnamed informant in the warrant will make this more difficult in court. I would prefer we name her. If we lose in court, the people of this county might support Big John rather than us."

"Sheriff, they tried to kill Cindy because they merely suspected her. If they find out what she knows, they'll come after her with everything they have. I'd rather not use her, but we must," Matt argued.

Sergeant Oliver then joined with his concern. "How are we going to protect her after the raid tonight?"

Matt answered, "I need commitments from both of you for a protection detail until she testifies in court."

The sheriff asked, "And how long will that be?"

"It could be for a month or two. If we can't protect her, I won't submit this to the judge, and the raid is off," responded Matt.

"Hold on there. You're talking about some money, Matt. Plus, this will shoot my troopers' work schedule all to hell," complained the sergeant.

"My boys can help some, but I also have limited resources," joined Sheriff Lawrence.

"Well, we do, or we don't. I know the press has been down our backsides over the Brown murder. The case hasn't moved forward an inch. Now, we have an informant with half-decent information, and there are too many coincidences for this not to tie into the Brown murder. So, gentlemen, it's your call," Matt stated his argument as forcefully as he could.

"Well, may I use your phone? Richmond will have to approve this," asked the sergeant.

The answer from the Virginia State Police came back faster than expected. The Richmond papers had been scalding the state police brass over no reported progress on the murder of a state prosecutor. Approval was granted on the fast track. The raid was a go, and there was a promise of protection for two months by the state police.

The sheriff left to organize things for the evening. Matt and Sergeant Oliver drove to the courthouse to see Judge Carlton. He read the affidavit, asked a couple of questions, swore in the trooper, and signed it.

"You boys know you're about to kick over the hive, don't you?" commented the judge.

"Yes, Your Honor. But if we don't do something, I don't think we'll ever solve the Brown murder," responded Matt while the sergeant stood silent.

"Does this little raid of yours have anything to do with that shootout near Chatham?" asked Judge Carlton.

"You know about that?" asked Sergeant Oliver.

"I do. Judges have their network. I expect this informant of yours is going to need a little protection. You got that worked out?"

"We do, Your Honor. We just hope we can get in and grab some good evidence. We think this all ties together," affirmed Matt.

"Well, good luck. I think you might need it," concluded the judge as Matt and Sergeant Oliver took the papers and left.

The sergeant left to gather a raiding party composed of troopers, and Matt walked into his courthouse office for the first time that day. He greeted Mrs. Harvey, who looked up at him and smiled.

"Mr. Cubley, it's good to see you're alive and not all shot to pieces," she said.

"Mrs. Harvey, there's not a single article in the paper, but everyone knows about my trip to Pittsylvania County. So why do they even bother to publish a paper that only prints old news?" Matt joked.

"I often wonder that myself," she responded, breaking from her typical severe manner.

The day wore on, and Matt became more and more anxious. He needed this raid to go off successfully. Everyone was to meet at the elementary school at nine o'clock. The sheriff thought that location might throw off certain people who might be watching. Plus, heavy rain was expected from Hurricane Connie tonight, which would help conceal things but make the night miserable for the men.

Matt returned to Cubley's Coze in time to see Richard Baker, Skip, Kent, and Billy return from their trip to the lodge. He wanted it to appear that no one was staying there and no preparations were being made for future guests. However, Richard's report spoiled his plans to move Cindy to the lodge after the storm. Matt decided Cindy best continue in the attic room. The strange hiker made Matt fear the worst.

A deputy picked up Matt at eight-thirty. Sergeant Oliver, Troopers Giles, Lusk, Quinn, and Franklin arrived at the school with two additional troopers from another area. The sheriff supplied his chief deputy, Ed Barnes, and ten other deputies, making a total of twelve police cars. This was turning into quite a caravan.

Since steel doors were involved, two deputies each brought a twenty-pound sledgehammer, and one deputy had a portable cutting torch. If they couldn't convince someone to let them in, they'd apply some good old-fashioned muscle.

Loading up, the sheriff and Ed Barnes rode in the lead car, followed by Sergeant Oliver and Matt in car number two. The rest were in a long line of red lights and loud motors.

The sheriff and state police sergeant parked in the first two guest check-in spaces, and the raid leaders ran into the lobby with the search warrant. The rest of the raiding party stopped wherever they could find room to park, which blocked the hotel's front entrance road.

Sheriff Lawrence walked quickly to the front desk where Bill Grogan, the resort's general manager, was working. The manager looked shocked and then mad when he noticed the sheriff with a posse following him, dripping water all over the lobby floor.

"Sheriff, what in Sam Hill are you doing? You're going to scare the sh...you're going to frighten our guests," exploded Mr. Grogan, and his face turned red.

"Bill, we have a search warrant to search the premises for gambling equipment and un-tax-paid liquor. Now, we need to go to the party room in the basement. Will you take us?" asked the sheriff.

"There's no party room in the basement. You just hold on until I can get Mr. McCulloch over here to straighten this out. You know Big John's going to be mad as hell," growled Mr. Grogan. The man moved to his left two steps and pressed something under the edge of the counter. It was now evident to Matt and the others that the man had just sent out a warning and was stalling for time.

"Bill, don't play me for a fool. I'm going down to the basement on that little elevator over by the potted plants. I know you just warned them. So, to make up for your little mistake, I need you to bring your key along. We don't want to bash down any doors," concluded the sheriff.

"I don't have a key! Even if I did, there's no way I would use it without Mr. McCulloch's okay."

"Boys, it looks like we gotta do this the hard way. You two stay up here with Mr. Grogan. The rest of you, come with me," said Sheriff Lawrence, pointing to two deputies who got the duty of holding down the lobby and babysitting the hotel manager.

Matt knew that two deputies and one trooper had gone to guard the rear in case someone tried to use the freight elevator to go out the back entrance.

Now, four at a time, officers crowded onto the tiny elevator and slowly took it to the basement. They found two security guards in the vestibule, blocking their way.

"Step aside there, you men," ordered the sheriff rather bluntly.

"Gentlemen, I'm Sergeant Oliver of the Virginia State Police, and I order you to step aside. We have a search warrant for these premises. If you obstruct the service of these papers, I'll have no choice but to arrest you."

The two men didn't move. That's when four more deputies arrived on the elevator and stepped into the basement with their tools and a torch. So now it was eight versus two. The two stepped aside and stood against the wall.

When the sheriff tried the steel door, it was locked. He turned to the two guards and asked them to open the door.

"It only opens from the inside. You can ask politely, but I doubt they are gonna let you in," said the smaller of the two guards with a smirk on his face.

The sheriff pushed a button on what looked like an intercom and explained why the officers were there. The person on the other side opened a peephole in the center of the steel door.

After a moment, he announced through the intercom, "The only way I'm opening this here door is when Big John or Little John gives me the okay! This is a private club!"

The sheriff stepped back and waved the men forward with the sledgehammers and the torch. The deputies went to work. At first, there was only the hissing noise of the torch where the torch man guessed the lock's latch and the door hinges could best be cut. Then, the deputies went to work with the hammers. After a few blows, they decided to swing together. After six or seven impacts of two twenty-pound sledgehammers striking the door at the same point and at the same time, the door became loose in its frame. Finally, on the eleventh blow, it swung open.

The man on the other side, dressed in a tux, was holding his left hand. He thought he could keep the door closed and got a sprained wrist for his effort. A deputy arrested him for obstructing the service of a court document.

Behind the door was a large room filled with poker and roulette tables. Thirty guests in evening clothes were in a panic to leave. The problem was there was nowhere for them to go.

Two deputies and a trooper went behind the bar and found a bartender crouched down, trying to hide while pouring bootleg down the sink. Behind the bar was a small kitchen containing a gas grill with three steaks cooking. Most of the bootleg whiskey had been destroyed, but four gallons remained. It was seized, and the bartender found himself in handcuffs for obstructing a search by destroying evidence.

The sheriff and the sergeant decided they would take down the guests' names and addresses since none wanted to speak. However, when one of the young men tried to say something, he was stopped by an older man who turned out to be his father.

The sheriff held up both of his hands for quiet. He put two fingers in his mouth, and a piercing whistle got everyone's attention.

"Folks, hear me out. It's a real shame that the names of all you fine people who refuse to talk to me will be published in all the local papers. Of course, anyone who cooperates will be treated as a confidential witness. No press, no names. You decide. Now! Once my men have your names and addresses, you'll be free to go on home. I'll need you to come to my office this coming week for an interview. Thank you for your cooperation."

All the employees, including the two guards, were arrested for operating an establishment where un-tax-paid whiskey was present. Despite a thorough search, they found no books or records. There was a guest register, but all the pages had been torn out. They had gone down one of the toilets in a bathroom, Matt surmised, and thus, the register of losses and money owed to the Casino had been destroyed; those debts would no longer be able to be collected. This would hardly hurt the gambling house but would irritate Big John like a slap in the face.

Matt was disappointed at the lack of evidence. However, there was enough to justify the search. They would need some luck getting the employees and guests to talk. If they could get one or two to give evidence, they might gain some leverage over others to speak. Matt also had the police take Bill Grogan to jail and keep him away from the other staff. He figured he might decide to talk.

Just as they were wrapping up the raid and the force was back in the lobby, Big John and Mr. Southwall arrived. Both were soaking wet and mad. Things got heated. Matt was threatened with everything from being fired, sued, and run out of town on a rail to more colorful punishments. The sheriff was told he might as well pack a bag because he wouldn't be able to get elected as the county dog catcher. Big John didn't forget the state police sergeant.

"Sergeant, you'll be lucky to get a post in west Grundy, directing traffic in and out of a two-bit, rundown, rat-infested coal mine."

The sergeant asked Big John to please calm down because he needed to ask him a question. "Mr. McCulloch, you're not under arrest and are free to go, but my men found a quantity of bootleg whiskey on this premises. The state police would like to know from whom you are buying your illegal whiskey?"

Matt thought Big John would pop a blood vessel. Mr. Southwall attempted to get Big John to go with him into a nearby office. While the company attorney was calming Big John, two of Big John's security detail pushed the sergeant back. When they touched Sergeant Oliver, Troopers Giles and Lusk had handcuffs on them before they knew what was happening. Trooper Quinn and a deputy also grabbed another guard, who tried to intervene. That guard was wrestled to the lobby floor and handcuffed.

Big John was still screaming insults as the raiding party left with their three new prisoners and departed for the jail. Finally, Mr. Southwall gave up trying to calm his boss.

Friday morning, Matt returned to Cubley's Coze at dawn. Not a single employee had made a statement that would incriminate Big John. The man with the broken wrist, who claimed the boss was the only one who could authorize him to open the door, could not remember his boss's name. Several employees did squeal on Bill Grogan, who they said was running things. However, Bill Grogan would not utter a word. He even refused to give them his full name.

However, bonds for all the employees were set at one hundred dollars each by the justice of the peace. Matt had asked for two hundred, knowing Big John's company could afford ten times that amount. Sure enough, by nine o'clock a.m., Mr. Southwall had bonded out every employee using a single check drafted on the account of Green Mountain Resort, Incorporated.

Matt got to bed when the last employee was being driven away from jail. He told himself he was trying. Someone had shown

Big John McCulloch that there was still some law in Green Mountain County. Not a lot of law, but a little.

The people in town spread the news of the raid, not the local paper. Afterward, no one had to explain what raid or where. All one had to say was, "The Raid." This two-word reference was often followed by, "And that's something I'll be telling my grandkids about!"

CHAPTER 39

BILLY, KENT, AND THE ATTIC ROOM
Friday, August 12, 1955

I t might as well have been Friday the thirteenth instead of Friday the twelfth. I was grounded, and with school starting in only sixteen days, this town, in one summer, had ruined my life!

Where was a circus, any circus? I wanted to run away. I'd clean up after the elephants if they'd only let me join a traveling circus.

I brushed my teeth, washed my face, and wet my hair with my hands. My hair was lopsided, with my curls on one side and short hair on the other. I was doomed. That's when things got even worse.

Scotty missed the toilet. I wanted to kill him. Kill him right on the spot. Turn me in and spend the rest of my life in prison. It had to be no worse than Highland.

How could two people living in the United States of America sentence a child to confinement without bike privileges and call themselves good parents? I smacked Scotty on his head and told him to aim for the toilet.

He screamed, but I didn't care.

"Billy, what did you do to your little brother?" Mom shouted from the kitchen, but it sounded more like criminal charges were being lodged against me than Mom asking me a question.

"Billy hit my little head," called Scotty, the stool pigeon.

"The little brat peed on the floor," I yelled back, knowing my defense would make little difference in Mom's eyes. A smack was a smack.

"Billy, I'm trying to cook breakfast. You clean it up. Tell Scotty to come down here."

"Hey, Snotty, go downstairs before I kill you," I stated.

Mom heard me call him Snotty. "Stop being so mean to your little brother. He isn't even three yet. You better straighten up and fly right!" Mom shouted.

"Scotty, someday, I hope you're stuck with a little brother. It would serve you right. Now get, or I'll make a wish for the stork to drop a little brother and a little sister at the back door!"

I was mad at the world. I fully expected to get whacked before this day was done.

I cleaned up the mess, got dressed in old clothes, and tossed my clothes from yesterday along with my pajamas on the closet shelf since they were only shelf dirty.

I slowly took the stairs to the first floor. I felt like I was on my way to my own hanging.

"Billy, hurry up. Your dad's going to drive you and Kent to work. Take that look off your face, or I might just give you something to frown about. Now, don't forget to call me when you're done. You answer me, young man!"

Mom was on the edge of whacking me herself. She and I both knew it.

"Yes, ma'am. Call when we get done," I answered her in the nick of time. I started walking faster to get out of the kitchen before I caught it good.

I put on my raincoat and a ball cap because it was pouring. When I got inside the garage, Dad spoke from under a customer's car, "Billy, Mr. Skelton will to run you and Kent up to the hotel. I'm busy with a tune-up and oil change."

Like I cared who drove me or why.

"Son, stop causing your mother trouble, or you'll have trouble with me," Dad warned me and waited for an answer. "You better answer me."

"Yes, sir. Mind Mom. Ride with Mr. Skelton. I don't see why I can't ride my bike. It's not that far." I knew I was pushing it. I also remembered my bike was at the hotel.

"In the rain?" There was a pause, then Dad finished with, "One more word. That's all it's going to take, boy. One more word."

"Yes, sir, I'm going," I said as I climbed in our Buick with Mr. Skelton. We drove over to Kent's house and picked him up.

Kent looked about as down in the dumps as I felt. Mr. Skelton tried to cheer us up, but neither of us said much. He dropped us at the loading dock behind the hotel. Rainwater was cascading off the side of the building. It was like running under a waterfall to make it onto the dock and out of the rain.

We got our breakfast plates, and Boo gave us each a poke on the arm. She's even nice when it rains.

We sat down to eat, but no Polecat or Mr. Cubley. That's when Boo came out to the loading dock.

"Boys, Mr. Cubley's been up all night with the police. He's sleeping, so don't make any noise."

We both said, "Okay," and she went back into the kitchen.

I felt like being quiet anyway. Besides, how much noise could a kid make with a paintbrush?

A wet Polecat arrived with his papers wrapped in an old oilcloth that had more dirt than oil on it. The front page had a great article about the shootout in Chatham. Kent and I each swiped a paper. We read about the gunbattle that Mr. Cubley and Trooper Giles had fought and barely mentioned. When you're a former Marine sniper, leaving dead people all over a farm's no big deal.

Polecat came out with his food and caught us reading his papers. Usually, he would chastise us, his word, not mine, but today he just passed by and sat down to eat. I finished my paper first, careful to put it neatly back on the pile. Kent finished next.

"Master Clark, Master Gunn, how is your constitution on this fine monsoon morn?" asked Polecat.

"Fine," we said, which was not the truth, but I doubted he cared.

Polecat seemed happy and launched into, "Once again, historical events have transpired in the streets, byways, and lanes of this fine metropolis. Great matters of political importance occurred in the wee hours nocturnal. *Highland Gazette* reporters expostulated with the paper's editor, but his decision to censure the news was absolute."

I looked at Superman; he looked at me. Neither of us had the slightest idea of what Mr. Smith had just said.

After a back-and-forth set of questions and answers, we finally learned about the raid. The news was spreading, and Polecat had heard bits and pieces at the fire station, police department, sheriff's office, pool hall, and the newsroom. However, the editor of the *Gazette* refused to publish any mention of the raid. His son-in-law threw a temper tantrum, but the old man refused to budge.

Polecat said it would make no difference. The story would spread faster, and its credibility would be enhanced because the paper refused to publish it. The plant workers and merchants in town were praising the sheriff, the state police, and Mr. Cubley. The bigwigs were casting those same individuals into the fiery pit of elitist public-opinion hell, according to Polecat.

Boo and Teresa Long came out onto the dock and joined us. They also had gossip to add. Everyone talked or listened until Mrs. Johnson threatened us with disembowelment if we didn't return our dishes and get to work. We ignored her because even Mr. Tolliver had come outside to listen. Finally, Mrs. Johnson broke up the gathering by coming to the kitchen door, waving a meat cleaver.

Kent and I let Mr. Tolliver go into the kitchen before we delivered our dirty dishes to Toby to clean. Polecat followed behind us at a distance—the chicken.

As Polecat left, he reported that most people in town were saying Mr. Cubley was a hero, bona fide, and the sheriff was favored to win the next election. Many were predicting that no one would run against the sheriff. Why did they think Big John would permit that to happen?

Kent and I went quietly up to the second floor and down the east wing to get ready to paint. When Skip came by with several buckets of paint, we three talked about the raid. He said he knew all along Mr. Cubley was top-notch.

Mr. Baker arrived with our instructions on where to paint. Before we started, he asked us to go upstairs to the top floor in the west wing to move a dresser. When we slid the heavy piece out for the maid to clean behind it, it made a screeching noise. That's when we heard a noise from the attic room directly above us. This was the room Mr. Cubley's uncle added for him when he was our age. It was also the room that Trooper Lusk used when he was trying to catch the sniper. We asked Mr. Baker who was using it, but he said he didn't know and it was none of our business.

When we returned to painting, Kent and I wondered about the noise. We decided it must be one of those hotel secrets that Mr. Cubley made us swear an oath never to reveal. Was it someone famous? If it were a cowboy or movie star, we would die if we didn't get a chance to meet the person.

We started painting and heard Mr. Cubley getting up. We knew it was that loud dresser's fault. Kent and I felt terrible because Boo had asked us to be quiet. I thought: *today, with being grounded and nowhere to go, how could we get into a scrape? But here we were, in trouble for waking our boss.*

The door to the room we were painting had been left open to help with the smell. Mr. Cubley peeked in to check on us. I was surprised that he never fussed about waking him. We asked him about the raid, and he chuckled.

"Boys, I'm afraid it wasn't much of a raid."

Kent asked, "Was there any shooting?"

"No, Kent, but there was a lot of yelling," he said and laughed.

"Who?" I asked.

"Big John, for one. He put on quite a show. I don't think he thought anyone would ever have the nerve to raid his hotel. I hope we can get some of the gamblers to testify because it appears that not a single employee will roll over."

Kent and I looked at each other.

I began thinking. *Maybe we could talk to Misty. I bet she or Cindy might testify.*

"Mr. Cubley, Cindy might talk. I mean, those bad men shot at her on the farm. If you know where she is, she might help you." I was trying to be helpful.

I got a frown for my efforts. "Billy, let's not mention Cindy. That's one of those secrets we don't talk about. Also, I need your help with something."

"Sure," we both said in unison.

"I called Misty but had no luck. Her dad claims she's not there. Do either of you know where she might be staying?"

Kent and I both looked horrified as we shook our heads no. How did Mr. Cubley know we had been talking to Misty? Neither of us had ever mentioned her name to him. I messed up and called her she, but I never said her name.

"Mr. Cubley, how do you know a certain person's name?" Of course, I said it all secret-like, but I knew the cat was out of the bag.

"Cindy told me. She knew her best friend had sent us looking for her. She's thankful Misty did, or she and her grandparents might not be alive right now."

"Oh," I exclaimed, thinking *I should have known Cindy would know Misty would be worried and send help. Gee, I was dumb*! Kent looked like he had the same thought as me. We could tell stuff like that about each other.

Then, I knew the sound in the attic room was Cindy. It just came to me. When Mr. Cubley went downstairs to work in his office, I whispered it to Kent.

Kent nodded and said, "BB, I bet you're right. That's who we heard."

"Yeah, that explains why Boo's been taking plates to a guest instead of the normal waitresses. Boo's a spy, working for Mr. Cubley."

"Yeah, I bet she's had to take oaths like you and me," said Kent.

Later, I had to go out to get some turpentine. I saw a trooper that I had never seen before. He backed his unmarked patrol car under one of the white pines at the end of the employee parking lot. It was like he was trying to hide it, but any dummy could see it was a police car. He got out in plain clothes with two rifle cases.

Mr. Cubley came out in the rain to meet him before he got to the loading dock. The trooper gave Mr. Cubley one of the gun cases, and they went into the hotel through the kitchen.

I told Kent what I had seen.

"Sure, that guy's here to protect Cindy. I bet Mr. Cubley has people all in the woods with sniper rifles, bazookas, and all kinds of stuff," said Kent.

"Superman. Really? Bazookas in the middle of a hurricane? Let's finish up this last room, clean our brushes, and check out the attic. We got to be careful. Our moms would kill us if we got shot by a trooper," I said, and then I realized what I had just said.

"BB, are you trying to be funny, or did you just pull a whiz-bang?" Kent asked as he laughed at me.

"Not as many as I've heard from you lately. After we finish here, let's see if we can talk to Cindy," I said.

"What about?" asked Kent.

"Let's ask her to write a note to Misty, asking her to talk to Mr. Cubley. They are close, and that should do the trick!"

We finished our work for the day, stored our painting stuff in the room's closet, and went up to the top guest floor. We tiptoed over to the door that led up to the attic. Kent eased it open. That's when we heard a shotgun being racked to load a round.

"Don't shoot! It's just BB and Superman!" yelled Kent, who let the door swing all the way open as he stepped back with both hands raised. There was the trooper I'd seen a little while ago. He had one of those twelve-gauge shotguns. It was pointed right at us, but he quickly pointed it up in the air.

"Boys, Mr. Cubley warned me about you two. In fact, Troopers Giles, Lusk, and Quinn warned me that you two would find this hideout before I was here a full day. But, doggone, it only took you scamps two hours."

Kent lowered his hands. "Sir, we don't want no trouble. We're on a mission from Mr. Cubley and need to ask Cindy to help us. That's all," Kent responded with a quiver in his voice. As soon as he said it, I knew we were in big trouble.

The frown on the trooper's face said it all. He took the shotgun and stashed it on the top landing. After knocking on the door and telling Cindy something we couldn't hear, he took us by the arms and marched us down to the lobby.

First, we got chewed out by Mr. Tolliver, and it was a good one. Better than my mom. Then, Mr. Tolliver took us in to see Mr. Cubley, leaving us with our boss.

Mr. Cubley closed his office door, and darn if he didn't laugh. He told us he knew we would cross paths with one of the troopers guarding Cindy sooner or later. He just thought it would take us a day or two.

We told him how we figured out where she was hiding. I explained, "We were going to get her to write us a note telling Misty to come see you."

Kent added, "We thought we were helping!"

He made us take an oath of silence and promise to stay away from Cindy and the attic room. "You two talk to Misty only if you meet her by accident. You are not to go looking or asking for her."

He made it very clear that police protection for Cindy did not include us getting in the way. This time, he was quite stern.

Mr. Cubley also told us he was keeping a sniper rifle and his shotgun loaded and handy. If we saw either one of those guns, we were not to touch them. We promised.

He ended our little meeting by calling my mom and telling her she could pick us up because we were finished for the day. I was thankful he didn't rat on us about almost getting shot by a trooper.

Well, Superman and I weren't ready for Mom to take us home, but I kept my mouth shut.

Mom picked us up within fifteen minutes and, right away, took part of our wages for college, which left us only half of what we had earned. Also, we got no tips working for the hotel. Life was so not fair.

I was thinking about where Kent and I might find a circus when I saw what was coming down the street. Kent was looking at a dog chasing a cat and was missing it.

I punched him in the arm.

"BB, what was that for?" he exclaimed.

"Look up ahead," I announced, pointing up Green Mountain Avenue.

A police car with its red light on, the Koehler Funeral Home Ambulance with its red lights on, Big John's Cadillac, and another police car, bringing up the rear, were all driving down the road. When they got to Big John's street, they all turned in front of Mom. She had to stop to avoid them.

"What is all that," Kent said.

"It could be Lou, I hope," answered Mom.

I was sure Lou was coming home, and he wasn't dead. The hearse only turned on its red lights when it was being used as an ambulance. But what shape was Lou in? Was he even conscious?

357

When we arrived home, Grandma gave us a telephone message. Mr. Henry Watkins, the Special Prosecutor, wanted a meeting of all the seventh-grade children and their parents at the elementary school auditorium on Tuesday, August 16, at ten o'clock sharp.

Yeah, things just got worse!

CHAPTER 40

A SERIOUS DATE

Saturday, August 13, 1955

Matt was almost ready after shining his shoes and shaving. He suppressed thoughts of canceling their plans because he was only meeting a friend. This was not a date. So why did he feel so guilty?

The hurricane had tracked north, and despite heavy rain, the dry weather before the storm meant much of the water had soaked into the ground. Some flooding had occurred in the eastern part of the state, but Green Mountain County was only soggy. Linda had agreed the weather was no reason to cancel their evening.

Another wave of guilt washed over him. But why?

His history with Linda included a couple of lunches and several limited conversations on living with crushing grief. After one long phone call and a recent meeting, she had helped him understand the recovery process after losing a mate. They were just friends being friends, helping each other through terrible times.

With one more look in the mirror, he set aside his doubts and took the stairs to the lobby.

"Matthew, you should take this," insisted Chuck.

Chuck had prepared a corsage for Linda. Would she feel that the flower was too much? He guessed that Chuck had called her to be sure the colors were correct. The man was very meticulous when it came to his flowers. The corsage was even in a small box for protection.

Matt took the flower because he felt he must. He didn't want to hurt Chuck's feelings.

Puddles lingered on the road as he drove to Linda's house. He went to the door, and it opened before he could knock. Linda greeted him with a smile, wearing a dress of the latest style. Not that he knew anything about ladies' fashions, but he had seen a similar one in *Life Magazine*. Her green eyes lit up when she saw the corsage he was holding.

"Would that be for me?" she teased.

"It is. Chuck made it," confessed Matt.

"Would you pin it on?" she asked Matt, moving closer.

"Oh, my. Well, I guess."

It was not easy, but Matt was able to pin the corsage on Linda's dress without stabbing her with the hatpin. Where Chuck had come up with an ornate hat pin, Matt had no notion.

They arrived at the General Wayne Hotel in Waynesboro just a few minutes after seven. The waiter took their order and brought them sweetened iced tea and a basket of hot homemade rolls. Then, Matt ordered shrimp salads for their appetizer, and they could now chat undisturbed.

"Matthew, since you've become the Commonwealth's Attorney, things have gotten rather interesting around the courthouse," stated Linda.

"A lot more so than I would have liked," Matt responded

"The judge and I were talking about what happened to Mr. Albert Winston Brown. Who, among the hundreds of suspects, might have done it?"

Matt thought for a moment before he answered. "The Brown murder has all kinds of issues. I'm in the middle of a swamp, looking for a branch to grab but having little luck finding a solution. We need a break," stated Matt, trying to hold up his end of the conversation. He started to butter a hot roll but put it down, forgotten. He was depressed, and the raid was adding to and not helping lighten his load.

"Matthew, you look worried. What's bothering you?" Linda asked with a shift in the subject.

Matt decided to confide in her. "Linda, I'm starting to have bad dreams. I had to save the boys and Richard from the sniper and fired my gun without thinking. These recent killings at the farm, though, were different. I meant to kill those men. The second man was running away when I shot him. How can I ever be forgiven for that?"

Linda reached across the table and gently placed her hand over Matt's.

"Matt, what you did was justified. All those men were killers. You saved a trooper, that farmer and his wife, his hired hand, not to mention that young lady, Cindy. Now, hush! You're a hero to everyone except Big John and his cronies," she insisted with a smile, then looked up while the waiter deposited the shrimp salads in front of them. She thanked the waiter for his service. He smiled back, thinking her recent smile was for him.

Linda changed the subject back to Big John and the raid. "Matthew, will you be able to get timely convictions on the hotel raid? The governor's old law firm notified the court that they'd joined Southwall in representing most of the defendants, and they're good at delaying things."

Matt picked up his salad fork but put it back down. "Ben Southwall is the counsel of record, and, so far, no delays from him. However, every single employee of Green Mountain Resort has refused to talk. All the guests are playing dumb except for one couple. That couple had never been there before, and I don't think they knew what they were getting into."

"How did they get invited?" asked Linda, breaking off and eating small bites of a roll as they talked. She was leaving her shrimp salad until Matt started eating his.

"Another couple brought them, and the invited couple swore they had no idea moonshine would be served. However, they did admit that they had been told that gambling would be part of the evening's entertainment. I believe them. The trouble is, two versus a crowd of witnesses gives us zero."

"Who was running the party and providing the illegal whiskey? If not Big John, then who?" asked Linda.

"I'm certain we can show Bill Grogan had guilty knowledge of the gambling. Mr. Southwall is trying to make us believe one of the guests brought the bootleg, bribed the bartender to serve it, and the rest of the staff knew nothing about it."

Matt was stabbing a shrimp with such force he was moving his salad plate across the table.

Linda laughed. "Matt, go easy on that poor shrimp salad. You're going to break the plate." She began eating her salad in a much more ladylike fashion.

"Oh, sorry." Matt countered and changed subjects.

"I feel bad for the children. They've started to mimic what the adults are doing. I know Kent and Billy, along with most of the kids in Miss Jones's class, attacked the two Lockhart brothers. What those kids did may have taught those two bullies a lesson, but that's not how this town should raise its children."

"You said two bullies. I thought there were three?" said Linda with mild surprise.

"You're correct. But Lou seems to have changed," Matt revealed.

The conversation then centered on Lou's attempted suicide and why he did such a terrible act.

Matt added, "Billy claims that Lou changed after he got his bike back."

"Matt, do you think Billy and Kent hurt Lou to get back their bikes?" Linda asked, growing more concerned.

"No, Billy and Kent had nothing to do with that, and who was involved remains a mystery. But all the kids gathered and pulled off the Lockhart ambush."

"The courthouse gossips say the same," stated Linda as she finished her salad.

"I can understand why they did it. When Richard Lockhart and Big John gave their boys fake alibis, that's when the kids took matters into their own hands." Matt made a vigorous gesture with his right hand, and his fork flew out of it and clattered on the floor.

A waiter hurried over to see if everything was all right. Matt apologized for dropping his fork.

"Well, what now?" Linda asked with a smile, hoping to lighten Matt's mood.

"Miss Jones is trying to get the kids on the right path, and most of the parents have agreed to help her. However, the Lockharts and the McCullochs refused."

Their dinner arrived, and Matt and Linda changed their conversation to the weather, good food, and other topics. The rest of the evening passed very pleasantly. Neither ordered dessert and after Matt paid the bill, the couple strolled down Main Street, looking in shop windows.

Driving out of town, Linda asked Matt if he would stop at the top of Afton Mountain to enjoy the view. The lights of the homes sparkled below them in random patterns with patches of fog here and there. The moon was in its third quarter, with only a few clouds passing in front of it. Nevertheless, it gave enough silvery light to be romantic.

Matt leaned over and took Linda's hand. She placed her other hand on top of his. They shared the moment until Matt straightened in his seat, took a deep breath, and started the car. Linda took his right arm, hugged it, and leaned onto his shoulder while he drove them back to Highland. Arriving in front of her house, he walked her to her door and kissed her cheek. She was disappointed but kissed him back on his other cheek, and they parted.

His mind was not on his driving on the way back to the hotel. He arrived at half-past ten, and all was quiet. Matt went up to his room, changed into some old clothes, and not feeling sleepy; he went to his office to read some mail. He remained conflicted over his feelings and decided to chat with his night clerk.

He was leaving his office when the outside line on the front desk rang. Cliff picked it up immediately.

"What did you say? Who is this? Son, if this is some joke, I don't think it's funny. Who? This better be for real. Hold on." Cliff called to Matt, "I think you better take this!"

"Hello," answered Matt.

"Are you Mr. Cubley?" said a small voice, almost whispering.

"Yes, I am. Who's calling?"

"I can't tell you my name. But you need to know that men with guns are coming to kill Misty somebody tonight! I don't want that! Please do something!"

"Why would they do that?" Matt asked with alarm.

"She knows things she shouldn't, and if they can kill this Misty, the missing bookkeeper will be afraid to talk. Please don't let them do this! She was nice to me!"

"Do you know where this will happen?"

"They're coming to her dad's house to kill everybody. Tell the Brotherhood I helped! Goodbye," and the line went dead.

Matt called the sheriff at home, woke him, and gave him the details. He explained the phone call and identified the families of the two targeted girls and who had called. The sheriff assured Matt that he would get some officers over to Archie Johnson's first, secure the family and Misty, and then have the Hairston household picked up. Matt revealed to the sheriff that a trooper was at his hotel guarding Cindy.

"Sheriff, can we lay a trap at each house?" Matt asked. "I think we might be able to snare us some assassins. Also, to keep Lou McCulloch safe, let's keep his identity just between you and me. Can we do that?"

"Good idea. Okay, first, I'll have Shoat go to Archie Johnson's house in his private car and slip them out the back. Then, we can set men watching the house and see who we catch," Sheriff Lawrence suggested.

"Good. Bring the Johnsons to the hotel. I have protection here already for Cindy, and I think I can get more from Sergeant Oliver," advised Matt.

"Should I have my men bring Cindy's parents to Cubley's Coze?"

"Absolutely," confirmed Matt.

"Also, we need to get the state police to cut off all the escape routes. No sleep for the men tonight."

Matt spoke up, "I'll call Sergeant Oliver while you get your men moving."

"Matt, be sure to remind them to stay off the radio. Ears may be listening," commented the sheriff.

Matt handed Cliff his twelve-gauge shotgun, briefed him on the strange call, and instructed him to lock the lobby and first-floor doors.

"Lock the doors. Right. I need a key." Cliff requested as he checked the shotgun to make sure it was loaded. It was.

"Here," Matt said, handing Cliff his set of keys. "Make sure all the doors and windows are locked. I need to call the state police."

Matt's next call was to Sergeant Oliver's home. The sergeant said he would have troopers ready to block the roads out of town. He agreed to send Matt a couple of troopers to reinforce the hotel. Also, he would pass along the sheriff's request to stay off their two-way radios.

Matt hung up, ran upstairs to the attic entrance, and informed the trooper guarding Cindy of the recent events. He gave the trooper keys to the first two rooms, second floor, east wing, with instructions to move Cindy to that location in case someone knew about the attic room.

Matt and the trooper woke Cindy and moved her to the new room. The trooper established a new guard post in a corner office with a view of the front and east wing halls. Matt told the trooper that the third and fourth east wing rooms were being painted and were empty, giving him a clear field of fire.

Matt then ran back to his office and loaded the sniper rifle loaned to him by Trooper Lusk. Suddenly, he heard glass shatter in the kitchen.

Matt worked the bolt to seat a round, flipped off the safety, eased open the master electric box in his office, and killed the lights in the lobby and his office. Then he slowly cracked the door from his office to the kitchen, dropped to the floor, and pointed his rifle through the crack.

He waited. When no one fired, he silently opened the door wider.

The lights were on in the kitchen, which cast Matt in a shadow for cover. He saw movement by the waitress's counter and aimed.

"You in the kitchen. Drop your weapon! Raise your hands where I can see them. Do anything stupid, and you're dead," Matt shouted.

"Don't shoot! I give up!" cried Cliff.

"Cliff, are you alone?"

"Matt, for gosh sakes, you just gave me a heart attack," Cliff responded.

"Who broke a window?" asked Matt.

"I knocked some glasses off the counter with my shotgun. Sorry, I'll pay for them. It was an accident."

"You almost gave me a heart attack. I thought someone was breaking into the kitchen. Don't worry about the glasses. I'm thankful it was only you," Matt said with relief.

"I still need to lock the loading dock door," added Cliff.

"I'll finish locking up. You guard the lobby. Just know, I killed the lights. Grab a flashlight and keep it on the ready," Matt instructed his night clerk.

Matt secured the ground floor of the hotel and returned to the lobby. He had focused on Cindy and underestimated the threat to Misty. He kicked himself for allowing the family to refuse protection. His mistake may have cost Misty, her mom, and her dad their lives.

Now, all he could do was pray.

CHAPTER 41

SHREWD
Saturday over Sunday, August 13 & 14, 1955

Matt was positioned just inside the dining room door with his rifle. Cliff was inside the entrance to Matt's office, holding a twelve-gauge shotgun. He could see over the front desk and across the hotel lobby. The lights were off in the lobby, the main staircase, and the dining room, with a single bulb burning in the kitchen near the loading dock door. Lights remained on in the halls of the upper floors.

The hotel guests were in bed for the night. Matt prayed that they stayed there. The hotel was quiet, except for an occasional pop or creak as the building settled down because of the cooler night temperatures. Sometimes he thought the old girl talked to him at night.

Best of all, Chuck was sound asleep in his apartment, unaware of what was happening around him. Of course, Matt would try to keep it that way.

Three cars arrived and stopped in front of the hotel. Trooper Lusk knocked quietly on the front door, more of a tap, tap, tap than a knock. Matt opened the door, minus the rifle.

Confirming with Matt that all was quiet, Trooper Lusk waved to the Johnson family seated in Deputy Lincoln's personal car. Archie, Louise, and their daughter, Misty, hurried up the veranda steps and into the hotel. Mr. Johnson carried a small overnight bag, but that was all the family's luggage.

Cindy's parents had refused to come to the hotel. Instead, they would rely on the story that Cindy had run away and on Mr. Hairston's six-shot revolver that was loaded and holstered on his hip. Plus, there were two deputies posted outside the Hairston home.

Matt asked the three Johnsons if they would like food or drink, but they declined. He took them up to the second floor, where he called softly to Cindy's guard. When the trooper was certain that

Matt and Lusk were bringing up only friendlies, he stepped out into the hall to wave the group forward. Matt and the troopers took the family to the room next door to Cindy's room. Before the guard could use his key, Cindy threw open her door with a bang. The two young women grabbed each other in a mutual embrace.

Cindy and Misty retreated into Misty's room as Cindy's parents were shown into the adjoining one. Trooper Lusk initially conferred with the trooper on guard duty, then returned to the lobby with Matt.

Deputy Lincoln had already left to join the sheriff. Trooper Lusk and another trooper, Matt didn't know, checked outside and moved the other patrol car to the employee parking lot. When they returned after checking the grounds a final time, each had a rifle, a shotgun, and a bag full of ammunition boxes.

Trooper Giles had driven his patrol car, which was still out front. He was in the lobby and told Matt that the sheriff had set up traps at the Johnson and Hairston residences. Also, deputies were parked behind the elementary school to either block the exits from town or rush in as backup for the other officers. An Amherst area trooper was stationed to the west along State Route 22, another was ready to set a roadblock on State Route 655, which led from the plant into Nelson County, and Sergeant Oliver was in hiding to the east on Route 22. If something went down, the police were ready.

Trooper Giles asked Matt to bring his portable typewriter and some typing paper in case they needed a search warrant. Matt carried those items to the trooper's car and placed them on the back seat, where he saw a sniper rifle and pistol. Trooper Giles loaned Matt those weapons in case they ran into trouble.

The two men rode to the elementary school and parked with the other deputies. Since they were under strict orders not to use their radios, the arrival of Trooper Giles caused a bit of a stir among the deputies in hiding until they saw who it was.

The waiting was causing Matt to squirm in his seat.

"If you need to pee, the woods are available. The men's room is the third tree on the left," joked Trooper Giles.

"No, all I need is for this to be over. I hate waiting."

"I thought Trooper Lusk told me you were one bad sniper instructor, and expert at waiting?" teased the trooper.

"I'm out of practice. Besides, it's been a long day. If I don't keep moving, I'm liable to doze right off," Matt replied and yawned.

Suddenly the radio came to life.

Sheriff Lawrence yelled, "Shots fired, one man down. A 1954 Chevrolet pickup is headed west on Elm Tree Lane with one occupant. The truck is a pop-eye. Get him!"

Sheriff Lawrence was transmitting over the sheriff's radio; however, Matt and Trooper Giles could hear it despite not being on the sheriff's frequency because they were parked beside a deputy. The windows were down on both vehicles.

Trooper Giles had his blue and gray started and in motion first. He spun gravel, backed off, got traction, and swung out onto Main Street. Matt braced for a hard right turn, but the trooper made a hard left.

"Bobby, you're going the wrong way. Elm Tree Lane is the other way," cried Matt as he tried to recover from the surprising turn.

"If this old boy is smart, he'll head out of town. I want to be where he's going, not where he's been," Giles said.

The trooper drove to the Liberty Bell Gas Station at top speed, turned right in a partial slide, and only slowed near the McCulloch Wood Products Plant, where he pulled into Bear Creek Road. The trooper turned around, killed his lights, put his car behind some shrubs, and waited.

"Bobby, what if he turns west, not east? You don't read minds, do you?" asked Matt, concerned that the trooper was going to miss the pickup.

"Matthew, have a little faith. Now, here is what's happening. This 1954 pickup will make a few turns in town and circle north on Main Street. The truck will no longer be a pop-eye. It'll be burning two headlamps, not just one, and the driver will be Sunday driving just under the speed limit. He might even stop at the Liberty Bell Gas Station for a pack of cigarettes or a cold pop. Meanwhile, the deputies will be tearing up the streets all over creation, looking for a one-eyed pickup. Our suspect, driving with one headlight, will have vanished. I'll intercept him as he drives the shortest route to his base."

No sooner had Trooper Giles explained it than a 1954 Chevrolet pickup, model 3100, with two headlights and both taillights burning, drove slowly past the Bear Creek Road headed east. Not a deputy was in sight.

Trooper Giles called his dispatcher and asked that car three-three be notified he was requesting a ten-seven for food at Tom's Grill.

"Bobby, isn't ten-seven out of service?" asked Matt.

"Yep, Sergeant Oliver now knows I'm on my way to his location, but no one listening will think anything."

Bobby Giles let the pickup drive a quarter of a mile past the plant before he pulled out. He didn't hurry, even though the truck was out of sight in the curves of East Gap. Finally, however, the pickup's taillights came back into view on the other side of the mountain. The trooper followed the vehicle through its left turn onto Afton Mountain Road. When the Chevrolet crossed over the hill, Trooper Giles reached under his dash and flipped a switch. Suddenly, the trooper's left headlight went out. He sped up, caught up with the pickup, and when the two vehicles reached a straight stretch on level ground, the trooper followed at twenty car lengths.

Both vehicles climbed Afton Mountain. Trooper Giles reached down and picked up his radio mike.

"Dispatch, this is three-zero-one," he said.

"Three-zero-one, go ahead," said the dispatcher.

"Advise three-three that I'll be ten-seven at Tom's in four," said the trooper.

"Bobby, what was that?" asked Matt.

"I told Oliver we would be at the rendezvous location in four minutes. He now knows we are still following our man and are undetected. I don't need him to take over, not yet. If I thought our boy had spotted us, I would have said to disregard my request," explained Bobby.

"Do you know where this guy is going?" asked Matt.

"Not exactly, but close. With luck, we'll watch him park and then grab him. I'm thinking he hasn't arranged for blocking cars tonight. He knows the fewer who know about this job, the better. We should be able to follow him all the way in," stated Trooper Giles. He pointed to a side road. Matt didn't see a thing, but a set of headlights flashed on when they passed.

"There's the sergeant," remarked the trooper.

Through the City of Waynesboro, Trooper Giles followed at a respectable distance. The sergeant traded places in his unmarked car from time to time. Trooper Giles switched between two headlamps to one headlight.

Tonight, Giles was right on the money. No blocking cars interfered because murders were done best with few witnesses. Finally, the pickup pulled up beside an old warehouse on the north side of town. A man got out of the truck, opened the garage door, and pulled into the large warehouse. He came back and closed the sliding door.

"Dispatch, this is three-zero-one, have everyone move in."

Suddenly three state police cars and two City of Waynesboro cruisers drove into the warehouse parking lot and cut on their red roof lights. Spotlights were also turned on and pointed at the warehouse. Several City officers ran to the rear. The rest of the men went to the garage door. It wasn't locked, so Sergeant Oliver grabbed it and pushed it open.

The pickup driver had parked in the warehouse near some stacked boxes. He was immediately pulled from the truck and thrown to the ground before he knew the police were there.

"And that's how it's done," announced Trooper Giles.

However, Matt had a frown on his face.

"Bobby, I hate to be the bearer of bad news, but we don't have a search warrant," Matt stated, shaking his head.

"Don't need one. I was in close pursuit of a fleeing felon who had just participated in the attempted murder of three people. Also, someone got shot. I just hope to hell it wasn't one of ours," exclaimed the trooper.

"But you didn't have your red lights and siren on," stated Matt.

"The close pursuit cases don't require it...do they?" responded the trooper.

"I never had that question come up. If we can prove it's the same truck, I guess it was a close pursuit. We were close and in pursuit. One big problem is that the one we needed to catch was a pop-eye. This vehicle has both headlights burning," proclaimed Matt.

Trooper Giles walked to the pickup and started the engine with the key still in the ignition. He reached under the dash and flipped a switch in the same spot as the one on his car. One of the headlights went out. He flipped it again, and it came back on.

"Well, I'll be dipped in...never mind. That's some trick. How in the world did you figure.... Oh my." Matt leaned over and whispered in the trooper's ear, "Is it who I think it is?"

"Bullseye. The man has talent. Now, don't you say anything. We need to keep this quiet for the sake of a certain family. All their lives may depend on it," said Trooper Giles.

Giles approached the man being held by his sergeant near the warehouse office.

"Trooper Giles, would you do the honors?" asked Sergeant Oliver as he swung the suspect around and into better light.

"Thomas P. Rosser, I'm placing you under arrest for participating as an accessory in the attempted murder of three members of the Johnson family. The crimes took place in the Town of Highland, County of Green Mountain," said Trooper Giles in a clear, loud voice. "What have you got to say for yourself?"

"Nothing, I ain't telling you the time of day, you bellhop with a badge," taunted Mr. Rosser.

Sergeant Oliver had already searched Rosser for weapons and recovered a switchblade knife, a pistol, and a lead sap. Each weapon was placed in an evidence bag while Matt watched Giles handcuff the prisoner.

One of the city officers approached the sergeant. "Sergeant, I think you better come see what else we found."

The policeman pointed to six cases of bootleg whiskey located just behind where the pickup was parked. Two were open and in plain sight. A search of the Chevrolet revealed it was registered to Angus Wallace MacDonald of Waynesboro, Virginia.

"Let me guess. In addition to all these charges, I bet your boss will claim this truck was stolen. So, Rosser, unless you talk to us, you're going down for a long time," announced Trooper Giles.

"I ain't saying jack. I'll be sprung before the ink is dry on these pumped-up charges, flatfoot," snarled Rosser.

Turning to the Waynesboro officers, Sergeant Oliver told them to take Mr. Rosser to jail. To ensure the prisoner didn't get misplaced or escape, he sent one of the troopers along with them. The remaining officers got busy seizing the truck, piling the bootleg in the truck's cargo area, and logging in all the weapons. These weapons would be going to the forensic lab for examination.

Walking outside and watching them put Rosser in the patrol car, Sergeant Oliver noticed that Trooper Giles' car only had one headlight burning.

"Giles, I just gave you my car, and look, your headlight's out. Get it fixed before your next shift!" ordered Sergeant Oliver to the trooper.

"Sergeant, it must be a loose wire. The darn thing was working fine when I left the house."

Bobby walked over to Matt and whispered for him to flip the switch when he got under the hood. Bobby raised the hood and yelled to Matt, "turn off my lights." Giles pretended to work for a few seconds and then yelled, "Okay, turn 'em back on."

Matt reached under the dash, flipped the hidden switch, and pulled the light knob to the on position. Then, of course, both headlights came on. The sergeant gave Giles a funny look and walked back into the warehouse. He was now aware of the switch on the Rosser vehicle, and he suspected Bobby was matching tricks with the crooks. However, he was too busy to worry about it.

The state police dispatcher called the sergeant to advise him that the man injured at the scene of the attempted murder was none other than Chill Dawson, another known employee of Angus MacDonald. The arresting officer at the Johnson's home recovered a shotgun, two pistols, and a lead sap from Chill.

Dawson's sap was larger and a favorite weapon of certain criminals when they wanted to knock someone unconscious to kidnap them. One blow and the victim would not be making a sound. It took some skill to knock a person out and not kill them. Matt guessed that Chill was an expert using lead saps.

Matt concluded that Chill Dawson and Tom Rosser were going to kill the parents, take Misty and make her talk, then kill her. Those two men were rotten to the core.

Matt had to figure out how MacDonald was connected to the Brown murder. Did MacDonald kill Brown without Big John ordering it? Was Big John a killer in absentia? A ton of questions and a bunch of loose ends to tie up.

Since this was in the City of Waynesboro, Sergeant Oliver called their Commonwealth's Attorney to write a search warrant for any remaining bootleg hidden in the warehouse. Bootleg not near the pickup and not part of Rosser's close pursuit and arrest would need to be seized pursuant to a proper search warrant.

While the state police and the Waynesboro City police were handling things at the warehouse, Sergeant Oliver had one of the troopers from Appomattox take Matt back to the hotel. Matt noticed that the Johnson neighborhood still had two sheriff's department vehicles parked on the street. Other than that, things looked quiet.

When Matt arrived at the hotel, Cliff had the lobby lit up with the kitchen coffee pot going. Trooper Lusk was still on the premises, but the other trooper had left.

Trooper Lusk had found half of a spice cake and was eating a quarter. Matt finished what was left with a mug of coffee. Chuck was awake, rushing around the lobby in a nervous twitch.

Sitting in the lobby in a comfortable chair, sipping his coffee, it hit him. What if he had not left Linda's but had gone inside? He would have missed Lou's warning, and the Johnson family might be dead.

He heard noises coming from the kitchen.

Footsteps? No, no one was in there.

Something popped.

Was it the old hotel's weary bones creaking?

Another sound of the wind was like a whisper.

Was Janet letting him know he'd made the right decision this evening? But what made Lou call him? Had the Lord brought Lou out of his coma just in time to sound the warning?

He sipped his coffee and reviewed the evening's events.
Trooper Giles had been brilliant to out-think Rosser.
A longer, windy sound came from the loading dock.
*He could have sworn it sounded like someone whispering
the word "shrewd."*

CHAPTER 42
A MONDAY MUDDLE
Monday, August 15, 1955

Monday morning, Matt arrived early at the courthouse. He was concerned that his most prominent case was not going well and wanted to discover what might solve it. The Brown murder was becoming a cold case. The older it got, the harder it would be to solve, and the press was becoming more hostile. He had been hopeful that Rosser and Dawson would confess. However, when Trooper Giles tried to obtain statements from the two men Sunday afternoon, neither would talk.

Charges of possession of un-tax-paid whiskey had been filed against Rosser by the Waynesboro Commonwealth's Attorney, and the Waynesboro PD night-shift boys had done a perfect job finding, securing, and cataloging the warehouse evidence. The Waynesboro prosecutor now had a good case and leverage over Rosser, but at present, the man refused to break. Rosser also faced charges in Green Mountain County, but he seemed not to care.

It was not unexpected that Angus MacDonald had called the Waynesboro police early Sunday morning to report his 1954 Chevrolet pickup stolen. He was told it was at the Waynesboro City Police Department impound lot. This was beginning to look like a case of history repeating itself. He had done the same thing when his driver, Doc Hathaway, was caught with a load of liquor. One big difference between the two events, Doc's truck had been a total loss, with Doc hospitalized.

After the Monday morning arraignment of Mr. Rosser in Waynesboro, Sheriff Lawrence's deputies transported Rosser to the Green Mountain County courthouse to be arraigned as an accessory on the attempted murder charges. Matt left orders with the sheriff that Rosser was not to be given a cell near Chill Dawson.

During a morning recess, Sheriff Lawrence and Sergeant Oliver told Matt how the interviews were going with some of the casino party guests. A deputy and two troopers had begun obtaining statements. The Farthington couple admitted to the gambling but were unaware bootleg was being served.

The rest of the partygoers were protecting Big John McCulloch by refusing to talk or claiming they saw no bootleg until the cops arrived. The implication was the bootleg whiskey had been planted.

Matt, the sheriff, and Sergeant Oliver agreed that the bootleg charges at Big John's resort could only succeed against the general manager, Bill Grogan, and the bartender. The bartender's case was solid because the officers saw him pouring the illegal liquor down the sink. However, against Big John, a conviction was looking impossible unless some employee *in the know* talked.

Since they were outside the locked door, the casino lobby guards would probably get off with the old "I didn't know" defense. But the doorman with the broken wrist was sure to be found guilty of obstruction.

After those phone calls ended, Mrs. Harvey buzzed Matt to tell him the governor's old law firm in Richmond was on the line. The firm was signing on officially to represent Bill Grogan and the other defendants from the Green Mountain Resort.

A law firm from Harrisonburg called twenty minutes behind the Richmond firm's call. The Harrisonburg firm would represent Chill Dawson and Tom Rosser on all their charges. The senior partner announced, "Mr. Dawson intends to plead guilty to the whiskey charges."

Matt immediately knew Angus MacDonald was paying Dawson for this plea, which would cost MacDonald a lot of money, but he could afford it. Matt was told Rosser would, of course, plead not guilty to his charges. However, Matt was confident that Rosser could at least be convicted for possessing his concealed weapons. However, the possession of the bootleg liquor charge regarding the cases located behind the pickup might fall, and the police couldn't prove a connection between him and the cases of illegal whiskey found in the Waynesboro warehouse. They were in a different location and sealed in boxes addressed to a vacant lot.

The Harrisonburg attorney next told Matt that the stolen vehicle charge was a big mistake, and he requested it be dropped.

"Mr. Cubley, Chill Dawson might be guilty of unauthorized use of the pickup, but Mr. Rosser is innocent of vehicle theft. You see, Mr. Dawson lied to Mr. Rosser about having special permission to use the Chevrolet."

Matt responded, "You expect me to believe that?"

"Mr. Cubley, when Tom Rosser drove the truck from Waynesboro to Highland, it was at the request of Mr. Dawson. The trip was to help Chill collect a debt. An old debt owed to Mr. Dawson by an old drinking buddy who lived in Highland. There was no conversation about killing anyone, and Mr. Rosser had no ill feelings against the Johnson family because he didn't know them."

Matt knew that if the judge or jury believed this tall tale, the Commonwealth couldn't prove criminal intent. Thus, regarding his role as an accessory to the shootings in Highland, Rosser would go free.

The Harrisonburg attorney concluded, "My client, Mr. Dawson, will plead not guilty on the attempted murder charges because an address error caused all of this. He had no intent to hurt anyone. Also, Mr. MacDonald knows that Mr. Dawson used the truck after hours without authority, but the man's a good employee. His boss wants to forgive and forget and requests that you drop the theft charge."

Matt almost laughed. "Sir, we are not dropping the grand larceny of the pickup charge. Dawson didn't have permission, and that's what the court will find."

The other lawyer came back with, "Look! My client, Chill Dawson, will plead guilty to charges of unauthorized use of Mr. MacDonald's truck and misdemeanor assault and battery on the officers. I urge you not to be hard-nosed about this man's poor judgment. The exchange of gunfire didn't injure any officers. Only Mr. Dawson suffered a serious injury. Again, he used poor judgment, going to collect a debt at that time of night. The man had no idea police officers were even in the area. We request suspended time only."

Matt had grown tired of this nonsense and tried to end the call with a short answer. "Sir, I'll have to speak with my counterpart in Waynesboro, but I doubt that we would be interested in your plea bargain. We'll be in touch."

Matt heard the other attorney make a surprised squeaking sound. After a moment of silence, the man blurted out, "Sir. I'm seriously trying to settle this matter. Please, don't insult my good efforts!"

Matt ignored this last comment and came back with a question.

"What about Dawson and the moonshine?"

Another pause, a rattling of some papers, and then it sounded like the man was reading a script. "My client, Chill Dawson, was given some shine by a friend for a big party that Mr. Dawson was planning. My client's a good person who made a mistake. He would never be involved in selling the stuff. It was all for personal use at his party."

Matt repeated that he would discuss these requests with the Waynesboro Commonwealth's Attorney since the bootleg charge was not in his county. However, Matt mentioned one contrary fact.

"Do you know there were six cases, each containing four one-gallon jugs? The police found ten more similar cases nearby. A little much for a party unless your client was inviting all the citizens of Waynesboro."

No additional argument from the other side was made, and the two men ended the call.

Matt had no sooner hung up the telephone when Mrs. Harvey knocked on Matt's door. She stuck her head in to tell him that Chief McCulloch and Officer Roger Younger needed to see him.

Matt let out a long sigh but told her to invite them in. This day was getting better and better.

Chief McCulloch walked up to Matt's desk and said, "Mr. Cubley, we need to talk. Okay?"

"What can I do for you? Have a seat." Matt answered in what he hoped was a cheerful tone. Based on prior meetings with Little John, the man was being half nice. Something had to be up.

Both officers ignored him and remained standing. Officer Younger had his police officer's hat in his hands. He was nervously turning it around and around by the brim.

Chief McCulloch began in a soft voice. "My boy, Lou, came home on Friday."

"How is he?" asked Matt, concerned for several reasons.

"Lou's fine. The youngster appears to be healing with no major problems."

"Chief, that's good news. Excellent news!" exclaimed Matt with a smile.

"Yes, it is. And Lou tells me he shot himself by accident. A terrible accident! Roger's boy had nothing to do with Lou getting shot. Uh, almost nothing. Little Roger loaned Lou the gun, which was a damn-fool thing to do, but he didn't shoot Lou. So, you gotta dismiss the charges today!" demanded Chief McCulloch. A demand, not a request, which was the usual way the McCulloch family thought and did things.

Matt was irritated by the demand and needed to talk to Lou. The boy had called him with that warning, and Matt was confident that Lou might share more information.

"Chief, I'll need to talk to Lou. I'll also need to have Sheriff Lawrence or Sergeant Oliver present as a witness to verify all of this," Matt interjected.

"What?" Why the hell do you need to do that? My boy's been through enough," shouted Little John. And, by the color of his face, his temper was causing a rise in his blood pressure.

"Chief, I can't go to the judge and tell him I want to dismiss felony charges based on the victim's father and the defendant's father, both of whom work together, saying this or that. The judge will surely ask me for Lou's version! We have Roger's statement in my file. If Lou's statement matches it, no problem," Matt explained with his temper also rising. "Roger, you do want your boy's charges dismissed, don't you?" Matt asked, turning this on Officer Younger.

"Yes, sir. That's why we're here."

Roger looked at Little John to see his reaction.

"Cubley, you always want to make things difficult. All right, you call the house. Run along, talk to the boy, and waste your time. I have important business to attend to," proclaimed Chief McCulloch, who then turned and marched out of Matt's office, not waiting to see if Officer Younger was following.

"Roger, I hope you realize I'm insisting on this for your son's sake. I want to be sure the judge agrees that we have the facts and signs off on the dismissal order. Understand?"

Officer Younger was walking out of the office, looked at Matt over his shoulder, but gave no reply. However, Matt was sure that he'd heard him.

What a day, Matt thought. *A little good and a lot of bad.*

He looked at his watch and saw it was time to return to the courtroom. The cases for the hotel raid were set next, and he was almost late.

The arraignments or reading of the charges against Bill Grogan and the other resort employees happened as expected. Bonds remained the same as set by the justice of the peace. The defense attorneys surprised Matt when they asked for immediate dates for the preliminary hearings and trials. Matt didn't object. Getting this over might take the threat off the two witnesses secreted at Cubley's Coze.

Finally, Chill Dawson and Tom Rosser were brought into court after a short recess and arraigned one after the other. The young attorney from the Harrisonburg law firm arrived for their arraignments. All his motions for personal recognizance for the men were denied. The court set the two bonds at one thousand dollars cash each, which was a bit low in Matt's opinion.

Matt suspected that the law firm's fee was five times the bond amount for each man. They were getting the best legal defense that Angus MacDonald could buy. Had Matt known the legal fee for each defendant was ten thousand dollars per defendant, even he would have been shocked. MacDonald was tight-fisted, but not when it came to saving his own skin.

After court ended for the day, Sergeant Oliver and Sheriff Lawrence came to Matt's office for a conference. It had been set to begin at four, and Matt was only ten minutes late—a minor miracle.

The men knew from Misty and Cindy that Mr. Brown had been buying bootleg for the Green Mountain Resort over a long period of time. The illegal whiskey was for the parties at the fish cabin on Bear Creek and the special parties at the hotel's casino. It was obvious that Angus MacDonald had been selling to Brown, the purchasing agent for Big John.

According to Matt, who was familiar with the state's major bootleg families, MacDonald had to be hauling for the Woody family because only the Perry family transported Perry whiskey. Matt began throwing out questions.

"Gentlemen, we know from Cindy Hairston that Brown had been skimming money off the bootleg orders. Big John was paying more than MacDonald was charging Brown. Could Big John have found out about the stealing? Did Big John order Brown to be killed?"

After a discussion, the three doubted he would have had his corporate attorney killed—too much mess and publicity at his own doorstep. Big John might have ruined the man financially but not ordered him murdered and allowed the body to be dumped near his plant.

The sheriff asked, "Okay, who would have the most reason to kill Brown?"

Sergeant Oliver answered at once. "Brown got greedy, and we know the Perry family has always wanted to extend its operation north and east. My sources tell me they tried to deliver to Green Mountain County years ago and got into a bloody war that profited neither family. What may have made old man Woody try this time was being approached by a potentially large customer, Brown, not a bunch of small fry nip-joint owners. He might have thought it was worth the risk to try to break into MacDonald's territory."

Matt added, "I see where you're going with this. If the Perry family undercut MacDonald's price, Brown could pocket a bigger difference. Brown's greed would entice him to buy from Perry and dump MacDonald. A risky move."

Sheriff Lawrence joined in with, "If Angus MacDonald found out about Brown trying to switch suppliers, he would kill Brown and dump the body faster than a scared rabbit goes into his hole. Angus MacDonald would never tolerate the Perry family cutting in on his territory. Yep, they tried it once, and Angus made sure they got their fingers burned. If Angus found out what Brown was doing, killing him would be what he would do."

Sergeant Oliver scooted his chair closer. "I think Big John probably didn't know who killed Brown until after the fact. Let's say the Perry family contacted Big John after Brown went missing. The man's no dummy. He would have checked the books. Then, seeing what happened to Brown, Big John wouldn't dare risk the wrath of Angus MacDonald, even if he could save a few dollars. He'd keep buying his hooch from MacDonald."

Sheriff Lawrence finished with, "No, Big John isn't stupid. And any investigation to catch Brown's killer might wreck his party business. He depends on that business's benefits—the influence it creates over others and the money. And that's why he's so uncooperative."

Matt stretched in his chair, and the men heard his chair creak. "You know, I wondered why Sam Perry came up here alone. He was making a play to talk Big John into switching his business to the Perry family. That's why there was no hooch in his car, and being deep in MacDonald territory, Angus MacDonald's men could ambush him easily enough."

Sergeant Oliver continued with, "After MacDonald's boys shot Sam Perry, the next domino would have fallen. The Perry family retaliated against the Woody family. The web pulled here in Green Mountain County would have pulled strands down in Franklin County. Thus, the big shootout in Franklin County."

Matt's group decided that they must find the pistol that killed Brown. They all hoped the bullets recovered from Brown's body would match one of the pistols recovered from MacDonald's men. The motive was there; the opportunity was substantial; they just needed something to tie MacDonald and his men to the murder.

The discussion on the Albert Winston Brown murder ended with a sobering thought from Sheriff Lawrence. "We solved the murder. Now, all we must do is prove it!"

Only time would tell, and that's when their talk turned to politics. Sheriff Lawrence was worried about his upcoming election. He knew Big John was going to withdraw his support, financial and voter-wise. He was placing all his chips on the workers in town voting for him. After the raid, his campaign budget would be mostly out of his own pocket.

Matt shocked him by pledging him a one-thousand-dollar donation. Once again, Matt's inheritance would be for the community.

Mrs. Harvey interrupted the meeting with more news. The Pittsylvania County sheriff had called her from Chatham to tell her the four dead men at the farm had been identified. The Baldwin Detective Agency admitted they had worked for the agency ten years ago but not recently. A lawyer for the detective agency was sending the authorities affidavits to confirm this information. Also, the uniforms the men wore were made by the same company that supplied uniforms to Baldwin. However, these uniforms, without any markings, were bulk sale items sold to various uniform stores. So, there was no way to trace them or tie them to Baldwin—another dead end.

When Matt was alone, he reviewed the arrest warrants on the Green Mountain Hotel employees to try to figure out a way to prove the participants knew there was gambling and bootleg. Unless someone talked, it was going to be difficult.

Cindy, his star witness, knew about the ledger. But would a judge or jury believe she could recite two full pages of figures, having seen them only once? If she was believed, it proved Brown was dirty, but how about Big John? Also, Matt had to keep Cindy alive to testify. Matt suspected Big John was behind ordering the attack on her uncle's farm.

Misty also had supplied good intelligence, but it was secondhand from a hotel guard. Such evidence wouldn't be admissible in court. The rule on hearsay would block it, making her a lot less valuable than her friend, Cindy.

The one man who knew the operation, Bill Grogan, wasn't talking. Matt wondered if all Big John's employees would support their boss with silence.

Matt called Linda to help his spirits and thanked her for their date. She said it was her pleasure and for him not to be a stranger. That comment made him feel both better and worse. Perhaps he'd not ruined his chances with her by only kissing her on the cheek. On the other hand, her final comment bothered him. Did she feel neglected?

The drive back to the hotel after work was beautiful as dusk caused the lights from the Green Mountain Resort to reflect upon the water as he crossed the bridge. He was starving when he arrived at Cubley's Coze. No wonder, he realized, he had missed lunch.

The Johnsons, Misty, and Cindy were in the lobby, waiting for the dining room to open. When they saw him arrive, they asked Matt if he would like to join them for dinner. He accepted.

At that moment, Boo announced that the dining room was now open. There was the usual rush, but she quickly seated Matt and his companions at a large table in the rear of the room. Boo had judged correctly that this party would like some privacy. No one was seated near Matt's table for the moment.

Cindy touched Matt on his arm. "Mr. Cubley, I asked Mr. Tolliver about my hotel bill. He said I needed to ask you because he didn't know what to charge me. I don't have much money because Mr. McCulloch didn't pay me much, and I'm not sure when I can go back to work. I need to make arrangements," whispered the young lady.

Matt noticed her trooper was in the lobby with an eye on the front door. There was no way he could allow Misty or Cindy to check out.

"Cindy, I doubt Big John will take you back, nor would it be safe for you there. How about you, Misty? What are your plans?" Matt asked the young lady.

"I don't know, Mr. Cubley. I don't want to leave my parents. Plus, I have friends here. I'm also at a loss," said the young lady.

"Well, perhaps I might be of some help. My maître d' is leaving for school. Mrs. Hathaway is taking over her job, but I need someone to run the front desk when Mr. Tolliver is off. Also, I need a second someone to act as maître d' when Mrs. Hathaway needs to be off. If truth be told, I'm getting behind on the hotel accounts, and my bookkeeping is lax. Mr. Tolliver helps, but neither he nor I are accountants. I thought I could make do, but with my new job as Commonwealth's Attorney, things are becoming a mess."

Matt let that sink in, and he waited while their dinners arrived. Once everyone was settled and eating. He began again.

"Cindy, I need a bookkeeper who can also run the front desk. Misty, I need someone who can handle the position of maître d', waitress some, and fill in at the front desk. I was wondering if either of you might be interested?" Matt placed the question in front of them. He hoped their responses would be yes.

Cindy looked at Misty, and Misty looked at Cindy. They both exploded with, "Yes." The response was loud enough that it caused the other diners to look in their direction. The trooper in the lobby also rose and checked the dining room. Seeing all was well, he returned to his seat in the lobby.

The rest of the dinner was a discussion of how, when, and of course, the amount of their pay. Matt suggested an immediate start since the two girls needed to remain in the hotel under guard. He would charge them a quarter of the standard rate if they cleaned their own rooms. That was agreeable to both. Not only would this solve the money problem, but both were getting bored with nothing to do. Jobs would keep them busy.

The summer help would be leaving for school soon. Not only would Boo be going, but so would several of the waitresses, waiters, groundsmen, and maids. Having Cindy and Misty available to fill in during the hunting season pinch would be good.

Boo and Mrs. Hathaway had heard the commotion and knew what was happening. Matt had asked them for their recommendations earlier. They were pleased with the outcome.

Matt finally retired to his apartment and got undressed. His eyes fell on the picture of Janet and Jack on his dresser.

His heart grieved. He knelt beside his bed and prayed. He prayed their spirits were at rest in each other's arms. He no longer desired to join them in death because he was past the point that he wanted to kill himself. He was ready for a graveside visit. He thought a trip to Roanoke would be a comfort, not an agony, as his last visit had been.

He rolled into bed, exhausted. As he drifted off to sleep, his last thoughts were of Janet, Jack, and Linda. A slight bit of guilt but more of reconciliation that one part of his life was closing, another beginning. Then nothing, no dreams; he rested.

CHAPTER 43

BILLY AND JUSTICE DENIED
Tuesday, August 16, 1955

I clearly remember that Tuesday in August. It began with Mom calling me—more than once.

"Billy, get up. We have to be at the school by ten. I'm not going to tell you again!"

I knew this was number three, and if Mom had to call me a fourth time, I was in for it.

Today was not the day to make Mom mad. It was the day Kent and I might be getting arrested along with our seventh-grade class. This school year could start with everyone absent. I guess they could hold lessons at the jail, like when kids get sick; they send a home-bound teacher. Would they call it having a jail-bound teacher?

Heck, I wasn't sure they even let teachers teach jailbirds.

I got up, loaded my toothbrush, and began brushing my teeth. While I brushed, I used the toilet to save time. That was a mistake. I was brushing my teeth with my right hand, aiming with my left. Things got crossed.

I finished my teeth, then cleaned up the mess. But, of course, that would be the time Scotty picked to wander into the bathroom.

"Billy, why are you crawling on the floor?" he asked.

"Scotty, I'm cleaning up a mess you made."

"Not neither. It was you! I'm going to tell," Scotty proclaimed in his baby voice. A sound that made me want to whack him on a good day. Today was not a safe day to punch my little brother, so I changed tactics.

"Go ahead. Next time it storms, I won't let you sleep with me. The thunder monster will come and carry you off," I teased him.

"Billy, please don't let the thunder monster get me. I won't tell," he said, changing to his scared voice. Now I felt bad about teasing him. He was terrified of the thunder monster.

I looked over my shoulder, "Scotty, if you behave, I'll let you sleep with me next time it storms."

I gave the floor in front of the toilet one more swipe. When I stood up, he was smiling at me. I think he'd forgotten what he was going to tattle about.

We each finished in the bathroom and got dressed without any additional arguments. I followed my baby brother downstairs to the kitchen without giving him a finger thump on the back of the head. I wanted to but didn't.

"Billy, you march right back upstairs. Put on clean clothes. You wore those yesterday," Mom ordered.

Not wanting to provoke anything, certainly not today, I did as I was told, knowing it was stupid. Those clothes had only been worn half a day after church and then on Monday. One tiny drop of mustard on the left leg of the pants. You could hardly see it. They were shelf clean and not near ready for the laundry. No sense in arguing. Nope, not a good day to light off Mom's fuse. I might need her to bring me pop and comics to the jail.

Breakfast was quiet. I think even Grandma believed I was a goner. She wanted my last meal to be pleasant—no fights, not even a minor fuss. She was calm, cool, and collected—a bad sign.

Dad finished eating and returned to my parent's room to get dressed. He was going with us. That's how I knew I was headed for the big house.

Dad would go to an occasional ball game at my school, but only if there was nothing better to do and only when I was going to play, not ride the bench. Getting him to a PTA meeting or teacher's conference rarely happened.

Kent arrived with his mom, who was on her way to work. Her mean boss wouldn't even let her off to say goodbye to her only child as he was going behind bars. How awful was that?

I thought I saw a tear journey down her cheek. She made Kent hug her before she let him out of the car. Superman's face blushed as red as a fire truck.

Kent, going with us made me feel some better. We had talked about asking the sheriff to let us share a cell. Gene Autry in *The Blazing Sun* spent a night in jail when he made the sheriff mad because he wouldn't join a posse. After today, we would have something in common. Of course, Gene Autry was grown, not twelve.

When we arrived at school, cars were already in the parking lot. In fact, I think most of the kids beat us there.

Inside the auditorium, no one was talking. No one greeted us, and we didn't call out any greetings to our friends. The parents didn't look at each other. Friends didn't act like they knew friends; this room had become a room of strangers.

The Lockhart family came in and sat near the door. Both parents were with Carl and Dickie. Those brothers looked mean as ever, and their dad's scowl was like he had been skunk sprayed.

I saw Roger Younger with an older adult. When I leaned over and asked Mom who Roger was with, she whispered back that it was his grandfather. Roger's mother arrived and sat with them. His dad wasn't there.

Neither Lou McCulloch nor his parents were in the school auditorium. Of course, Lou hadn't been with Carl and Dickie for the ambush. But if I was going to jail, I thought Lou should go too. He did clobber me with a baseball bat, and later, he helped beat Kent and me up when the three bullies stole our bikes—fair is fair!

Miss Jones stood by the side door of the auditorium. I figured she was waiting for Mr. Henry Watkins, the special prosecutor. I was right. Mr. Watkins arrived with Mr. Cubley at five to ten. When the three met at the door, they walked up onto the stage, where there were three chairs.

At ten o'clock, Miss Jones introduced Mr. Watkins and told everyone he was the special prosecutor from Amherst County. He would speak to the group first, followed by Mr. Cubley, our new local prosecutor. She asked everyone to hold their questions until the end of the meeting. I heard grumbling, but no one objected.

Mr. Watkins stood and walked up to the podium. First, he told us about himself and his position with Amherst County. This included what a special prosecutor was and his assignment for Green Mountain County. Then, things got serious, and he raised his voice.

"Our courts depend on good citizens. Good citizens who are truthful, regardless of their position or status."

Like a revival preacher, he took right off by going back to when I got hit in the head with the baseball bat in the town park on the Fourth of July. He described all his attempts to find out what happened. How the only witness, Roger Younger, said first one thing and then the opposite. He looked at Roger, who I'm sure wanted to crawl under his seat.

Poor Roger about died when Mr. Watkins told how his father beat him. He shouted, "Not to tell the truth, but to tell a lie. Beaten by his father, a police officer, to tell a lie."

No one moved. There was not one sound.

I thought, *it sure is good Officer Younger isn't here. He would kill his boy over this embarrassment.*

Mr. Watkins then spoke in a softer voice. Several people leaned forward in their seats to hear.

He told about the attack on Kent and me behind the furniture store.

"This was not a schoolyard fight! It was a crime that amounted to robbery by force, which is a felony for adults!"

After a pause, he continued in a normal voice.

"The two victims identified their attackers. There was no doubt in their minds."

Once again, he got loud when he told the crowd the bullies, their parents, and relatives lied. "One parent falsified employment records. Another parent claimed his son was at his grandfather's home, and I believe the grandfather also lied."

There was a lot of shuffling and whispered noise. I thought Mr. Lockhart was going to get up and leave. Instead, his wife pulled on his arm for him to sit back down. He stayed, but I could tell he was boiling.

Dickie and Carl turned and looked at me, which meant I was in for it. I hoped we wouldn't share a cell. Not even Gene or Roy would survive being locked up with those two.

Mr. Watkins started quoting stuff from the Bible. "The leaders of this community are encouraging deceitful behavior. You sow the wind, and all of you will reap the whirlwind."

I had studied that passage in Sunday School.

Then he got around to the ambush out at the school. He lit into us, "good fashion."

"I find bullies on one side and child vigilantes on the other. You are raising a generation of thugs and liars. You, the adults, are at fault. The children of this town are taking the law into their own hands. Why? Because the law no longer protects them. This community has abandoned its children, leaving them to the mercy of wolves!"

The lecture by Mr. Watkins reminded me a lot of the sermons we heard at our last revival. That bald preacher would rant even better than my grandma, and I figured after his second sermon, our town was bound to be visited by angels just like Sodom and Gomorrah. Now, I feared angels were on the way as Mr. Watkins accused all of us of being liars and criminals. That's when he got to the meat of his sermon, as Dad would say.

"I can't do my job when witnesses aren't trustworthy. One must have credible witnesses, and in this town, there are no credible witnesses."

Mr. Watkins paused and looked around the crowd. He placed his hands on the sides of the podium, and I thought he would push it off the stage. He did shake it as he spoke.

"Therefore, I will not bring charges against anyone. The boy hit in the head in the town park will not find justice. He and his friend, who were beaten and had their bikes stolen, will not find justice. The man who had his hardware store burglarized will not find justice. The corporation with broken windows and a log yard set afire will not find justice. And the two boys who were set upon by a gang of child vigilantes will not find justice. This injustice I lay on you, the adults of this community. You have failed your children."

Mr. Watkins was done. There was silence in the auditorium. Finally, he turned and walked out of the school, just like the Lone Ranger did at the end of each TV show. He rode off into the sunset, except there wasn't a sunset.

Several of the moms started to cry. Some of the men began to talk in whispers.

Miss Jones stood up and asked for quiet. She got it quickly. Looking across the auditorium at Mr. Cubley, he rose, and she took her seat.

"I'm a new resident in Highland, but I've been visiting here since I was a child. This is my home, my town, and I'm your current Commonwealth's Attorney. Mr. Albert Winston Brown was murdered. He died because corruption had crept into this community. I agree with everything that Mr. Watkins just told you. This town is failing not only the children but itself. We must start making changes and clean up this mess."

He paused and looked over the auditorium. People began to squirm. He stopped and held out both hands. It looked like he might ask for an offering, but that wasn't what he was doing.

"As your prosecutor, I need your help. If you don't do it for me, do it for the children," and then, Mr. Cubley turned and took his seat. Again, things got very quiet. Before the whispering started, Miss Jones stood and walked to the podium.

"My friends and especially my students. My heart is sad. Today is the day I call on you for a change. Students, who will be in the next seventh-grade class, I ask for your promise to be truthful. When one of you says, 'on my word of honor,' it must mean something. I leave this in your hands, and may God bless us all!"

Miss Jones then walked over to Mr. Cubley, and they walked off the stage together. There was no sound for twenty seconds. Then, someone in the back began to clap, and everybody started. Several cheered, and several had tears. I saw the Lockharts leaving by the side door. They looked angry, except for Mrs. Lockhart, who looked sad.

I turned to Kent and grinned.

He grinned and spoke over the noise, "I guess we don't get to share a cell."

I responded, "Yeah, we won't need that hacksaw blade I put in my shoe."

Mom punched me on the arm. She must have heard us.

The trip back to the garage went better than I thought it might. Mom and Dad never mentioned that we all had lied about going fishing. They talked a little about how the parents would have to start with some changes, but mostly they were silent.

I started thinking about how I didn't see Big John McCulloch changing much. Things at that end of town would remain the same.

When we arrived home, Superman and I went up to my room. I asked him if he had told his mom the truth about Carl and Dickie. Kent said he told her last night and admitted that he had whacked Carl and Dickie with his belt.

I knew Kent would cave in eventually. He almost always did when his mom was involved. But he held out longer than I expected.

He asked me if I had told my parents the truth.

"No, not so far, but I'm sure Mom knows."

I told Kent if Mom or Dad asked me again, I would tell them the truth. Mom had already told Miss Jones some of our family secrets.

It was time I confessed to my buddy. "Superman, we both broke our word to our class by telling Miss Jones the truth during our meeting."

"BB, what are we going to do?"

"We better tell the truth most of the time, but I'm not telling on my dad and his army buddies. They got our bikes back."

"I agree, and they must have scared Lou because he's leaving us alone," stated Superman.

Kent and I agreed. Neither of us saw any reason to rat on Dad or his buddies; no reason at all.

"BB, we need to let each other know when to tell the truth and when we should keep things secret," Kent suggested.

"Superman, I plan on waiting to see if things change. No sense jumping into something, not knowing if the alligators are waiting with open mouths," I replied.

"Okay, but do you think Carl and Dickie are going to leave us alone?" inquired Kent.

"I think the opposite. I think we're in for it. Mr. Cubley meant what he said, but he's a good person. The Lockhart brothers are rotten mean. How do good people fight bad people when bad people run things and lie all the time?"

I felt sad and wasn't convinced good people could fight bad people. Besides, I was tired of getting whacked in the head. I still had headaches from the Fourth of July and the furniture store scrapes.

"BB, I don't want to have to lie to my mom. Do you?" asked Kent.

That was the one thing that worried me. Lying to my mom made me feel bad. Well, unless it was about laundry or Scotty. I had gotten used to a little fib now and then at home.

"Superman, there are big lies and little lies. Miss Jones is right about the big lies, especially when I tell them to Mom. I'm cautious about telling a big lie to my dad. I'm afraid of my dad. I love him and all, but you know?"

Mom called us to get a move on. It was time for Kent and me to go to work, and she had an appointment at noon. She drove us up to the hotel because we were still on confinement, which meant no bikes. Our bikes had remained locked in the hotel maintenance shed since Hurricane Connie. Things were still rotten for us kids.

Now Hurricane Diane was due into town, right on the heels of Connie. So first, the rain, then being grounded, and now, more storms. I wasn't sure how much longer Superman and I could stand it.

After Mom let us off in front of the hotel, we began painting the second room for Mr. Cubley. Kent got the supplies from the maintenance shed, and I got a step ladder from our first room and moved it into this second room.

We made good time painting when Mr. Cubley came up to see how we were getting along.

"Were there any surprises?" he asked, getting right to the point about the school meeting.

"Yeah, me and BB thought we were going to jail for sure," said Kent.

"Superman, it's BB and I thought we were going to jail. Right, Mr. Cubley?" I said, all proud of my correct grammar and being wise to change the subject.

"You are correct, Billy, but don't try to change the subject. You know Miss Jones told me that the both of you admitted that the story about going fishing was a lie," he said.

"Yes, sir, but what were we to do?" I was pleading my case, I hoped.

"Mr. Cubley, no one would help us," added Kent.

"Boys, why do you think Mr. Watkins didn't place any charges?"

We both said we didn't know, which was the safest thing to say in any situation involving adults.

"Mr. Watkins wanted to be fair. If he charged one side, he would have to charge you all. He was afraid the bullies and their parents would continue to lie. The man didn't want the good kids to be punished and the bullies to get off. Now, we must figure out a way to stop the bullies and not lie to the police to do it."

"How is that possible?" Kent asked before I could.

"Well, boys, the first thing is to help Miss Jones. She will try to get her class to promise to tell the truth about the important stuff. Okay?" asked Mr. Cubley.

"I guess so, but...." I was at a loss as to how to finish my sentence.

"What has you worried, Billy?" Mr. Cubley wanted to know.

"Mr. Cubley, my mom won't let me ride my bike because Chief McCulloch is out to get me, and the same goes for Kent. We're the victims, not the bullies. How do we fight that?" I asked.

"Well, let's see. How about I have Richard follow you and Kent in the wagon if that storm holds off? Hurricane Diane is not due to hit us until the middle of the night. Perhaps you two can ride your bikes home today. I know that's not exactly what you want, but the hotel car won't be obvious. Isn't that better than nothing?"

"Sure, if he stays back, it might fool our friends," said Superman.

"Also, if something happens, he can tell me. I have a little say over court cases, right?" asked Mr. Cubley.

We said yes, but Kent and I wanted to ride our bikes all over, not just back and forth to Cubley's Coze.

We talked about wanting to ride to other places. He suggested that the boys and girls of Miss Jones's class stick together in good ways. If we had a group of six or seven, the bullies and the town cops would be afraid to start something.

So, the day ended with me telling Mom that the fishing business wasn't true. She said she knew I lied from the moment I told her, but she thanked me for admitting it. Mom also said I could start riding my bike to work since Mr. Cubley had called and Richard Baker would look out for us. In addition, the sheriff's deputies would be keeping an eye out for certain bullies. Most of the parents were talking about how things needed to be changed. Perhaps there was a change coming.

When I brushed my teeth before going to bed, I thought about making a wish for things to be better. Then I remembered what happened when I wished for Kent and me to have an adventure. That mirror didn't know when to stop. I wondered if someone had wished on their bathroom mirror for rain. I knew it had been dry, and the farmers needed water. That would explain why we were about to get our second hurricane within a week.

Yep, I bet that's what happened. Some other mirror didn't know when to stop.

CHAPTER 44
NOT THE RIGHT GUN
Wednesday, August 17, 1955

Matt looked out his bedroom window and Hurricane Diane pouring water on farms and fields. According to the radio, many roads were flooded around Richmond and Washington. Hurricane Connie had soaked the ground a week ago, and Diane was making things much worse. Green Mountain County had swollen creeks with the Smith River over its banks by two feet. The only good news was that this second hurricane should depart to the north on the heels of the first later today.

Matt dressed casually because he and Trooper Giles were going to meet with Lou McCulloch. Lou's mother, Willa McCulloch, had consented to the meeting and was much more agreeable than her husband. She informed Matt that Lou's father would not be at the meeting because he was working on a plant security matter, but the Chief had left instructions that the meeting must take place at Big John's mansion.

Matt descended to the hotel kitchen, where he heard Boo, Maddie, and Karen Hathaway in a friendly discussion regarding a future menu. Cindy and Misty were joining in with suggestions.

Matt had been afraid that Cindy and Misty wouldn't want to work with Karen because her husband, Doc, had worked for Angus MacDonald. But Boo had explained about Doc being framed for the theft of several payroll envelopes. When he was released from jail, he was forced to deliver bootleg for MacDonald to feed his family. It was common knowledge that the local troopers were now helping to clear Doc of the theft charge at the plant. Mrs. Hathaway's kind demeanor won over Misty and Cindy after Boo explained things.

Cindy proved to be an incredible mathematician and bookkeeper. She asked permission to change some hotel accounting procedures after reviewing the books. The changes provided Matt and Chuck with a weekly report that was easy to read and contained more information on the hotel's operation. Matt and Chuck were pleased with the improvements, making it easier and faster to track profits and losses.

Also, Misty demonstrated her ability to master dining room operations. After Boo and Mrs. Hathaway coached her, she could handle most of the dining room tasks. And she was learning not to irritate Maddie. It might take her longer to learn the head cook's likes and dislikes, but Boo told her not to worry; Maddie hadn't stabbed a single person this summer.

Boo informed Matt that she had to report back to the university on Monday, August 29. That day saddened Matt for two reasons: Boo was leaving, and Kent and Billy would also return to school.

Matt realized the old hotel would be different without Boo, BB, and Superman. Life was moving on and dragging Matt with it, whether he wanted to go or not.

Maddie handed Matt a plate with an admonishment, "Stop standing around. I'se got plates to get out."

He smiled at her, grabbed a cup of coffee, and hurried to join Kent, Billy, and Polecat, on the loading dock near the hotel wall to stay out of the rain. The others were discussing the recent raid on the Green Mountain Resort Casino.

Matt knew that everyone in town was still talking about it. Most of the workers were on his side. Those workers against the raid were only a handful, and it was because they were afraid their jobs might be affected. However, all the plant supervisors and county bigwigs were against the search, being regulars at the casino.

Matt refrained from joining the group discussion until Kent began moaning about school starting in just over a week. Next, Billy joined in complaining that the summer had been ruined from the start and the fall was going to be worse.

Matt almost laughed because he knew both boys were pleased that Miss Jones would be their teacher and were looking forward to school. Their classmates were now a tightly knit group, having survived the troubles with the bullies.

Matt wished his boy Jack could have known these two. Known them, despite the fact Jack would have been too young to hang out with them. He missed his boy so much. Deep in thought, he was startled when he heard his name.

"Mr. Cubley, are you going to talk to Lou today?" asked Kent.

"How did you know about my meeting?" demanded a surprised Matt.

It was Polecat who answered him. "Mr. Cubley, the whispers at the Highland Police Department this morning are of that ilk. Would that gossip be truthful or a canard?" responded Polecat in his obtuse way.

"No, Mr. Smith, the rumors are correct. I'm having a meeting with young Master McCulloch this morning. His mother says he's sufficiently recovered for us to meet."

"Mr. Cubley, would you tell him something for me?" asked Billy.

"I might. What would you want me to tell him?" Matt responded with more than a little curiosity.

"Tell him thanks. Tell him that he has nothing to worry about...uh, well...the people he was worried about...will, er, now know what he did."

"Billy, you better write him a little note. I'm not sure I have the slightest clue what you just said," responded Matt, although he thought he might know.

Billy got up and went into the kitchen. He returned with a note from the pad on the front desk. The message was folded with Lou's name on the outside, but the boy opened it for Matt to read. Matt read it, took it, and placed it in his shirt pocket for safekeeping.

The next part of the morning was spent going over account information with Cindy. She left just as Chuck told Matt that Trooper Giles was in the lobby. Matt rose to greet him.

"Morning, Bobby. Care for some breakfast?" asked Matt, giving the trooper a firm handshake. "Maddie's made sweet rolls that'll melt in your mouth."

"No, I ate at home and need to watch my waistline. My gun belt is starting to get too tight." The trooper frowned and handed Matt an envelope. "I have something you don't want to see, which took my appetite, and it might take yours."

Matt opened the analysis report on the firearms removed from Chill Dawson and Tom Rosser. The guns were 38's and were the same calibers as the two intact bullets recovered from the body of Mr. Albert Winston Brown. The problem was clear because the shots fired into Brown did not come from either gun.

"I was afraid of this," responded Matt after reading the report.

"Yeah, Dawson is slow but not that stupid, and Rosser's way too smart to get caught holding a murder weapon. I'm afraid they tossed the gun where we'll never find it," said Trooper Giles.

"This murder is so frustrating," exclaimed Matt, and now both men were wearing frowns. "I'm sure Angus and his two henchmen are guilty, but I can't prove it. I don't think we will solve that murder unless someone talks.

Giles spoke as he shrugged, "No use crying over it. This won't be the first time old Angus MacDonald has beaten the system. He has money and connections, his people are covering for each other, and he's no dummy. A hard combination to best."

Matt rode with the trooper over to Big John's mansion. Trooper Giles wore civilian clothes at Matt's request, thinking Lou might speak more freely if they didn't look like cops but regular people.

When they got to the front door, they were met by Willa McCulloch before they knocked. She was small with a boyish figure and limp brown hair cut short. Her striking sky-blue eyes were her best feature in contrast to the rest of her. Matt had often heard her described as mousey, but her cordial nature revealed an inner beauty.

"Come in, gentlemen. Lou's in the front parlor," she said, greeting Matt and Bobby with a warm smile. A servant took their dripping rain gear. Lou's mother escorted them across a large marble entrance hall and past a massive mahogany staircase opposite the front door. A twelve-foot-tall grandfather clock chimed the hour with deep cathedral tones.

For an instant, Matt's mind flashed to a movie he and Janet had watched every Christmas. He saw the title in his mind, *A Christmas Carol*. The 1938 film with Reginald Owen as Ebenezer Scrooge suddenly distracted him. The clock in that movie, as it struck the hour before each ghost appeared, had sounded like this one. He had the feeling that the spirit of Christmas past might appear.

When they entered the parlor, Big John McCulloch sat beside Lou. Next to his grandfather was Mr. Southwall, the new family and corporate attorney. Beside Lou on the other side, a nurse sat perched on the edge of her seat. She was wearing a white uniform with her nurse's cap pinned on the back of her head in defiance of gravity.

Lou's mother suddenly stopped and stood aside. She didn't stay in the room with her son but departed quietly, closing the door—her actions more like a servant than a mother.

"Mr. McCulloch, I was hoping we could speak to Lou alone. I think it would be easier on him," stated Matt without a greeting. He figured he was in enemy territory by the look of things, and a greeting would be a waste of time.

"That's not going to happen," responded Big John, who was still recovering from being shot. His voice had a breathy, labored sound, and he winced when he spoke. Matt wasn't sure if the nurse was for him or his grandson. The oxygen tank within the older man's reach was obviously his.

Next, Mr. Southwall spoke. "Mr. Cubley, I insist that Master McCulloch have counsel present, a caregiver, and of course, his grandfather, the patriarch and protector of the family. This is a consensual meeting. We want to be sure the young lad isn't upset by insensitive questions."

Mr. Southwall flashed a smile that was as sweet as cyanide.

Matt was determined to make the most of their little meeting. "I understand. So, Lou, I'm happy to see you're recovering from your injury. I'll keep this brief. May I ask you a couple of questions?" Matt inquired, and as he did, he picked up a chair from some distance away. He brought it over and set it down right in front of Lou. He gave the boy a friendly smile. The boy smiled but made no answer.

Trooper Giles remained standing at the door to the parlor. He moved to the side and tried to blend into the woodwork. He noticed Big John McCulloch started to object to Matt sitting close to his grandson, but Mr. Southwall shook his head slightly to cut off Big John's objections.

"Lou, I understand you received a gunshot wound to the side of your head. Would you please tell me how that happened?"

The boy looked at his grandfather, then at the floor. He took a deep breath and began, "I borrowed a gun from my friend, Roger. I borrowed the gun to do target shooting. I thought I'd better clean it, but it went off when I tried to unload the gun. I shot myself by accident. I'm very sorry to have caused my parents unnecessary worry. That's all I have to say."

Lou recited this statement in a sing-song fashion. His answer sounded like a memorized script written by an adult, rehearsed many times, and regurgitated without thought or emotion.

Matt asked, "Your friend, Roger, wasn't present when you accidentally shot yourself?"

"No, sir, Roger wasn't there," said Lou in a normal conversational manner of speech. This time, his statement sounded like it wasn't rehearsed. He even looked at Matt when he answered.

"Lou, why were you cleaning your gun on the tennis court?" asked Matt.

"Stop!" interrupted Mr. Southwall with a frown. "Lou's answered all he needs to answer, Mr. Cubley. Where he cleaned the gun is none of your concern."

Mr. Southwall stood and moved behind Lou, placing his hands lightly on the boy's shoulders.

Big John started to speak, but Matt beat him to it.

"Well, I guess that's all I need. Lou, thanks for seeing us."

Matt looked at Trooper Giles, who gave him a slight nod that was barely visible. They both knew that this meeting was a lost cause. Lou might have some information they could use, but today Big John and his attorney had blocked their efforts. Being pushy would only hurt the boy and get them tossed out of the mansion.

Matt thought he might try to slip Billy's note to Lou. He saw, however, that Mr. Southwall and Big John were not moving. Neither man made a move to escort him out. Instead, they were watching Matt's every move. Finally, Big John called out, "Willa," as one would call a domestic.

Willa must have been just outside the door because she opened it immediately. Matt and Trooper Giles followed her out into the atrium. A servant closed the doors to the parlor as soon as they had departed the room. Then, at the front door and out of sight of the others, Matt whispered to Willa, "Ma'am, a friend of your son has written him this note. Would you please give it to him?"

She at first hesitated. Looking back at the parlor, seeing the closed doors, she took the note and quickly put it in the side pocket of her dress without even looking at it. The same servant returned their raincoats, and Willa thanked the men for their kind visit in such inclement weather.

Back in the trooper's car, Matt interposed, "Well, that was useless, wasn't it?" He wasn't expecting an answer but got a surprise.

"About as useful as fishing without bait. I saw you slip Mrs. McCulloch that note. Think she'll give it to Lou or hand it over to Big John?" asked Giles.

"Well, I hope she gives it to her son. If she gives it to Big John, I don't think he could figure it out. Billy wrote it almost in code. Anyway, we tried."

The two men rode back the short distance to Cubley's Coze in silence. Trooper Giles was thinking about where the murder weapon might be hidden. Matt was thinking about how the kids of this town were seeing the worst side of the adults.

Once at the hotel, Matt changed into a suit. That afternoon, he had a short trial, which required him to dress in a suit and tie. Driving to the courthouse, he was wondering what Lou McCulloch was thinking. That poor boy knew at least some of what his grandfather and father were doing—scary stuff for a youngster with no one to talk to—very scary stuff.

Matt entered his courthouse office and showed Mrs. Harvey the report on the three pistols. She read it and filed it without comment.

Next, he called Linda to see if she was available for lunch. She was, and they walked together under his umbrella to the Black Panther. They enjoyed a nice lunch, talking about things other than work. When they left the restaurant, the rain was ending. Matt felt much better about life when he returned from lunch.

The afternoon circuit court trial went smoothly. He won his case in front of Judge Harland, and after that trial, he visited the judge of the county court and moved that court to dismiss the warrants against Roger Younger. Judge Carlton asked him about

Lou's statement, and Matt reported what Lou had said. He left out telling the judge that he thought Lou had been reciting a script or that the boy claimed to be cleaning his gun on his grandfather's tennis court. He cleared Younger without mentioning the troublesome details, and the judge never asked.

Matt worked the rest of the afternoon trying to organize the raid evidence, plus he did the same for the MacDonald gang charges. He knew the two cases were related, but again, no proof. Lies were stopping his best efforts.

Driving back to the hotel after work, he passed Billy and Kent riding their bikes home. Richard Baker was seventy-five yards behind the boys. Glancing in his rearview mirror, he saw two other boys on bikes pop into view. These other two boys had just come out of Court Street behind Billy and Kent, making it clear they were trying to catch up.

Matt waved at Richard to stop and told him he would follow the boys. Then, he made a quick U-turn and raced after Kent and Billy.

Were these the boys' friends or the Lockhart Brothers? He needed to catch up to find out.

After his U-turn, Matt should have seen Kent and Billy ahead of him, but he saw nothing. Neither Billy, Kent, nor the two boys following them were in view.

Which way?

Matt drove past Seventh Street, Firtree Lane, and then Sixth Street. Still, he found no boys.

He tried to calculate how far they could have gotten. He knew they had to be close. He took a chance and turned into the back parking lot of the Green Mountain Baptist Church. That's where he saw four boys in a circle—two on two at the far end of the lot. Billy and Kent versus Carl and Dickie. Those two bullies would just not stop their attacks.

Matt coasted into the lot, stopping thirty feet from the boys. Carl and Dickie had their backs to him, unaware he was present. Matt also observed the pastor, Dr. Joe Johnson, walking toward the group.

Even though Carl and Dickie had the advantage over Kent and Billy by height and weight, Matt noticed that Kent and Billy weren't backing down.

He heard Carl call out, "Give us your bikes, or we'll stomp you until you look like sidewalk stink!"

"You're not taking our bikes!" yelled Billy.

Dickie picked up a stout stick from under a big elm tree. He swung it at Kent.

Kent jumped back. The club missed him by less than an inch. Much to Matt's surprise, the pastor grabbed Dickie's arm, the arm not holding the stick. He jerked the arm before the boy could take another swing at Kent. Dickie swung without looking, hitting Dr. Johnson on the side of his head.

The pastor rocked back on his heels but remained on his feet. He grabbed the stick and jerked it out of the boy's hand. Blood dripped onto the pastor's white collar from a cut on his ear.

Matt walked up behind Carl and grabbed him by the arm. Carl drew back his fist, saw who it was, and decided he better not.

"Kent, Billy, you two boys go home," Matt told Kent and Billy. So, the boys picked up their bikes, did running mounts, and rode north.

The two adults marched the Lockhart boys into the pastor's office. Matt bandaged the pastor's ear from a church first aid kit. Then, Dr. Johnson called Richard Lockhart, who came right over.

Matt left it up to the pastor to explain to Mr. Lockhart what had transpired. When Richard Lockhart tried to claim the other two boys must have begun the fight, the pastor would have none of it. Instead, he blamed Carl and Dickie for picking on boys smaller than them and trying to steal the younger boys' bikes.

Matt added he had seen the Lockhart brothers following Kent and Billy, not the other way around. The pastor told how his ear had been cut.

Dr. Johnson accusingly said, "Mr. Lockhart, it's past time for you to handle your boys!"

Mr. Lockhart changed his tact and apologized.

The pastor warmed up his Sunday sermon preaching voice.

He started with, "You better give these two boys some love. They need a lot of love. Why aren't you setting a good example for them?"

When the sermon was over, Mr. Lockhart told his boys to get in the car. He tossed their bikes in the trunk. Leaving the church parking lot, a lot of finger waving was going on by the father at the boys, who were hunkered down in the back seat, looking at their feet.

Matt added a second bandage to stop the bleeding on the pastor's ear.

Dr. Johnson surprised Matt when he said, "That man needs to be buggy whipped, and a good spanking would probably do his boys some good." The pastor was so mad that he called Sheriff Lawrence to report the incident.

Matt left thinking this pastor was old school. If he ever started attending a church, this one would be his first choice. Janet would have wanted him to start back to church. Perhaps it was time.

Arriving at the hotel, Chuck informed Matt that the Highland Business Owners Association's meeting, which had been canceled the night prior due to the storm, had been rescheduled for tonight since the rain had stopped. The kitchen had been in a tizzy all afternoon, trying to get all the food cooked and ready. Chuck had a profound twitch over one eye; Matt sensed there was more to be told.

"Matt, that's not all. Once the tables were set in the second-floor banquet room and all the food was in the final stages of preparation, Big John called to cancel his party of four for tonight's supper meeting. Five minutes later, Richard Lockhart called and canceled all the reservations. He let slip that there's a big meeting at Big John's house this evening. So, what are we to do with all this food?"

Matt thought for a moment and decided. "Tell all the employees that supper's on me. Have them invite their families. We have food prepared, so let's have a party."

That evening, Matt attended the employee's party in the banquet room, and even the Clark and Gunn families attended. But he was bothered by a nagging question. *Why did Big John call a special meeting at his house?*

406

CHAPTER 45

TRIALS OR CIRCUSES?

Friday, August 19, and Wednesday, August 24, 1955

Matt's week had been a mixture of horrible and pleasant. Throwing a spontaneous free meal for the employees last Wednesday night had lifted everyone's spirits, including his own. But, from then until today, he had been swamped getting ready for today's trials. Setting his alarm for four in the morning and driving to the courthouse to prepare for today allowed him quiet time to finish his preparations. However, scheduling the casino trials this quickly was like trying to turn the Titanic in time to save it. Was he about to slam into an iceberg?

He did have a few good witnesses, but with so much deception pouring in from the other team and so few facts to staunch the flow, he felt like a Captain Smith. This might be the day he went down with his ship.

Polecat had kept Matt abreast of some of the preparations by the other side and provided hints about the subject of that hurried meeting at Big John's house. The defendants and their legal team were fabricating a breakthrough defense. Courtesy of Polecat, scuttlebutt from the Highland Police Department revealed the defense would call three surprise witnesses, but who they were was a closely guarded secret.

The courtroom was overflowing with witnesses, press, and spectators. Cindy and Misty would testify for Matt, and the Farthington couple would add the little they knew about the gambling operation. But much to Matt's surprise, his case went on without many objections from opposing counsel.

The Richmond law firm failed to attack Cindy on her exceptional memory. Something Matt had been sure would happen, and he warned her to expect a vicious attack on her incredible memory. The two ledger sheets she recited were reduced to writing and accepted by the judge. Then, only two innocuous questions on cross-examination on minor points were asked.

Also, Cindy was allowed, without objection, to testify about the second-hand knowledge told to her by the guard about how the police delivered boxes to the secret basement party room. Not a single defense attorney rose with the expected hearsay objection. Matt became uncomfortable because he knew something was up.

No objections were made to the search warrant. All the officers he called told their observations with only a few protests and limited cross-examination. This was not the usual way this law firm conducted trials for defendants. Matt rested without a motion to strike his evidence from the other side. Even the judge was astounded when none of the opposing counsel made a dismissal motion.

Then it began. The defense called their first ten witnesses. They testified that the hotel had provided a room for this private party. In addition, the regular patrons testified that they had never seen a casino on-premises except for this one night, and there was no illegal gambling going on the night of the raid.

Staff swore the house didn't take a cut of the table proceeds, and all the money used at the gaming tables was destined for charity. The winnings would be donated under the winner's name to a church, and not a penny would go home with the pretend gamblers.

Three local churches were the recipients of the donated money. The three surprise witnesses were area pastors. These men of the cloth testified that they had been promised significant donations, and each complained that the sheriff was holding their charity money as evidence, keeping them from using it for good works.

One elderly hotel employee took the stand and admitted he was the keeper of the "bank" for the games. He kept track of each winner's pot, and the top winner would receive a cake—a chocolate cake from the hotel kitchen.

Regarding stories of the town police hauling in boxes, yes, the police had delivered party favors and decorations to the hotel basement on prior occasions. These items were for birthday parties or holiday dances in the hotel's main dining room.

When asked about the guards and the locked steel door, Bill Grogan testified this basement area was a storage area that had been cleaned out and used to provide a realistic party atmosphere. The steel doors had been installed years ago for fire protection.

Mr. Grogan testified that he was aware of the charity but failed to mention it the night of the raid because the police were causing such a ruckus that he couldn't think straight. So, the Richmond lawyer's final question for this witness was, "Do you know who brought in the illegal alcohol?"

There was a quick reply. "It was Mr. and Mrs. Farthington, that's who. They were strangers invited by another couple, who were regular patrons. The Farthington couple must have lied about the bootleg not being their whiskey to escape punishment."

Matt asked several questions of Bill Grogan, but the hotel manager stuck to his version of events. He was sorry that he was so distracted that he missed telling Matt and the police about the charity.

He admitted that guests would have too much to drink at hotel parties, but the resort didn't provide the alcohol. So instead, the guests brought their own bottles to the event and often left them at the hotel until the next party in special lockers installed for that purpose.

The gentleman, who had invited the Farthington couple to the party, was called to the witness stand. He told the court he and his wife only slightly knew them. He would never have invited them if he'd known what awful people they were to bring bootleg liquor to a respectable establishment like the Green Mountain Resort. "Never in a million years," were his exact words.

The bartender took the stand and swore he thought the bootleg was tax-paid whiskey and poured in bottles to make it look like bootleg to add color to the party. He would never jeopardize his employer by serving un-tax-paid whiskey to resort guests.

When asked why he was trying to pour it down the drain, he said he didn't want the police to think it was bootleg since it wasn't in the original bottles. He further stated that he had no control over the alcohol brought to the party by the guests. It was their alcohol, and he just mixed their drinks. The hotel only provided and charged them for the mixers.

Witness after witness, some of the most well-to-do people in Highland and the surrounding area testified under oath for Big John's charity casino. Matt now knew why the defense had left his witnesses alone. These lies would sweep the criminal intent right out from under the prosecution. Finally, the finger for possession of bootleg liquor was pointed at the one couple who had told the truth. Now, they looked like criminals.

Judge Carlton had little choice but to dismiss the gambling and bootleg charges against the guests and Bill Grogan. He convicted the guard with a broken wrist of obstruction for not admitting the police when they had announced their authority. Party or not, the police had a right to enter with a search warrant. The charges against the other guards were dismissed. He convicted the bartender of possessing un-tax-paid whiskey since it was technically bootleg when he had accepted bottles without the proper tax stamps. Both men had clean records and were given suspended sentences. The bartender was prohibited from that line of work for one year.

After the court handed down the verdicts, Big John stood up and requested the money seized by the sheriff be turned over to the three pastors. The money belonged to the Lord and not to him or his resort.

Sheriff Lawrence and Matt only got the satisfaction of knowing that Big John had lost the proceeds from one night's operation of his casino—plus some bad publicity for his hotel.

Matt took Thursday night off and spent it with Linda at her place. She provided an Italian dinner with light conversation. Neither mentioned the recent trials.

The following Wednesday, the twenty-fourth, Matt proceeded with the felony preliminary hearings and the misdemeanor trials for Chill Dawson and Tom Rosser. Judge Carlton was the presiding judge. The prosecution began its case against Dawson with Trooper Giles, who testified how the police set up the trap to stop a murder.

Matt had decided to protect Lou; there would be no mention of his name or the telephone call. The trooper could only say what he knew. He had been following orders to protect the Johnson family and had never spoken to the person who provided the warning.

He, along with the sheriff and several local deputies, had removed the family from their home. The police then waited to see who might show up.

Chill Dawson stipulated he was at the scene and shot at the deputies. Deputies testified about the arrival of Dawson in a truck driven by Tom Rosser. Then, when the deputies announced who they were, how Dawson had opened fire. None of the deputies were hit, but Chill Dawson had been shot twice in the one-minute gun battle. Dawson's wounds had not been life-threatening. He was fortunate.

The defense began with Chill Dawson testifying he was only trying to collect a debt and had gotten the address wrong. He denied knowing that the people shouting at him were deputies. He claimed he saw men in the shadows with rifles and thought his life was in danger. That's why he began firing.

At the close of the defendant's case, Chill Dawson's attorney made several motions to dismiss. After the judge considered them along with the legal arguments from both sides, he announced his decision.

The charges of attempted murder of the Johnson family by Chill Dawson were dismissed. The evidence of a debt collection gone wrong was credible, and the Commonwealth could prove no motive for Dawson wanting to murder the Johnson family. The judge ruled there was ample evidence that Chill Dawson had fired on the police after receiving notice of who they were. Defense counsel asked for a short recess, which was granted.

After the recess, Chill's attorney suddenly changed his client's plea to guilty on the charges of assaulting the four deputies by firing at them. The defendant received twelve months in jail and a fine of five hundred dollars on each of the four charges.

The bailiff called Rosser's case next. Dawson testified Mr. Rosser had no knowledge of any wrongdoing. The charges against his friend Rosser were a big mistake. All the charges against Mr. Rosser in Green Mountain County were dismissed.

Matt also attended the trials in Waynesboro that afternoon as a spectator. Dawson admitted possession of the bootleg in the warehouse in Waynesboro and testified Mr. Rosser didn't know anything about it. Dawson claimed he used his boss's truck earlier that night to buy the whiskey from a stranger at a pool hall. The stranger, whose name he couldn't remember, drove a black pickup truck—make and model unknown.

Mr. Angus MacDonald testified that if he had known Chill needed the truck, he would have let him borrow it after work, so long as it was for a legal purpose. He did not abide by the drinking of spirits and would never allow one of his vehicles to be used to haul bootleg or any other type of whiskey. He and his wife were devout Christians and did not believe in drinking.

Upon hearing this, several troopers and two Waynesboro officers almost lost it. The judge gave them a frown to keep order in the court.

The Waynesboro City Court sentenced Mr. Dawson to twelve months in jail for the unauthorized use of the pickup truck belonging to his boss, but that sentence was suspended on one year's good behavior.

Dawson got one year for possession of the un-tax-paid whiskey he had left in the MacDonald warehouse, and all of it was ordered to be destroyed. The truck was returned to the owner.

Thus, all in all, Chill received four and one-half years to pull with half of his time off for good behavior by statute. He would be back in two years, give or take a few months. Mr. Dawson's attorney had arranged for the sentence to be pulled at the Waynesboro City Jail on work release. The man would continue to work for Angus MacDonald.

Tom Rosser was tried in Waynesboro on his charges. He received a fifty-dollar fine and thirty days for the concealed knife, pistol, and lead sap. However, the charges on the warehouse whiskey were dropped when Chill Lawson explained the liquor belonged to him.

Matt returned to the hotel, gave everyone the news, and urged Cindy and Misty to stay at the hotel for the present. The young ladies said they would consider his offer at their special rate.

Misty's parents moved back home and tried to return to normal. Mr. Johnson purchased a twelve-gauge shotgun and taught his wife how to use it. It was kept loaded in whatever room they occupied.

There was some good news that Matt heard from Polecat and later from Sheriff Lawrence. Polecat had stopped by for an emergency loan of two dollars, and in exchange, he favored Matt with the local news that Carl and Dickie Lockhart had been grounded for two months. Their father worked it out with the Baptist minister, who agreed not to press charges, provided the boys were grounded and attended church with their parents every Sunday for two months.

Kent and Billy were elated to learn the brothers would not be riding their bikes for two whole months. They had already informed Matt that all seventh graders were on guard, and the class had pledged to look out for each other.

The elementary school teachers had banded together with Miss Jones as their leader. They were going to stress good citizenship, and the parents had also signed on to help. Many eyes would be watching.

At least the last week of August had ended happily for the seventh-grade children. The two bullies had been grounded.

CHAPTER 46

BILLY AND KENT'S SURPRISE VISITOR
Friday, August 26, 1955

"Billy, hurry up and get dressed. You don't want to be late for Boo's party, do you?" Mom called from the foot of the stairs.

"No, ma'am. I'm almost ready," I said with conviction, but that hair of mine would not smooth out. Mom had evened it out some, which helped. I had wet and brushed it fifty times. Well, not quite that much, but it had been a bunch.

Tonight was the party to celebrate Boo going back to school. It was to be a big Friday night bash. This party would have been perfect, except Mom made me wear a suit.

I felt sad Boo was leaving. Boo was so nice, and I would miss her around the hotel. She often prevented Maddie from killing Superman and me. Not that we were terrible. Sometimes a fellow could get in a scrape and have no way of knowing it was coming for him.

Walking down the stairs, I was careful not to fall. My new shoes were stiff and hard to walk in. The bottoms were slick as ice. I asked to wear my tennis shoes, but Mom said, "Absolutely not, young man. Tonight, you need to look like a proper gentleman." According to my mom, looking good was worth the risk of falling down our stairs, breaking a leg, maybe two, and spending weeks in the hospital.

Grandma Harris was keeping Scotty at home. He had another cold, which he frequently got at his age, his snot factory was working around the clock, and he was fussy. So was Grandma, but I dared not say that out loud. Getting whacked was not on my dance card for tonight.

Mom and Dad were both dressed up. Dad was pulling at his collar, and I knew the feeling, but I was smart. I had unbuttoned my collar after my necktie was on. Then, I cinched my tie, but not tight, so my collar looked like it was still buttoned. With luck, I could get through the evening that way. If not, I could always say I had no idea how it came unbuttoned—it must be the fault of another cheap shirt from Sears and Roebuck.

We picked up Mrs. Clark and Superman since only three of us were in the car. We had plenty of room.

Superman also wore a suit, but he didn't know the trick about the top button. Later, I took him into the hotel bathroom and showed him.

When we arrived at the hotel, Mr. Cubley and Mr. Tolliver came outside to greet us. They had on dark suits and looked like they were dressed for a funeral. Not that we needed any more of those.

Mr. Skelton came over and greeted us. He was also in a suit. Boo had told us how much trouble it took to get her dad into one. He looked nice, but I could see he was miserable. He was also pulling at his collar.

I thought about showing him my top button trick but decided adults could figure it out on their own. No one helped me with mine!

Mrs. Carlisle and Miss Jones were talking to each other in the lobby. They wore pretty dresses. I wished I was as old as Mr. Cubley when I saw Mrs. Carlisle; she had bare shoulders. I nudged Kent, and he poked me back. I had to whisper for him to look because the dummy thought I was poking him for a *gotcha*.

Boo came over and hugged Kent and me. Have I mentioned how nice I think she is? She told us about her school and how much it meant to her to finish at the university. She treated Superman and me like we were adults. I listened to everything because I wanted to go to a university someday.

Sergeant Oliver and the local troopers were in a group by themselves. They were friendly if they knew you. But when there were several of them, they stuck together. Troopers are like that.

Sheriff Lawrence arrived with his chief deputy, Mr. Barnes. I heard them say Shoat, that's Deputy Lincoln, was working at keeping the county safe tonight. This was going to be a big party. More and more people were showing up.

I noticed Mr. Cubley asked Sheriff Lawrence and Sergeant Oliver to go with him to his office. This looked important, so I punched Superman and gave him the sign to follow me. We followed them at a distance, and after they closed Mr. Cubley's office door, we went behind the front desk, picked up some hotel newspapers, and pretended to read them. No one was near us or paying attention because they were all in a crowd near the lobby entrance, greeting each other and talking.

Kent and I listened at the passthrough and heard it all.

"Sheriff, Sergeant, I hate to break into our party time, but I need to tell you the latest. If his client would talk, I offered Chill Dawson's attorney a reduction in Dawson's sentence. I thought solving the Brown murder case was worth cutting Dawson a deal," stated Mr. Cubley.

The other two men agreed.

"Well, he turned me down, so we're at a dead-end!"

Sergeant Oliver concluded, "It sure sounds like it."

The next voice was Sheriff Lawrence saying, "Yep, we're dead in the water!"

Mr. Cubley continued, "I firmly believe MacDonald had Rosser and Dawson kill Brown. That old Scot was not about to let the Perry family cut into his bootleg profits. We know it, but we can't prove it!"

Sheriff Lawrence spoke up, "I agree. We need that murder weapon or for Dawson or Rosser to blab. Doing anything more on this case would be a waste of resources, right?"

Sergeant Oliver said, "That's how I see it!"

"Lady Justice just died from a dose of liars poison," concluded Mr. Cubley.

That's when Mrs. Hathaway walked into the lobby and called for Boo's party guests to come upstairs to the second-floor banquet room. Then, she announced to the hotel guests waiting in the lobby that dinner was served in the main dining room!

Ten minutes later, the main dining room was almost full of townies and hotel guests. The kitchen staff was busy filling orders and trying to attend the upstairs party in shifts. Tonight was a night to stay out of the kitchen and avoid Maddie until the rush was over.

Kent and I scurried back to our parents. We made it before Mr. Cubley and the officers came out of the hotel office. Then, we all trooped upstairs, almost filling the second-floor banquet room. Our salads were waiting, and dinner was terrific, as always.

Cindy was helping with orders tonight. We had three choices for what we wanted, and I noticed she never wrote down what people told her. Even when they asked for special-order items, not a single order was wrong. My memory's pretty good, but not that good. She and Polecat are the best anywhere.

Misty was helping seat people, and she came over and gave Kent and me each a hug. I think Boo told her to do that. I noticed how pretty Misty was tonight, and she smiled a lot more now that she was working for Mr. Cubley. Mr. Tolliver recently had to call Cindy and Misty down a few times for joking around.

Skip and Barry Hathaway sat at the table with Trooper Giles and his family. Back in June, I would have told you such a thing would have been impossible. Back then, Skip and Barry hated the police because of their dad being framed. Now, it was not even a little bit remarkable. They were all old friends. What a summer of changes.

We all had dinner, and then the speeches started. I was shocked when Mr. Cubley and Mr. Skelton told us some things about Boo that I didn't know. She was so smart that her university was going to give her a full scholarship to graduate school after she graduated. Miss Jones added some things about Boo's grade school years. Her dad was all smiles, and Boo was blushing at the praise.

Even Mr. Tolliver stood up to say how everyone at Cubley's Coze agreed that the hotel staff would miss her terribly. They all chipped in with a present of cash for her books. He also invited her to visit every time she was back home.

Many brought gifts for Boo. My mom gave her a warm sweater from all of us, Miss Jones a pair of mittens, and Mr. Cubley gave her a full-length wool coat. It was fun watching her open the presents, and it wasn't her birthday or Christmas. She thanked each person like they were special.

The final part of the evening was when all the waitresses and waiters came out with big slices of spice cake fresh from the oven. There were sparklers on the top of them. I would have to tell Scotty about the "fire workers," his goofy name for fireworks. The family had given up trying to correct him.

The cake was delicious, and if that wasn't enough, we had big bowls of ice cream on the side. I learned this was Boo's favorite dessert. Mine too, but no one had asked me.

Mr. Cubley then announced that Boo had an exceptional card from an admirer. He had almost forgotten to give it to her. I was trying to figure out from whom this might be. When Mr. Cubley pulled it out of his inside coat pocket and handed her a small envelope with a big stain on it, I knew it had to be from Polecat.

That made two cards our friend had given out this summer, one for me when I was hurt and now, one for Boo. A record for Polecat, who I bet was out on the loading dock, eating spice cake.

When Boo opened the card, two dollars fell out. Mr. Cubley broke up. I guess he thought two dollars was funny for some reason. Adults do such nutty things at times and for no reason. I refuse to be that nutty when I get old.

We all talked and visited until Mr. Tolliver came to our table. He whispered first to Mr. Cubley, who shook his head, yes. Then Mr. Tolliver came over to my parents and Mrs. Clark and whispered something to them. Dad and Mom looked at him in a weird way and then at me. I heard Mom say, "I guess so. Really?" Then Dad said, "Okay."

Mr. Tolliver came around the table and told Kent and me there was someone in Mr. Cubley's office on the first floor who would like a word with us. Dad leaned over to Mom and whispered something in her ear. She looked at me and said, "Go on, boys!"

I thought this odd, especially when Mr. Cubley got up and escorted us down to the first floor. When we got to the lobby, I saw Mrs. McCulloch, who Mom calls Willa, sitting in a chair near the front desk. Mr. Cubley walked to where she was seated and greeted her. I saw her smile. He motioned for us to go on, so Kent and I walked into his office without him.

Sitting in one of the chairs was Lou McCulloch. He stood, and I took a step backward, bumping into Kent. I saw he still wore a head bandage, and his hair on that side had been shaved. I knew all about how hospitals liked to scalp people, but only halfway.

Then I saw it. My note was in his hand. He looked at Kent and then me, looked down at the floor, and just stood there for at least ten seconds.

I looked at Kent, and he shrugged his shoulders, but we didn't know what to say.

Then, Lou took a deep breath, looked up at us for a moment, and said in a still, small voice.

"BB, Superman, I'm sorry for hurting you and taking your bikes. And thank you for telling the Brotherhood I helped. Now, I would like to ask you something."

He paused, and Kent and I waited until he said a shocker.

"May we be friends?"

ABOUT THE AUTHOR

R. Morgan Armstrong, born in Martinsville, Virginia, was a prosecutor, trial attorney, and General District Court Judge there. He attended Virginia Military Institute, received his BA degree from Duke University, and his law degree from the University of Richmond. During law school, he worked summers as a park ranger for the Army Corps of Engineers at Philpott Dam and during the summer of 1972 as a police officer for the City of Virginia Beach.

While a prosecutor, he helped organize and supervise a special police unit composed of state troopers, county deputies, and town police. While a judge, he wrote the Unauthorized Practice of Law section of the Virginia District Court Judges Bench Book.

He joined the National Ski Patrol (NSP) in the fall of 1980. Armstrong served in every line officer position and most instructor positions. He was elected director of the Southern Division, then elected to two terms on the National Board of Directors for the NSP, chaired the Governance Committee, and in 2019 was inducted into the National Ski Patrol Hall of Fame.

Upon his retirement from the bench, he moved to Wintergreen Resort with his wife, Jo Ann, and their dog, Bailey. He enjoys working with the local ski patrol and writing.